LEAH HAGER COHEN is the author of four non-fiction books, including *Train Go Sorry* and *Glass, Paper, Beans* and three other novels, most recently *House Lights*. *The New York Times* has named five of her books 'Notable Books of the Year'. She is a frequent contributor to the *New York Times Book Review*.

ALSO BY LEAH HAGER COHEN

FICTION

House Lights

Heart, You Bully, You Punk

Heat Lightning

NONFICTION

Without Apology

The Stuff of Dreams

Glass, Paper, Beans

Train Go Sorry

"The book's brilliance lies in moments like this one, these shards of devastating insight. Cohen's empathy is sure-footed and seemingly boundless; her writing gifts its characters with glints of ordinary human radiance. It is the possibility of this glinting that ultimately becomes Cohen's most powerful gift to us, her readers, as well."—*San Francisco Chronicle*

"*The Grief of Others* is an engrossing and revealing look at a family sinking beneath the weight of a terrible secret. Leah Hager Cohen writes about difficult subjects with unfailing compassion and insight."—Tom Perrotta, author of *New York Times* bestseller *Little Children*

"In this subtle portrait of family life she shows the maddening arithmetic of marriage, the useless attempts to balance the equation."—*The New York Times*

"In this gracefully written, elegantly structured novel, Leah Hager Cohen has created an indelible cast of characters whose story is at once wrenching and redemptive. This is a beautiful book."—Dani Shapiro, author of *Family History*

"A gorgeous, absorbing, intricately told tale, as well as an intimate exploration of art and its place in our lives. She is a masterly writer on every level."—Lily King, author of *Father of the Rain*

"*The Grief of Others* is delicate, haunting, and lovely, and very difficult to leave on the shelf."—Susanna Daniel, author of *Stiltsville*

"A wise and compassionate novel that looks frankly at the ways memb[...], even when t[...], author of *The [...]*

"At once compact and sweeping. Cohen never strikes a false note in relating the complicated emotions of her characters. She has created a world both universal and particular. She illuminates all the ways it is glorious to be burdened with full-fledged humanity in the vast universe." —Robb Forman Dew, author of *The Evidence Against Her*

"With gorgeous prose, Cohen skillfully takes us from past to present and back again as she explores the ramifications of family loss, grief and longing." —*Kirkus*

"This is an ambitious novel offering insight into the rift between the public and the private, and illuminating the many ways in which we deal with tragedy." —*Publishers Weekly*

"Cohen's stunning writing and ruthless, beautiful magnification of soul-crushing sorrow that threatens the Ryries' day-to-day family life mesmerizes, wounds, and possibly even heals her readers. Her courageous novel (she knows of what she writes) is to be savored." —*Library Journal*

"The death of a newborn triggers the slow collapse of the Ryrie clan in Hager Cohen's richly layered new novel . . . Affecting." —*More*

"With this incredibly moving commentary, Cohen has secured a place in the lineup of today's great writers." —*Bookpage*

"The Grief of Others has a lyrical bent and is affecting in its examination of unresolved sorrow." —*Age*, Australia

THE

Grief *of* Others

LEAH HAGER COHEN

THE CLERKENWELL PRESS

This paperback edition published in 2013

First published in Great Britain in 2012 by
THE CLERKENWELL PRESS
an imprint of Profile Books Ltd
3A Exmouth House
Pine Street
London EC1R 0JH
www.profilebooks.com

First published in the United States of America in 2011 by
Riverhead Books, part of the Penguin Group

10 9 8 7 6 5 4 3 2 1

The author gratefully acknowledges permission to quote from the
following:
'Cigars Clamped Between Their Teeth', from the *Dime-Store Alchemy*
by Charles Simic. © 1992 Charles Simic. *Funeral Customs the World Over*
by Robert W. Habenstein and William M. Lamers. © 1960 The
National Funeral Directors Association

Book design by Nicole Laroche
Printed and bound in Great Britain by
CPI Group (UK) Ltd., Croydon CR0 4YY

The moral right of the author has been asserted.

A CIP catalogue record for this book is available from the British
Library.

ISBN 978 1 84668 627 6
eISBN 978 1 84765 832 6

to Reba and Andy

and to Mike

Cigars Clamped Between Their Teeth

I've read that Goethe, Hans Christian Andersen, and Lewis Carroll were managers of their own miniature theaters. There must have been many other such playhouses in the world. We study the history and literature of the period, but we know nothing about these plays that were being performed for an audience of one.

CHARLES SIMIC, *Dime-Store Alchemy*

PROLOGUE

Last Year

When he was born he was alive. That was one thing.

He was a *he,* too, astonishingly—not that anyone expected him to be otherwise, but the notion of one so elemental, so small, carrying the complex mantle of gender seemed preposterous, the designation "male" the linguistic equivalent of a false mustache fixed above his infant lip.

His lips: how barely pink they were, the pink of the rim of the sky at winter dusk. And in their curl—in the way the upper lip rose to peaks and dipped down again, twice, like a bobbing valentine; and in the way the lower bowed out, luxuriant, lush, as if sated already from a lifetime of pleasures—how improbably expressive were his lips.

His hands like sea creatures curled and stretched, as if charged with purpose and intent. Five of his fingers closed around one of his mother's and held it while he slept. He was capable of this.

His toenails: specks of abalone.

The whorls of his ears were as marvelously convoluted as any Escher drawing, the symmetry precise, the lobes little as teardrops, soft as peaches. The darkness of the ear hole a portal to the part of him that wasn't there, that hadn't fully formed, that spelled his end.

His mother had been led to believe that the whole vault of his skull would be missing, raw nerve tissue gruesomely visible beneath a window of membrane. She'd pictured a soft-boiled egg in an egg cup, the top removed, the yolk gleaming and exposed. She'd braced herself for protuberant eyes, flattened nose, folded ears, cleft palate: the features of an anencephalic infant. But the opening in his skull was no bigger than a silver dollar, and all his features lovely. She believed, at first, triumphantly, that the diagnosis had been made in error, that now the doctors, seeing the baby, would be forced to downgrade their diagnosis to something less serious—still severe, perhaps, but not lethal.

He was out of the womb and alive in the world for fifty-seven hours—a tally that put him in rare statistical company and caused in his mother an absurd sense of pride—during which time she kissed his ears and insteps and toes and palms and knuckles and lips repeatedly, a lifetime of kisses.

She could not bear to let him out of her arms. He belonged to her, exclusively, a feeling she had not had when her other children were born. This one was bound to her in ways no one knew. Just as she, having hidden his secret these past four months, was bound to him. She would let no one else hold him, not even the baby's father, who asked only once and then, with great and terrible chivalry, pressed her no further.

During the hours she held him she could not make herself believe how fleeting his life would be.

His breath, above all, gave incontrovertible proof of his being. With grave equanimity, eyelids closed, mouth relaxed, he took and expelled hundreds, thousands, of the most exquisite wisps of air, amounts that might be measured in scruples and drams, and which his mother imagined bore their own delicate hues, invisible to the human eye. They, his breaths, were the one thing she wished could be saved. In her state she almost believed it possible (it seemed a matter simply of having the right vial in which to stopper them . . . what were they called, those special vials for holding tears?— lachrymatories, yes; if only she had one intended for breaths: a *spiratory*), and although she did not allow herself to sleep properly during all those fifty-seven hours, still she had some passing dream or medicated fantasy in the hospital bed, while she savored the feel of his inaudible, numbered breaths still stirring against her cheek, in which she glimpsed herself with an actual such vial on a chain around her neck, an amulet she might wear forever.

He wore, during his short life, a white cotton shirt with a single, covered, side snap, a white flannel receiving blanket, and a white cotton cap, fitted so gently over the opening in his head. He was given two diaper changes, the second proving unnecessary.

His mother found that once he was in her arms, she didn't want to name him anything, not even the name they'd picked out, Simon Isaac Ryrie, a name she had loved but which struck her ears now as a terrible quantity of pricking syllables. It was not that she was trying to resist forming an attachment, nor that she wished to deprive him of any blessing, any gift or token, but only because once he was in her arms it became obvious that a name was too clumsy and rough and worldly a thing to foist on such a simultaneously luminous and shadowy being.

She tried explaining this to her husband, and also to the nurse and the midwife and the neonatologist, and then to the lady who came with the forms that had to be filled out, and to the resident with the beautiful sad eyes and the accent that made her think of anisette cakes and tiny glasses of thick coffee (his name was Dr. Abdulaziz, which she remembered because of the way he kissed the feet of her fading child each time he came in)—but she couldn't seem to produce words that matched the authority of her conviction; her voice encountered obstacles, so that the easier and ultimately more rightful thing to do was abandon speech and simply hold her baby swaddled against her chest. This was all she could do and she did it absolutely. In the end it was the resident, Dr. Abdulaziz, who dissolved her resistance to naming the child, not by design or conscious effort, not even knowing he'd played such a role. Yet when he stopped in to visit her, visit them, for the last time (he explained it would be the last time, as he'd come to the end of his shift), he called the baby by name, in so low a voice, his accented syllables seeming to drape the baby in a beautifully embroidered garment as he pronounced, with care and not a speck of fanfare, almost as though it were private, not intended for either parent but for the baby's sake alone, "Simon Isaac," and bent to touch once more his mouth to the soles of the baby's feet.

And so she let her husband inscribe the name they'd chosen on the forms. What did it matter? She recognized her child as he truly was: all-spirit, his limbs pale as candles, his eyes never open once, innocent of all terms.

PART ONE

This Year

1.

Shortly past noon on the first Friday of the month, Biscuit Ryrie approached the low brick building where she attended fifth grade. She had ridden her bike a mile already and her lungs were sharp with the sweet-onion sting of early April. Against the wind her cheeks felt tight as marble. The day did not look like spring. It was white: white sky, a pallid sheen on every surface, clumps of snow lingering here and there. In a week's time, these last remnants of winter would be gone.

The sight of her own classmates gave her a start. She'd counted on their being safely ensconced in their classroom around back, instead of filing out of the building just as she drew even with it. Each student was carrying something, she saw, an identical brown sketch pad. Only then did Biscuit remember Mr. Li's announcement that today they were to begin making a visual record of the shape and size of the buds on the trees and bushes around the school. Too late to avoid being seen, she scrunched her already small frame lower over the handlebars and veered toward the far side of the street.

"Hey!" shrieked someone, importantly, hilariously. Most likely Vanessa Sett. "There goes Biscuit Ryrie. On a bike!" Laughter followed, and hooting. Biscuit kept her gaze forward, her speed steady. Someone whipped a chunk of petrified snow into the road; it smacked against her front tire and flew apart as stinging crystals. A few of them sprayed her hand and cheek.

If Biscuit had simply stayed at home like other truant children, watching reruns on cable, eating chocolate chips from the bag and peanut butter from the jar, informing her parents when they got home from work that she'd had a stomachache and could she please have a note to bring to the teacher in the morning, nothing might have come of it. But it would no more have occurred to Biscuit to skip school in order to watch TV and eat junk than it would have occurred to her that she wasn't entitled to make her own decision about attending. She did not look around to see who had flung the chunk of ice, nor did she look when Mr. Li himself called her name in his diffident baritone, which seemed to trail along after her, lofted on a question mark, before she pedaled past the northern edge of the school and went safely around the bend, heading toward the Hook.

That Biscuit was small for her age (newly ten) suited her. She regarded the fact of her size like a convenient bit of camouflage. If she'd been in command of picking her form in the first place she might have chosen different, might have opted for that of an aquatic mammal, or perhaps something avian. But all in all, diminutive human female was acceptable. Of course, she'd had no say over what she would be called, either, yet this, too, had worked out to her satisfaction. Her given name, Elizabeth, had been dispatched by her older brother within days of her birth. Paul, then three, had fixed exclusively upon the last syllable, which he'd rendered *bis* and gone around the house proclaiming with great gusto. Their parents had been so charmed by his enthusiasm that they'd followed his lead, and from there it had been only a matter of time before they'd appended the *-cuit*.

Now, with school well behind her, she let up on her pedaling and even coasted a bit. The air blew gently against her forehead. She thought not about school, not about consequences, but about her destination, her intention. She thought about the *tchok tchok* sound the teaspoon had made as she'd gathered ashes from the fireplace earlier, the bowl of the spoon tap-scraping the charred brick each time she scooped another heap of gray powder from the hearth. These ashes now resided in a folded-up washcloth stuffed inside the pocket of her parka, along with a few chicken bones she'd fished from the kitchen garbage that morning after everyone else had left. Into her other pocket she'd slipped an egg.

Tchok tchok. She had a thing for certain sounds. She had a thing for lots of things. Images, too, but usually only the narrowest bits. Slivered images, fragments: the way a little piece of ice had been nestled in a crook of the split rail fence in front of the neighbor's house when she'd left. Even though she had only just set out, she'd had to stop and get off her bike in order to examine it, this piece of ice all curled in on itself like a tiny hand, when nearly all the other ice and snow around it had melted. She'd leaned her bike carefully against the fence and squatted down with her face right up close to the frozen coil. She'd noticed the play of colors in its semi-transparency, and also the gleam of wetness from which she'd deduced, with a moment's grim satisfaction, that this bit of ice would shortly be going the way of its brethren. *The melt is upon it,* she'd thought, not in her own voice but in that of a white-coated scientist confirming with a brusque nod a colleague's more tentative speculation.

She'd gone more than a mile and it was one mile more, straight along Broadway, from her school to the Hook, whose sheer rock face she could already see looming in jagged patterns of red-brown and gray. It appeared deceptively close. Although it was near midday the sun was barely distinguishable from the overcast sky: a white dinner plate on a white tablecloth.

Broadway stopped abruptly at the foot of the Hook, where a small wooden gatehouse, closed for the season, announced the entrance to Nyack Beach State Park. Biscuit flew past it and rode the brakes down the steeply winding road, at whose bottom she coasted to the end of a small parking lot, dismounted, and propped the bike against a tree. The kickstand was broken. It was a boy's bike, having first belonged to Paul. It had five speeds and was the metallic gilt-green of a bottle fly.

The wind coming off the Hudson held some warmth, or a promise of warmth to come. Biscuit inhaled, open-mouthed, and got a foretaste of rain. Oh well, she had on the hooded parka (another of Paul's hand-me-downs) and two pairs of socks inside her scuffed work boots (Paul again). She set out along the cinder path that ran north from the parking lot, banding the Hook like a hat brim. To her left rose wooded and talus slopes, broken up by the occasional jumble of boulders. These always looked heart-stoppingly precarious, as though they might resume tumbling at any moment, even though Mrs. Mukhopadhyay, the children's room librarian, had taught her that the cliff had been formed some two hundred million years ago, at the end of the Triassic Period.

To her right the river spread broadly. It was smoke-colored today and choppy, its stiff-looking waves patterned like cake frosting. Biscuit's father had made a cake from a mix yesterday, a yellow cake with whipped cream for her mother's birthday. The thought of the cake, and of her mother's subdued reaction, made her bite the inside of her cheek.

People passed, not many. An elderly couple, the woman wearing a clear plastic rain hat, heading toward the lot. A thin young man with reddish hair and a bearlike dog, off-leash, who overtook Biscuit and soon disappeared around a curve. A middle-aged woman carrying a folded umbrella, who looked Biscuit over appraisingly. Biscuit made fleeting eye contact, gave a curt nod, and did not slow. This was a routine she had perfected. When her father had taken Paul and her to visit their mother and brother in the hospital—this had been a year ago; they'd been twelve and nine—he had explained to them that the policy was no visitors under twelve, but that he didn't suppose anyone would stop them if Biscuit carried herself the right way. "The trick," he'd said, "is to walk like you own the place," a concept and phrase that appealed to her appetite for self-sovereignty. With no further coaching, she'd adopted a cool-as-you-please, look-straight-ahead saunter that had gotten them all through the vast lobby without a hitch. By the wordless glance he'd cast her once the elevator doors had closed behind them, she saw that her father had not been expecting such quick mastery of the technique.

The same instinct or skill served her now, although the farther she walked along the path, the fewer people she encountered. The threatening weather seemed to be a factor, for those she did see were all heading in the direction of the lot. Sure enough, just as she found a spot suitable to her purpose, it began to rain, or to mist, really, a speckling sort of moisture breaking out all around her. She left the path and climbed down onto a rocky slice of beach framed by a short spit of rocks on one side and the natural curve of the shoreline on the other. A squat, bent-necked tree craned out over the vertex of the little cove. Biscuit understood that if anyone were to see her doing what she was about to do, it would invite scrutiny, or possibly actual intervention. But she also saw that from this position, the ashes would not reach the water.

She peered over her shoulder. The cinder path was empty. The mist had become rain. The chances of anyone else coming along seemed slim. All right, she'd do it properly. She left the shelter of the tree and the ice-littered shoreline and went onto the spit, picking her way out along the rocks.

Light rain dashed her face. At the end of the spit, a few inches back from the darker, slippery outer rocks, bearded with yellowish rime, she stopped. The egg first, she decided, and removed it from her pocket. She squatted, tapped the shell smartly on a rock, and broke it over the water. The yolk slipped out, seemed to float on the waves, then was swallowed by them. Strands of the white hung from the broken shell in long, viscous trails. Biscuit let go. The halves of the shell floated like two round-bottomed boats.

She straightened and took the washcloth out of her pocket, unfolding the corners carefully. It felt heavy to her. She almost forgot it wasn't the real thing. She checked again over her shoulder. No one. Then looked out across the heathery expanse of water, squinting past the drops. Along the opposite shore, a train snaked silver past Philipse Manor and Tarrytown before slipping beneath the Tappan Zee Bridge. Biscuit imagined, as she sometimes did, the gray lady riding that train, the lady who was able to look out the moving windows and take note of her far across the water. Biscuit could not remember a time when she hadn't had this idea of the gray lady. She was a kind of friend, or not quite. She was sad and just and mute, and she traveled along the border of Biscuit's life and could see all Biscuit could see and all that she could not.

Biscuit gathered a small handful of ashes, along with one of the chicken bones, and threw these gently toward the water. A lot of the ashes blew back and stuck to her jeans. The rest floated on top of the waves like pepper. The bone floated, too. She paused to see whether she felt anything.

Her mother had not liked the cake. She hadn't said so, but Biscuit could see that she hadn't. She had said, "Thank you, John," and Biscuit's father had smiled at her with such relief that Biscuit had felt a little sick, and let down by them both, and then the cake, which she had been looking forward to, had tasted just so: of disappointment.

She was here on the spit because of them, because of the way her mother and her father had fallen down behind themselves. She thought of it like this, like the way a book can fall down behind all the others on a shelf, and in this way it's missing, only you don't know it to look at the shelf: all that you see looks orderly and complete. Her parents seemed like the books you could see: they smiled and spoke and dressed and made supper and went off to work and all the other things they were supposed to do, but something, a crucial volume, had slipped down in back and couldn't be reached.

She was here, too, because of Mrs. Mukhopadhyay and the library book. Mrs. Mukhopadhyay whom she hadn't seen in almost a year, and the library book which she'd stolen.

And of course she was here because of the baby. To sever *its last earthly ties.*

The rain was falling harder. Biscuit raised her hood and fingers of rain tapped on it: *Hello, hello, Biscuit.* Silver drops like Mrs. Mukhopadhyay's silver bangles, which fell up and down her wrists, singing, as she checked out books. *Good girl,* tapped the rain, in Mrs. Mukhopadhyay's lilting, practical voice. *Come on, then: get on with it.*

She ought to speak, Biscuit knew, or at least to think some words. She squinted through the rain, trying to remember the words from the book, which had been too fat and heavy to stuff inside her parka and so was back at home where she kept it hidden underneath her bed. She was supposed to beg the water to bear the ashes safely away. *Please, dear water,* she began, but that didn't seem right and she faltered. Then words did come: *Blessed be,* less for meaning than pure sound: *blessed be, blessed be, blessed, blessed, blessed be.* It was something you might skip rope to. She saw girls skipping rope, tap-scraping the ground with their hard-bottomed shoes.

But she was not here for skipping-rope girls.

This was about the egg, the ashes, the bones, the baby.

The baby's name had been Simon.

Blessed be, Simon Ryrie.

She reached again into the nest of ash and bone. Before she threw the second handful, something big and hard and soft pushed against the backs of her legs, and her knees buckled, her feet slipped out from under her, and she slid, as if amenably, into the river.

2.

Just before one, just as he was about to start priming the second flat, the theme song from *Scooby-Doo* sounded from within John Ryrie's pants. He transferred the brush to his other hand and fished among keys, loose change, crumpled bills and receipts, for his cell. His thirteen-year-old son was in the habit of swiping it, downloading a new ring tone, and replacing it all without John's knowledge, so that he never knew precisely what tune or sound effect was going to emit next. John recognized his son's high jinks for what they were: love notes. Usually they pleased him, although once, while riding an elevator that happened also to contain his department chair, an admissions rep, and a bunch of prospective students, he'd suffered the indignity of having Jay-Z's "99 Problems" (explicit version) issue from the region of his groin; he'd admonished Paul, lightly, for that.

Now he glanced to see who it was, and flipped it open. "Hey."

His wife. No preamble. "Upper Nyack called."

The elementary school. "What's up?"

"They wanted to know if Biscuit's all right."

"They couldn't ask her?" He aimed for Groucho Marx, even as he felt the sinking in his gut.

"John, she skipped again. Do you think you could get over to the house?"

John refrained from sighing into the phone. This was their daughter's fifth unexcused absence this year, her third since winter break alone. They'd been called in to discuss the matter last month, after the most recent incident. He and Ricky had sat down with the principal, Biscuit's teacher, and the school guidance counselor, and they'd had a lengthy, convivial, and unilluminating conversation, not so much about Biscuit as about curricular benchmarks, hormones, childhood depression, pharmaceutical research, and the works of Carol Gilligan, Mary Pipher, and Rachel Simmons. The meeting had ended with John feeling touched by the concern of the school personnel, Ricky seething at what she characterized as their prepackaged condescension, and neither of them one whit closer to understanding what was going on with their daughter.

John was baffled. All he could think was that Biscuit seemed awfully young to have truancy issues. When he'd been ten he would no more have thought of playing hooky than robbing a bank. "Did you try calling the house?"

"I did." Her brevity told all.

Still, he hesitated.

"Do you think you could drive over?" she asked again; he could hear her working to make it a request.

Now John did sigh. He looked at the glistening paintbrush in his hand. The four students in the scene shop with him, currently applying soy-based theater paint to a dozen flats, would be unable to go beyond that task without his guidance. He'd counted on cutting the brick wall out of Styrofoam this afternoon. It would take at least an hour and a half to go home, register his and Ricky's concern with Biscuit, and make it back to campus. And it wouldn't be fair to the students, who were required to work in the scene shop for course credit, to ask them to rearrange their schedules and come back later in the day. Which meant he'd wind up giving them credit for hours worked, while he himself would cut and paint the wall alone tonight. In fact, despite the relative minimalism of the set, and the fact that John was largely recycling an old design (*For Colored Girls Who Have Considered Suicide/When the Rainbow is Enuf* was a perennial favorite at Congers Community College; this was its second production during his short tenure there), the opening was only four days away, so he could pretty well prophesy at least one all-nighter in his immediate future.

When John first met Ricky Shapiro, when they'd first begun dating, it had not been uncommon for him to spend entire nights in the theater. Back then he'd earned a living (after a fashion, Ricky would qualify) teching professional shows at Broadway and regional theaters. He had many happy memories of her visiting him at work on a set after midnight, when the world at large was dark and oblivious, and all light, all life seemed temporarily concentrated within whatever minor world he was constructing. She'd bring in food and they'd sit at the edge of the stage together—he in his painty, sawdusty clothes, she looking so clean and smelling so good—with little white cardboard take-out containers spread out around them. Their love had sprung up, taken root, and run rampant in half-realized forests and tenement houses, castles and kitchens, drawing rooms and hospital rooms, and once in heaven, and once in Denmark.

Back then Ricky—a freshly minted financial engineer (a "quant," as they called themselves, as she called herself, with a kind of utilitarian pride), not long out of graduate school and playing her new role to the hilt in hose and pumps, pencil skirts and tailored shirts—had been captivated by all his tricks of the trade: how you'd mix perlite (the tiny white balls in potting soil) with paint in order to bring texture to an interior surface; how you'd spray a little paint on the artificial flora, in order to pull it into the world of the show; how, for a big backdrop, you'd spray fixative on charcoal, then tint it and build up a few layers of paint to give it the depth and richness of an oil painting. She'd loved the lingo of the scene shop: scumble painting, scenic fitches, pounce wheels. She'd loved the tools of his profession, from flogger to feather duster, chicken wire to Cellupress; even the most banal piece of equipment—the hair dryer he'd use to quick-dry a patch of paint in order to check the end color— fascinated her in its theatrical context. With a kind of busybody intensity he found sexy, she'd insist he describe to her, in detail and in language she could understand, exactly what he was working on, on a given night, and why he was going about it in that particular way.

"All make-believe," she would say. "All this for just pretend." Her tone of wonderment at once paying tribute and poking fun.

"But this stuff is real," John would counter, rapping his knuckles against the wooden brace holding up a painted storefront, fingering a sharktooth scrim. "Your stuff's pretend."

"My stuff!"

"What are derivatives? Stuff you can't touch. Futures. Swaps. Forwards. Backwards."

"There's no backwards, smart guy."

"Oh, no?"

"No . . . oh."

Already he'd have turned her around, positioned her tight against his hips, begun to peel her skirt up slowly from the hem.

The truth is he'd never been particularly interested in her world. Volatility arbitrage had sounded exotic—hell, had sounded hot—when first she'd uttered it, tucking a piece of hair primly behind her ear as she did. And it was a rush when he'd realized how flat-out smart she was, how quick and sharp, in a way he'd never be; her interest in him seemed to confer on him a sort of attractiveness he hadn't suspected he possessed. But in another respect, although John avoided thinking of it in such terms, he found Ricky's profession beneath him. He thought of her and all her ilk—not only other quants but the whole phylum: investment bankers, hedge fund managers, speculators, risk-management analysts—as so many self-absorbed children playing an elaborate game of make-believe, running around dressed in the costumes of power brokers, issuing decrees in gobbledygook, trading promises like wads of play money. Sipping air from plastic teacups. Although he was both too considerate and too uncertain of this view to voice these impressions outright, his general opinion of her field was not exactly a secret. Even before their marriage it had begun to show.

As for Ricky, what had started as genuine interest in John's work transformed over time not into feigned interest but frank resentment. At first, and really, all throughout Paul's toddlerhood, she'd continued to be at least nominally supportive. If she'd tolerated John's late nights and sporadic employment with more stoicism than grace, she'd made only the occasional, concertedly factual observation of the strain it put on her. After Biscuit was born, however, Ricky had put her foot down and John had given up this work, with its gypsy schedule and irregular paychecks.

In fact, John knew the phrase "put her foot down" did Ricky a disservice—for any number of reasons, one being she had *not* actually put her foot down but merely registered her preference; another being John had not been unhappy to accept the job at Congers Community College's Llewellyn-Price Theater. The Llewellyn-Price, a five-hundred-seat performance center, was used (or "utilized," as CCC brochures unfailingly put it) not only for campus productions but also by amateur and professional groups from around the county. John, whose official title for the past nine years had been Lecturer in Theater Design, taught one course each semester covering the basics of stagecraft and lighting; managed the scene shop; designed sets for a four-show season; helped supervise the student work crews; and served as technical consultant for outside groups using the space. An insane job. Which he did not pretend not to love.

This was precisely what complicated matters on the phone now with his wife. Ricky, who for the past three years had headed the research group of Birnbaum and Traux in White Plains, hated her job as passionately and openly as he loved his. The work itself had once captivated her: the search for patterns in apparently random systems, the idea that one could forecast future volatility, devise models of what was "true in expectation." It wasn't simply that she'd loved the notion of hidden order, of discernible outcomes. It was that she'd cast her lot with it, banked on its existence. It was almost not too much to call it her principles, her faith.

When they first met, Ricky'd been contemplating going for a doctorate in the philosophy of mathematics. Sometimes John wondered, with a kind of confused, guilty perturbation, how things might have turned out if she'd gone this route. She'd have been happier, he supposed. They might all have been. Even if it meant they'd still be paying off student loans, renting instead of owning, borrowing instead of investing. He couldn't help his rather embarrassingly rosy image of what their life would have looked like then—chillier house, older cars, rattier sweaters, more pasta, less steak: happier.

At the beginning of the economic crisis, and during the long plummeting months of recession, he'd lived with the fear that she would lose her job. Daily he rehearsed receiving the news, offering consolations, making adjustments, weathering loss. The dread was a pressure in his chest, a gnawing in his bones. His very teeth ached with it. Yet when things began to bottom out, when the layoffs tapered off and the market began to evince feeble signs of life, he was aware of a bashful, bewildered disappointment. They had been left unscathed, untested. Only then did he wonder if such a test might have been their saving grace, the very thing that would have shaken them awake, restored to them their vitality, their happiness. Like that summer at Cabruda Lake, when, tested, they'd risen admirably to the occasion, surprising themselves a little, discovering within their relationship something heartier, at once more stalwart and accommodating than they'd known.

Ricky never complained about what she did, the work itself, but she griped volubly about the accoutrements of her job: the twice daily commute across the bridge; the fact that she had to leave the house each morning before the rest of the family was awake and arrive home each evening too late to cook dinner; the fact that she had to wear "clothes," as she put it (she had a special, contemptuous way of pronouncing the word in this context); and, perhaps most of all, the fact that she earned three times as much as her husband, making her job pretty much unquittable. John knew all of this, including the fact that the last part was not, strictly speaking, true, that Ricky could quit if only he were willing to do something that paid more. That this was a possibility they had never properly discussed loomed over him at all times.

It was because he lived in trepidation of such a discussion, because he lived with the burden of his unspoken (by either of them) indebtedness, that he knew he would give in to Ricky's current request: would go to the house, check on Biscuit, and scold her in some weary fashion, even though he felt there was little to be achieved by such a gesture. And because he knew, and knew Ricky knew, that he would ultimately give in, John took a moment to dispute the necessity.

"You don't think it can wait?" He spoke softly, angling his body so that its bulk afforded him some privacy from the students. "I mean, we've all been here before. What am I even going to say? That we haven't already said."

Ricky sipped in a quick breath. Clearly she'd prepared her answer. "It sends a message, though. If you go home now. If we confront—sorry, if *you* confront her right away. Then at least she gets a sense of the urgency. That we're not taking this lightly."

"Yeah." He stroked some paint across the top of the stretched muslin, using up what was already on the brush. "You're right."

"Thanks."

"Don't do that."

"Yeah, but—thanks, John."

He slipped the phone back in his pocket. It wouldn't be so bad, returning later tonight. Lance Oprisu, the Llewellyn-Price's technical director, who ordinarily bore chief responsibility for executing the sets that John designed, was on leave this semester, which had turned out to be both burden and blessing. Although John's workload was more stressful, he had found the increased solitude, the sheer number of hours he'd been spending alone now in the theater, welcome. Tonight he'd have the scene shop to himself, a ready supply of Diet Coke from the vending machine down the hall, The Doors blasting on the stereo, and no students around to mock, however affectionately, his musical tastes. He knew when he got in the right groove he could work solo with as much efficiency as an entire crew of students. Nor would it be awful to spend a night out of the house. He set the brush across the top of the paint can and turned around to face the students, none of whom looked up.

Amy and Pureza were working, minimally, on a single flat; mostly they seemed to be deep in conversation, Pureza doing the majority of the talking, Amy murmuring at intervals, *"Claro. Claro, que sí."* Iryna wasn't working on the set at all, but applying color to her face instead, from a seriously impressive eye shadow kit; at a glance it contained some twenty cakes of color. Vivi was wearing red earbuds and grooving to whatever music she was absorbing through them, but she had, bless her heart, finished one flat already and was halfway through her second.

"Ah, people," said John. His inclination was to say, "You guys," but he had learned that this didn't go over well with his students, predominantly female, first-generation college students, almost a third of them first-generation Americans. Addressing them as "women" seemed too stiff, "ladies" too sexist, "folks" too grass-roots, and "kids" too insulting. So: "People?" said John again, louder, and they turned to him. He waited for Vivi to remove one earbud. "I'm going to have to take off early today. I'd like you to finish up these flats, but then you can go. It's my screwup, not yours, so you can still sign the crew sheet for two hours. Iryna."

Sighing, eye-shadow wand in hand, she turned from the little round mirror balanced on her palm. "I'm leaving you in charge of making sure all the brushes get cleaned. And you're responsible for making sure the paint cans have their lids pressed on. Tightly. Yes?" She nodded with an air of bored self-pity that John ignored.

From the start he had placed a similar degree of trust in his students as he'd placed in the professionals with whom he'd built Broadway sets, and nearly always his expectations were duly met. In return, the students wound up respecting not only him but, more important, the craft—or so their course evaluations often stated. He knew the students regarded him warmly, too, from the way they gently teased him. John was a tall man, burly, with curling dark hair on his head and face; over the years he'd been mostly amused to hear himself likened to Paul Bunyan, Bluto, the Brawny paper towel man.

When he left the building a thin rain was falling, and the drive from Congers to Nyack was a palette of grays, broken up by licorice-stalk trees and spectral flashes of snow at the side of the road. The Ford Ranger's wiper blades needed replacing, something John had been reminding himself and then forgetting to do for months. He took the winding roads slowly: no point hurrying. Lately, something had gone wrong with the car speakers, too, and after a minute of staticky classic rock, he switched the radio off and listened instead to the wet tires, the metronomic wipers. His thoughts were troubled, but not by his daughter, never mind that she was the cause of his leaving work early; it was his wife who preoccupied him as he drove.

Ricky had turned thirty-seven yesterday. In the afternoon, she'd gone to adult lap swim at the Y and John had baked a yellow cake from a box. He'd topped it—his own inspiration, of which he'd been pleased—with cream he whipped and strawberries he sliced. While he'd been making the cake, the kids had walked into town with a twenty and a ten he'd taken from his wallet and instructions to pick out gifts for their mother. Biscuit had returned with a mood ring and a Whitman's Sampler, Paul with a wooden-handled cheese knife. John—who found it harder to pick out a gift for his wife every year, and who, although Ricky always expressed gratitude for whatever he gave her, felt increasingly inept at pleasing her (this in turn leading him to make progressively more outlandish choices)—had already bought her a mandolin. It arrived complete with padded case, instructional DVD, practice book, tuner, and set of picks. He'd been excited about it when he ordered it online, then in doubt ever since.

Part of the problem was his fluctuating inclination over how much to spend. When he bought her something expensive he felt sheepish about the fact that it was so obviously her earnings that allowed him to do so. Yet when he bought her something modest he felt just as sheepish and like a spoilsport, besides. Thus the schizophrenia of his gift-giving over time: one year daisies and a water pitcher; another platinum and emerald earrings; one year a Kiva gift certificate; the next a Kindle. This year, he'd half consciously striven to balance the extravagance of the mandolin with the humbleness of the food. For the birthday supper he'd served tacos and black cherry soda, which had seemed a jolly, festive menu back in the supermarket but inadequate, collegiate, once they were all actually sitting at the table. Ricky looked ten years younger than her age in an enormous SUNY New Paltz sweatshirt and holey jeans, her still-wet hair combed straight past her shoulders. The wavy white-gray strands that had begun to striate the brown this past year were invisible now, weighted down by the dark damp lot. Seeing her this way, as if polished and pared by her swim, and smelling the chlorine in her hair, John could not help but imagine her in water. He could envision the precise stroke of her limbs, the supple way she sliced through liquid, although it had been years since he'd actually seen her swim. After cake she'd opened her presents, and despite the attentive way in which she thanked them each by name, John had the distinct impression the only gift she genuinely appreciated was the Whitman's Sampler.

Later that night John had carried the instrument upstairs and set it on the foot of the bed, where Ricky, wearing the giant sweatshirt as pajamas, sat up reading *The Economist*. "Have you opened it yet?" he asked.

She'd given him a look that combined, he believed, contrition and resentment before laying aside the magazine. Her hair, now dry, had regained its measure of gold, and it shone in the lamplight as she bent forward to unzip the padded case. A wing of it, faintly threaded with gray, fell over her shoulder, curtaining her face. He'd reached over and with a thick forefinger tucked it behind her ear, a movement that felt at once tentative and bold. She hadn't reacted at all, neither withdrew nor softened under his touch, but gazed steadily at the instrument in its case, surveying its glossy tobacco surface, the curves of its f-holes, the mother-of-pearl inlays on its fingerboard. At last she'd looked up at him and smiled. "It's beautiful, John." He was aware she had not touched it. She zipped the case shut, placed it on the floor beside the bed, retrieved her magazine. Later, under the covers, the backs of her slim bare legs had fit un-protestingly against the bulky warmth of his.

Ricky never got mad at him anymore. Once, he might have considered her volatile, might even have called her hot-blooded. Feisty. He thought of her in their courtship days, the salty sting of her, the way she might look up from the table and spike the air with her fork, the way she'd fill a doorway and bring the heel of her boot down. The crack of it, the candor. Now she never expressed anger toward him. Under direct questioning, she claimed not to possess any. Nor could he think of any crime, any infraction, for which she might blame him. And yet. John found himself repeatedly, increasingly, preparing for a sort of imaginary defense, as though he might be brought up on charges at a moment's notice. Though she no longer roused herself to anger, it felt like she was furious. It had been this way since before the baby's death.

Ricky's crimes were well documented. They numbered two: the ancient infidelity and the more recent one, both of which he'd forgiven, been so broad as to forgive. These events had not broken them. Here they were a year after their greatest trial, standing proof, something very like intact. Thanks in large part to his exercise of tolerance, so impressive to them both. Why, then, with such ample reserves, such stockpiles of goodwill owed him (if you were going to think of it in such terms, make an equation of it, a balance sheet, though of course that was more Ricky's domain than his), why did he worry he'd done wrong?

Turning the truck onto their street, he had actively to remind himself of the task at hand: it wasn't Appeasing Ricky, but rather Confronting Biscuit. He supposed he agreed with Ricky that one of them ought to deal with the issue straightaway, but despite what he had to admit would at this point be called his daughter's chronic cutting, he couldn't manage to summon real anxiety over Biscuit. If he did not understand her, neither did he worry about her. Whatever her idiosyncrasies, she struck him as being herself untroubled by them, which was in a way what mattered most. Sometimes he had the odd thought that of them all, Biscuit alone seemed to know what she was doing, what she was about.

John parked in the gravel driveway, cut through the rain over the scrap of front lawn, and strode up the steps to the porch. This porch had been the great hook back when he and Ricky first saw the house, on an October afternoon eleven years earlier. They'd been living in the city then, in a one-bedroom way over on West Twenty-ninth, near the river. They had borrowed Ricky's parents' car in order to take little Paul, then two, apple picking in Rockland County. The day was unseasonably hot, the orchard packed, the remaining fruit all on the highest branches, the ladders all taken, and to top it off John got stung by a bee. But then they'd gone and had lunch in Nyack and a river breeze wafted up the hill, and afterward, as they'd been strolling down the sidewalk toward ice cream, with Paul asleep in the carrier on John's back, they'd paused to look at the photos in the storefront of a real estate office, and popped inside on a lark.

It had been premature: they didn't really have the money for a down payment (this was before Ricky had been recruited by Birnbaum and Traux, back when she'd been working downtown part-time as a consultant), nor had they convinced themselves they were ready to leave the city for the suburbs. But as luck had it, one agent had been sitting idle and fairly pounced on them with an offer to show a handful of properties straightaway. For the next several hours, as they'd viewed house upon house in the hilly, residential neighborhoods, their sense of themselves as essentially urbanites only increased. But the fifth time they'd emerged from the agent's car—this time stepping out into eighty-degree heat just a block from the main drag, where a small public park sloped down toward the river—and saw the FOR SALE sign marking a perfectly modest dwelling in the middle of the block, they'd both felt something neither had ever known before: house lust.

In a village architecturally dominated by Victorians, this house had been small and plain as a swallow's nest. A big fir shaded the low structure, whose stucco was the color of shredded wheat, and it had covered the diminutive lawn with pine needles, a blanket of bronze. The clay tile roof had a few bald patches, and the chimney a visible crack. There'd been something of a witch's cottage about the dwelling, echoes of a house under an enchantment. What tilted it away from outright cheerlessness and delivered it instead—just—into the realm of charm, had been the wide front porch, disproportionately deep, disproportionately gracious, the entrance framed by the sinewy branches of a wisteria. It had been well past the season of its blossoming, but its leaves hung thick and heavy, the lush gold of ripened pears.

Instantly, John began playing the game he occasionally played: if this were a set he had built, what would have been his intention? What would its design have been meant to convey to an audience, even before the play had begun? A haunting tranquillity? A disheveled haven? Indulgence? Humility? Beauty? He could not decide.

The block ran downhill, sloping steeply at the bottom toward the river's edge. The water on this day of unseasonable heat had looked quenching and calm. Ricky, whose second pregnancy had just been beginning to show on her slight frame, and John, with the sleeping Paul drooling a dark wet patch on his shoulder, had reached out at the same moment and found each other's hands. The agent, shrewdly enough, had taken note and said nothing, giving the fantasy time in which to colonize her clients' hearts. She had let them be the ones to initiate movement toward the house, materializing before them somewhat magi-

cally as they approached the door and handing the key—this
had been the master touch—to Ricky. Turning it in the lock,
Ricky had slid John such a look as he had never before seen
on her face: like a cat scenting cream, almost sultry with deter-
mination.

Many times over the ensuing years of variously stressful
mortgage payments, insurance premiums, and property tax
increases—not to mention broken hot water heaters, windows
that no longer fit snugly into their casements, and roof jobs gone
awry—one or the other of them had looked up from a clutter of
bills and contracts to curse the real estate agent; it was their private joke that she had indeed been magic, an evil sorceress. But
beneath the jest, it was understood that he and Ricky remained
in the house's thrall, and having bought it was one thing they
never regretted.

As John crossed the porch now, rain beat on the roof loud
as pebbles on tin. A broken drainpipe caused a cascade beyond
the eastern end of the porch, making an opaque curtain of water
there. John wiped his feet and went in, called out to Biscuit and
was answered by the shrilling of the teakettle. If he had paused to
consider, he might have found this odd, as his daughter was not
a tea drinker. But he did not, and it didn't occur to him until he
entered the kitchen that he would find there someone other
than Biscuit.

3.

Gordie Joiner, an only child, aged nineteen, was not minding the rain. He took it as affirmation of his own melancholy and did not let it alter his unhurried course, but continued in a northerly direction along the cinder path. It was slightly past one, and he had nowhere he needed to be. Not this day, nor the next. Nor, for that matter . . . but it did no good to think along those lines. Only when his dog cast him a series of questioning looks, head cocked, mouth ajar, and then gradually lagged behind him, ultimately declaring her reluctance by coming to a stop, legs slightly splayed, in the middle of the path, did he relent.

"All right. Sissy."

Ebie, who was mostly Newf—that enormous, double-coated breed famous for having both the ability and instinct to perform water rescues—was not a sissy. She relished being in water, any form of water—ocean, river, pond, bathtub—anything except rain.

Now she swung about, her wild approval of the decision to retreat making a puppy of her. Somehow an ear had become inverted, giving her a ridiculous, spastic look. She glanced over her shoulder: *Coming?* Her tail knocked out raindrops right and left. Gordie caught up, smoothed down her ear and gave her rump a tap. She sallied forth erect, all bearish one hundred thirty pounds of her. The rain fell greenly, pocking the remnants of crusty snow that banked the curving, riverside path.

He did a double take when, coming around the bend, he saw Ebie take off from the path and trot—for a moment it looked like this—out across the water, messiah-like. Then he blinked and squinted through the rain, which had become a downpour, and his perception was corrected: she was in fact picking her way across a spit of rocks that jutted some fifteen yards straight out into the river. Gordie's confusion at this unlikely sight was compounded almost immediately by another, that of a peculiar figure at the very end of the spit: a dwarf in hooded cape. Or child in large green parka. Ebie's Newf instincts, however partial, however misplaced, had kicked in: she was off to the rescue.

Gordie whistled for her, one sharp commanding note, knowing even as he did that it was futile. When she sensed danger, she would not be dissuaded. He sighed and began to climb down onto the rocks himself, then froze. Ebie, too, had stopped, just three or four feet from the child, who seemed not to have noticed the advent of company. He or she seemed to be holding an object in one hand, and with the other hand scooping and throwing . . . *something,* toward the water. Ashes, from the look of it, fine, dark ashes and a few chunks of something denser, bone. Gordie would not have known if he hadn't done it himself that winter.

For the first time since he'd started this walk, he felt the cold. His oversized jacket—really a heavy, woolen lumberjack shirt that had been his dad's—was finally soaked through at the shoulders, and the thighs and cuffs of his jeans, all drenched to the skin.

Ebie moved then. He could tell she meant to use her head, her bulk, to nudge this person away from the edge of the spit, toward dry land. The rocks out there at the edge must have been more slippery than she'd judged. He saw first his dog slip—her paw faltered and went out from under her—and then, as she scrambled with canine dexterity to gain a solid foothold, he saw her shoulder plow against the child's legs, and the child's legs buckle at the knee. There was a vanishing and a splash, and he could not have said which came first, they happened so fast.

The child didn't go underwater, at least not all the way. Her head—he could see now it was a she—remained visible, and an arm, one bare hand clinging to the jagged rock upon which she had been standing. Behind her, on the water's shimmering surface, something pale appeared to float momentarily, and then was gone. Ebie, her own singular shortcomings now in full display, declined to go in after the girl but half stood, half sat anxiously at the water's edge, wagging her tail as if in mad apology or frantic encouragement: a real hero manqué.

Gordie leaped off the path onto the crescent of sand and tore out across the rocks. He had a light body, a wiry build, and managed the uneven surface nimbly; even so, he almost lost his footing twice. At the end of the spit, he squatted beside Ebie and thrust out an arm. The girl's face was white, stunned, blue-lipped. She did not take his hand, but tried to heave herself up on her own, scrambling with her feet against the submerged part of the rock. He thought she had it, but in the end she slipped back, this time going all the way under. Gordie plunged his arm into the water and grabbed the hood of her parka. He pulled her above the surface and she spluttered and blinked, appearing, even through her chattering, rather affronted by this intervention. But Gordie got a two-handed grip under her arms and hoisted her out.

She stood bent, shivering and dripping on the rocks. She looked to be eight or nine, he thought—he was no good at telling, really—and had on heavy work boots, jeans, and the oversized parka, which must have weighed a ton. She looked at him with light brown eyes he found disconcerting; she did not appear aloof, exactly, so much as unduly composed.

"Is someone here with you?"

She shook her head. Gordie looked around rather stupidly, as though she might be mistaken, but there was no one else in the pelting rain, only the two of them and the dog.

"Well—God, I'm sorry about this. Look, my jacket's a little drier than yours—you're obviously freezing—please." He slipped off the woolen lumberjack shirt and made a fairly hapless movement, as if miming tugging at the sleeve of her parka. He supposed he ought not actually undress a strange child. "You should take that off," he urged, "and we'll get you—well, a little—warmer." She fumbled at her zipper, but her fingers were stiff with cold; it wouldn't budge. She surprised Gordie by extending both arms, wrists turned skyward, in a gesture that clearly meant *do it for me*. So he unzipped her, conscious of Ebie wagging and whining softly beside him, and eased the parka off her shoulders. It slid from her slight frame and sunk to the rocks, leaded with water. Ebie took a step toward the girl and licked her palm.

"*You're* a bumbling oaf," Gordie informed the dog, draping his woolen shirt over the girl's shoulders. The pattern was a large plaid of green, red, and black. "I really am sorry," he repeated.

"W-w-what for?"

He leaned back and squinted at her. She had her hand on Ebie's neck, her fingers buried deep in Newfie fur. "Well, because she's my dog. Not that she meant to knock you in. I think she was trying to herd you away from the water. It's her lifeguard instinct. But she's a bit of a clod. Really, I'm to blame. Look, my God, you're freezing. Do you live around here? We should bring you home. My name's Gordie Joiner. Can I give you a ride? Or call someone?" As he spoke he scooped up her sodden parka and attempted to usher her back over the spit to land. She let herself be brought along. With one hand hovering lightly on her shoulder, steering, he could feel her shivering violently through the jacket. They went slowly, under the press of rain, so as not to lose their footing. Once on the little slice of beach, Ebie gave herself a mighty shake, firing droplets three hundred and sixty degrees, and the girl surprised Gordie again by laughing at this.

"Look. Let me take you home, yeah? I'm parked in the lot."

The girl shook her head.

"You just—you really need to get warm. I know you don't know me," he repeated.

"'S-s-s-s not that." Her teeth were going like mad; it was an effort to make out her words. "B-b-b-b-biked."

Gordie looked around for the bicycle.

"Th-there." She jerked her chin in the direction of the lot.

"No problem. I've got a station wagon."

They climbed up the bank to the path, using the knobbly tree roots as grips. Gordie whistled for the dog, who clambered along belatedly and then, with an air of saving face, barged out in front at a trot, as though she'd suddenly remembered she was supposed to be guiding this tour. They made their way back without talking.

Gordie was nearly certain of what he had witnessed: the girl had been flinging ashes into the river. He tried to unhook the act from its most obvious, funereal interpretation. There could, after all, be other reasons a person might toss ashes. Though none came to mind.

He studied the girl surreptitiously. How old *was* she? He'd have thought seven or eight from size alone, but her bearing was decidedly older. Her hair was plastered wetly to her head. His dad's plaid jacket hung to her knees: a clown suit on her, within which she remained inscrutable. Anyway, it was the middle of a day on a Friday—why wouldn't she be in school? He considered whether she might be a runaway, an orphan, perhaps. He wanted to ask her about those ashes.

At the lot she showed him the bike propped against a tree, and Gordie hoisted it toward his dad's station wagon, one of only two cars that remained, the weather having chased most visitors away. The other vehicle was a brown Buick. With a glance he could just make out, past its streaming windows, an elderly couple eating sandwiches. They looked cozy, dry, unhurried. The sight brought him up short, riddled him with feeling. He didn't know what to do about it, besides look away and open up the back of his dad's station wagon. The middle seat was already folded down flat, with a dirty fleece blanket spread across. He stowed the bike, arranging it horizontally on top of the blanket. Ebie whined, gave a short bark. "Hush," said Gordie. "You'll have to squeeze."

She whined again.

"Go on, get in."

"Why can't she ride up front?" asked the girl, her longest utterance by far.

"Oh, she'll be all right. You go ahead and get in." But only after Gordie had coaxed Ebie in next to the bike did the girl comply.

"So what's your name?" he asked once he'd sat, turned on the ignition, and blasted the heat. The car still smelled of cigarettes. He did not mind this for himself—the smell had used to bother him, but these past few months he'd come to like it, even to hope it might linger forever—but for the first time, because of the girl, he was sorry about it, self-conscious.

She drew a breath and paused. She still looked tiny, wan, half drowned, but color was beginning to come back into her lips and cheeks. She also still looked, for one so small and sodden, uncannily poised. But in the protracted silence, he began to wonder if she felt unsafe with him, now that they were in the car with the doors closed and the cigarette smell.

"Or, I mean, of course you don't have to tell me. I know I'm a strange . . . a stranger." He'd been about to say "strange man," but it sounded ridiculous, a phrase from a police blotter. "All I really need to know is how to bring you home."

"No," said the girl, regarding him thoughtfully. "It's not that you're dangerous. I was just thinking what name to tell you."

Gordie was a little deflated by her cool assessment. He covered his embarrassment with an attempt at wit. "You have an assortment?"

She sighed. "I have a nickname and a real name."

"Got it."

"Biscuit and Elizabeth," she explained.

"Right. Well, like I said, I'm Gordie." He jerked a thumb toward the back. "And that's Ebie."

They both turned toward the dog, who responded to the sudden attention by jutting her face forward, open-mouthed. A great hammock of saliva hung from her upper lip.

"You're very big," Biscuit told her. Ebie responded to this statement by closing her enormous mouth for several seconds. Then she resumed panting. "I live on Depew," Biscuit told Gordie, turning. "You know Depew? Across from the park."

Gordie nodded and pointed the station wagon up the hill. "Your parents know you're out here, Elizabeth?" As soon as he heard himself say it, he knew it was wrong—both the assumption that she had parents (he of all people ought to know better), as well as the way it made him sound like a truant officer.

But she replied simply, "Yes."

"So"—he cleared his throat again—"sorry, but—I have to ask: What were you doing out on the rocks?" He offered an apologetic grimace.

"Oh." She shook her head, just a little toss, and turned to look out the passenger window. "Nothing."

"It didn't look like nothing."

"Nothing much." This was barely audible.

Still he pressed. "To be honest, it looked like"—he coughed—"like you were scattering ashes. Was it . . . ? Do you know what I mean? I mean, you seem . . . well, for one thing, awfully *young*."

"I'm not," she said flatly.

"Okay. You're young*ish*, though." By shifting the focus to her age he was, he knew, yielding to her, allowing them to move beyond the subject of the ashes, and Gordie was disappointed by this, his own inability to press on, his curiosity unsated. He resisted the impulse to tell her about his own loss. "I mean," he said, another attempt at humor, "you *are* a kid and all?"

"I'm ten," she said, in a tone that might as easily have implied contradiction as concession.

After that a small coolness descended upon them and they rode most of the rest of the way in silence.

The rain made a din. The wipers eked out their steady lullaby. Ebie was redolent, the specter of every skunk she'd ever chased summoned up by the wetness of her fur plus the waft of the heater. The trees along Broadway arched heavily over the street. Gordie began to feel almost drowsy, under an enchantment made up of rhythms and textures as old as childhood. He thought for some reason of his dad coddling eggs. That was something Gordie had always loved to watch, though he never cared to partake of eggs cooked in this fashion. But he'd loved watching his dad butter the insides of the porcelain cup, crack the eggs one-handed, give a few twists of the pepper mill, sprinkle salt with his fingers, screw on the metal top and immerse the lot in a pan of simmering water to cook, *"gentle-like, mind you,"* for exactly seven minutes.

The girl Elizabeth spoke. "The next left."

"Got it."

The house she pointed out, in the middle of the second block, sat just as she'd said, smack across from the small green park. Gordie was glad to see a vehicle in the driveway if it meant someone was home, although the fact that said vehicle was a beat-up pickup gave him a moment's pause; he associated such trucks with guys with big guts and short tempers. "I'll get your bike," he told her, pulling up by the curb. "You go on ahead."

"Don't worry. It wasn't your fault," she said kindly, and for an instant he thought she'd read his mind, but she wasn't talking to him. "Good-bye, girl," she said, offering her cheek, which Ebie swiped with her tongue. Then she patted the dog's glossy crown and slid out.

Gordie wrestled out the bike and carried it, along with the sopping parka, onto the ample porch. The girl, having left the warm station wagon for the damp and the wind, stood hunched and shivering again. "Is it open?" asked Gordie. "Or do you ring the bell?" Whether she shivered or shrugged he could not tell, but as she didn't move to let herself in, he reached out and pressed the button.

The man who came to the door was indeed large, and darkly bearded as well, but he looked more disconcerted than angry and when he spoke his voice was mild, even faintly musical. "Well! Biscuit. What happened to you?"

"I found her at the Hook," Gordie announced. "It's my fault she's all wet."

"Your fault?" The man peered confusedly at the pouring rain. "Please, come in."

Gordie looked at the girl, thinking she'd take up the tale, but she remained both silent and unbudging. "She fell in the water, but it was my dog—my dog basically knocked her in."

"The water? Both of you, please come inside."

Now the girl melted sideways past her father into the front hall and Gordie followed, despite protesting, "I don't want to drip on your rug. Yes, the river. My dog kind of shoved her, accidentally."

"The river!" Light dawned. The man stared at his daughter, seeming at last to absorb just how thoroughly drenched she was: much more so than Gordie, or than anyone who'd simply been out in the rain. "Biscuit, are you all right? You fell in the Hudson? Where?"

"The Hook," she said, and arched her back and stuck out both arms in such a way that Gordie's dad's wet lumberjack shirt slid to the floor. Her father picked it up and spread it on top of the radiator, and then took a big fleece jacket (from the look of it, his) from the coatrack beside them and wrapped it around her, rubbing her back and arms as Gordie detailed more plainly the course of recent events.

"I'm grateful you were there," said the father, when Gordie had more or less summed things up.

"Oh, no," Gordie demurred, and tried to clarify that if he and his dog hadn't been there in the first place the girl would have needed no rescue. But then she spoke up, for the first time in

Gordie's presence betraying a hint of garrulity, insisting that she hadn't needed a rescue in *any* case, since she'd known how to swim since she was four.

Nevertheless, the father looked at Gordie with heavy gratitude. "John Ryrie," he said, extending his hand.

"Gordie Joiner."

The man's grip was fantastic.

"Well: I'm indebted. This one"—he looked at the girl—"has been something of a concern to us lately." His voice seemed tinged with private rue, something like self-reproach. The father laid a broad hand on top of his daughter's head. She caught Gordie's eye then with a look of insolent amusement, and he was taken aback. It seemed to imply a connection, a complicity between them. Had they shared something, he and this child who had snubbed his attempts at conversation in the car? If so, what? An adventure? A secret? He felt hopelessly slow.

"Um, Mr. Ryrie," he said, and cleared his throat. He decided he would, he must, mention what he'd seen this Biscuit-Elizabeth-girl doing just prior to her plunge. By intervening in the first place, by delivering her home, he'd incurred a responsibility.

"John," the father corrected him.

"John. I don't know whether I should say . . . I asked in the car, but . . ." He cleared his throat again. "I just wondered if you knew—"

But he broke off in mortification at the sudden arrival of Ebie, who came nosing-and-shouldering her massive way through the open front door. She circled the front hall rapidly, the ungainly sway of her hips and damp thwack of her tail making the space seem very cramped, and threaded among the humans, blithely disseminating her gamy perfume.

Gordie tried to grasp her collar. "Ebie!—sorry—*come, girl.* Sorry. I don't know why she's— Ebie, no!" She ended up by Biscuit-Elizabeth, on whose foot she trod once before inserting herself decorously between girl and coatrack. There she sat, giving the distinct impression of hoping to go unnoticed.

The girl's hand floated to the dog's neck, fingers twining deep into the fur.

Gordie shrugged, let his hands fall to his sides. "She apparently likes your daughter."

"I see that." John rubbed his cheek with two fingers. He looked at the dog. Ebie, apparently conscious of being under scrutiny, did not make eye contact with her observer but thrust her face slightly in his direction and thumped her tail. John laughed. "Well. Gordie, right? And Biscuit. You're both soaked." He gestured ironically, as if to acknowledge he'd stated the obvious. "Bis, go up and put on dry things. And if you"—he turned to Gordie—"could possibly spare the time, I'd like to offer you tea or . . . coffee, cocoa? A dry sweatshirt? And to hear what you were starting to say."

It was unsettling how glad the invitation made Gordie, how almost relieved he was to receive it.

Before he could respond, however, the girl spoke up. "Who's she?" Pointing a finger toward the doorway that led from the hall.

A young woman leaned against the frame. She had short dark hair and wore a dark turtleneck and faded jeans. Her feet were bare, her arms folded across her chest. She was observing them all with a half-smile, a look of loosely reined amusement. Gordie had no idea how long she'd been there. She alone in the room appeared wholly unconcerned, comfortable in her skin. He found himself interested in this, if slightly unsettled by it.

4.

Paul and Baptiste sat at the counter of the Skylark polishing off an order of fries, their backpacks slumped soggily at their feet. They'd known each other since Baptiste moved to Nyack in third grade, but had not formed a friendship until last year, when both happened to join cross-country, the only team that didn't make cuts. They'd become at that time not so much best friends as each other's only friend. What had begun as a vague affinity (based on their finding themselves, practice after practice, bringing up the rear together) developed into something more when they discovered they shared an appetite for comics and a talent for drawing. But what cemented their friendship was death. Paul had had to miss a few days of practice last spring while his mother was in the hospital. When he came back and told Baptiste why he'd been out, it became the occasion for Baptiste's disclosure that he had lost a sibling, too. His little sister. Also his father. Back in Haiti. Last year.

"Dude. At the same time?"

Baptiste made the slightest movement with his shoulders; the shrug would have been seismographically undetectable. "Their bus," he said, and took one hand out of his back pocket to show how it had tipped on its side.

The boys had clocked many hours together last summer sprawled on the floor of Paul's bedroom or out on the Ryries' front porch, working on what was at first going to be a comic book and then morphed into a graphic novel, the heroes of which were kind of alter egos, the one a lean and princely boy who could change at will into a black panther; the other a hulking, trench-coated private eye who could make himself invisible. By the time they'd begun seventh grade, they'd completed sixty-three pages and had more or less woven together the two story lines in a mixture of pencil, blue ballpoint, and black India ink.

The clock behind the cash register said three-fifty. The rain had stopped and the sun come out, its brisk light slicing sideways through the air. Through the plate glass they saw things snapping in a freshly risen wind.

Baptiste could now head home. He was not allowed to go straight home from school because his grandmother, with whom he lived, worked as an aide at the hospital and didn't get home until four, and she had a fear of someone with a knife breaking into the apartment when Baptiste was home alone. This was the explanation Baptiste had given when he and Paul were first beginning to confide little things in each other, and although Paul found both the rule and the specificity of the concern bizarre, he had never voiced that opinion. In truth, he was a little awed by the dignity with which his friend honored his grandmother's wishes. Paul had met Mrs. Lecompte only a handful of times, and his impression was of wearily maintained formality. She spoke little in Paul's presence, although Baptiste said her English was good. She had an imposingly straight back and a heavy, mineral countenance.

Ever since Paul first learned of Mrs. Lecompte's prohibition on Baptiste's arriving home before four o'clock, he'd fallen into the habit of keeping Baptiste company after school on days they didn't have practice. Baptiste had at first seemed leery of such omnipresent companionship, then tolerant, and eventually content with it. The boys would walk down the hill from the middle school together, cutting through the old apple orchard and across the thruway overpass into town. Some afternoons Baptiste came over to the Ryries' house; some days they walked down to the public library and got their homework done; some days they kicked around the shops and wound up by the river, chucking rocks into the water. Lately they'd begun frequenting the Skylark, at least whenever they had enough cash between them to order a piece of pie or plate of fries. They were thirteen, and the experience of patronizing a restaurant without an adult was novel enough to constitute a small thrill in itself.

"How much you got?" asked Paul. "I got one-eighty." He was thinking maybe they could split a plate of scrambled eggs, the fries being nearly gone, but when Baptiste counted up his money they were short. "Oh well. I guess we better be going, anyway."

"Yeah."

Baptiste, whose aptitude for math was understood by both to exceed Paul's, figured the tip. They deposited a small pile of bills and coins and left, slinging their backpacks over their shoulders as they stepped out into the brisk and newly sunstruck afternoon. Puddles glimmered everywhere. Leftover drops shook and sprayed from the Skylark's awning, the scalloped edge of which was flapping madly in the wind.

"Want to come over?" Paul issued the invitation halfheartedly, not because it was insincere, but because he knew what Baptiste's answer would be.

"Can't. My Grann."

"A'ight. See you."

"See you."

They went their opposite ways on Main Street, Paul downhill, Baptiste up. Baptiste and his Grann lived in four rooms on the first floor of a house on Elysian Avenue. The apartment was north-facing, spartan and dim. Paul got asked in only rarely. He'd been surprised the first time he saw Baptiste's room, two full walls of which were papered with pictures cut from newspapers (a lot from sports, but a fair number from the travel section, too: a Kyoto temple ringed by mist, a Thai beach at sunset, an okapi eating leaves off a tree in Zaire). Not only which pictures had been selected, but also the way the images had been arranged, what their art teacher would call the composition, had been arresting. From across the room, the whole thing made a colorful abstract, a work of art in itself, apart from what the individual pictures showed as you moved in and examined them more closely. There was a sense of exuberance in the project that had surprised Paul, a capacity for investment that was nowhere evident in the Baptiste he knew at school.

The air was astringent after the rain and thin-feeling, as if it had just been pruned. Paul's jacket was still wet from the downpour; he and Baptiste had been caught smack in the middle of it as they walked to the Skylark. He felt a bit penitent now about having eaten all those fries (just yesterday a girl in his class had called him "Chub" to his face), and at the same time wistful about the eggs. He would have put ketchup on them, and salt on the hash browns that would have come alongside.

Baptiste, though equally slow in track events, was not hampered by extra girth. Although he could hold up his end just fine when it came to scarfing a plate of fries, he was pretty much a pipe cleaner. Paul didn't quite get how Baptiste could be so slow—the thought had once come into his head that what weighed his friend down was something along the lines of sorrow, but immediately he'd chided himself, embarrassed at what seemed to him the girlishness of this speculation.

The walk home from the Skylark was only four blocks, but it seemed long to Paul, today and every day. The straps of his backpack dug into his shoulders through his wet jacket and the wind brought tears to his eyes. His feet slapped heavily in their Doc Martens. He did not like his body or the way it felt to move it: like drudgery, like a slightly disgraceful chore.

He hadn't passed more than a few shops when he heard his name belted out: "Ryrie!"

He shouldn't turn his head. He turned his head. It was Stephen Boyd, hanging out in front of Turiello's, his jeans hanging eight inches off his waist, his jacket on the sidewalk. He gave a laugh that meant nothing to Paul and jerked his head in greeting. "How's it hanging?"

"Hey," said Paul, nodding back. He'd stopped, a mistake; it would look as though he expected more conversation. He should have said hi and kept walking.

But Stephen, ruddy-cheeked and scruffy-haired, smiled as if to commend him, as though he'd said something incomparably witty. It was true—that was the thing of it—asshole that he was, that Paul knew him to be, Stephen had an irresistible smile, mischievous and oddly flattering; it seemed to convey that anyone who could elicit such a smile must be of special worth. It confused Paul for a moment, made him think the bluff greeting had been in earnest. Maybe it was. Who was to say his time of social hell wasn't coming to an end, a natural conclusion as unpredictable as its inception had been, back at the start of sixth grade?

"Where'd your friend go?" asked Stephen, a not unreasonable question. Paul figured he must have noticed him and Baptiste parting ways up the block. Yet he hesitated.

Stephen raised his brows encouragingly. Remnants of smile lingered on. He had ridiculous amounts of charm—even teachers seemed uncertain, at times, about whether Stephen was cracking wise or speaking in earnest. His boxers—the exposed two-inch swath of them—were striped blue and green. Some of the boys hanging out by the door of the pizza place sauntered over; Paul hadn't noticed they were with Stephen. Two were eighth-graders.

"*Where* is he?" he repeated, amiably enough, as though Paul had already replied but Stephen hadn't quite caught his answer.

When Paul went to speak his voice rattled phlegmatically; he should have cleared his throat first. "Home." He wanted to stab himself for that—for answering, obeying. He could not help it; there was no clever retort, or if there was, he couldn't think of it. Anyway, it was a simple fact, hardly incriminating; why not answer directly? Only the way they all stood around, clumped and grinning, made it into something else.

"That's too bad," Stephen said. Again, low chuckles, from his cronies this time. Not overtly nasty. Almost, those chuckles could be read as affectionate, sympathetic. Then, "Dude, he's blushing," one of the older boys said, and the laughter turned grosser, and the tone of the whole preceding exchange turned unambiguous. Paul hurried away, having the guts to give them the finger, but holding it tucked against his chest so they couldn't quite see. The worst of it was that he really could feel the blush.

"You see him checking out Boyd's shorts, man?" one of them rasped behind him, and there were hoots.

It had been this way, more or less, for almost the past two years. He had no idea why. He'd been liked well enough in elementary school. Of course, it hadn't helped that his best friend, Alexi, had moved to Florida at the end of fifth grade. But it wasn't as if Alexi had been his only friend. In fifth grade, fifteen kids had attended his birthday party, brought him gifts in colored paper, played capture the flag with his mother's dish towels, sung to him. By the following autumn most of these same kids, if they did not actually abuse him outright, would greet him in the hallways abstractedly if at all. And not one rose to his defense when other kids, those who had never been his friends, targeted him with their teasing.

"You're smart, and you're sensitive," his mother said when he confessed through tears, the second month of sixth grade, what was happening—though whether she offered it as explanation or compensation, he couldn't tell. "Rise above it, if you can," his father said. "Think how insecure they must be, to feel they have to tease others. You could think in terms of feeling sorry for them."

He practiced being sorry for them the rest of the way home. He thought the words *I'm sorry for you* and *I pity you,* but what he meant was *I'm sorry for your mother having to look at your shitass face every day* and *I pity you for being such a sorry fucking scumbag.* His thoughts were bullets shot from a gun. Hollow-point, armor-piercing. By the time he reached his block, Paul had killed Stephen Boyd and his cronies several times over. He felt, if not better, at least a few yards removed from the epicenter of hatred and shame. He also felt—how could this be?—hungry again, empty in the gut.

His father's truck was in the driveway. Paul registered the fact with a twinge of minor curiosity. It was not routine, yet neither was it bizarre. Depending on whether or not a show was going up soon, his father might get home from work in the afternoon or not until late at night. He went across the porch, pushed open the door, and shed his wet backpack and jacket in one motion, letting both lie where they landed on the tatty hall rug. "Dad?" he called, heaving off his boots.

"Paul?" His father answered from the back of the house. "We're in here." Walking through the passageway, Paul detected multiple voices, and when he rounded the corner he saw that the kitchen was seriously populated. His father sat at the table.

So did a wiry young man with red hair, wearing one of Paul's father's sweatshirts. It was far too big for this stranger; even rolled up, the sleeves fell past his knuckles. Cross-legged on the floor, leaning against the radiator, sat his sister, Biscuit. She wore her pilly lavender bathrobe and was eating a banana in that overly attentive way she had, while stroking the side of a vast black dog, which lay on the floor beside her with its chin on her thigh. Finally, leaning against the stove, both hands laced around the chunky, lumpy alphabet mug Paul had made in second grade, stood a young woman with dark hair cut spikily short and a spark of a smile between her pursed lips.

"O-*kay* . . ." said Paul from the doorway, shaking the long bang that drove his mother crazy out of his eyes.

"Come on into the room, Paul." His father sounded so expansively casual that Paul knew he was tense. "You remember Jessica? I don't know how old you were, the last time we were all together."

"Paul!" burst the woman at the stove, and it was too much. As if she'd thought the same thing, she tamped down the enthusiasm, following her initial utterance with only a low "Wow."

She was not as he remembered. She looked shorter, plainer, denser. All her thrilling miles of hair hacked off.

There seemed to be a mass of cotton in his throat. "Uh, I think so," Paul mumbled, casting an interrogatory glance at his father. "Jessica as in *Jess*?" As if he wasn't sure.

"Our sister," Biscuit put in helpfully, although for her it must be brand-new; she had been too little to have any previous memory of Jess.

"O-*kay*," he said again. "Great. Hi." He clasped his hands

together audibly. It was a consciously comical gesture; he had recently discovered he had a knack for delivering a certain kind of stand-up, a flattened, staccato, affectless patter. It went over best with older audiences, his parents and their peers, and he'd begun to use it as a cover when he was feeling anxious or agitated. "So. Why's Biscuit wearing a bathrobe, since when do we have a dog, who's *he*?"—pointing at the red-haired fellow—"and by the way"—pointing at Jess—"that's my mug."

Jess, to his consternation and delight, did not seem flustered but hoisted the mug in small salute and gave him a nod.

Biscuit said, "The dog's Gordie's."

His father said, "Paul, my son. This is Gordie Joiner. He helped your sister out today."

The dude's ears turned red. "Well, not exactly."

Then, overlapping:

"Your sister skipped school—"

"Actually, it was my dog—"

"I can swim perfectly well—"

"Gordie was kind enough—"

"Newfs have this instinct—"

"—like I would have learned anything I cared about."

The more confusedly their voices entwined the more stolid grew Paul's silence. Jess, it was impossible not to notice, held herself equally still, so that through their very inaction, a commonality was forged. Paul stole a glance. She really looked completely different from the last time—the only time—he'd seen her. Then she'd been willowy, almost gangly, with hair to her waist. She'd worn braces on her teeth, been tan and freckled, towered above him. Now his father's first child was his height or a hair shorter, and her skin moon-pale, and her figure filled out. She was solid-looking, the way a bird can seem plump without being fat. He forgot what their age difference was—ten years, eleven? She must be in her early twenties.

His father and Biscuit and the scrawny red-haired dude finished up their story. Paul waited a beat and turned to his father. "What does all that have to do"—inclining his head toward the stove—"with her?"

"Nothing," his father admitted. "A coincidence. We're having an unusual afternoon."

"You think?" Paul knew his father would probably have welcomed some help juggling the company, but he did not feel it within him to offer any. He wasn't sure why seeing Jess should make him angry, but he was aware of wanting to hit something. He flashed a sardonic smile. Then, in a manner he understood was rude, he crossed to a cupboard, leaving a trail of large damp sock prints on the floor, and got down an unopened package of Hydrox. He turned to face the room at large and executed a small bow. "A pleasure. Now if you'll excuse me." And strode through the doorway toward the front hall.

"Hey, Paul . . . ?" His father's voice sought after him.

"Book report," Paul yelled back, fraudulently. He grabbed his backpack and clomped up the stairs in the way his mother had spoken to him about many times. In his room he kicked the door shut, peeled off his wet cargo pants and socks, pulled on a pair of sweats, switched on his desk lamp, tore open the Hydrox, and inserted a cookie in his mouth, all in fluid progression. Then he sat very still, not chewing.

Though he'd met his half sister just once, a long time ago, the memory was vivid. It had been summertime; he must have been just about to turn six. Biscuit (precocious in many things but not in toilet training) had been, at three, still in diapers. They'd spent two weeks together, his whole family and Jess, upstate where his mother's parents had a cabin on Cabruda Lake. Jess had been a teenager then and accordingly remarkable to him, with her guitar, her braces, her friendship bracelets, her long, heavy hair.

He'd felt rich on that holiday, rich with the sudden acquisition of her. He'd known, because his parents had told him, what "half sister" meant: *Daddy is her father but her mother is another lady.* Even so, he couldn't fully dispel the impression he'd formed, upon first hearing the term, of a mythical being, half sister and half something else, the way a centaur or a mermaid was half-and-half. And half *his,* too, for that was what sister meant, only in this case the word seemed far more exotic and advantageous than in the case of his other sister, never mind that Biscuit was a hundred percent his: she cried and stank and was liable to put his things in her mouth.

This one played with him. She threw him like a torpedo through the water and taught him how to spit high in the air like a fountain. She showed him how to make food for the fairies she said lived in the woods, grinding pine needles and tree sap into a sticky porridge, which they set out on leaf-platters upon tablecloths of moss. She combed his hair, after swimming, into a Mohawk, and used some of her own mousse to make it stiff. She instructed him on how to dig fingernail X's into the mosquito bites she couldn't reach on her back. She sang along to folk songs she played on her guitar; other times, she let him strum it while she made chords. She teased him, too, as no one had ever done. She called him Paolo instead of Paul, said "Pee-yew" and held her nose whenever he took off his shoes, and sang, with a pronounced, insistent twang, *"Why don't you love me like you used to do?"* at random intervals to him during the course of the holiday. *"How come you treat me like a worn-out shoe?"* When he'd shrug in hapless embarrassment she'd say, "That's cold, man." Her teasing had the strange effect of making him feel both overwhelmed by the privilege and on the verge of tears.

Her name was Jessica Safransky, impossible to resist chanting several times in a row, and Paul had chanted it a lot, during that holiday and in the weeks following, after they'd returned to their respective houses in different parts of the state. Jess had been only on loan, it turned out, from the Safranskys. That was the curious phrase his mother had used, as though Jess were a library book. During their time at Cabruda Lake Paul had given no thought to the provenance of her last name; it had seemed fitting that such a fantastic being should come bearing her own distinct appellation. Only afterward did its implications dawn on him. Weeks after the vacation he'd asked when they would see Jess again, and was by way of indirect answer given this piece of information: the Safranskys lived in a town far, far up the Hudson River, past Albany. Albany: even the word sounded distant, milky and cool as a train whistle. He'd envisioned a citadel on a hill, white flags rippling from the spires. But, wait—Safranskys, plural? Well, yes: Mr. Safransky was Jess's father, having married Jess's mother long ago. But wasn't Daddy her father? Daddy, it was explained, had never been married to Jess's mother. He had once been Jess's father, it seemed, but now there was another who'd taken his place. And so. In this way Paul lost his early sureness about the world. Fathers could be interchanged; sisters could come in fractions. The easy manner with which his mother explained these things made them only more distressing.

Still, Paul had hopes of a repeat holiday. For a while he persisted in asking every now and then when they might get together with Jess again. "We'll have to try to work something out," his father would say. But when the Ryries went back to Cabruda Lake the following summer it had been without Jess, and no other plans for a visit ever transpired. He began to think of her less frequently, though when he did, the thought still caused a great prick of interest, and continued, in a vague way, to seem like a treat yet to happen, a promise on the horizon. Then one day when he'd been in second or third grade his mother had replied to his latest inquiry, with what he took to be inexcusable offhandedness, that the Safranskys had moved some time ago to California. After that he'd stopped wondering when Jess might visit them again. If he wondered anything, it was how that single summer's holiday had ever come to happen.

As he grew older, a few more details of the story had filtered through: how young his father had been at the time of Jess's conception, and how foolish. That it had been the mother's decision to raise the baby alone, that she'd actually refused his father's involvement. That only when the teenage Jess had rebelled, insisting on meeting her birth father, did the mother begrudgingly allow it. And that mere months after the summer at Cabruda Lake, the Safranskys uprooted and moved clear across the country. So that the picture Paul formed of Jess's mother was of Rapunzel's witch: a woman so jealous she locked her daughter away from the rest of the world—or, at least, away from the Ryries.

To see Jess today in real life, real time, to stand before her in the kitchen and have her look so diminished, so ordinary, had been like having a trick played on him. It was like something Stephen Boyd might do: set him up in order to deflate him. It wasn't so much that Paul had exalted her in his memory; it was that his memory of her had functioned to exalt *him*. That holiday at Cabruda Lake had become, in the uncanny way of a select few childhood memories, a storehouse of symbolism. They had fallen for each other, the little boy and the teenage girl, in a way that remained unparalleled. He believed that no one since, no friend or teacher or babysitter, not even his parents, not even Baptiste, had seen in him such promise, or reflected back at him such delight. The notion of this Rapunzel, this distant half sister vaguely in need of rescue, who'd seen him more purely than anyone else before or since, had been itself like a promise.

For her to show up now as she was—shorn, short, pale—and see him as he was—overweight, awkward, acned—was a double blow. He felt duped. He longed for Baptiste to have come home with him, but whether as buffer against Jess or in order to flaunt him before her, Paul didn't know.

The cookie had become a perfect disk of chocolate-and-cream paste on his tongue. Paul swallowed and inserted another. He slid open the top drawer of his desk, removed a spiral sketchbook and a bottle of Winsor & Newton Black, selected a pen from a mug full of drawing tools, and stuck in a nib. Then he flipped open the sketchbook and riffled through its pages, more than half of which were covered with drawings, or bits of drawings, fits and starts of images and designs that had coalesced, collage-like, into a world of his and Baptiste's making. There, on one page, crouched the black panther, muscular and scowling in the shadow of a garbage can. There, behind him, stood the private eye, lantern-jawed and stubbled, slouched in his trench coat. Paul dipped his nib in the ink, then blotted it on an old wadded-up T-shirt he kept for this purpose. His breath slowed and he brought his head so low the fringe of his bangs brushed the paper. There, on the facing page, with no idea yet of what it would contain, he began to sketch in the next frame.

5.

Ricky never crossed the bridge from east to west without seeing herself driving off it. This didn't happen when she was going in the opposite direction, on the way to work each morning, for example, or when they went to Tarrytown to visit John's mother, or to Manhattan to visit her parents. But without fail every time she spanned the Hudson in a westerly, homeward direction, she imagined herself pointing the car—or allowing the car to point itself, more like—toward the shoulder, bursting through the guardrail, nosing toward the waves, disappearing from sight. She didn't imagine anything beyond death, beyond breaking through the silvered surface of the water. She never considered particulars such as the rate at which the car might sink, or flood, or for that matter what the physical sensations would be: the impact, the temperature of the water, how drowning would affect the heart and lungs. The engine of her imagination always cut out at the moment of the car shooting beneath the river's skin, the moment of her vanishing.

She'd begun having this fantasy almost a full year earlier, as soon as she'd started back to work after the baby. For the first few months it would come on so strong, so like a premonition or compulsion, she would begin to sweat as soon as she'd passed the tolls at the entrance to the bridge. She was convinced that only the most dedicated act of concentration would keep the car in its lane. Her palms would be wet on the steering wheel, her back muscles tight with effort, the whole way across. Over time the vision of a fatal plunge did not fade, but its fearful grip abated. After a while, not only did it no longer induce sweats, it no longer even disturbed her. In fact its effect was reversed. Familiarity in this case had bred good company. The fantasy became almost a necessary traveling companion, the morbid daydream having taken on the aspect of a good-luck charm. To have it was to ensure that she would get home safely.

On this afternoon, when she was halfway across the bridge, traffic slowed to a crawl. Ricky leaned back against the headrest and looked out across the river, toward the faraway shore. Earlier that afternoon it had rained. For about ten minutes, the windows of her office had turned nearly opaque with the streaming, and so noisy was the cloudburst that she hadn't been able to hear Silvio, the risk manager, on the phone; she'd had to call him back. Now the sky had cleared, and the lowering sun shone, apricot-colored, through scudding clouds. She tried to enjoy it, to will herself to experience pleasure from it. Tried to *see* it (it?— beauty, she supposed) instead of the rush-hour traffic in which she had once again found herself stuck.

All senior-level staff at Birnbaum and Traux not tied to trading desks were allowed to set their own hours. At least on paper this was true. Ricky had found that in order to get the job
done, she could not avoid rising in the dark nearly every month
of the year, leaving John still basking in warm slumber, the children still oblivious in their beds. Similarly, she rarely managed to
leave the office before six or get home much earlier than seven.
As a result, most nights the Ryries ate frozen dinner, take-out, or
else John's simple, mannish fare: hamburgers, spaghetti. This past
January she'd made what seemed a perfectly reasonable resolution: she would leave early on Fridays. She'd announced it to her
family on New Year's Day, framing it, if not quite as a concession,
then as an offering to John, as though he'd been after her to
spend more time at home. Truth was, the resolution had pleased
her: the idea of beating traffic, of stopping at the grocery store
on the way home and walking into the house with kale and
salmon, lemons and fresh bread, making a simple, hot dinner
from scratch. One day a week. One single evening on which they
could play happy family. Of course—she should have known—
this had not turned out.

Somewhere up ahead a car must have stalled; now traffic
halted altogether. Every couple of seconds it inched forward.
Someone, somewhere, beeped, as if that might get things going.
In fact, the cars ahead of her did begin to flow, slowly at first,
then picking up speed. Girders cut the sky into a succession of
geometric shapes; as she drove under them the shapes shrunk
and pinched off and expanded into other shapes. A sudden
bloom of taillights; Ricky braked. Another standstill. Wind
sang, ghostlike, through the girders. Ricky thought she could

feel the bridge sway. Down below, the breeze spanked curt waves from the surface of the water, and these were spangled by the post-storm light. Hardly noticing she was doing it, Ricky took stock of the distance between her car and the guardrail.

Her phone rang. She fished inside her bag on the passenger seat and checked the ID: HOME.

Flipping it open, "Hey. I'm on the bridge."

"How is it?" John asked. "It looks slow."

Ricky wondered at which window he stood. At this time of year, the Tappan Zee was visible from the den as well as from their bedroom upstairs. By late spring, once the trees filled in, only the upstairs window would offer an unimpeded view. For her part, she looked out now beyond the latticework of cables, across the wide river toward Nyack, toward the very spot where she knew their house to be. "Yeah, it's not really moving. How's Biscuit?"

"She's fine—well. I'll have to fill you in. She actually fell in—"

"Sorry?"

"—the river, sort of."

"What?"

"She went to the Hook."

Ricky looked at it through the window: Hook Mountain, jagged and darkly shadowed at this hour. Biscuit had gone there? And fallen in the river? For an ignominious moment Ricky felt she'd been trumped. Wasn't that her move, the card she'd been hiding up her sleeve? She looked over at the guardrail—perhaps twelve feet away—and then her heart seemed to slow and she was falling through the air, crashing into the river, her limbs tearing the water into soft ribbons that curled apart and knit effortlessly back together in her wake.

". . . but she's fine," John was saying. "A guy brought her home. Can you hear me?"

"A guy?"

"A nice kid. With his dog. It's been a weird"—he sighed—"well, day. Listen. I mainly called to tell you, to prepare you: Jessica is here. Jess."

Ricky, creeping forward, saw that all the cars were merging into the left lane. She put on her blinker. Only when the car in front of her turned did she see the flares in the road, the flashing lights ahead. For once she was thankful for the state law banning cell phone use while driving "Wait. John? I'm going to have to hang up—there's an accident or something."

"Okay. Did you hear what I said about Jess?"

"Yeah, I just—there's a police car. Bye."

She tossed the phone back in her bag. Had she heard what he said about Jess. Ricky began to cry. Just like that, stupidly and not very convincingly. A swelling behind her nose, a surge of self-pity. A rough bleat loosed itself from her throat: half sob, half bitter laugh. A collapsing feeling in her chest. Everything present but the tears. She waited, but no: tears were not forthcoming. Was she not unhappy?

As far as Ricky knew, beyond an occasional postcard, twice a year at most, Jess had not communicated with the Ryrie household since she'd moved to California with her parents. Some, what, seven years ago? John rarely spoke of her. Paul never did anymore. Ricky herself hardly even thought of her; sometimes she practically had to remind herself the girl existed: that's how nominal a factor she was in their lives. Yet the whole time Ricky had been bracing herself for the reappearance of John's grown daughter, knowing all the while two things with equal certainty: that it was inevitable and that it was a thing to dread—not because the girl was in and of herself dreadful, but because of, well, simple economics: supply and demand. Or for that matter, because of basic maternal instinct, the innate drive to protect her own. No, it was not mean-spirited of her; if anything it was Darwinian. Keynesian. Sensible.

Here she paused to let a driver merge from the right, signaling him on with a wave. He mouthed his *thanks* and she was warmed by this acknowledgment of her own magnanimity.

So Jess was, at this very moment, in her house. Odd. She searched her feelings for discomfort, for violation. She was aware only of a sense of grim vindication. Ever since the vacation they'd all taken together at Cabruda Lake, the prospect of Jess's reappearance had loomed, Damoclean, above their heads. Never mind that John virtually did not speak of her, let alone pine. Never mind that as the years passed with hardly a sign, hardly a word from the girl, Ricky had almost fooled herself into believing the sword wouldn't fall. In her heart she had known that one day the single hair on which it was suspended would break, that Jess would reenter their lives, lay claim to them, awaken their rightful shame.

But that was not quite right. That was not really how the story went. And in fact she did feel something other than grim vindication. Something anticipatory. Eager. A somewhat untoward gleam of possibility renewed.

Now she was close enough to glimpse the accident, a car and a van at ugly angles. A gurney. A figure inside the car, the front of which was tightly crumpled. A state trooper in a big hat, standing by the driver's side. Now she was passing it. Crimson flares, diamantine glass salting the asphalt. The stateliness of the paramedics, moving in. Now the right lane opened up again. Now she was past the cantilevers and onto the causeway portion of the bridge. More space between cars, unobstructed sky above. The flashing lights of the ambulance grew small in the rearview mirror. She breathed. It wasn't that accidents frightened her more now. It was that they made her feel more tired, as if by possessing a fuller understanding of the complexities of loss, she could not help experiencing more particularly the losses of others.

Ricky had known about John's out-of-wedlock daughter since early in their relationship, learned of her almost as soon as she and John began seeing each other exclusively. "There's something I have to tell you," he said seriously one night, spreading his fingers flat on the purple tablecloth in a little Indian restaurant on East Sixth. Ricky's stomach had pitched, less from fear than excitement; she'd experienced so little real drama in her life. Over bits of pappadum dipped in chutney, John had told her about the child he'd fathered, a girl by then eight years old. He had, he said, no contact with the child or her mother, a woman he'd been with (his phrase) for only a few months in college. It had been the mother's decision to raise the child alone; she'd been adamant about wanting no contact, no money, nothing to do with him.

"Okay," Ricky had said, wondering whether she ought to

mind, whether there was something wrong with her. She'd found the announcement titillating, and the man himself more interesting than she'd hitherto thought.

It was only later, when she had the affair (or not even affair, but dalliance: a single misguided, electrochemical weekend) three months before their wedding, that John's having a child with another woman came to seem like a blessing, like good luck. Even, if you went in for this sort of thinking, like part of a grand, intricate design. Meant to be. Because in fact she thought of her affair this way, too: as having about it an aura of inevitability—hadn't she been built for transgression; didn't she possess, not outright badness, but an errant streak? Wasn't this the message she'd received indirectly again and again from her mother and father, her judicious, compassionate, secular human- ist parents who never said but managed silently to convey that they were mildly wounded by the person their daughter turned out to be?

John was like them. Endowed with native decency, uncom- plicated good. Almost, it sometimes struck Ricky, insultingly so. For if he loved her brazen appetite and air of mischief, if these were the very things that made him gaze at her besotted, didn't there also lurk in that same gaze a kind of wary bemusement, even faint reproach? Wasn't it that very gaze that had propelled her, in a way, into bed with Parker? (*Parker* of all people, that ar- rogant dolt, that callow, blond, Brooks-Brothered, prep-schooled, disastrously magnificent lay.) Even while it was happening, she'd felt a little sick. Even while he'd been sucking tequila from her navel, sliding bits of crushed ice inside her with his thumb to make her gasp and claw at his arms, she'd been sickened to think of the truth she was proving: that she was unfit to be a good man's wife. But it turned out there was a providential symmetry, a reason she and John *were* suited, after all. For when John confronted her with what he knew (what he'd only guessed, actually, it would later emerge); when she confessed, broke down and begged, wretched, mascara-streaked, hating herself for the cliché of it all more than anything, when she pleaded for another chance, for him to trust her again—even in the midst of the squalor that was of her own making; even before John had, indeed, granted forgiveness—it dawned on her that he would.

He'd have to. In order to balance some larger equation. Hadn't he made mistakes, too, of a related nature? Hadn't he been irresponsible in the bedroom? Didn't the world hold living proof of this? And from that point, long before she'd ever met Jess, before Jess became remotely real as an actual person she might lay eyes on, Ricky had come to see the value of her. Jess was a kind of magic pebble, a trump card that could be played when other options had run out.

The first seven years of their marriage had passed as John foresaw, devoid of contact with his daughter. Then one day a letter had come, on orange-and-yellow daisy-strewn stationery, and this was followed a week later by a phone call, and this by a rainy Saturday when John had driven up to Elsmere, alone, and taken his daughter out to lunch. A month later there was another lunch, and then more phone calls: lengthier, leisurely, at a regular time (Thursdays after dinner)—and then a series of shorter, tenser calls between John and the mother as negotiations were conducted for a longer visit. Jess would accompany the Ryries on their summer holiday at Cabruda Lake. It was decided. Terms were agreed on. Arrangements put in place.

Ricky objected to none of this. She actively encouraged it. The shadow of her affair with Parker had proven durable, stretching its pall forward through all these years to chill them now and again, even without its being named. It seemed to Ricky that sewn deep inside the lining of every argument she and John had burned her infidelity. And so when Jess's mother somewhat surprisingly granted permission for Jess to accompany the Ryries on their August camping trip, Ricky found the prospect not unwelcome. She imagined that Jessica's arrival on the scene, her physical presence in their lives (even if only for a few weeks), might balance out that old wrongdoing of hers, serve as bodily reminder that John's own past was not spotless. With self-interest, then, as much as goodwill, Ricky had embraced the plan, submitting herself wholeheartedly to sharing their holiday, sharing what was after all her old family cabin, with John's daughter. If the girl turned out to be a nightmare, Ricky would have suffered it gladly.

In fact, Jess turned out to be a dream. In looks, she'd been a young fifteen, gangling and shy in her bathing suit, makeup-less, with yard-long braids and braces on her teeth. But in character she'd proven mature, stepping eagerly into the role of big sister and proving genuinely helpful with the kids, Paul especially. The two of them had developed, even in that short time, an undeniable bond. Nearly every afternoon during Biscuit's nap, Paul had tramped off adoringly to the beach with his new relative, who somehow got him to swim underwater and jump off the dock without holding his nose. She wove him wreaths of clover, which he'd actually worn, even allowing himself to be photographed thus festooned. The whole family had been absurdly symbiotic, John teaching Jess how to chop wood; Ricky teaching her how to paddle stern; Jess teaching them card games they'd never heard of—Russian Bank, Liverpool, Beggar My Neighbor—and strumming her guitar, and baking John's birthday cake in the propane gas oven, which Ricky showed her how to use.

That had been part of the holiday's success: the cabin itself, built by Ricky's grandparents half a century ago. She'd gone there with her parents every summer of her life, and up until last year the Ryries had spent two weeks there each August. It was fairly isolated; the forest grew thick around it, so you could not easily walk to any of the other cabins that dotted the banks of Cabruda Lake, and the town was a thirty-minute drive over marginal roads, so that once you were there at the cabin, you were *there,* the little group of you, alone together. The northern woods held, for Ricky, a feeling of timeless virtue, a quality that had charmed her as a child, but which, in adulthood, sometimes struck her as daunting. The cabin had neither electricity nor plumbing; the sleeping bunks were built into the walls; the woodstove got lit for warmth each morning, even in July; the original tin-lined cold pit dug into the ground beside the cabin kept the perishables cold.

Ricky had guessed Jess would feel put out by the lack of amenities—admittedly this was in part because she herself, as a teenager, had hated the imposed separation from shower, hair dryer, television shows. But from the day she arrived there with them, Jess had embraced the spirit of the place, seeming to understand beyond the capacity of most modern adolescents that physical labor was a large part of this spirit. She'd assigned herself the job of hauling buckets of wash water from the outdoor spigot to heat on the stove, and after supper when Ricky did the dishes, Jess had stood beside her with a faded orange towel and dried. She'd delighted in being allowed to feed items into the garbage fire they had outside each evening, delighted in being the one to sweep the previous day's sand and pine needles out the front door each morning. Seeing Jess take to these tasks, Ricky was reminded of the way life at the cabin—its scale, its primitive specificity—had the feel of playing house; now it lent itself to their playing family.

For Ricky there had been one unpleasant aspect to Jess's model behavior: she felt shown up by it. That was ridiculous, of course, not only because Jess could have no knowledge of Ricky's disappointing history—all those summers she'd gone to the cabin with her parents only to gripe and sulk the entire time, refusing to help with chores, doing a deliberately sloppy job when she did help, and volubly scorning everything she knew they loved about the place: the tall, piney woods; the wobbly cry of the loons; the broad, inky lake, the pleasures of performing simple tasks by hand. It was ridiculous, too, because John had not known her during those years, and would be in no position to draw unflattering comparisons, yet it was he she feared being shown up in front of. As though Jess's genuine graciousness might be just the thing to stir loose the ghost of Ricky's former self, exposing it to John, resulting in his certain disenchantment.

One evening early in their two-week stay stood out in Ricky's memory. Jess had taken it upon herself to light the gas lamps, airily declining John's offer of a preliminary tutorial. She knew how, she said, from watching him and Ricky do it. On her first try, she'd touched the tip of the match to the mantle, with the result that it promptly disintegrated into a pile of white ash. Teary with embarrassment and contrition, she had declined to try again, but Ricky said quietly, "No. Now you have to," and she'd taken a fresh rayon mantle from the drawer and demonstrated how to hold the match so that only the flame made contact, and John's daughter had then succeeded in lighting the rest herself. Ricky's feelings toward the girl were never warmer than in that instance, with her own firm benevolence burnishing the image. But the memory's real source of heat derived from the impression, almost physical, of John observing her throughout. She could feel, as clearly as if he'd spoken it aloud, his adoration of her, and, in it, something like absolution.

She'd thought of that summer as giving them a new beginning, a clean slate. She was startled now to think how young she'd been: only twenty-nine.

Idyllic as it was, Ricky was not dismayed when the holiday at Cabruda Lake had failed to lead to more like it. The Safranskys moved away and Jess moved on, her need, her curiosity, whatever it had been, apparently sated. She'd drifted backward out of their lives with nary a ripple. John had seemed only mildly let down when the phone calls and letters waned. Life was busy, and he had Biscuit and Paul on whom to lavish his paternal energies. All in all, Jess's withdrawal from their lives was as seamless, as easily accomplished, as had been her brief appearance. This, perhaps, was the crux of Ricky's unease, the reason her excitement was edged in shame: children are not supposed to be easy to lose.

6.

Nearly midnight, and no one is asleep.

Biscuit had been asleep, but now her voice broke seamlessly into the quiet of her bedroom, without any indication (no little clearing of the throat, or yawn, or sigh, not even any telltale gravel to her timbre) that she had transitioned from one state to another. In fact, she was not aware of waking, simply of being, all at once, awake. "Are you praying?" she said.

Jess opened her eyes. This strange young woman who was yet familiar—who was, as Biscuit had been informed that afternoon, her half sister, out of the picture for eight long years—sat lotus-style on the air mattress Biscuit's mother had made up with flannel rosebud sheets on the floor of her room. The glow of the night-light cast Jess's shadow high on the wall behind her, a silhouette at once epic and primitive, like a cave painting.

"I thought you were sleeping," Jess gasped, hand flying to her heart.

"What religion are you?" No preamble, was the Biscuit way.

"Not any."

"Then how come you were praying?"

"I wasn't, I was only thinking."

"What about?"

"About . . . the last time I met you."

Biscuit doubted this, but the topic interested her nonetheless. "I don't remember it."

"You were very small." Jess eased out of her lotus position and leaned back on her elbows. Biscuit sat hugging her knees.

"What was I like?"

Jess gave it a moment. "You had a pocketbook."

"I did?" She loved this answer.

"You went around with it all the time, dangling off your arm. You'd go around in just a diaper and your pocketbook. It was white, kind of shiny. Vinyl."

"What did I keep in it?"

"Spare diapers. Canadian coins."

"Canadian coins?"

"And mints."

Then Biscuit said, very slowly, "I think I remember that purse." She did no such thing, but wanted to play along. She had a hunch it *was* a matter of playing along; that Jess had made it all up out of whole cloth. "Did it have one of those metal ball-clasp things you pinch open?"

Jess laughed softly. "Mm-hm."

Emboldened, she tried: "And sequins?"

"In the shape of a bird."

"I thought it was a bug."

"What kind?"

"A ladybug."

"Yes."

Not bad. Biscuit studied her half sister. Jess had removed her glasses, which had the effect of making her look, in the four peachy watts of the night-light, oddly featureless and smooth, like an ancient statue whose face has been worn to mere suggestion. Her pajamas were a pair of scrubs, like the nurses at the hospital had worn. Jess's were pale blue. Around her neck she wore a thin gold chain with nothing on it. Biscuit knew that Jess had come by bus from California, and that she'd brought with her a single, very fat duffel bag. It was over there now, in the corner by her bookshelf. There'd been a guitar, too, when she started out, but that had been stolen along the way, Jess said. Somewhere outside Julesburg. Biscuit didn't know where Julesburg was, why Jess had come without telling them, or how long she was staying. Apparently no one knew that last bit, not even Biscuit's parents, not even Jess herself.

"Can I ask you a question?" Biscuit whispered.

Jess let out the tiniest laugh: a breeze blown through grass.

"What?" Biscuit didn't get the joke.

"You've already asked me like thirty."

"Do you have a boyfriend?"

"No. Do you?"

It did not sound like teasing. Biscuit experienced a kick of pride. "No."

After a bit: "Thanks for letting me stay in your room."

"Oh," said Biscuit. "You're welcome." This was not an adequate response but she didn't know how to say that she was thrilled and unnerved to have Jess sleeping on her floor, that it felt like a prize, like something she'd won in a drawing, but also it felt daring, potentially dangerous, not least because her gladness did not seem evenly shared by the rest of her family. She had observed them closely at supper: her mother's special brightness, her father's near-silent watchfulness, and Paul's desperate chameleoning between acting bored and acting clever. Biscuit wished she could protect him from trying so hard. If she were magic she would make his acne vanish, and all his extra fat, and also the blond fuzz above his lip. She would make his voice reliably low, make him smell the way he used to smell, and she would make him nice.

"Can I ask *you* a question?" Jess whispered.

"'kay."

"What were you doing today? When you cut school?"

*Every*one wanted to know. The thought clutched Biscuit's insides with something like glee, but an awful glee, secretive and inside out, glee's nasty, stunted cousin. She imagined her parents at that very moment sitting up in bed and talking about her latest antic. Today's had managed to be more serious than the others. Thanks, in large part, to the man and his dog. Biscuit conjured the moment of Ebie's pushing her into the river. In truth, Biscuit might have made more of an effort not to go in; there was a moment, minuscule but definite, when, instead of resisting, instead of fighting against gravity and the slippery moss, she'd let it happen, given in to the fall. Not because she wished herself harm, but more from a sly curiosity, a wish to see what would happen if she took this whole thing one step further. She would not have done it if not for the man, Gordie, glimpsed from the corner of her eye, standing back on the path. As it was, he had been witness; because of him, the story had traveled back to her father, and she was pleased with this, the fact that he'd been told about the ashes and bone.

Biscuit knew Gordie had told, although he'd waited till the end and till he thought it was private, standing with her father on the front porch just before he left. She knew because she'd hidden herself inside the front hall closet, a spy among coats and boots, smells of caked mud and damp wool. She'd heard them clearly through the half-open door. When Gordie said it was none of his business and then proceeded to describe in detail what he'd seen, she'd had to bite a mitten to keep still. It wasn't laughter, exactly, that threatened to erupt. She didn't know what it was.

"Biscuit?" prompted Jess.

She did not answer. She made her breaths long and slow. She thought of the stolen library book under her bed. Did she dare show Jess, dare explain about the egg in the water, about the ashes and the cloth? About *its last earthly ties*? Who was this woman, this girl, her half sister, who came unannounced and served them tea, who made up easy lies about a white pocketbook, a sequined ladybug? Was it possible she would be of help to them?

"I know you're not asleep," whispered Jess, doubtfully.

Yes. No. She was a spy again. Russian, like in movies. Svetlana. She had straight black hair like velvet drapes, smoky eyes, a beret.

She specialized in feigning sleep. *Shhh,* Svetlana told herself. *Keep eyes closed. Wait and see.*

Behind her lids she saw peppery specks drifting, flitting through rain-speckled sky, floating on heathery scallops of water. *Blessed be, blessed be. Wait and see, wait and see.*

TWO DOORS DOWN Ricky and John whispered, John with his head resting in the space between Ricky's stomach and breasts, turned so that he could see her face, which was made ethereal by the bluer-than-white streetlamp outside their window. They had been talking softly in this half-light for close to an hour, ever since bidding Jess good night.

"I think she should stay with us," said Ricky now.

"Really?"

"I don't know. Yes."

"How long?"

"Straight through. Until the baby comes. I mean, and then some."

This had turned out to be, as far as they could tell, the reason for Jess's visit: she was with child. Not that she had asked them for a place to stay. Nor had she spoken of her pregnancy as the motivation for reconnecting. She'd simply felt the urge to travel, Jess said. She'd bought a cross-country Greyhound ticket and spent the past ten days making her way across America. Visiting friends here and there—an old family friend in Salt Lake City, a college roommate in Chicago. Eating at bus stations, highway rest stops. Reading *Leaves of Grass* (she produced the well-thumbed paperback with a small flourish, as if it were some sort of credential). Getting her guitar stolen: the one sour note. It disappeared from the bus while she'd been sleeping, she said, somewhere between Julesburg and Ogallalla, and the way she pronounced those names told Ricky she'd managed to make even that occurrence something not all-sour.

Only once the bus had left the Lincoln Tunnel that morning, pulled into the bowels of the Port Authority Terminal and discharged its passengers in the diesel-smelling dawn, had she decided to look the Ryries up.

John and Ricky had glanced at each other. It seemed strange, they said mildly. To have come three thousand miles, to have gotten herself within thirty-five miles of their house, and not have thought of seeing them until that morning.

Oh, it had been in the back of her mind, Jess said (and was she backpedaling, or simply clarifying?). It's just that she hadn't been sure she wouldn't get cold feet. Even at Port Authority, searching out the booth for Rockland Coaches, she got such a thumping headache she nearly hadn't bought the ticket to Nyack. She'd considered that the headache was a sign, a warning. She'd seriously deliberated leaving the line, picking up a packet of aspirin at Duane Reade, sitting down to wait for the next bus west. She already had her return tickets. Tickets, plural, because that was how they came, each leg of the journey printed on a separate sheet, all of them accordioned together like a Jacob's ladder: she got that out of her bag to show them, too. Another credential. That was why she hadn't contacted them in advance, because she hadn't been certain, up until the very moment she'd let herself in through the unlocked door of their empty house, that she would make it all the way without chickening out. And no, truly, she didn't want anything from them. Just a chance to see them again, say hello, find out how they were doing.

It still seemed strange, they both thought but did not repeat aloud (communicating only with the subtlest of glances, which served, in the moment, as a jarring reminder of the intimacy they still shared), that she would come all the way across the country, in her condition, by Greyhound bus, and then up to Nyack by Red and Tan, lugging that enormous duffel, simply for the purpose of saying hello and seeing how *they* were doing. Yet they couldn't disagree that she possessed a distinctly un-needy quality. They could almost believe she wanted nothing from them except a reacquainting.

It also seemed strange, Ricky thought (and felt lonely thinking it, certain the coincidence would not strike John), that Jess had shown up nearly a year to the day after the baby's birth, the baby's death, shown up rich with the very gift they had lost, knowing nothing of their sorrow. She didn't, did she? Ricky asked when they were alone, and John confirmed he had never told her.

Ricky appreciated Jess's thoughtfulness in waiting until after Biscuit and Paul had gone to bed to tell them of her pregnancy. It had become evident, over the course of the evening, that Jess *was* waiting for something, a little glow of concerted patience burning brighter within her during the hours leading up to the children's bedtime. Neither Ricky nor John had any inkling of what she wanted to say, but by unspoken agreement had convened in the kitchen after Ricky finished making up the air mattress on the floor of Biscuit's room and saying good night to both kids. John and Jess were already there, John scooping

Rocky Road into three bowls, Jess standing by the Dutch door, peering past the black panes that looked out on the backyard.

"Well, I do have some news," said Jess when they were all seated. She proceeded to explain, with considerable gentleness, that she was pregnant, that she would keep it, that she was nine weeks along, that the guy was someone she had no future with, that her parents were dismayed. They wanted her to have an abortion. Here she paused, her eyes flicking briefly first toward John, then Ricky. In appeal? In order to gauge their reactions? At any rate, it seemed a testing moment, swollen with something she wanted or expected. Neither John nor Ricky spoke.

Well, Jess continued, she wasn't going to have one. And when she'd told her parents, they'd kicked her out.

"They kicked you out?" John sounded gruff, either from anger or confusion.

"They don't want anything to do with me. Well—it." She spoke with a lack of bitterness that struck Ricky as unlikely. Her head was tilted a little to the side, her eyes were mild, forgiving. She'd laid it all out with such poise, such tact, that Ricky thought if ever some blow were going to be dealt her, she'd want Jess to be the one to do it. In her mind's eye she saw briefly, from earlier in the day, the stateliness, almost courtliness, of the paramedics.

John, having taken the announcement of the pregnancy with apparent equanimity, became visibly upset when Jess described her parents' reaction. "How can they say that?" he'd demanded. His consternation grew as it emerged Jess apparently neither had a plan nor felt the need for one. He kept asking different versions of the same question: "Where are you headed?" And later, "But how will you manage? What will you *do*?"

To which she'd repeated, patiently, that she hadn't worked any of it out yet; she'd simply wanted to stop in and see them along the way.

"Along the way where? What's your plan?"

"I'm not trying to be difficult." She smiled. "I just honestly don't know."

Ricky heard the disclaimer not simply in practical terms, but as a larger, existential truth. *I just honestly don't know.* She rocked in the rocking chair by the radiator and the ice cream melted in streams in her bowl. Of course what Jess said was so for everyone, for all time. You never knew what was going to be.

John cleared his throat. He rubbed his fingers audibly against the bristles on his face. Ricky felt tender toward him then as she would toward a fretful child.

John said, "Well, you need a plan."

Jess, betraying a shred of defensiveness at last, and sounding childish for the first time that evening, said, "I'm twenty-three. Four years older than you when you got my mother pregnant."

John's brow darkly furrowed. "Well," he'd growled, glaring for a long moment at his own bowl of runny ice cream, "I'm not sure how that relates to the present situation."

Ricky had laughed.

The other two looked at her.

"Sorry," she said. "It's just . . . well, not *funny*, I don't mean, but . . ."

She was aware of the yellow softness of the kitchen, and how small, how nearly doll-like they were, the three of them, sitting in their three chairs, sitting with their three bowls and spoons. The warmth she'd always held in reserve for Jess—well, perhaps not; but the warmth she'd always felt as a latent possibility—swelled, as though finally having received its cue, and she found herself resisting the urge to put her arms around the girl, make her promises. She'd settled for announcing, at last, that there'd be lots of time for talk in the coming days, and that now it was time for everyone to get some sleep.

Once in bed, however, Ricky had felt untired, as had John, and they'd lain awake a long time dissecting and analyzing the situation from every angle, taking the aerial view and then zooming in to ground level, referencing the past, wondering about the future, until the quality of their talk developed a leisurely, almost recreational, rhythm and purpose of its own. Rather than wind down toward sleep, Ricky had grown to feel more lively as they talked, and John, if not entirely understanding this then liking it anyway, had been emboldened to move in and rest his head on her stomach.

Each was surprised when her fingers found their way into his curls. It silenced them. John closed his eyes. He drifted toward sleep (he could do this very rapidly; it was the envy of his wife, this ability to slip so easily from consciousness into R.E.M.). Then all at once, he jerked himself fully awake: he had neglected to tell Ricky what Gordie had said about Biscuit and the ashes.

John had confronted Biscuit about it, going to her room before dinner and closing the door behind him. "So what was that all about?" he asked.

She'd played dumb. Ashes? What?

He pressed and cajoled, tried concern and then anger, but she refused to acknowledge, let alone explain, her actions, until,

"This is serious," he'd said, raising his voice. "You could have drowned!"

To that she'd responded with a small, sweet smile that walked the line between contrition and condescension. "Dad. I wouldn't have."

The maddening thing was, he agreed with her; he could not help feeling she was right, that she was essentially not in danger. But what, then, was she up to? Why all the mysterious absences? Now, as every time, she would not say. She either remained stubbornly, serenely vague or affected lack of comprehension.

At last John had heaved a sigh, rubbing a hand across his brow and down his beard. "It's got to stop, Bis. That's all I can say."

Although she had not voiced any argument, he knew already, as he left her room and went downstairs to start dinner, that his words would prove ineffectual and that he'd come no closer to understanding what lay beneath either her truancies or any of her peculiar, largely secretive activities.

John knew he ought to fill Ricky in on all of this now. He would. He'd count to five and then bring it up. But how he dreaded saying even the word "ashes." For all it would invoke.

He'd already made sure, of course, that Biscuit hadn't somehow found them. He'd done that first, before going to speak with her in her room. Right after saying good-bye to Gordie he'd gone straight up to their bedroom and looked in the closet, feeling around on the back of the high shelf where he'd buried the corrugated cardboard box beneath a mothy old sweater. He was the one who had hidden it, the only one who knew where it was, Ricky having asked him to take charge of it almost a year earlier. "Put it away somewhere," she'd said dully from the bed, her eyes closed, her face turned away.

But Biscuit was such an avid spy, and knew no bounds when it came to property or privacy. So that afternoon when John checked, he'd been relieved to find it still in its place, still sealed with clear packing tape. Relieved and then clobbered, blind-sided: in his hands, in this small box, this small definite box with its definite dimensions, its definite significant weight, rested all that remained of his son, the son he'd never held in life, in flesh. It made the walls reel about him. He'd replaced the box beneath the holey wool and gone unsteadily from the room.

John drew a breath to tell Ricky about Biscuit, but the mattress quaked then and Ricky was in flight, having extracted herself from under him and sprung from the bed in a single move, childlike in her fleetness. He propped himself on an elbow and watched her cross in the direction of the closet. For a moment he thought she'd read his mind, was searching out the box of ashes. But she went to her dresser instead.

He waited, but she did not offer any explanation. "What are you doing?"

"I think . . . I still have . . ." She was fumbling in the top drawer, groping around at the back, her arm thrust deep. She withdrew it, victorious. "Yes—I didn't throw it away." She brought to their bed a plastic bottle: turquoise, he could just barely make out.

"What's that?"

"Prenatal vitamins."

"Oh, Ricky." They'll be expired, John thought but did not say. "Are you crying?"

"No." And it was true: her voice held no sound of tears. She set the bottle on her nightstand and got back under the covers. He wanted to comfort her but she seemed almost giddy, and it was she who placed a hand on either side of his face and guided his head back to rest on her sternum. He listened to her heart, felt it like a small animal stirring within her ribs.

The ashes. Biscuit's "ashes," whatever they had really been. They had to talk about Biscuit. He lifted his head again, made a sound preparatory to speech.

But, "Shh," she told him, touching his mouth. "Don't worry about me. Don't worry so much." And she undertook to stroke his face, the wiry coils of his beard, the smooth depression of his temples, his lips again. He held himself still and wondering, propped above her on his forearms, his breath shallow. She traced the frill of his ear, then the cord that led from the base of his ear to his clavicle. Drew the backs of her hands down his stomach. Slid her fingers inside the waistband of his pajamas. Here, without warning, was more intimacy than she'd offered since before the baby's birth. He would not speak now to save his life.

AT THE FAR END of the hall Paul was sitting up in bed, wearing pajamas and the porkpie hat he'd bought at a vintage clothing booth at the street fair last fall. He was drawing. He drew in bed whenever he couldn't sleep. In the past his mother had reprimanded him for getting ink on the sheets, but as no sign of reform ever made so much as a cameo, she'd resorted to looking the other way (at which point Paul had spontaneously decided that pen and ink were too troublesome to manage in bed; now when he drew from a reclining position his implement of choice was his antigravity pen—the kind used by the astronauts—which wrote like a ballpoint but worked at any angle, even upside down).

At the moment he was working on a portrait of his alter ego, gaunt and brooding. He wore a trench coat with the collar turned up. On his head, a porkpie hat, angled low. He leaned against a lamppost. Paul gave him dark shadows under his eyes. His own eyes burned with fatigue. He closed them a moment, the lids fairly creaking shut, like the metalwork door of a birdcage elevator. That was pretty good. If he were representing it in a strip, he'd draw it that way, two little metalwork elevator doors for eyes, and he would write in the word "CREEEA-KK."

Sleep eluded him by and large. It had for years. When he was younger, he'd get up out of bed five, ten, as many as fifteen times a night, going to his parents with minor, revolving complaints (tangled blanket, stomachache, strange noise, itch), which sometimes progressed, as the night wore on, to tearful, wordless appeals. His parents would resolutely walk him back to his room, and he would submit to being tucked in again, over and over, until exhaustion finally overtook him and ended the cycle until the next night. Paul had been aware, even at the time, of his parents' efforts to suppress their frustration at these dramas that dragged into the early hours of the next day, and in a way their success at this was harder to bear than their occasional failures. Twice his father had punched a wall; several times his mother had wept and once she'd hissed at him to stop being such a *baby*. In the course of their desperation they had offered him, variously, relaxation tapes, warm milk and Benadryl at bedtime, a system of star charts and rewards for staying in bed, a system of time-outs and loss of TV privileges for *not* staying in bed, a beautiful green suede–covered journal in which to vent the ungainly thoughts that were supposedly keeping sleep at bay, and karate classes three times a week in which to vent his physical energy—all to no avail.

Around the time he entered middle school, Paul had simply stopped going to them for help they'd never been able to provide. While the period that elapsed between hitting the sack and dropping off still often lasted several hours, it had become less fraught, if only because the guilt he'd felt over inflicting so much grief on his parents had been removed from the list of worries that continued routinely to visit him. Contrary to what his parents had so often assured him would happen, the worries, or state of worry, had not subsided with age. Some of the worries were concrete: he'd left his French book in the cafeteria, they were starting floor hockey in gym, he was confounded by cosine and sine, there was another birthday party he hadn't been invited to. Worse were the nameless ones. When he'd been younger, they'd all been nameless. Paul could still remember hovering, pajama-clad, on his parents' threshold, his throat and chest tight, his nose prickling with tears, and being utterly incapable of formulating a single word in response to his mother's exasperated query, "What is it now?"

Sometimes he suspected that his gravest worries remained nameless, that the concrete, identifiable ones that amassed in his mind were illusions, diversions in the service of a malevolent force whose sole purpose was to prevent his ever resting easy. It seemed to him that as the nameless worries were supplanted, or obscured, by more tangible ones, he was actually moving further and further from the possibility of freeing himself from their root cause. He didn't like to think about this, but sometimes couldn't help it, in the way that he couldn't help picking at his hangnails, even when they bled and scabbed over. Sometimes he wondered if this all meant he would one day likely become crazy.

All his worries, named and nameless alike, shamed him. Back when he used to go in distress almost every night to his parents, they had reminded him how lucky he was, how safe and privileged to live with his whole family, in a house, in a riverside village, in America—as though that would provide him with consolation instead of another burden, proof of his deficiencies. He was old enough to know his troubles were nothing compared with other people's, to know the world was full of people with a reason, a right, to be unable to fall asleep. His own best friend, for starters. Baptiste spoke little of his life before moving to Nyack. The name of his village, Jacmel. That he'd worn an ironed shirt every day to school. That his mother still lived there, that she worked in a hotel, that she hoped eventually to come to the U.S. The very starkness of these details—and more, the stark way his friend delivered them, as if each fact were a single dry bean—convinced Paul that if anyone had cause for insomnia, it was Baptiste. Yet Baptiste exuded calm. Not calm: peace. As though everything yet to come had already happened. Sometimes, when Paul got worked up about some future event, Baptiste would try explaining that whatever was going to be would come about *si Bondye vle,* if God willed it. Paul was made uncomfortable by the submissiveness implied by his friend's belief, but he couldn't help envying Baptiste his faith.

Paul envied Biscuit, too. His sister seemed never to worry, not even when, in his opinion, a little worrying might be in order. Today, for instance. It wasn't so much the playing hooky as it was the biking right in front of her school, for crying out loud, and the part about going to the Hook and falling in the river, even though she'd sworn she hadn't fallen, or wasn't at fault, or whatever. Who else but Biscuit would manage to get herself knocked into the Hudson River by a rescue dog? And then there was the question of bringing home the strange man.

Paul's objection to this last was not on the grounds of danger. All you had to do was glance, briefly, at the guy—jockey-sized and watery-eyed, with his too-bright red hair and raw-looking mouth—to know he wasn't dangerous. It was on the grounds of weirdness. Paul had pegged him as a misfit, an odd bird, and that was one thing this family didn't need more of. Certainly it was one thing Biscuit didn't need more of. Paul hated it that his sister had no real friends, no school friends, peers. His parents, inexplicably, did not seem to consider this a problem. But Paul knew what it could be like if you didn't blend in, if you didn't pass for being like everyone else—especially in middle school, where people were capable of calling you "Chub" to your face and your best friend, "Yo, Haitian"; of blowing milk through their straws into your tray of Fiesta Nachos or Teriyaki Chicken Dippers; worst, of ignoring you so comprehensively that it didn't even seem intentional, until bit by bit the friends you'd had all through elementary school excluded you not out of malice but because you'd fallen off their radar screens—and you found yourself fair game for all the maggot-faced Stephen Boyds of the world.

He gave his alter ego a knife, and with a few short lines showed how it gleamed under the streetlamp.

This Gordie might be a nice guy, but encouraging a friendship between him and Biscuit—between him and anyone in this already too-weird family—was clearly a step in the wrong direction. Paul couldn't help but blame his father, who'd not only invited the guy in but clothed and fed him, too. Not that he should be shocked; both his parents had already proven themselves legally blind several times over. They couldn't seem to detect anything wrong with Biscuit, never mind that she had no friends her own age, cut school, and could frequently be heard whispering to herself in ridiculous accents. They couldn't seem to detect anything wrong with him, never mind that he'd rapidly transformed from a happy-go-lucky kid who got invited to twenty birthday parties a year—everyone in his class—to a misfit loser with one measly friend—a friend who hardly ever even came over because of *his* misfitty Grann. They couldn't even seem to detect anything wrong with each other, never mind that his mother had been silent for most of the past year, or that his father, for all his apparent optimism, was beginning to show fissures. But no, to hear his folks tell it, things were swell, everyone doing admirably, chins up, noses to grindstones, business as usual, soldiering on—like the very fact they'd all come through the past year made them heroes. Break out the purple fucking hearts.

And now into all this appeared Jess, magically, like someone stepping through a looking glass, like a character in a book made flesh, standing in their kitchen, smiling at him, holding of all mugs his alphabet mug, like a sign, an omen, but that was stupid, but maybe things were about to change, maybe they'd already begun. Paul was still unnerved by the confusion he'd felt upon walking into the kitchen and seeing her there. He'd had a feeling it was her straightaway, although of course he'd needed his father's confirmation, so many years had passed. "Jess as in Jessica?" he'd asked, pretending to be unsure but in reality covering for his shock, the mix of happiness and anger that had flooded him. It was as if he'd popped a handful of joke-shop candy, a rush of sweetness followed by the vinegary tang of having been tricked.

But no one had tricked him. His parents had been in the dark themselves, as taken aback as he by her unannounced arrival. And if she seemed different than he remembered, that was hardly a betrayal. People changed. So she'd lopped off her spectacular hair—why shouldn't she? Eight years had passed. Neither was Paul the towheaded, baby-toothed, loose-limbed boy he'd been. For all he knew Jess was as disappointed by the changes in him as he was by the changes in her. Except that was presumptuous. To imagine even for a moment that his inconstancy mattered to her.

He scratched out, viciously, the guy he'd been drawing. Started over on a fresh page, drew a girl this time, not some mud-flap ho but a badass chica with cargo pants and spiked hair.

If Paul had long nursed an infatuation for Jess, it had been more intense for its childish clarity, more tenacious for the innocence of its inception. Although he hardly thought about her anymore in a concrete way, he'd never really stopped expecting, anticipating her eventual return. As though the prospect of her resuming a role in his life had lent the future a necessary luster. But the joke was on him: it turned out the idea of her retained its power on the condition she not reappear.

That evening at supper Jess had shown him the same quality of attention she'd offered Biscuit, no more, no less. Paul had been unable to detect the slightest indication from her of their preexisting bond, and he took this absence as confirmation of something he'd begun to suspect: that he was in a kind of decline, growing more deeply unappealing every year. He thought of them down the hall now, Biscuit and Jess, side by side, sleeping, probably, but still he was jealous of them for having each other as company. He imagined he could hear their breathing through the wall, slow and inflated with sleep, rising and falling in tandem, lining the nest of Biscuit's night-lighted room with its downy sound.

In fact he could hear nothing. Only, straining, the insect whine of electricity within the walls. The clock beside his bed read 12:58. An hour ago he'd been aware of low voices from his parents' room. Odd that this still held some power to comfort. The house had since grown relentlessly quiet. He wished for the sound of rain. That was a thing that helped, some nights— the sound of rain on the eaves. But it had rained once today already, and the front had come through.

ON THE CRAMPED BALCONY of the second-story condo that he had until this past January shared with his dad, Gordie Joiner sat with a wool blanket wrapped around him, his feet propped against the railing, and regarded his own breath as it traveled in sparse veils from his mouth. It was not unusual, now, for him to sit out here quite late at night. The balcony had room for little more than the molded plastic chair in which he sat and a single milk crate, on which rested a clamshell that still held a few extremely weathered cigarette butts. Beneath the chair his dad's old radio played, tuned to the same soft rock station that had been on when his dad had left for the hospital that final time. Plugged into the outdoor outlet, it had been playing continuously these past four months.

The condo complex was built into the crook of the thruway entrance ramp, and the whoosh of traffic, though diminished at night, never entirely stopped. Gordie's dad had used to say it was like living by the sea, comparing the sound to that of the surf, not a nuisance but a lullaby. So Gordie tried to think of it now. Below, from the darkness, came the sound of bottles being tipped into a recycling bin. Someone in one of the other units yelled out a window: "Sheila! Get in here!" A car started up and pulled away slowly, out of the parking lot and into the elsewhere until Gordie could no longer follow the sound of its engine. He closed his eyes and inhaled deeply. The rain earlier in the day had stirred all manner of intricacies from the soil, and the air, though almost painfully cold in his nostrils, smelled plainly now of spring. It was, literally, no longer the season of his orphaning.

Will Joiner had entered the hospital on December twenty-third with complications from lung cancer. It had metastasized to the liver, lymph nodes, and spine. He died just short of his fifty-fifth birthday. Gordie's mother had died nine days after his birth. Postpartum toxemia. The loss made bitterer by the fact that nowadays, in a developed nation, such a death ought not to have occurred. Will Joiner put the blame squarely on their native stoicism, his and Bronwyn's both, and throughout Gordie's life his dad had always erred on the side of caution, medically speaking, in all ways but one: the cigarettes he could not, would not, give up. Red and white pack. Peeping out of his breast pocket or tossed on the kitchen table. The cellophane sleeves, run through with their strip of gold, always lying about. Even after the scan showed cancer, even after Gordie moved home, as much to police him as anything else, his dad persisted in sneaking smokes, out on the balcony or in the bathroom. Eventually he did not bother to sneak, but smoked again in broad daylight at the kitchen table, or in his leather chair before the TV, or brazenly, sitting up in bed, until Gordie had given up lecturing, given up hunting down the hidden packs and squirreled-away loose smokes he'd find rooting through his dad's nightstand and sock drawer and the pockets of old sport jackets hanging neat and idle in the back of the hall closet.

Gordie told himself he sat out here to avoid being overwhelmed by his dad's random clutter, still untouched inside the condo: papers, books, shoes, newspaper clippings, hand tools, prescription bottles, saucers of loose change. Yet the bulk of the clutter was not random at all; it comprised the trappings of what had been Will Joiner's singular passion: diorama-making. He'd used shoe boxes, mostly, but also shirt boxes, cigar boxes, chocolate boxes, and a tall oak one that had once held a bottle of very good scotch. An autodidact partial to the *Encyclopædia Britannica* (for which Ebie had been acronymously named), Will Joiner had taken for inspiration anything that struck his fancy. Some of the scenes he built depicted precise, if apocryphal, moments in history: Archimedes saying "Eureka!" in his bath (a speech bubble stuck to his mouth with a bit of wire), or Alexander the Great about to slash through the Gordian knot (with a translucent blue cocktail sword). Some drew their inspiration from literature: Cyrano hiding beneath Roxanne's balcony while Christian stood in the moonlight; Alice at the Mad Hatter's tea. Some came from his dreams: a woman hanging laundry on a clothesline, a boy leaping off a bridge.

Their construction was at once crude and exquisite in its pains. Cheap plastic dollhouse furniture mingled with hand-stitched curtains; a landscape cut from a magazine was juxtaposed with real sand and a glue-gunned birch bark canoe. Some of the boxes had Christmas lights or flashlight bulbs rigged to shine through holes cut in the backs or tops. Some had movable parts you could work by pulling paper clips attached to strings. Some had tiny crank-handled music boxes duct-taped to the outside. If you turned the handle on the back of Lincoln's assassination, for example, you'd hear Brahms' Lullaby. Or on the scene of a magician sawing a lady in half: "O Sole Mio." Gordie's dad had worked in the same post office branch for twenty years and not a single colleague had ever known of his hobby—this had dawned on Gordie only at the funeral.

A noise at his back made Gordie turn. It was Ebie, wanting to join him on the balcony: a thing she rarely did. Gordie slid open the glass door and filled with gratitude for the delicate industry with which she pressed herself past his legs, brought her rump around, her tail striking the bars of the iron railing, and wound up sitting beside him. She pushed her nose up against the ceiling of his palm, and he stroked her glossy crown and murmured, "You're a good girl." He had not ever seen her react to someone as she had to the girl Biscuit. He saw again how she'd torn out along the spit, how she'd knocked the girl in, how she'd then pushed her way into the Ryries' front hall and planted herself not by Gordie but by the girl. He might almost have felt jealous if not for the fact that he, too, had wanted to plant himself, to stay in that house—which he had, for nearly two hours, accepting a cup of tea and the loan of a sweatshirt while his own soaked jacket went through the drier, chatting with the father and the grown daughter, revealing bits and pieces of his story, gleaning bits and pieces of theirs.

Two whole hours. It embarrassed him now, to think how long he'd stayed. As if he didn't mind their realizing he had nowhere better to go.

With a sudden, almost violently decisive movement that made Ebie prick up her ears, Gordie reached beneath the chair and felt around for his dad's radio. After a moment he located the power switch, and after another he pressed it. For the first time since December it went quiet. Then there was only the susurration of the thruway, and the hard black smell of new spring.

PART TWO

Last Year

1.

The diagnosis had been made the same day she learned it was a boy, during a routine ultrasound in the fifth month.

Anencephaly was such a pretty word. It might have been a Victorian girl's name, or that of a minor deity: goddess of apocrypha, muse of nonsense verse.

Instead it was the name of a neural tube defect that meant her child would be missing the major portion of his brain and also the top of his skull and scalp. His head would be open to the sky. The radiologist there in the obstetric ultrasound suite explained that the condition was "incompatible with life," a phrase that took Ricky several seconds to understand, but which then struck her not as sneakily euphemistic but as surprisingly elegant and apt, free of judgment. A numbing fog sifted down upon her, an etherizing blanket. She experienced the overwhelming desire to sleep.

Yet something was not right, some vital fact was escaping her, something she knew she must bring to the radiologist's attention, what? A sort of contradiction. Medically significant. She furrowed her brow, ransacking her mind, then struck upon it with a rush of near-nauseating adrenaline. "But—I've felt him— moving. Just in the past week." She flushed furiously; sweat stood out along her brow.

The radiologist nodded, rested her eyelids a moment, lifted them again. "Yes. The anencephalic fetus quickens, just like any other baby."

When she did not continue, Ricky looked in confusion at her own hands. *Oh.* Somewhere, far away, too far for her to do anything about it, a train wreck was in progress, tons and tons of metal collapsing on itself, whole compartments combusting, grass bursting into flame and smoking alongside the tracks.

She and the radiologist were alone in the room. John, who had been present for Paul's and Biscuit's ultrasounds (uneventful both), had a show at the Llewellyn-Price going up in four days, and only just the previous day had learned the director needed part of the set to revolve. He'd looked haggard and harried that morning at breakfast, cradling his coffee in the lopsided alphabet mug.

"You sure it's okay if I don't go?"

"I'll bring you a picture," she'd promised, with a cavalier flourish of her fingers. "You already know what it's going to look like, anyway."

"Some kind of weather." That had been their joke with the other two, whose fetal images resembled, they agreed, nothing so much as the radar maps used by meteorologists. They'd referred to Paul, before his birth, as Gathering Storm; Biscuit as An Area of High Pressure.

Both children had already left for school. Ricky was having an unusually decadent morning, lounging about this late. She'd scheduled her ultrasound for the earliest available time slot, nine, which meant leaving the house at eight-forty, more than an hour past her normal departure time.

"Exactly," she said, shrugging to minimize the importance of the event, then kissing his weary brow (he'd stayed at the theater till two the night before). "Go make your set spin, sweetheart. I'll see you tonight." And pulling on gloves, she'd left the house.

It had been December, so frozen the air seemed to rustle as she crossed the porch, and the little lawn to creak under her tread. Her shrug was a dissimulation. She was in fact giddy with excitement. The moment, that moment, of seeing the little profile! In the car, she fantasized about coming home from work that night with the promised item: an impossibly grainy square of black-and-white, which she'd stick up on the fridge, displaying a certain outward irony to acknowledge that showing it off in this way was very white, suburban, bourgeois. But she imagined with real pleasure Biscuit and Paul, in turn, wandering over, wrinkling their noses at the image, demanding to know if they had been that funny-looking, too. John would declare it a good-looking bugger no matter what (and mean it), and Ricky would tease him lightly about making this categorical pronouncement based on only a blurry shadow, while inwardly basking in the ambient glow of his happiness. As for herself, she would already have pored over the image a dozen times at her desk that day, marveling tenderly over its slopes and protrusions, inferring from them a whole life, a distinct person.

That had been her fantasy an hour ago, while making her way here in the wan light of the winter morning. Now she did not know whether the day had turned out sunny or overcast. The ultrasound room was windowless and dim, although the monitor had been switched off and Ricky no longer lay on the examining table but sat in an oversized modular chair of vaguely Scandinavian design. The radiologist, herself a large-boned woman of vaguely Scandinavian design—blue eyes; bland, implausibly symmetrical features; blond hair sculpted in a bun at her nape—was speaking gravely, methodically. She was not warm, offered no recognizable expression of sympathy. Ricky found herself grateful for this, the clinical reserve and uninflected formality of the radiologist, of whose words only a fraction penetrated the fog that had settled, mercifully, over her.

Rate of occurrence was about one in ten thousand. A rudimentary brainstem might be present but not the cerebrum, without which there could be no thinking, no feeling, no consciousness. Anencephalics who were not stillborn had a life expectancy of a few hours or days. Rarely, weeks. She could choose to terminate now. Most did, the radiologist added.

"I'll carry to term." The strength and alacrity of her assertion surprised her.

The radiologist nodded but said, "You'll want to talk with your partner. You don't have to decide anything now. We'll notify your doctor of the results."

He kicked then. Ricky put her hand on the spot. He pressed

out against it, and she cupped whatever it was—elbow, heel—with a wild ripping of her heart.

"Is there"—she tried to sound nonchalant, as though her interest were merely clinical—"a margin of error?"

The radiologist looked nonplussed for just a fraction; then her features resolved into an expression of terrible sympathy. She said nothing but held Ricky's gaze, until Ricky, blinking, looked at the floor.

The radiologist made a move as if to stand, and Ricky looked up quickly. There must be some other question she ought to ask, some way of forestalling the end of this meeting and its commensurate conclusiveness. "Can I have a picture?" she said. Again, her utterance—both the assertiveness of her voice and the fact that she had the wherewithal to think of the request—surprised her.

"Sorry?"

"Of my baby."

The radiologist made a tiny sound inside her mouth. "Of course."

She had to get back on the table, push the stretch panel on the front of her maternity jeans back down over the small hump of her belly, pull up her shirt, have more of the warmed gel squirted onto her skin. In the radiologist's unbroken silence—she said nothing more from that point on—Ricky read reluctance, possibly even disapproval, but the woman guided the transducer unhurriedly, pressing the button to print not one but two images, and before she left the room nearly undid Ricky's composure by placing her large hand on the top of Ricky's head and keeping it there for at least three seconds, an unexpected and very nearly shattering benediction.

Ricky took home the two squares of baby weather map, not in the evening after work as planned, but straightaway, in the middle of the morning, direct from the complex of medical office buildings in Nanuet. One she stuck on the fridge. The other she brought, the edge held delicately between finger and thumb, as she climbed half blindly the stairs to her room, where she barely managed to conduct her body to the big wooden bed before, like the princess who has pricked her finger on a spinning wheel, and without first calling John to tell him what had happened or the office to say she was going to be out sick, she succumbed to the most instantaneous oblivion, a sleep as viscid and nullifying as tar.

2.

Biscuit lay before the fire, lost in the flickering light and colored marbles nested in tin. She was playing alone, purple against black, opposite points of the star. The purple was good, a creamy lilac, all sweet and bitable, but the black was even more intoxicating, the inkiness so liquid she wanted to drink it, wanted to roll the onyx orbs about on her tongue, grind their glossy surfaces together inside her mouth.

She lay with her chin resting on her stacked fists, luxuriantly yet imperfectly lost. Somewhere on the edge of her awareness, treading lightly but refusing to retreat altogether, was the fact that Paul was angry again, had gotten mad at her during this very game of Chinese checkers and flung a handful of his pieces at her before storming from the room, so that even now as she continued her move without him, she knew the game could not be played to completion. Somewhere even further from the center of her thoughts, the bigger worry loomed.

The fire was gas, the logs fake. The gas made a queer whistling sound, faint in Biscuit's ears. Even the embers were not real but some sort of molded ceramic that only seemed to glow from within. It was her grandma's fireplace, lit today not only because of the unseasonable cold, the last gasp of winter trespassing on the first full month of spring, but also because of the sad reason for the children's visit: a curative. Not that anyone said this straight out. Her grandma hadn't even mentioned the reason they were here. But Biscuit could tell because her grandma, a woman not given to excess of any kind, had declared the lighting of the fire (the turning of a knob) a "special treat."

This was her father's mother. She was called Polly, a jolly name that did not suit her. She was a kind woman who expressed her kindness in a bossy, fretful sort of way. She kept Handi Wipes in her purse and doled them out at picnics, pressed odd morsels (tapioca, prunes) on people between meals, and was forever touching her lips to foreheads suspected of being too warm. When the children had been informed, yesterday afternoon, that instead of going to school the next day they were to be dropped off at their grandma's, Paul's first response had been, "I'm not going," and his second, "This family sucks," followed by a rat-a-tat tear up the stairs and the gunshot sound of his door smashed against its frame.

Biscuit's favorite spot in her grandma's house was the cupboard behind the fire. It was filled with toys and books that had once belonged to Biscuit's father and aunt. Along with the Chinese checkers, it housed a basket of wooden houses, a metal spyglass, dominoes, a set of matryoshka dolls. Among the old picture books was one inside whose front cover Biscuit had once discovered her father's name (well, *Jonh*), written in laborious, wobbly strokes. It had been thrilling, oddly humbling, even farfetched to think she was touching the very pages *he* had touched at five or six. Now Biscuit got up from the tin tray of marbles and rummaged through the cupboard, searching for the book, suddenly longing to confirm her memory of it. But though she inspected the flyleaf of each volume, she did not find his name.

Her father had driven them across the bridge early. The sky had still been dark. They'd had to wear their puffy coats, which they hated, and to bring their suitcases, which had made them balk. They would be staying in Tarrytown until tomorrow or the next day, or possibly even a day or two after that; the duration of the visit had been left alarmingly vague.

The car radio had said it would snow today. It was April second, but never mind that—four to six inches, the radio had said. April second: already Biscuit had made a talisman of the date. Their brother's birthday. The day their mother was scheduled to give birth. The birth had to be scheduled because the baby wasn't coming on its own. Sometimes with this kind of baby that was going to die, it had a hard time getting born. There was something terribly confusing about all this—not about the baby and that it was going to die, but about the way her parents explained it all: with a kind of ready candor, as if to suggest there was nothing they would not share. Yet Biscuit knew this was not so, and it left her feeling muddled and hard.

Their father hadn't come into their grandma's house that morning, but only stood on the stoop. He'd been in a hurry to get back across the river before the snow started. That had been hours ago. It was snowing now and had been steadily for some time. Out the windows on either side of the fireplace, flakes the size of minnows swam by. Biscuit's grandma was in the kitchen making egg salad. Biscuit could smell it. Earlier, she'd heard the eggs bumping lightly against the walls of the pot, and now she knew by the smell that her grandma had taken off the shells and was mashing them with a fork. She didn't care for eggs herself.

The egg salad was being prepared especially for Paul, who'd entered the house that morning shuffling heavily, his shoulders up by his ears, his eyes not leaving the floor. Biscuit had heard her father's low voice: "He's having a hard time," and her grandma's reply: "What would he like to eat?"

"Ask him," her father had said, already on his way back down the walk to the car, whose engine he'd left running.

But when she did, Paul had only shrugged. "I don't know. Nothing."

It was Biscuit who delivered the answer on Paul's behalf, later, when it was nearing noon, after their grandma had put the question to them again: "How about some lunch?" She'd appeared on the edge of the room, and clasped her hands at her waist. "Paul, what's something you like to eat?"

Biscuit looked at him. Her brother's face was largely obscured, first by the angle—he was studying the bright pentacle with its arrangement of marbles as though it contained the secrets of the universe—and then by his hair, a dirty-blond, uncropped thatch that he lately never bothered to comb. "I'm not that hungry," he'd said.

"No? Biscuit, what about you?"

"I'm okay."

"Really? It's getting on toward twelve." Their grandma stood doubtfully in the door frame a moment before heading back to the kitchen.

"Go," prompted Paul, nodding at the game board.

Instead Biscuit said, "One sec," and sprinted into the kitchen. "He likes egg salad." She felt quietly noble, supplying this information without consideration for her own preference, and the way her grandma's face brightened at this tip inspired her to add, "If you have olives, he likes those, too."

But this good deed turned out to be the very thing, once she'd revealed it with a little shy pride, that made Paul scoop up a handful of his pieces and fling them, hard, at her (or a calculated centimeter to her left), saying, "Butt out, Ass. You don't know what I like," before clomping from the room.

Biscuit contracted with regret. She'd done it again. Her knack for maintaining good cheer in the face of everything that made Paul miserable—he always seemed to take it as rebuke, as though her little gestures in his behalf were made for the sole purpose of rubbing in the fact of his glum nature. Biscuit stared into the fire. A few tears rolled down her cheeks and dried there, tight on her skin. *There, there,* the gas seemed to whistle. The false embers glowed like a tiny city half hidden in the grate. In that city was a building, and in that building was a room, and there her mother lay in a bed with nurses bustling softly around it, preparing for death. There were white sheets and white snowflakes out the window, and the gray lady stood hushed at the edge of the room, knowing, seeing. *There, there,* the nurses whistled like the gas.

There, there, whispered Biscuit to the baby. Her grandma came into the living room, wearing an apron over her jeans. "Ready for lunch? Where's Paul?"

"He left."

"Left? What do you mean? I've got lunch all ready."

Biscuit shrugged. She understood that at her grandma's house today there would be no mention of the baby, or of the hospital, or of her parents. She knew her grandma would refrain from speaking out of a conviction that children were best served by protective silence, and she knew she and Paul would steer clear of the subject in deference to their grandma.

"Well, you come, anyway. Wash your hands."

But she didn't. She followed her grandma, who went looking for Paul, who turned out to be not far, only halfway up the stairs, hunched on the window seat on the landing. This was Biscuit's second-favorite spot in her grandma's house. The window seat was shaped like a wedge of pie, and bore a pie-shaped cushion covered in faded green velvet. The house, tall and narrow, stood on half an acre of steep hillside, and this window looked west, toward the Hudson and home; over the tops of the still-bare trees, whose branches were now shoring up nests of snow, she could just glimpse the palisades across the river.

Paul's sketchbook was open and propped against his knees, which he drew in closer to his chest, secretively, without looking up.

"Well, there you are," said their grandma. "Lunch is ready."

It was as if he hadn't heard her. For long seconds, his pencil was the only sound. Biscuit felt its rude skritching in the base of her throat.

"Come on, now," their grandma tried brusquely. When still he did not look up, she went over and knelt on the carpeted landing. It looked as though she might be going to put a hand on his arm. But then, abruptly, Paul did acknowledge her presence, by shutting the book with a violent snap and bending his head lower, glowering determinedly at his lap.

Biscuit, one step below, gazed at her grandma's wide, flat backside, at the apron strings trailing crookedly over the expanse of pale blue pants. It struck her that her grandma could not see her own apron strings, could not know the rumpled paths they made over her bottom, nor the indignity with which one traced the middle seam and dangled like a tail between her legs, and this seemed briefly terrible, lamentable beyond proportion. Biscuit's chest contracted. She had little faith in her grandma's ability to reach Paul, retrieve him from the terrible place he'd consigned himself to. What did her grandma know that might equip her to do the job? Was it possible to reach someone whose sorrow you didn't acknowledge, let alone understand?

"I'm not a dummy, you know." Their grandma spoke tartly, and though the comment was directed at Paul, Biscuit jerked in surprise. "I wasn't born yesterday." Oh no, Biscuit thought, wishing there were some way she could signal her grandma that a bluff tone would only make things worse. Paul might possibly be reached with kindness, very gingerly proffered, but never with chiding. "I did raise a son." Their grandma gave a sniff. "Not to mention a daughter. If you think I don't know the silent treatment, well. You should have known your father."

It was a funny thing to say—of course they did know him— yet Biscuit imagined what her grandma meant: her father as a boy, as *Jonh,* not the person they knew at all but an alien, an impostor, almost fearsome in his ignorance of her—she who did not yet exist—incapable not only of loving her but of possessing even casual interest in her. Biscuit gazed over at her grandma and Paul at the snow out the window, darting this way and that like schools of tiny fish. She was suddenly hungry to see her father, to be in the same room with him and her mother both, to squeeze their hands and have them look down and see her, too.

"Oh, he could be rotten," her grandma was saying in her comfortably testy way, describing their father when he was Paul's age and gave her nothing but trouble. "Trouble and lip. And attitude. His hair was even worse than yours." She added, with a rough sort of fondness or pride, "He brought me to tears on a daily basis."

At some point during this Paul had lifted his chin and turned to look out the window. A silence came and bathed the little landing while all three of them took up the identical task: watching the snow, the flakes that had grown smaller and wilder in the darkening midday sky. Biscuit reached out and very softly ran her grandma's apron strings through her fingers.

In the kitchen they had egg salad on rye and three Mallomars apiece from a brand-new box. Paul did one or two small things for Biscuit during lunch—leaped up and got the paper towels when she spilled her milk, rolled his eyes in commiseration when their grandma complained for the hundredth time that she did not know how a girl with such a healthy appetite could stay so skinny. It was easy to forgive him, easy to welcome him back. He had a harder time than she did, every single day, a fact so plain to her it hardly bore remark.

After lunch, their grandma announced she was sending them out of doors for fresh air. They groaned in a protest more requisite than heartfelt. Deep down they were both relieved to get out, and put on their boots and mittens and awful puffy coats with little fuss. Biscuit yanked open the front door. The snow had stopped and the world, heavy and hushed, was coated with flakes so airy and light that every bush and branch seemed aquiver, and the lawn sloped off as smooth and steep as a pitched roof; she fairly lunged toward the steps. But Paul stopped her. "Hang on," he grunted, and disappeared back into the kitchen where they'd left their grandma doing dishes. Biscuit could hear his rising tone, the impatience, the creeping belligerence; some request was being denied and he was arguing, persisting. Biscuit's stomach knotted. Why, oh *why* didn't he know how to give up, let go of things?

But then Paul was back, not scowling but grinning in victory, scampishly displaying his plunder: two garbage bags, heavy-duty black ones. "Come on," he said, pushing past.

She followed him into the clean-coated world. He strode to the high point of the lawn, the ledgelike spot right before it dropped away downhill. Snow displaced by his stride sprayed into the air before him. Some small animal, a bird or squirrel, disturbed by the sudden human activity, fled its branch, leaving behind an ivory cascade.

"Come here."

She trotted up beside him. He spread one of the garbage bags flat on the ground, holding the plastic smooth while she positioned herself on it, then instructed her to grip the sides and fold them in over her lap.

"Ready?"

She barely nodded before she felt his hand on the middle of her back, pushing her forward, off the ledge. She was skimming, speeding downhill, spinning, then tumbling, before she came to a halt at the bottom, somersaulted into a mouthful of cold.

"You okay?" Paul called down.

She nodded, dazed. Her face felt covered with stars.

"Look out, then!" He came bulleting down on his own gar-bage bag, headfirst on his stomach. She did not take her eyes off him. His cheeks, as he drew closer, were ruddy, slashed with red, and his eyes burned with the danger, the importance, of his mission. Although he was not smiling, Biscuit believed he was as happy as he ever got these days, which was to say as far from whatever troubled him as he could get within his own mind.

3.

Will Joiner was making gold-rimmed goblets. His tenth day home from the hospital. He sat at the kitchen table cutting a clear plastic straw into thumbnail lengths, then dipping one end of each section into a puddle of Elmer's. The glue formed a membrane across the opening that would dry clear and so form the bottom of the glass. Next, he dipped each open end into a puddle of gold paint. The paint, less viscous, would not form a seal but only deposit a gold ring around the lip. The goblets were for a wedding. Specifically, the scene of his and Bronwyn's wedding supper. Thus the photo album splayed on the kitchen table along with the glue and paint: he had gotten it out for reference.

None of his other dioramas represented a scene from his own life. Ordinarily he would have been sheepish about what might seem like self-regard. But it wasn't for himself, this box, and that made the difference.

His eyeglasses had slipped low on his nose. They and the nasal cannula that led to the portable oxygen concentrator made his face front-heavy; he had to tilt his head somewhat back to compensate. The sustained effort was giving him a crick in the neck, and the bright light he'd trained on his workspace was making him very warm, but he took note of these discomforts without strongly minding them; he had begun to notice himself relishing even unpleasant sensations.

He'd had a lobe removed a year ago, followed by chemo and radiation. Then this recurrence, and another tumor removed, and more chemo scheduled. They'd wait and see how he responded. They were loath to offer any prognosis. He had no illusions about what this meant.

Bronwyn, who would not appear in the scene—it would be entirely unpeopled, a table set in anticipation of guests—had been dead nineteen years, so many more than the four he'd known her. Her youth, more than anything, is what he remembered of her. Her skin had been smooth and firm as a bar of soap. She'd had a tiny mole at the corner of her mouth that did not mar but rather enhanced her polished elegance; it looked endearingly like a toast crumb.

They'd had a civil ceremony followed by a restaurant supper, a private room rented out for them and a dozen relatives and friends. Bron, in the photos, which lay under protective film, was lovely in her knee-length ivory A-line dress, her dark hair flipped up at the ends. Will admired her handsomeness and did not grieve at the sight of her. It was the images of himself that stabbed. Bron, after all, had been relatively unchanged at the time of her death from the bride in the photos, whereas the man he was now bore little resemblance to the pictured groom. In the pictures he was lean and lanky and wore his happiness, along with his shaggy hair and skinny tie, quite unabashedly. At fifty-five he was thickened and wheezing, tethered to tubes and metal canister: such a far cry from that other person—whom he yet distinctly remembered being—that he felt a flash of the old bitterness, the sense of helpless, stunned betrayal that had knocked him flat upon her death.

In the months after Bron's funeral Will had worked hard to counter with an outwardly mild manner what he knew to be his envenomed core. He did this in the interest of others, not only his infant son but also his colleagues, relatives, and neighbors, and the well-meaning outreach workers who would call or come by with bereavement brochures, donated diapers, tins of formula. To his surprise, discipline became habit: his sweet ways built up, over the years, around the old mordant kernel, like peach flesh around its stone of cyanide. So that Gordie not only grew up with a dad who displayed no sign of having been damaged from that early loss, but might in turn believe in the possibility of recovering from future losses; might see that sweetness could follow upon suffering.

Will sighed as deeply as his body would let him, until the queer, frightening pull in his chest stopped him abruptly—the rude sensation of climbing into a short-sheeted bed—but this was only adhesions, the nurses had reassured him, a normal result of the surgeries he'd had. He found it strange but not dishonorable the way they offered reassurance on this matter without pretending he was not dying. He hadn't talked about the fact of his dying with Gordie.

The ersatz gold-rimmed glasses done, set upside down on yesterday's weather to let their Elmer's bottoms dry, Will took inventory of what other pieces he'd assembled: an antimacassar for the lace tablecloth, a thrift shop earring for the chandelier. A small batch of homemade white play dough, which Will would mold into a three-tiered cake. (He'd had an inspiration for the bride and groom figurines: rice, he thought he'd try, two raw grains of it, painted with a pin dipped in ink.) The dinner plates were the white tops of pill bottles.

At his feet, Ebie's tail thumped and she gathered herself to rise, navigating backward out from under the table, her toenails scrabbling on the linoleum. She was one, still a pup, or now a teenager, Will supposed. On the cusp of adulthood. Like his son, just nineteen and a freshman at Fordham. Or, officially, on leave from Fordham. Gordie had insisted on taking leave, against his dad's vigorous protests, as soon as the diagnosis had been made.

"You're staying in school," Will had growled. "Won't have you quitting." Neither he nor Bronwyn had attended college. "I've got all the company I need," he'd said, stroking the top of the dog's head.

"Ebie's great, Dad, but she's as much burden as companion."

What Will could not bear was Gordie's air of overripe consternation, the rawness of his helplessness. But he had a method, a means of delivering them both from these scary slicks. "What do you know about burdens?" he snorted.

"I'm saying. She's a *dog*."

"You think you're that much better?" And Will made a

mincing expression, tilting his head from side to side. It worked: Gordie shook his head and rolled his eyes. The pretense of irascibility never failed to bring them back to more familiar, less starkly terrifying ground.

It was Gordie the dog had risen to greet just now, her ears having distinguished his particular footfall in the hallway outside their unit even before his key turned in the lock. She'd always been more Gordie's than Will's, never mind that they'd adopted her expressly to provide company for the elder Joiner when the younger went off to school. Oh, she was affectionate enough with Will, but anyone could see she considered herself Gordie's dog, almost as though she knew what lay ahead: that Gordie would be the one, in the end, in need of company.

He came in bearing a gallon of carrot and spirulina juice and several pharmacy bags containing Will's prescription refills.

"I'm not drinking that," offered Will in the rote manner of an oft-repeated refrain.

Gordie ignored this, setting his bags on the counter and crouching to greet the dog effusively. "Hel-*lo*, Ebie. That's right, that's right." She bucked her head forward and licked her chops at him drippingly. "You're a good girl, aren't you?"

Will scoffed ostentatiously, on cue.

This was how it had been ever since the diagnosis: a pretense of animosity had grown between them, a kind of ongoing, low-level dyspepsia. As surely as the disease itself, this new pattern of behavior divided present from past. Will didn't regret it. The enormity of Gordie's having given up school to be his caregiver—the enormity, for that matter, of his own imminent mortality—seemed to require such a charade. Will understood it not as an avoidance of true feeling, but as the most tenable means of expressing it. It translated, in a way he couldn't begin to explain, into a high order of intimacy.

"I'm going to you-know-what the pooch," Gordie said.

"Right." Will picked up a bit of play dough and began to roll it between his palms.

But Gordie, despite his declaration, remained where he was, palpably miserable, it seemed to Will. Ebie whined once, twice, then gave up and lay back down. Gordie said, "What are you working on?" and wandered over to the table.

Will felt his son standing behind him, breathing, taking in the elements of the scene, piecing together what they must mean. Beneath the clumsy freight of his eyeglasses and oxygen tubes, Will felt his face grow hotter. He was blushing. Never before had he intended any of his dioramas to convey a message. Never before had he made one expressly for someone else. But that's what this was: a little box of meaning, a memorandum, a wish. Another minute passed before Gordie next spoke, during which time Will continued, as nonchalantly as he was able, to shape the small cake. His fingers, however, were trembling.

Gordie's question came out shy, thimble-sized. "Can I help?"

4.

For a time she believed herself to be in love with the pediatric resident Dr. Abdulaziz. That this was irrational she knew full well, having interacted with him only a handful of times, all during the first twenty hours of her postpartum stay. But when was it love's business to be rational?

She lay in bed at home for the better part of a week after the baby's birth and death, grateful for every tablet she'd been prescribed to dull the afterpains, grateful for every minute she managed to dispatch asleep rather than awake, above all grateful for her fantasies of Dr. Abdulaziz. Ricky held in her mind a picture of him: obsidian eyes; unkempt, rather swirly black hair; the faint shadow on his jaw which appeared darker with each subsequent visit he made to her room. As for his voice, she couldn't quite replay it in her mind, couldn't quite remember how it went, only that it had been beautiful, soft and deep, his syllables intricately worked, like something carved of ivory or sandal-wood. She lay in bed imperfectly conjuring him; her effort, more than its result, was the companion that made the long hours endurable. Hours, at the beginning, were quite simply her foe: the entire future spread out before her like inhospitable terrain through which she must slog. So the flights of thought that delivered her into the calm, expansive arms of Dr. Abdulaziz, delivered her ruched brow to the smoothing stroke of his fingertips, her offered throat and wrists to his slow and mindful ardor, her anguished sobs to the consoling pressure of his mouth—her ability to entertain such fancies came as a welcome surprise, and she threw herself into them with willful abandon.

She tried, and failed, in those early days, to summon gratitude for her husband, for her living children, for her own life and health, for spring itself: the just-now-unpuckering forsythia, the way the ground yielded underfoot, the high-stepping return of mildness to the air. She tried, with partial success, summoning gratitude for the fact that she had carried her baby to term and had a live birth, that she'd shared fifty-seven hours in the world with him, that he'd drawn his last breath from the nest of her own arms.

But once he'd left her arms the force of her grief gouged her. She'd had no inkling it would be like this: not simply lonely-making, but corrosive. She was filled with hatred. Some of it for herself.

She had never told John what transpired at her routine five-month sonogram.

"Anencephaly," the radiologist had said. Her hair a blond knob at her nape. "You could choose to terminate now. Most do."

Most do. Those words followed Ricky home from the medical complex, rode with her in the car, slipped into the house, climbed with her into bed, taunting, suggestive. They were two nasty things, two wicked sticks that rubbed together over and over in her mind. Until, after a hundred repetitions, suddenly they were not. They blazed into focus. How had she missed it? *Most do.* And those two words galvanized her, provided her with focus, with intention: to do the single thing, in the midst of crushing, unbearable helplessness, that was within her power. She would not be most. Her child would not be most. They would defy most. But only in secrecy could they prevail. This much was clear—she could not risk telling John. He would want her to terminate. She could see it just so: the way his eyes would go, the way his lips would tighten in the darkness of his beard, the way he'd take it like a man, quickly and all at once. He would want her to react the same way, would want to spare her the drawing out of pain. He would say it was her decision, would claim to support her either way. And no he would not pressure, not bully her—except that he would, with his worried gaze alone: silent, imploring, following her around the room, around the house, studying her. Weighing, beseeching. For four months. She could not risk trusting him to agree to such pain.

From here it was a quick leap to deciding there was no one she could tell. Everyone would want to spare her in the same way. She would be forced to explain, to argue, to justify her choice. The thought exhausted her. All the familiar faces—those of her family, her coworkers, the parents of her children's friends, the cashiers in the supermarket who recognized her after all these years and clucked so nicely over her burgeoning belly—took on in her mind the placid countenance of the radiologist with her preternaturally sleek bun. Who even knew what she'd looked like? Her features had been erased in Ricky's memory; all that lingered was a kind of bland veneer, a plaster mask. And Ricky had a horror of this face, this smooth sameness, which she saw everywhere, animating everyone she encountered: the embodiment of malevolent dispassion.

She'd drawn a line that December afternoon, that bitter day when she came home and went straight to bed. She fooled herself that it was a gentling sleep and not a narcosis brought on by rage. On one side of the line stood Ricky and her baby; on the other side, the uncomprehending world. Ricky did not perceive her rage. She saw only the fault of an arbitrary universe. Of the diagnosis she said nothing. That evening, she shared with John and the children the sonogram (this one, ironically, less of an abstract weather map than the others had been; you could make out the profile clearly: the dear funny bump of the nose, smaller hillocks of lips and chin), and if she seemed unusually quiet, it was easy enough to blame it on the fatigue of pregnancy; and if, over the ensuing days and weeks, John noticed an alteration in her, she encouraged the assumption that it was only womanly, hormonal.

All the while the baby grew. With every new movement, so did her hope. She visualized his brain developing from bud to half-blown to full-blown rose: a flower in a time-lapse display, completing itself. The intricate bones of his skull meeting all around; the architecture of flesh and skin, all of it forming, all of it beautifully realized. Between months five and nine stretch sixteen weeks, a long time, she reasoned, time enough to make up for lost time. Ricky the quant, good at math and all things rational and all things rationalizing, told herself these fairy tales, willed herself to believe in them, to adopt their skewed logic. Within this logic her dissembling was justified, for she let herself believe that secrecy was her part of the compact, the price she'd bargained for the baby's life. And if, when John bent to kiss her now, she had a tendency to turn and give him the side of her face, and if when he lifted her sweater to place his hand on her naked belly she gently pulled it back down and remembered she'd left something in the other room, these were only small rebuffs, tiny deceptions, part of a greater good, which was hope.

Not until the end of the ninth month did she deliver the sad news. He cried. She held him. He was sitting on the foot of the bed and she, standing before him, stroked his curly head. Even then she lied. She told him the doctor had only just spotted the flaw. And she made up odds. She felt compelled to—and this part couldn't really be called a lie—because by this point she'd come to believe there *had* to be a chance, however slim, of survival, whether because of medical anomaly or misdiagnosis. The figure that came from her lips was seventeen percent. He might look it up, might research it on his own and dispute her, but then she could claim to have found it on the Internet—anything could be found on the Internet—and anyway, she knew he would not. He would take her at her word. So: a seventeen percent chance, she said, that the baby would be born with enough of his brain to survive.

Why did she invent this? Why further complicate the lie, and why, in particular, frame it so? Enough of his brain to survive. Ricky thought of it as a way of softening the blow, but was it possible she meant to test him, too? And if so, was she hoping his reaction would justify what she'd done? Or was it just the opposite, was she hoping his reaction would prove her wrong?

She waited, her hands still lingering about his face, while John grew silent, digesting this, and then, looking up with reddened eyes, he'd asked: "But how compromised would he be?"

And Ricky, though she touched his shoulder once before letting her hands return to her sides, realized, coldly, that she had been right not to tell. With this question he identified himself as belonging definitively and abhorrently to *most*. Until that moment he had, in his enforced innocence, remained in the realm of ally, of friend: she'd been able to conceive of her secrecy— her dishonesty—as a means of protecting him. But now as he held her around the wide waist and heaved a sob, his head resting on the ledge of their imperfect child, she felt herself recoil, felt herself fill with a frightening dispassion of her own, as though she, in a final heartless twist, had become the radiologist with the flaxen bun.

This coldness toward John settled in her like conviction. She did not question it. Recklessly, she welcomed it: a kind of armor. She discarded her fantasy that the doctors had made a mistake, gave up meditating on the image of a fully blossomed rose. The coldness saw her through the last week of pregnancy, through the final, futile humiliations of the Cervidil, the Pitocin, the epidural, the pushing. Then the baby came and the baby breathed. For fifty-seven hours she held him in her arms; for fifty-seven hours the ice inside her abated. She and he hung suspended in time, and it was, if not a reprieve, then a respite. And then he died and the ice clamped on more solid than before, and when she looked at her children she had to hide the fact that she felt nothing, and when she looked at her husband she did not bother to hide it. She lay, in those early days home from the hospital, on their queen-sized bed, wishing she were sick, wishing she were dying, wishing for cancer, an aneurysm, an earthquake, a gun. Looking blankly, for hours at a time, at the horrid trees, river, bridge, sky.

On the third morning she found herself remembering bits of the Robert Louis Stevenson poem her mother used to recite whenever Ricky had been kept home from school with a cold or flu. "When I was sick and lay a-bed, / I had two pillows at my head, / And all my toys beside me lay / To keep me busy all the day." How sweet the experience of being bedridden when she was small. Yes, there was the achy head, the bilious stomach, the scratchy throat. But there was also the certainty that all would be well and right again in a day or two or three. And in the meantime, the luxuries! Pajamas all day, endless paper and crayons. Her parents' doting; the special snacks they brought as she regained her health: miniature portions arranged like delicacies, for maximal tempting, on the prettiest plates; the treat of having her father sit next to the bed reading out loud or telling from memory his favorite stories by I. L. Peretz, Isaac Bashevis Singer, Sholem Aleichem; her mother administering an alcohol rub while reciting the poems of her childhood. "I was the giant great and still / That sits upon the pillow-hill, / And sees about him, dale and plain, / The pleasant land of counterpane."

Ricky upon the pillow-hill five days after the baby's death saw about her the barren plain of bedclothes, the unpleasant coverlet rumpled and askew, the spiteful blankets and twisted, tormented sheets. The old towel she'd spread out under her hips to protect the sheets bunched up beneath her. Her lochia still flowed red, her perineum was still swollen, her breasts hard with milk, her husband at work, her children at school, her baby in ashes. They'd had him cremated. No doll-sized coffin, thank you. No lamb-topped gravestone in a leafy cemetery where passersby might pause and read aloud the dates, do the math, sigh: "Only three days, how sad," and go on with their pretty strolls.

Somewhere there was a box—a volunteer at the hospital had prepared it for them—containing the baby's hat and onesie, his socks and receiving blanket, a lock of hair from the base of his head (lucky, someone had commented, he'd been born with any), a few photographs, his footprints on a card. The meanness of these relics revolted her. John had put the box away somewhere. Ricky didn't care to think about that now.

She didn't care to think about John now, for that matter, or Paul or Biscuit, either. It wasn't simply that she didn't want to think about them, it was that she couldn't manage to care. On some level she knew that must be very bad. When she thought of them they seemed oddly abstract. They were like the paper dolls of her childhood, iconic figures of HUSBAND, SON, DAUGHTER, each adorned in the appropriate costume, arms akimbo, expressions fixed.

But: Dr. Abdulaziz. Of him alone could she think these days and be brought to softness, be returned to a state in which her old, unruined self seemed to have breath left in her. She dreamed up scenarios of going back to the hospital, roaming the building until she encountered him on the ward, or in the lobby, or in the elevator—"chancing" upon him and exchanging a wordless look, which would be filled with mutual sorrow and under-standing. Her fantasies, in which she received not only his suc-cor but also his passion, his desire, moved her to shed small, hot tears. She licked those that rolled by the side of her mouth and tasted salt.

When the pain medication ran out at the end of the week, Ricky rose from her bed without wishing for more. She no lon-ger needed the tablets for her physical symptoms, and no longer wanted them to mute her emotions. Her emotions seemed per-haps too muted already. Paul and Biscuit had come into her room various times over the past several days, Paul bringing sup-per to her on a tray and doing his homework on the rug; Biscuit sitting on the edge of the bed to have her hair braided after her bath. That their exchanges were skeletal ("What's sixteen times seventy-four?" "Tell Daddy he didn't get all the cream rinse out"). Ricky didn't find herself noticing until afterward, and then with only the most far-off flicker of regret. The vast, spearmint distance she felt between herself and everyone—everything—else was almost, she imagined, what royals must feel, and forevermore Ricky would link mourning with royalty, and royalty with mourning; for the rest of her days, the words *king* and *queen* would remind her of deep sorrow.

Sorrow, anyway, she could admit. Mourning. Not anger. She—who had made one grievous error in failing to recognize her anger back in January—made a second in consciously dis-avowing it now. She told herself that to be angry over the baby's fatal condition would imply the belief that it was unfair, which would in turn imply that she believed she and her child deserved a better outcome than they had gotten. An insupportable claim, in light of all the different varieties and magnitudes of tragedy that people faced on earth. Given how relatively fortunate, how unmarred by suffering, her life had been up till now, given how much others suffered by comparison, the loss of this one baby, in peacetime, to natural causes, when she had two healthy children at home—this tragedy, compared with those of countless others, was small. She resolved not to feel anger. It was nothing she was entitled to, and she would not commit the disgrace of grasping at it.

Sorrow. Mourning. Queenliness (a cupped hand oscillating from the window of a carriage). These might carry her through the motions, through the days. These she might claim, and would, and did. It was Friday. She threw out the empty pill bottles and showered and dressed and went downstairs. She did the dishes and took a walk and cut some pussy willow switches from the tree out back and put the cuttings into a pitcher of water, and then she went to the store and came home and made tomato soup and cornbread and did the laundry and after school she listened to Biscuit practice her recorder and she did geology flashcards with Paul and when John came home he found the three of them sitting on the living room rug having dragged out the old board game Sorry. When Ricky looked up at him with a shallow smile, and he returned it with a relieved, grateful one of his own, she knew she was unworthy of him, but not how to make it right.

5.

J ohn."

He set his teeth. He was getting used to hearing his name pronounced like that, in husky tones, dove-gray with pity.

"I just *heard.*"

The whole department had heard; it would have been hard to keep the news private. For one thing, his closest colleagues had all known his wife was expecting, so it had been necessary to break it to them when the sad news about her pregnancy emerged. Then he'd needed to tell the head of the theater department the specific date of the induction in order to get his classes covered. Furthermore, this being the theater department, communication flowed expertly while the practice of discretion was somewhat less well-developed. By the time he'd returned to work a week later, everyone from the campus police to his first-year students seemed to have heard of his misfortune.

Not every response had been unwelcome. The department had sent a vase of white hyacinths to the hospital, and a simple potted gardenia bearing a card signed by the college president had arrived at the house. Charlotte from the costume shop had baked lemon bars, which she'd offered with a merciful absence of fanfare, and his department head had told him he could get his midterm grades in after the deadline. But as many responses had felt invasive. A bouquet of crimson roses, of all things, had appeared on his desk, the accompanying cloying note signed by his most grade-grubbing student. There'd been a dozen condolence cards, awful, glossy, pastel things with ornately scripted Bible verses and soft-focus pictures of lilies and angels, which John had opened and promptly thrown away. The topper was a pious letter, sent by the dean's hopelessly well-meaning wife, announcing that a donation had been made in the Ryries' name to the March of Dimes.

All in all, John was relieved when the expressions of sympathy began to peter out. It was certainly easier to work without having to dodge the bullets of people's good intentions. The fact of his tragedy had seemed to foster in everyone around him a sudden, alarming presumption of intimacy.

As in the case of Madeleine now, belatedly shocked—she'd just returned from a conference in Denver—standing on the threshold of the scene shop, one hand clutching the door frame, the other having lit upon her artfully arranged décolleté blouse. Madeleine Berkowitz, associate professor of costume design, a perfectly respectable teacher and scholar who unfortunately undermined her own credibility by dressing on all occasions like a vamp. From the feet up, at this moment: ankle boots, patterned hose, a rust peau-de-soie miniskirt whose hue matched her mane of hair, a black blouse with plunging neckline and a heavy amber pendant nestled just at the point of her cleavage. At times her appearance provided a not unpleasant diversion or even comic relief, but right now, coupled with her desire to express bathetic condolences, it was the last thing John wanted to deal with.

"John," she said, making his name somehow two syllables. "How *are* you?" She crossed to where he stood by the industrial sink.

"Doing well, doing well," he answered briskly. "Thanks for asking." He shoved the brushes he'd been holding—half a dozen scenic fitches and badger hair flats—into a can of Murphy Oil Soap and lukewarm water to soak, then wiped his hands on the front of his coveralls. It was nearly evening and he was exhausted. All day he'd been catching up on postponed student conferences in between working in the scene shop; the set for *Twelfth Night* was behind schedule. The more significant reason for his fatigue, however, was that he'd spent the past few nights on the couch, pleading insomnia. His voluntary banishment was less about insomnia, though, than a grab at dignity. It was a refusal to submit passively to Ricky's indifference in bed. He didn't fault her for mourning, but the coolness stung. Why wouldn't she let herself be comforted by him? For that matter, why did she withhold comfort from him?

"I'm sorrier," Madeleine continued, "than I can possibly say."

"I know." He tried to make this sound both appreciative and final.

Yet she pressed on, her tone swelling with concern: "So, how's your *wife*?"

At this moment—John could have smooched him—Lance Oprisu called from the doorway, "Yo, John. You coming or what? Oh hey, Maddie."

She pivoted toward him. A hand fluttered to rest on the amber pendant between her breasts. "Hello, Lance."

"Uh, yeah," said John. "Let me grab my, uh, coat."

Lance was in his mid-twenties, with wire-rimmed glasses and a dirty-blond ponytail. He'd been hired as the theater's technical director only this past fall, but he and John had already constructed three sets together, and in the act of shared labor a mutual, un-voiced affection had grown between them. He and John had not made plans to go anywhere, and even at this moment, as John snatched up his green army jacket and tossed Madeleine an apolo-getic grimace, he had no idea what Lance intended, other than the obvious and noble cause of rescuing him from this encounter.

Twelfth Night was Lance's baby; John had offered it to him even before he'd known how difficult April would turn out to be. For being the first set Lance had ever designed for the Llewellyn-Price, it was admirable; John, for his part, had been glad to play first mate for a change. But work on construction was going slowly. Only a half-hour ago, they'd gotten the first coat of paint on the stage floor. Now, out in the hallway, Lance suggested they go get some dinner while it finished drying, then come back and put on a second.

"Good by me," said John. "And thanks for that." He tilted his head toward the scene shop.

The sky outside still held plenty of light, of the faded blue variety that always seemed it could linger in perpetuity—until that final moment when it was unceremoniously snuffed. John's truck was blocked in so they took Lance's Miata, a tight squeeze for John, but in its own way liberating, as it triggered memories of more carefree days. When he and Ricky first met he'd been carless, and they'd gone everywhere in her lame coupe, a Pontiac Fiero that was always breaking down, and in which he always felt uncomfortably compressed—and yet. It had been a sweet car, not least for the creative contortions it had induced them to resort to whenever they drove somewhere secluded and parked.

Lance drove fast, with the windows open an inch and the radio turned up loud. They went to Mero Mayor's, a dive on Route 303 halfway between Congers and Nyack, where they sat at the bar and ordered enchiladas and margaritas, one for Lance, and, uncharacteristically, three for John, which he downed like limeade. They watched the game on the wall-mounted TV. John was a Yanks fan, Lance hated their guts, and they wrangled about this amiably as they drank.

"You done?" Lance asked at last, with a show of impatience. He leaned in ostentatiously to eye the meniscus of John's glass, then rose from the bar stool. "Come on."

"No, no, wait. I'm buying the next round."

"Not for me, man." But Lance sat back down.

John called for two shots of Cuervo—again not like him—and, upon failing to persuade Lance to have his, consumed both and declared, jabbing a finger festively toward the ceiling, *"Otra más!"*

"All right," Lance said with some resolve, after John had nursed his second beer chaser for some fifteen minutes. He slapped the bar. "Come on, we got work."

"You know what I am? Honestly?"

"What?"

"Three sheets to the wind. Hey." He slapped the bar, too. "Did you know that?"

Lance took John's Corona and drained it. "No."

"The sheets aren't really the sheets. The sails. Did you know that? They're ropes. They're the ropes that tie down the other things, what do you call them?"

"What?"

"Sails! That's not what the sheets are. Don't ask me why. Now me, I'm saying, I'm three sheets to the wind. That's three ropes, get it? The ropes that tie down the . . . shit. What are they? The things. You know what I'm trying to say. When the ropes go to the wind, the. Uh. The. The *sails*. Go flopping and the ship goes off course. *Like a drunk*." Completing his thought with enormous satisfaction, John snatched up his empty bottle and tried for a drink.

"More like four, by my count," Lance muttered drily.

"Actually"—John turned to contradict the younger man with pedagogical flair—"that's wrong. Four's unconscious."

"We gotta go." Lance pulled out some cash. "I have a floor to paint."

"As do I."

"I don't know about that. I'm thinking I'll drop you home first."

"No, no. That's crap." John, too, pulled out several bills, which he placed on top of Lance's, taking great care to line up the corners neatly, yet none to check their denominations. "Come on!" He clapped his hands together once, louder than he'd intended; all around Mero Mayor's the customers, deeply unexcitable men all, glanced over.

Lance plucked John's contribution—four crisp twenties— from the pile and stuffed the bills back in John's coat pocket.

"Hey," John discovered warmly, "you're Antonio, and I'm Sebastian!" He was back in *Twelfth Night,* the shipwrecked sailor rescued by the sea captain.

Lance gave half a grin. He nodded thanks to the guy behind the bar and, with three fingers on John's back, propelled him toward the exit.

The air had turned cold and dark; it seemed to bear down on them. It was ribboned by a quick, snipping wind as they made their way to the Miata.

"Your car's no boat," John observed forlornly as they reached it.

Lance unlocked the doors and got in.

"Not many people know about this place," John declared, although now he was addressing no one. A car sped by, its engine noise rising, then fading. What he meant was that Ricky didn't know about this place. He didn't think so anyway. Mero Mayor was the sort of place he could imagine her driving by any number of times without actually seeing it. It was quintessentially male; nothing about it had been designed to appeal to women. A low white cement building, brown-roofed, hung with a string of yellow and red fiesta lights that managed to project an aura that was precisely the opposite of festive, and, at any given time of day, a handful of clunkers parked out front. On some level John liked it for this very reason, the fact that it was unknown to Ricky; but on another level this caused him anxiety, the thought that she had no idea—*could have* no idea— where to find him.

"Yo, Sebastian," Lance prompted. John opened the door and tucked himself into the passenger seat, drawing up his knees and elbows, feeling his frame pressed tightly against the limits of his space. And as if the act of self-compression had triggered a wave of sadness, he felt himself suddenly fighting—not *tears*, certainly, but a dizzying melancholy, which welled and surged through him and then as suddenly ebbed. He worried that Lance must have noticed, as if the wave of sadness were an odor or a noise he'd emitted.

All this, and the quantity of alcohol he'd imbibed, made it several minutes before he realized they were driving toward Nyack, not Congers. "You can't take me home, man."

"You can't operate machinery."

"No machinery—we're painting."

"I'm not sure you can operate a paintbrush."

John drew a breath. "Look," he began. And sighed. He would not argue the point. Lance was probably right in principle, although John firmly believed—*knew*, actually—that he could, in fact, operate a paintbrush. But all right: he would be an acquiescent, a dignified drunk. "Look," he said again. "Listen. I'm going to spend the night in my office."

His declaration was less dramatic than it might have been, since pulling the occasional all-nighter was a part of the job. He kept in his office, for that reason, an old foam love seat that unfolded into a lumpy bed. His declaration was merely unorthodox. Given his current state. Given the fact that they both knew he would not be contributing to the work of set construction this night.

Lance made no sign of having heard him, but at the next

turnout did a K-turn, let a few cars pass, and then pulled out again, crossing over to the far lane and heading back toward Congers.

"'Preciate it," whispered John. "I think my wife's having an affair." The thought had not actually occurred to him; he was surprised to hear the words come out of his mouth. Did his drunkenness know something his sobriety did not?

She had done it before, adultery. Though maybe not technically, since they hadn't been married. Though fuck technically. Infidelity was infidelity. His devastation could not have been greater had it happened post-wedding. The blow of discovery had been oddly somatic, like a two-by-four to the groin, and it was compounded by the awful banality of the sequence: suspicion, inquiry, denial, retreat; suspicion, inquiry, confession, disintegration of the known world. He remembered sooty tears, the sordid cliché of it, the mascara streaking her cheeks as she'd begged his forgiveness, not seeming to understand that this was a matter beyond his control. It made as much sense as begging for someone to love you. As though it were something you could choose.

When he explained that it wasn't as simple as that, as simple as making a decision, she'd had the gall to try putting the affair in just those terms: as something she hadn't actively decided upon, but that had "happened" of its own inviolable accord. The guy was some Wall Street coworker asshole; Ricky herself called him that. John never laid eyes on him and was glad. Ricky didn't care for him, she said. It had been a "thing," that's all, the word she used to dismiss it, and John saw it in his mind as just that: a shiny, dangling, tangible thing, a piece of tinsel, maybe, and she a witless magpie who couldn't help herself. The image

didn't help. She tried giving him some song about its inevitability, how she hadn't even wanted it; how in a way she felt he,
John, had expected it of her; how her actions had been predicated on his own self-serving perception of who she was. She
was a maestro of crazy feminine logic, he had to give her that.

Lo and behold, in the end he found he did forgive her. That,
too, a thing beyond his control, something he contrived neither
to do nor to resist. He forgave her, loved her, married her, made
a family with her, and still he was not certain he'd ever trusted
her again. It was not trust he felt so much as faith he exercised.
But maybe that was true of all marriage. "Fuck me if I know," he
said out loud. And then repeated, as though he needed to experience again how the words sounded, "My wife might be having an affair."

"Dude." Lance sighed. "Just to mention, you're wasted."

"That's true," John agreed. Then: "You think I'm wrong?"

"Look. What you and your wife have just been through must
suck. I'm just saying you've probably got to be . . . *delicate*. You
know? Give yourselves a break, some time, or some . . . I don't
know, just some fucking *delicacy*."

It seemed an unlikely word, coming from Lance. Both words,
actually. Fucking and delicate. In New York, their first apartment,
he and Ricky'd lived above a delicatessen. Old school, Italian,
sausages hanging from the ceiling, the whole bit. When she'd
been pregnant with Paul, Ricky used to ram her bare feet in
her rain boots and go down in pajamas to buy jars of stuffed
peppers. Then she'd sit in bed and eat them, one after the other,
putting a whole stuffed pepper in her mouth and working at it,
lips gleaming with olive oil. He liked to watch her eat them and

she ate them ostentatiously for him. Erotically, roguishly. Her mouth stuffed with the delicacy. In her delicate condition. Her indelicate condition, he had loved to watch, and she had loved it, loved him. What had happened to them? What had happened since then?

"Maybe you're right," said John. "Maybe she just doesn't like me anymore."

Lance did not reply. They turned in to the campus, wound around buildings and pulled up outside the theater. There he said, "You could crash with us."

Us meant Lance and his fiancée, with whom, John knew, he shared an apartment in Haverstraw. John had never been to their place, but imagined it furnished sparsely, optimistically, in Ikea and Target. He had met the fiancée only once, at the faculty holiday party. He could not retrieve her name just now, but remembered having thought she must be a student. She was Brazilian, agreeable, and attractively plump, as though the extra weight were no more than a surplus of youth. The thought of encroaching on her innocent hearth, denting her affordable modular sofa with his tequila-sloshed bulk, horrified him.

"No, no," John said. "Thanks."

He did not expect Lance to try to persuade him, and when the younger man added, "Estrela would be okay with it," he was touched and appalled. He felt an urge to seize Lance by the shoulders, to counsel him to be more doubting, less confident; to warn him of all the unseen dangers waiting to suck happiness out of life.

"You don't know," he heard himself propounding. He realized he was shaking his head from side to side in a manner that struck him, even in his current state, as comically equine. "You don't know anything, man. I'm saying that because I care about—about you. I care about you guys."

Lance smiled, nodded in the direction of the dashboard.

"Listen," implored John. He understood that he was rambling but he had an imperative—this much was suddenly clear—to impart a single profundity. An epiphany. He clapped his hands together again, held them clasped. "Lis—Listen to what I'm telling you. If you don't listen to anything else I say"—here he paused, momentarily distracted by the beguiling sound of *elsisay*—"Else. I. Say. Listen to this: don't think you know—don't give up your couch, man—don't—your couch—" He'd lost the thread of the message, but not the vehemence; on that he retained a firmer grasp than ever. "I'm saying don't ever offer your couch, man—hold on, hold on to your couch."

"Thank—"

"Don't let it get *away* from you."

"Okay, come on now." Somehow Lance had materialized on the passenger side of the car; he stood holding the door open. John swung a leg around, worked to free the other from the little space. He began to raise himself, lost his balance. Lance extended an arm and helped hoist him upright.

"Antonio," John remembered.

"That's right."

"Antonio." Very fondly.

"Let's go."

With care and a sense of virtue John shut the door behind him, then teetered and buckled against it as if buffeted by the wind, thrown off his very course.

6.

Feet up on the chair, knees drawn in, her eyes five inches from the book in her lap, wisps of hair come loose from her barrettes to form a fuzzy nimbus around her face, Biscuit read:

> Following the church ceremonies, the priests and a large number of people gathered at ancestral cemeteries and placed pancakes, pretzels, loaves of bread, and one or two decorated eggs on the graves. Sometimes they added a cup of meal or a bit of sweetened cereal. After the ceremony priests later gathered the remaining food and took it home. Finally, the priests said the office of the dead.

The office of the dead?

She pictured a large metal desk flanked by filing cabinets, a window behind with blinds drawn, blocking out all but a hint of flashing neon sign. A cloaked, hooded figure enthroned on a swivel chair, feet up on the desk, cigar burning in the ashtray, scythe leaning against the wall, old-fashioned rotary phone getting ready to jingle.

She herself was occupying an office at the moment: that of the children's librarian, Mrs. Mukhopadhyay. Just beyond the door, which was not shut, Mrs. Mukhopadhyay chatted with young patrons and their caregivers at the circulation desk. It was a rainy Saturday; prime time in the children's room. "How are you feeling?" one mother after another kept asking in knowing, confidential tones while Mrs. Mukhopadhyay scanned the bar codes on their books. They all said virtually the same things, as if reading from a script: a string of hopefuls auditioning for a bit part—"Are you tired? You look great."

Biscuit paid scant attention to the content of Mrs. Mukhopadhyay's replies, listening mostly to the rise and fall of her voice. She believed Mrs. Mukhopadhyay possessed the prettiest voice in the world. Sometimes at home, alone in her room, Biscuit would stand before her full-length mirror and chat sotto voce with her reflection in her best approximation of the librarian's Bengali lilt. It was a water voice, trickling and eddying and cool.

Tucked into the librarian's chair, half listening to her converse just outside the office; listening, too, to the Brahms chamber works wending softly from the librarian's portable CD player, Biscuit breathed contentedly over the fat book on her lap. It was from upstairs, the adult stacks. It had truly hundreds of pages. Nearly a thousand. Wafery, yellowed, vanilla-smelling pages that fell with a dense *plunk,* like a plank, when you flipped over a great sheaf at once.

Biscuit flipped just so now, idly, backward, traveling, much as a finger travels on a spun globe, from the Southeast Russian province of Saratov to land, by chance, among the Parsis, the Zoroastrians of Bombay:

> Vultures look hungrily on while the funeral-servants remove the body from the bier, lay it on the stone bed, and strip it of the white garments. After these are thrown into the well, the bier is borne from the Tower of Silence, and the vultures begin their meal. In the course of a few hours the bones are usually stripped bare.

Traveling forward again, to the Tanala of Madagascar, where her finger came down on this passage:

> To discover a body of a drowned person, a banana tree core encircled with a silver bracelet is cast on the water, in the belief that it will rest motionless over the spot where the drowned one lies. After this, if divers fail to bring up the body, the Ikongo conduct funeral services over the deceased's mat and pillow.

The customs, in their peculiarity and their specificity, had the quality of belonging to a fairy tale. Biscuit considered that they were only slightly more real than fairy tales. Even at age nine, she knew not to believe everything she read, not even in a library book from the adult nonfiction section. She was no budding historian (already in school she showed signs of being a poor history student, with remarkably little regard for the significance of dates), but even if the book were not so gorgeously redolent of age, even if its leaves and binding did not give off such an unambiguous waft of antiquity, she did know how to find a copyright, and this one told her that the book had been written long before she was born, before her parents had been born, too, and in her view this was enough to render it manifestly Old, belonging to that one vast, misty category that included everything from horse-drawn carriages and hoop skirts to typewriters and black-and-white TVs.

Sometimes, Biscuit knew, what had been perfectly correct in Olden times was not so anymore. In other musty books she'd found references to things that no longer applied: gramophones, polio, Negroes, beef tea, the admonition that ladies ought not swim. It wasn't only books. Her own grandma was always saying things Biscuit knew to be wrong. She claimed that drinking cold milk with hot soup would give a person a bellyache; that "Orientals" had an inborn talent for math; that the television remote could under no circumstances be programmed to work for the DVD player (Paul had rather rudely but effectively proven her wrong on this last). All these errors made Biscuit feel rather sorry for her grandma; but more, they told a cautionary tale.

And so she brought to this aged book of funeral customs a mixture of skepticism and indulgence, yet this made what she read no less satisfying or useful to her.

Leafing again:

The world outside first learns of a death when the family hangs blue and white or blue and yellow lanterns at the front door and pastes white paper over the red good-luck strips. In addition to this ceremony, it is customary in Peiping to station a drummer outside the front door, to the left of the entrance if a man has died, and to the right, if a woman.

Gold leaf and pearls are placed in the mouth of the dead in some parts of China, and a ball of red paper mixed with incense ash is tucked between the lips.

Mrs. Mukhopadhyay had helped Biscuit find the book. Never mind that it lay within the library's upper provinces, two stories above the cozy, underground children's enclave; Mrs. Mukhopadhyay's range knew no bounds. She had jotted the call number, 393–Death customs, on the back of an old card-catalog card, her bangles jangling cool music as she did, and then she'd explained exactly where that number would turn out to be in the stacks. "Alllll the way up, against the far wall," she'd said, tracing the route on a map in the air with a flourish that produced more silver-sliding notes.

Now Mrs. Mukhopadhyay came into her office carrying two damaged books: a Nancy Drew clinging to its binding by frail threads, and a picture book that looked as though a bite had been taken out of its cover. These she deposited into the plastic bin that she referred to as "the clinic"; bit by bit, as time allowed, she would triage its contents, mending the mendable and removing from circulation those volumes deemed past repair. For now, she went behind the desk and squatted to remove her boy-senberry yogurt from the mini-fridge.

"Should I get up?" asked Biscuit.

"No, I want to sit here." Mrs. Mukhopadhyay settled into the rocking chair in the corner, beneath the square window that gave a view of the roots of bushes, the undersides of leaves, and snippets of patrons' feet and legs. Once, gazing out this window during a downpour, Biscuit had spotted a clear-winged bug perched upside down on a rhododendron leaf: using it, in effect, as an umbrella. The cleverness of the infinitesimal! Now she watched as Mrs. Mukhopadhyay put her feet up on a low stool, leaned her head back and closed her eyes. Her belly was getting very big now, not unlike how Biscuit's mother had looked just a few weeks earlier.

"So," she asked, opening her eyes and unlidding her yogurt container, "how is your research going?" She said this without any amusement in her voice, without the speckling hint of laughter most adults would have sowed among the words.

"It's good."

"You are finding interesting things?"

Biscuit nodded.

"Read me something. For example."

Biscuit flipped a plank of pages: *plunk*. Landed in Bali. Read: "'At sunset the embers are quenched, and any charred bones and fragments are mounded, covered with palm-leaves, and placed in an urn fashioned from a coconut shell and covered with a white cloth, for carrying to the sea. When the procession reaches the shore, the priest enters the water, and after having begged it to bear the ashes safely away, scatters them on the waves.'"

"That has a beautiful sound to it," Mrs. Mukhopadhyay remarked, licking the back of her spoon.

Biscuit looked up, surprised, in perfect agreement.

"Is there more?"

She continued. "'Further offerings are dedicated to the soul. Its last earthly ties are severed'—severed?"

Mrs. Mukhopadhyay made a scissoring motion. "Snipped."

"Oh. '. . . are severed by the symbolism of burning a string and breaking an egg.'"

Mrs. Mukhopadhyay chuckled. "I like that: an egg."

Biscuit looked at the clock. Four-thirty. It was her turn to make supper: meat loaf and rice. She and Paul each got supper duty once a week now. The custom had been instituted in the Ryrie household several months earlier, under the banner of We All Have to Pitch in More Now with a New Baby on the Way, and it had not been amended to reflect the fact that the new baby was dead. Meat loaf was supposed to be fun for kids to make, or so Biscuit's mother had read or heard: the tactile experience of mixing all those ingredients by hand. Biscuit hated it, the cold, the greasy pink squish. "I have to go."

"Would you like to take the book home with you?"

You were only allowed to check out adult books on an adult card. Mrs. Mukhopadhyay was offering to bend the rules for Biscuit. She flushed with pleasure yet muttered no, suddenly tongue-tied. She did not want her parents to see the book.

Mrs. Mukhopadhyay put her spoon in the yogurt and leaned forward. She looked as though she were about to ask the question Biscuit had come most to dread, and which she'd find most especially dreadful coming from this, her special friend.

Everyone had been asking this question—teachers, friends of the family, grown-ups whose names she didn't know but who somehow knew hers. "How's your mother?" or worse, "How's Mom?" as if Biscuit's mother were their mother, too. "Tell her I send my best," they'd say. "Tell her we're thinking about her." As if they couldn't tell her themselves. As if Biscuit's mother had traveled somewhere far away, out of the reach of their voices, their words.

But it occurred to Biscuit that if Mrs. Mukhopadhyay were to ask about her mother it would not be the same thing at all. If Mrs. Mukhopadhyay asked, there would be room to respond with something other than a pinched "fine." There would be room to keep silent, or cry, or tell the truth.

Then Mrs. Mukhopadhyay's expression changed. She said, "Oh!" and placed a hand against her side. She looked up at Biscuit, her eyes wide. "A big one," she explained.

Biscuit got up from the librarian's chair. She still held the book of funeral customs, with two hands.

"You can leave it right there." On the desk.

"Thanks."

It was only a block to her house, too short. Biscuit walked it slowly, running her hand along the tops of low hedges where they lined the sidewalk. They were bare, bony, their twigs stiff brown bones. She had been to a funeral just once, when she was six. She remembered it very well, the physical details as well as the mood. It happened that on a summer evening just after she'd been tucked in, a sparrow had flown against her windowpane. She'd been lying awake, bored, looking out the window at the still-light greenness, and so she'd seen it happen. The thump of its body was terrible and quick. She'd run down the stairs in her short summer nightgown, slipped into the kitchen and out through the Dutch door. In her six-year-old mind it was a story that had already been written. She, its hero. Its ending, plain: with a stroke of her finger the sparrow would awaken and ascend in the dusk.

The backyard was bathed in shadows of nightfall, just beginning to be lit by fireflies. She'd been aware of enjoying herself. Her skin tingled in the cooling air. Right through her nightie she could feel it. She'd never been outside alone in evening before. It had a smell, the evening grass and evening dirt. She paused to inhale it: the scent of a story about a girl who mends a bird and is rewarded for her kindness. She whispered to the bird inside her head: *I'm coming.*

What reward? Every morning thereafter, the girl would awake to find a present under her pillow: a feather, a berry, a seed.

Finding the sparrow proved too easy. It lay directly beneath her window, unbloodied, its feathers and beak and claws all more exact, more finely formed and particular than she'd imagined. She touched it, but it did not stir. She gathered it in her palm and carried it inside, hopeful. Her parents took it from her.

The next day they'd all filed into the backyard. There was a shoe box coffin, lined with grass. Her father wore a necktie; her mother wore a dress. Paul, whose third-grade class had been doing limericks, recited a poem that began, "There once was a brown bird from Nyack." Biscuit helped to dig the hole under the bridal wreath bush. The ground was hard, not soft. She hadn't been able to make much difference; it was her father who got the hole big enough for the box. After, she helped to fill the hole back up with her hands and that earth was warm and crumbly. It stayed under her fingernails until her evening bath, in which she'd scraped out each caked half-moon: not regular dirt but funeral dirt. She soaked in it a long time, until the water grew cold. What she remembered best was the formal, slightly exalted feeling she had as she'd stood wearing her towel like a cape beside the tub after, watching her bathwater with its measure of ceremonial dirt circle the drain.

7.

Ricky came clean. Her first infidelity had lasted a weekend; her second lasted four months.

The night John got drunk at Mero Mayor's, he'd fallen asleep on the fold-out love seat in his office and woken at three, confused at first as to where he was but quickly oriented by the sick feeling in his gut, a feeling that had nothing to do with alcohol and everything to do with fear. He realized, then, with a clarity bred of waking at a strange hour in a strange setting, waking dead sober out of his drunkenness, that fear is what it was, what he'd felt, what had been eating at him these weeks since the baby's birth and death. Fear and not grief, and why was that?

Because Ricky was not Ricky; Ricky was different, changed, not changed, he believed, as grief might legitimately alter someone, but changed in a way that was causing him dread. He might have been babbling incoherently when he'd raised the idea of her having an affair, and maybe Lance was right to have shushed him, but he hadn't been entirely out of bounds. This he knew from the cold quiver in his gut. He knew it rising from the cheap love seat and stumbling out of his office down the hall to the men's room to pee. He knew it putting on his shoes, lacing his goddamn shoes at three in the morning in the empty theater building and then exiting into the parking lot, fumbling with his key in the cold on the barren campus with the stars out, and the moon: he knew the danger of losing everything was real.

It took him fifteen minutes to get home, which, if he'd been in a frame of mind to think about it, was scary: he was lucky he hadn't been pulled over, or worse. He came into their bedroom and switched on the overhead light and Ricky sat up immediately: blinking, blinking, a sweet little cat, confused, her hair all pushed about with sleep. Except it turned out she hadn't really been asleep, or not very. She'd been waiting for him to come home, she said. She'd been worried, she said, had kept waking, checking the clock, listening for his truck in the driveway.

"Why didn't you call?"

"What?"

"If you were worried, why didn't you try calling?" Tired as he was, exhausted, wanting badly to remove his shoes, his socks, his belt, his jeans, to lie on the cool white sheets, still he stood by the door, yards from her. She was sitting up in bed, cross-legged in a sleeveless nightgown, her hands folded in her lap, her eyes getting used to the light, her cheeks flushed, pink and pretty, like a cheap figurine of a schoolgirl.

"I didn't know if you'd want me to. You were the one who— Why didn't you call?"

So that much was out on the table: she thought he might not want her call. "You thought"—he wanted to get this right—"I was angry at you?"

"I don't know. I don't know, John. Why are you standing over there? Why don't— Why aren't you coming to bed?"

He shook his head.

"What does that mean?"

"You tell me." He could see she was afraid now.

"Why don't *you* tell me? What's wrong?"

He shook his head again.

"I don't understand." Her voice quavered.

"You tell me," he repeated, and waited, and she began to cry. He crossed the room eventually, and sat on the bed and touched her foot through the blanket. But when she reached for him, went to lean her head on his shoulder, he pulled back.

She sat up straight. "Tell you what?"

But he waited.

Something changed; something shifted in her eyes. Only then did he know he'd been right.

"You mean," she said, twisting the top sheet, "you mean about the baby. I knew. Before I told you. I didn't tell you right away. Is that it?"

He rose from the bed, hardly aware he was doing so, and backed away a few steps. "What do you mean you didn't tell me 'right away'? When did you know?"

Just audibly: "In December."

It was so far from anything he'd guessed. It was as if he'd braced himself for a burn and been knocked down by a wave.

She'd received the diagnosis of anencephaly at the five-month ultrasound, along with the statistics, the odds, and their options, and she'd kept it to herself—lied to him—not only throughout the rest of the pregnancy, which maybe, *maybe* he could have forgiven, could have tried very hard to understand, to chalk up to estrogen, the sanctity of a woman with child, all those things you were supposed to revere even though—or because—you could never understand them—but even after the baby's birth, even as she held the baby in her selfish, unyielding arms, even after he died in those arms and was taken from them, she had preserved the lie, this lie she'd jammed between them.

"Why?" John asked, holding himself very still, a necessary counterpoint to the maelstrom crashing within. The weather-map photo of the baby she'd brought home with her from that ultrasound and put on the fridge for the rest of the family to mull and coo over; this, too, he was realizing, had been part of the deception. It occurred to him there had been countless concrete instances between December and April when he'd made some comment about the baby, about the future, and she had let him, had actively allowed the untruth to flourish. The crib he'd bought and assembled. The newborn diapers. The mobile with the cloth moons and stars.

"I didn't . . ." Ricky looked at her hands, a piece of the sheet gathered in them in a small white knot. She released it, opened her palms to the ceiling. "I didn't want anyone to tell me to end the pregnancy."

"You think that's what I would've done."

"The woman, the technician, said it's what most people do."

"I'm not talking about the technician. You think that's what *I* would have done."

"I don't know." She'd shrugged her slim shoulders. They went up and down. She was a poppet, a little doll with alabaster arms and moving parts. "I didn't want any counseling." He watched her carefully, coldly. He had the feeling she was trying out explanations as they came to her. "Or consoling. I didn't want sympathy."

"Or interference."

"No." It was a statement of agreement.

"You didn't want my *interference*." The word coating his mouth like ground aspirin.

She shrugged again: the pale oblongs went up and down. He wanted to hit her then.

"You wouldn't let me hold him."

"I'm sorry," she whispered.

"No." He cut her off. "I don't want to hear you're sorry. I thought you were in shock, totally undone. I asked if I could hold him. You remember? You remember what you did? You didn't say no. You didn't shake your head. You did nothing. Nothing. You didn't respond. And I didn't press. I didn't ask again." He stood and ran a hand through his hair. "You weren't in shock. You'd known for months."

Ricky wrapped her arms around her knees, hugged them to her chest. "You can't sit on the same bed with me?" He didn't answer, and she answered herself: "You can't bear to sit on the same bed with me."

"And then after," John went on, as if she hadn't spoken, "when you still didn't tell me. When you kept up the act."

She looked up at him swiftly. Her pretty chin, her eyes even now spilling over. A trace of wiles? How could he ever know,

now, how could he ever now judge what was real and what play-acting?

"What good," she begged, "would it have done us?"

"If you have to—" He reached out a hand and it met the wall. He steadied himself. "If you have to ask," he'd said, "I don't know how we can be together."

"John." She rose from the bed so that she was standing, too, and he took a step back in case she thought she could touch him. "This is me. Please. I kept a secret. I thought it was the right thing. It wasn't right, but I thought it was. It was hard on me. I didn't cheat on you. It's not like an affair."

"It's *exactly* like an affair." He thought—they both must be thinking, of course, and it was strange to consider, even in that moment, all the intimacies and history they shared—of the affair she'd had before their wedding. "It's worse than when you had the affair." He struggled to say why, to think why. He looked out the window at the lights of the bridge. "That was bad. It was a secret and a lie, but you could say, in a way—a stupid way, but still, you could argue it didn't involve me. Directly."

He gathered up, almost absentmindedly, the extra blanket they kept folded on the window seat. He took a pillow from the bed.

"John? John." She followed him to the door. She was crying again. "You can't look at me?"

He looked at her. He looked at her. "This was my child. Too."

PART THREE

This Year

1.

In the little park across the street from the Ryries, Jess lay on the grass mulling the advantages of death. It was idle mulling; she was not suicidal, even if she was feeling somewhat melancholy. And she was, she thought with a sigh, practical enough to tell the difference.

Jessica Safransky was nothing if not practical. This was both a truism, cobbled from other people's estimations of her throughout her twenty-three years (she had in fact heard the very phrase "eminently practical" applied to her on two separate occasions), and a point of actual truth. Lying on her back in Memorial Park, arms folded behind her head, the grass young and cool beneath her, she reminded herself, bracingly, of her eminent practicality. Beside her rested her shoes, a pair of scuffed brown clogs.

Since leaving Berkeley, her moods had swung, uncharacteristically, between giddy excitement and dulling fear. These swings (reasoned Practical Jess) were hardly inexplicable. She was, after all, two thousand miles from home; hyperestrogenized; imposing on the kindness of a family that did not entirely belong to her; and, not to put too fine a point on things, lying to them. Still, the swings were disconcerting. She wished they'd go away.

She closed her eyes and opened them again. The sky was an extreme, almost rude shade of blue. Lording-it-over-you blue. Bluer-than-thou blue.

If she were dead all her mistakes would evaporate. Along with the puzzle of trying to unravel which things had actually been mistakes. She could tick off the possibilities on her fingers: sleeping with Seth; sleeping with Seth without a condom; not telling Seth the truth; telling her parents the truth; not getting an abortion; getting a Greyhound ticket; coming to the Ryries; lying to the Ryries.

Jess sat up and clasped her bare feet. It was the third Friday; she'd been here two weeks, and she meant to stay longer. She felt on an island here, exquisitely removed from the rest of her life. The days were a little boring, yes; she took walks, read, napped. The napping! She'd never been so sleepy in her life, nor found sleep so delicious. And the rhythm of the days was the rhythm of other people's lives, which was itself a kind of holiday.

She'd wake each morning, on the air mattress in Biscuit's room, to a distant electronic beeping, followed by sounds of shower and toilet, then of drawers being opened and closed, then of low-heeled pumps treading smartly down the stairs, and eventually of a car backing out of the drive. That would be Ricky. After a lull, in which she'd drift off, she'd wake a second time to a second round of sounds, some of them quite close by, some in other rooms: there were radio voices and live voices, the clamor of feet running down and up and down the stairs, of dishes set ungently in the sink, of the front door opening and shutting (many dozens of times, it always seemed), and finally the revving of a second engine: the pickup truck, departing. That would be John taking the kids to school and himself to work. Through it all, Jess would stay put, luxuriating in the dual freedoms of feigning sleep and succumbing to sleep. But the moment each morning when the house grew empty and still, the moment when she should have been able to settle back into real unimpeded slumber, she would find herself unalterably awake.

She would rise then, shower and dress, and go downstairs, her hunger propelling her toward the kitchen with an urgency she'd never experienced pre-pregnancy. There she'd stand, wolfing a bowl of cereal by the Dutch door, looking out at the neglected jumble of the backyard, its patchy crabgrass sprinkled with pine needles, its border crowded by bushes and shrubs all vying for what scant sunshine reached. A couple of squirrel babies put on a circus act each morning, using the clothesline for a tight-rope. As much clowns as acrobats, they performed their scrab-bling antics while Jess poured herself a second bowl of cereal and ate this one standing up, too, amused by the gaffes and re-coveries of the furry gray siblings.

Then she'd call her mother. Just the same, every weekday morning since getting here, as soon as she'd washed her bowl and spoon she'd pick up the phone and dial. Her mother would answer before the second ring. The mother she'd left in anger and for whom she yearned.

Deena Safransky was a potter. Back when they'd lived in Elsmere she'd thrown pots in the basement, and behind their current house in Berkeley she'd built a small studio in a shed, so Jess had grown up always close to the rhythms of wheel and kiln. Her mother's long, wavy hair had silvered prematurely, before Jess started grade school, and as a little girl Jess had assumed this to be a result of handling all that clay and slip, just as her mother's smock and jeans and fingernails were always stained and spattered, streaked and flecked with palest gray.

Strange to think it had been less than a month ago, that day—the day before she bought the Greyhound ticket—when she and her mother sat in the parking lot outside the obstetrician's office and her mother begged her not to have the baby. Pleaded with Jess really in spite of herself, in spite of her long-standing and voluble convictions that a woman should be free to make her own choice on the matter, also in spite of her professions of faith that Jess would make a good mother someday. The car windows had been shut and the air felt too close, with Deena streaming tears, blowing her nose, wadding damp tissues, making points. She'd talked and cried at mind-numbing length, making her case, by turns, passionately, irrationally, resourcefully. Through the windshield, Jess had tracked the progression of women in various stages of fat-belliedness go to and from the building. Nine women in the time she endured her mother's rant. Three alone, five accompanied. One with an infant in a sling. Deena argued, Jess began to think, with an intensity that suggested more than the moment, the particular instance at hand.

"It's what you wish you had done," Jess said finally. A realization as much as an accusation.

"It isn't as simple as that," Deena protested. After a moment: "And no, not in a million years."

But the order of her responses was as good as an admission, and the conversation had ended there, the tone of Deena's belated insistence lingering, like something faintly noxious, between them.

Her father, who practiced what Jess had long thought of, with amused affection, as a noninterventionist form of love, had not tried to influence her decision one way or the other. Bernard Safransky was ten years older than his wife. He was pear-shaped and wore bifocals, which, when he wasn't reading, perched unstylishly on top of his head. His law offices were downtown, at the top of a tall glass building from which you could see both the Bay Bridge and the Golden Gate. He played clarinet to relax, and sometimes went around the house with a reed sticking, half forgotten, out of his mouth, the way another man might go around with a toothpick. When he was informed not only that Jess was pregnant but that she had decided to keep the baby, he had thought—you could always *see* him thinking—and pursed his lips as though sucking on a reed. Then he'd bent silently forward and kissed the top of her head in a way that made Jess feel both grateful and ineffably sad.

It was Bernard who'd supplied Jess with her reading material for the journey—handing her, on the morning of her departure, his tattered paperback *Leaves of Grass*. "If you're setting out to see America," he'd said in his quiet, almost recessive way, "you could do worse for company." She'd been touched as much by the unexpectedness of the item as by the fact of his giving her something. Who knew her father cared for poetry? Jess was curious about this heretofore hidden side of him, and as she read deeper into the pages, more questions arose. When, near Flagstaff, she'd come to the line "I know I am restless and make others so," she'd lifted her head from the pages and stared out the window for miles, wondering what else she and her father might have in common. But Bernard Safransky was no good on the phone; she'd have to wait until she was home to explore it further. At any rate, she was not mad at him. It was her mother from whom she'd stormed in a huff ("Fine, then—you won't have to worry about it. I'm leaving!"), her mother without whom she felt lonely, lost. Her mother she called, perhaps compulsively, at the same time every day.

At ten in Nyack it was seven in Berkeley. Jess's father would have just left for work; Deena would be awake but not yet in her backyard studio. They never talked long. They said the same things: sorry, mostly. How are you feeling? Fine. Do you have morning sickness? No. When are you coming home? Soon. Do you have enough money? Yes. The banality of the exchanges soothed and irritated Jess.

But this morning, when Jess was once again vague about her return, Deena, unable to let it go, had fished. "Do you think you're getting whatever it is you went out there to find?"

"I didn't come to 'find' anything. This isn't a coming-of-age novel, Mom. This isn't the Oxygen network."

"I don't know what that is."

Jess sighed. "A cable station, Mom. You've watched it."

"I'm wondering if I should call John, speak with him directly."

"No. You should not."

"Why?"

"For starters, because I told them you kicked me out and want nothing to do with me."

A silence and then: "Why would you do that?" Deena sounded as though she'd been pricked by a hot needle. She sounded like the vortex of all pain. Jess was reminded of the morning in the parking lot, her mother's wet tissues and swollen eyes, her sense of injury, the tedium of it. "I can't believe you would do that."

"I'm just kidding."

"Jessica."

"What? Sorry."

"Do you think they feel put-upon?"

"What do you mean? No."

"You don't think you're outstaying your welcome?"

"I'm not."

"Don't be defensive. It's just, they have those two little children. And I don't know how the wife feels about you there. I don't want—"

"The kids aren't little. And Ricky likes me. She gave me her mandolin."

"But are you—oh honey, are you getting what you want from this visit, what you hoped for?"

"Mom. Yes. Whatever." Deena would be happy, Jess thought, with nothing short of a full renunciation of any interest whatever in the Ryries. "I don't hope for anything."

"Well," said Deena. "I hope that isn't true."

After they hung up a fretful melancholy set in. The way the call had ended. Jess shuffled over to the counter and began, almost without noticing, her third breakfast: the remains of the cake she'd brought back yesterday from the bakery in town. She liked to surprise the Ryries with little gifts, things. She picked at the remaining wedge with a fork. It had been left out on the counter in its cardboard box overnight and the edges had grown hard.

She did hope for something. She only didn't know what.

She'd loved the Ryries since that summer in her teens when she went camping with them. The fact that she'd narrowly missed being a full-fledged member of the family enhanced its allure, as did the fact that she'd had only minimal contact since. But her impressions of them, as well preserved and as limited in scope as the single roll of photographs she'd taken that summer on a disposable camera from the Cabruda Lake drugstore, did not mesh with what she'd found.

Back then John and Ricky had struck her as excitingly in love, a couple almost at the mercy of their own passion. They had been far more physical with each other than her own parents ever were, making them somehow seem at once more sophisticated and more innocent. Her memories of Biscuit were a toddlerish blur, but Paul had left a distinct impression: a slender stalk of a boy with white-gold hair and teeth like so many mini-Chiclets. She remembered him always moving, full of vigor and light.

The disconnect between these memories and the Ryries as they appeared now was disquieting. People changed, of course— but this was like a different family. It was like being a loyal fan, president of the fan club, and finally meeting the object of your adulation only to have your attentions dismissed. No, that was wrong—no one had dismissed her. It was more like finally meeting your favorite star only to find him flatter, more ordinary, than he appeared on screen. At least they had been kind, invited her to stay. Ricky of all people had been the warmest, shown the most overt interest. She'd made up the bed for Jess, had given her the bottle of prenatal vitamins, had offered, on the second day, use of her mandolin.

"It's gorgeous," Jess had breathed, sitting on the end of Ricky and John's bed and examining the instrument, running her fingers lightly over its bowl-shaped back, its mother-of-pearl inlays. She tried out some guitar fingering, then lightly stroked the neck. Looking up, she saw Ricky watching her with keen, almost hungry, interest. "Are you sure you don't mind me playing it? It looks brand-new."

"It is," Ricky answered. "John gave it to me for my birthday." And she pulled a little face, as if Jess ought to agree this made him somewhat ridiculous.

As for John, Jess saw how carefully he treated Ricky.

As for Biscuit, Jess saw how she hid things under her bed.

As for Paul, he might have been a changeling. Lumpen and darkly aloof, he'd barely said two words to her.

What she remembered of the Ryries, the memory she cherished above all of her time with them on that single summer holiday eight years ago, was how shiny she had appeared in their eyes, how good and honorable and clean. The happiness of those two weeks had been the happiness of having her worth gauged by strangers, of being seen fresh—it was her debut, after all, as an independent person, with no mother or father or teacher or friend to lend her context—and found estimable. She had not the least doubt about this, their regard. They'd expressed it amply, in ways both direct and indirect. Had she thought it would all come back so easily, that all she need do was show up, help herself to their kitchen and kettle, announce her condition, dissemble a little about her state of need, and be reinstated as precious, as prized in their eyes—is that what she'd hoped? Is that what she'd come for?

After hanging up the phone with her mother, after scraping up the dry last bit of cake, Jess had helped herself to a sweatshirt from the coatrack and taken her coffee out to the porch. The wisteria that grew up along the posts was winter-bare, its branches forming a gnarled proscenium. She'd stood at the edge of the top step, face tilted toward the thin bright sun, and took stock: she was twenty-three, two thousand miles from home, with a baby (and two bowls of cereal and a piece of cake) inside her. What did any of that mean, bode? The April air cut like scissors, the light spooling across the grass, and she stood on a kind of brink, a lip, pressing forward into the morning, but the park stood empty, the street stood empty, there was no one to see her: the world was blind.

So Jess had abandoned her mug on the shady porch and crossed over into the sunlight of the park, removing her clogs as she stepped onto the grass. And there she'd lain this past half-hour, at first feeling weighed by real misery, but eventually sliding into half-pleasurable, even improbably cheering, suicidal reveries. Now she propped herself on her elbows. The grass spread all around: new, slim-bladed, palest green. She thought of Walt Whitman, leaning and loafing, observing his spear of summer grass. She thought of her father as a young man, loafing in the grass with the very copy of Whitman he'd passed along to her. He was mysterious to her in this vision, someone she'd not guessed at. She could drum up, barely, wisps of memory: herself as a child in the grass with him, her father instructing her in the art of tying shoelaces, calmly batting away a wasp. Then another wisp, this one not memory but projection: herself loafing in the grass with her own child years hence, the two of them observing the green strands together, the intensity of the grass doubled. Whitman had a line about that, too, didn't he? Where had she come across it, Topeka? St. Louis? About a child fetching a handful of grass, displaying it as treasure. That was the silver lining, then, the sweet surprise of pregnancy: at best, it seemed to promise an antidote to loneliness. Someone else to witness the particularities up close, to share with her her vision, her singular perspectives and thoughts. It was a doubling, the prospect of an imaginary friend who would become, in a matter of time, incarnate. (Though there was a part of her that did not believe it at all. Was she fatter? Did she feel any different? Sleepy, yes, but nothing more. She wanted proof. She wanted kicking.)

Down the slope from where she sat, hidden from sight by shrubbery, younger-than-school-age children were frisking in the little playground. She listened to their high, purposeful voices registering thrill, and the countering voices of their caregivers, bent, from the sound of it, on squashing thrill. "Get down from there, Connor!" a woman ordered. "You know you can't go that high!" Jess smiled: evidently Connor could. One thing she knew for sure—if there really was a baby inside her, if she really was about to become a mother, she would never sound like *that*.

She knew who she hoped to sound like: her friend Annie. Annie had no kids, but she had a dog, a rescued greyhound she called Brokedown Palace, and Annie was great with her dog. Jess had met her at Conefucius, the ice cream parlor where they'd both scooped their way through college, and where Brokedown hung out during Annie's shifts, mostly out on the sidewalk, cadging the ends of people's cones, snapping lazily at bees, dozing in the shade of a fan palm. Once a customer had asked, "Is that your dog out front?"

Annie, looking up slowly from under the brim of her omnipresent Stetson, had given one of her slow grins. "Nope, she's her own dog."

It was the kind of thing that made Jess both admire Annie and want to crack her over the head. No wonder, in that land of anarchic shop owners, ice-cream-fed greyhounds, and cowboy-hatted girls, Jess got termed "eminently practical." Could that be the reason she'd gotten pregnant in the first place, the reason she'd quarreled with her mother, bought that epic bus ticket, and delivered herself so rashly into the house of her not real family, her alternative-reality family? In order to repudiate the designation?

Maybe. In part. Jess was at once too clear-sighted not to consider the possibility and too smart to fall sway to the kind of reductive thinking that would make it the whole answer.

It was Annie's younger brother, Seth, who was the father. Now there was a designation to make Jess snort. Better simply to say he was the one who'd gotten her pregnant—not that he knew or ever would. He was still in college—a sophomore, for God's sake—undeclared but leaning toward environmental studies, a lanky, unstudied heartthrob who wore an ancient Chinese coin on a cord around his neck. In her mind's eye he could be found eternally playing Hacky Sack in Sproul Plaza, his dirty-blond hair bouncing on his shoulders, his long, tapered torso naked and tanned, frayed cargo shorts hanging low off his waist. They'd met at a house party last fall; he'd filched Annie's Stetson off her head and settled it on his own, where, Jess thought, it showed to better effect. In fact, it had been the hat that caused her to approach him, the odd draw of a familiar object radically transformed by virtue of its placement in a strange context. Much the effect Jess hoped to gain for herself by coming here.

Jess, herself at that point six months out of Berkeley with a degree in English and no real clue of what was next, had been chatting him up with what she'd thought was big-sisterly interest, asking him about his classes and profs. It was two or three in the morning by then, the air sweet with pot and sleepy bodies. No one was dancing anymore. Someone had taken off Kanye West and put on Leonard Cohen. Seth was in the midst of some genial riff involving the Aztec god Quetzalcoatl and fair-trade coffee, when "Suzanne" came on and he interrupted himself first to listen, and then to sing, "And she feeds you tea and oranges that come all the way from China." But privately, unshowily, it had seemed to Jess at the time. Doing that thing men do with their eyebrows when they're straining to reach the high notes.

Then he'd shot her an embarrassed grin—it was almost the same grin as Annie's, though his was crazy sexy—and, shrugging, confessed, "My dad loves this song."

Who ever knew what it would take? It was always unexpected, she was learning, the thing that smote your heart, always something untranslatable, irreducible, something that refused to come through in the retelling, so that you felt the absurdity of it increase each time you tried to parse it. The moment that caused your chest to expand, the moment your shortness of breath let you know you had fallen for somebody new. Seth and Jess had fucked on and off then for the next couple of months in a sweet, blasé way—almost childlike, almost puppylike, their lightly pleasurable tumblings—each knowing there was no future in it, Jess sternly trying to keep her heart and hopes in line, to remind herself this was how it went with her generation; indeed, it was the very rubric of her generation. She knew no one her age who was in a long-term relationship, no one who seemed even to wish to end up with the person they were sleeping with.

By the time Jess realized she was pregnant, she'd neither seen nor spoken with Seth in five weeks, obviating the need to break it to him, or for that matter, break up with him. By then, neither she nor Annie worked at Conefucius anymore. Annie (improbably) had begun studying for the LSAT, and Jess (ironically) had taken a job in the career placement office on campus, assisting students with the very process that, in her own life, most baffled her.

Could *that* be the reason she'd gotten pregnant? In order to saddle herself with something she had to do, thereby precluding the need to figure out what it was she wanted to do?

All at once she heard panting near her ear, felt pungent breath on her face.

"No!" scolded a man's voice. "Come away from there! You dunce."

She propped herself on her elbows and squinted across the park. Already the apparent culprit, an enormous dog, had moved off. A slight red-haired man in a plaid jacket threw a stick for it. The dog caught it in midair with a hard snap of tooth on wood, then lumbered slowly back toward the man, slower, slower, before coming to a halt some distance away. It lowered its head suggestively. The man approached with stealth. The tail wagged. The man drew nearer. Nearer. At the last moment, just as he lunged, the dog bounded away, its entire massive body seeming to radiate laughter.

"Oh, so *that's* how it's gonna be," the man said to the dog, and they squared off against each other.

It was a hackneyed routine that remained somehow fresh, and Jess, who had recognized them both, did not suppress a laugh. At the sound the man turned toward her, shading his eyes. He looked hesitant, then surprised.

What was his name? Greg, Gregory? They'd sat in the kitchen together for a long time, the day she'd arrived. His presence had mitigated, in a way, the awkwardness of her own unexpected arrival. Was it Jordan?

Oh, well: "Hi!" she called, waving. She snatched up her clogs, began walking toward him. "It's Jess. We met"—jabbing a thumb over her shoulder in the direction of the Ryries' house and enjoying, even as the words flew out of her mouth unbidden, the absurdity of the statement—"over tea and Biscuit."

2.

M itosis." Ms. Nuñez put the word on the board as she spoke, the chalk clacking as if impatient. She was young, new to teaching this year (as she'd jauntily and perhaps unwisely announced to Paul's seventh-grade Life Science class on the first day of school last September), and had actually turned out to be pretty decent, except for her oddly hyped-up tempo. She talked twice as fast as anyone Paul had ever met, as though she'd taken to heart some mentor's warning that unless she did everything with Internet-era velocity she'd risk losing the kids' attention.

"Mitosis," she repeated, "is the process by which autosomal cells reproduce. So. What's 'autosomal'?"

When no one responded, she added this word to the board, the chalk flashing with such urgency that the final result was legible only by broad stretch of the imagination. Ms. Nuñez whipped back around to face the class. She wore her hair slicked so tight it looked painted on, except at the back, where her ponytail bobbed and swung.

"Autosomal: meaning the non-sex chromosomes. Okay? So mitosis is how cells reproduce asexually." She enunciated the last word deliberately, thereby eliciting smirks and laughter, as Ms. Nuñez, green or not, had to have known she would. She shook her head and rolled her eyes, pretending exasperation. But she'd warmed them up, brought them to attention, and on some level Paul understood she'd thrown in sex in order to ingratiate herself, to grease the wheels of teacher-student rapport. He didn't really fault her for it. In a weird way, she got his sympathy whenever she pulled something like this, some transparent effort to remind them she was hip. Still, he couldn't help regretting that she'd held the door so irresistibly open to rejoinders.

Here it came now, so predictable Paul could almost laugh, a jibe from Stephen Boyd, speaking low enough that his remark didn't carry all the way to the front, loud enough to set off a staccato burst of snorts and giggles around the desks in back: "That's how Ryrie's parents had him."

"That's mean," chided a girl, but admiringly.

The worst part was that the comment—which a year earlier would have blindsided him—only confirmed what had become his regular status, the miserable part he now played, the costume he wore through the halls of school like a heavy, invisible cloak. At least Paul's desk was toward the front of the classroom, so he could pretend not to have heard. He frowned intently at his book, as though contemplating a particularly challenging passage. But one comment was never enough.

"That's how Ryrie's parents do it every night," said Noah Prager, speaking for some reason in a television-cowboy drawl. He was a Stephen Boyd wannabe, but meaner than Boyd and lacking the charm; short, with an overdeveloped set of biceps and pecs to compensate. He shifted into a disgusting, whispery falsetto—"Oh. Oh! Oh-hh-hh!"—presumably simulating the sounds Paul's mother (or worse, father) made during sex.

Paul's heart thumped; his temples throbbed. He made his face dead stone, made his eyes dead fucking shit, drilled them straight ahead at the board.

"Noah, you're such an asshole," whispered someone—Fiona Conley, Paul guessed—and the sniggers flared up again and died out.

At the front of the room Ms. Nuñez was continuing blithely, sailing along on her newly fortified confidence. "A lot of your own body's cells reproduce this way. We're talking skin cells, hair cells, stomach cells, heart . . ." As she spoke she set up a series of cardboard diagrams on the chalk ledge: INTERPHASE, PROPHASE, METAPHASE, ANAPHASE, TELOPHASE, CYTOKINESIS.

Then she spun around and started waving her hand in the air. "But, Ms. Nuñez, Ms. Nuñez, how does this occur?" she said, in a kind of parody that achieved moderate success: she received polite laughter from the first couple of rows. After a moment's delay, however, she hit the jackpot in the form of Noah Prager singing out from the back in a faithful echo of her own eager cadence, "But, Ms. Nuñez, Ms. Nuñez, how does this occur?" He did this in a way that managed to suggest equally that he was her co-conspirator in the joke and that he was mocking her attempt at humor.

"Ah, Mr. Prager," she replied, "I'm glad you asked. Open your binders, people. New heading: 'The Six Stages of Mitosis.'"

Beneath the generalized shuffling and flipping open of twenty-eight binders, Paul heard Prager mutter, "He's fucking gay, anyway," and then the same female voice, Fiona Conley's, retort sanctimoniously, "*So*? That doesn't mean you should make *fun* of people," and it was the retort more than the crack—the retort that seemed to assume the veracity of the crack—that defeated him utterly, withering whatever shred of dignity he'd hoped to convey, even to himself.

Ms. Nuñez began to lecture. At first Paul took fastidious notes—not out of any scholarly impulse, but in an effort to appear thoroughly engrossed in the lesson and therefore oblivious to the words being traded behind his back. Baptiste wasn't in this class, and Paul was grateful. He didn't know whether Baptiste had heard any of this particular breed of comments, which had started up and multiplied over the past several weeks, the odd "faggot" or "homo" tossed with appalling casualness his way. He'd become used to other epithets, digs at his weight or his general unpopularity, but the references to sexual orientation were new. They made the earlier insults seem almost benign in comparison, and Paul worried about the effect they might have on his and Baptiste's friendship, should Baptiste become aware of them.

On two occasions during their friendship Paul had heard a racist slur directed at Baptiste. "Jesus Christ, another shitskin." An older boy from another school had said it at a track meet when the Nyack team had filed into their locker room. It had taken Paul a moment to figure out that the comment was directed specifically at Baptiste and that it referred to his color. The kid, a towering specimen of advanced puberty, had muttered it in a low voice, with apparently sincere revulsion: more damaging than if it had been delivered with spiteful glee.

The other time it had been a pair of quite small elementary school girls, cute in their dresses and patterned socks, sitting on the wall in front of the post office, next to a baby stroller, swinging their legs and singing with impunity, "Happy birthday to you, you live in a zoo, you look like a Haitian and you smell like one, too." Both times Paul's stomach had turned, and he'd wondered sweatily whether or not to comment. Both times he'd ultimately deferred to Baptiste's own silence, interpreting it as Baptiste's wish for how he, too, would respond. Yet afterward, both times, he'd been haunted by the worry that Baptiste had not wanted his silence, that there might in fact be nothing dignified in it.

On Friday the only periods the friends had together were art and lunch. Lunch was next. Paul stole a glance at the clock. All the school's clocks were an hour off, no one having yet adjusted them for daylight saving time. Its long hand juddered forward one audible notch. Twenty-six minutes left in the period. He smelled, or imagined he could, lunch: The school tuna (pinker, wetter, sweeter than at home), the school lettuce (iceberg, shredded noodle-thin), the school fries (skinny, hard, greasy). The sandwich rolls (dry, almost scratchy). The school disinfectant (a kind of inorganic citrus, acrid yet not altogether unpleasant), which provided the olfactory backdrop for every lunch period and which, alone, could stimulate Paul's appetite.

His stomach rumbled and he scuffed his shoes on the floor in an effort to mask the sounds. There was the pain of being ridiculed, which was the pain of knowing yourself to be despised for an isolated moment, and there was the pain of anticipating ridicule, which was the pain of knowing yourself to be the object of ongoing contempt.

He swallowed, and ground his teeth against tears, the effort to contain which made his head ache. He needed something beyond this room on which to focus, something to transport him from this place. Jess. Two Jesses, superimposed: the starry teenager he remembered from that long-ago summer at Cabruda Lake, and the plainer, more ambiguous figure she cut now. So that in his head he saw her simultaneously long-haired and shorn, slender and plump, quick and languid, teasing and decorous. She at once wore braces on her teeth and none; viewed the world unmediated and through lenses. Which was the true Jess, which the false? It felt that way, as though one version was a guise and the other genuine. Behind one lay the promise of his highest hopes for himself; behind the other, the explicit dashing of those hopes.

All week he'd largely avoided her, even while wishing she would seek him out, single him out for attention, indicate in some way that she remembered him as he'd been: the torpedo she'd shot, toes pointed, through the water; the willing accompanist who'd strummed her guitar while she fingered the chords;

her companion in the hammock as dusk fell and they pointed out to each other with their fingers the evening's first bats.

"How long is she staying?" he'd asked last night, as they'd all been eating supper. The kitchen table did not easily accommodate five; they had to remember to keep their elbows tucked in, and still they wound up jostling one another.

"That's rude," his mother said.

He knew it was rude. But, "What?" he said, "I'm not allowed to be curious?"

"It's okay," Jess told his mother. "Not long," she told Paul.

His mother had lain down her fork and knife. "You know you're welcome to stay as long as you like."

"Thanks."

"Really. We'd love you to—stay."

His father had reached over and squeezed his mother's shoulder, and it was far beyond Paul why this should have made him feel bad.

"Thanks," Jess said again. "I'm not sure the feeling's unanimous." She smiled at Paul, though, almost conspiratorially, and did not seem the least concerned.

Paul struggled not to betray himself. He bent over his plate, pretending to cut a piece of lettuce and hoping his fallen bangs masked his blush. "It's immaterial," he assured her. "This isn't a democracy."

"Paul!" snapped his father.

But Jess laughed.

"I apologize," Paul mumbled. "May I please be excused?"

He'd retreated to his room in near-giddy confusion. His parents might've been shocked at his rudeness, but with this rudeness, if that's what it was, he'd successfully captured Jess's attention; better, had made her laugh.

He did not think Stephen Boyd or Noah Prager would have been able to accomplish this. In some sort of contest—if only it had been public! if only it held currency in the arena of middle school!—he was capable of besting them.

3.

For the second time in less than two weeks a daughter of John Ryrie's was riding in his car. Gordie nearly made the observation out loud, but checked himself, turning, instead, to glance at her. Jess smiled back, her teeth gleaming apple-white, as if this were all perfectly normal, confirming Gordie's sense that he was incapable of judging normalcy.

His palms were sweaty on the wheel. Certainly, he was a bit giddy, a bit revved by the unexpected turn of events. What his dad would've called *in a froth*. "What are you all in a froth about, then, eh?" Imagine how surprised his dad would've been to learn it had to do with a girl. Behind him, Ebie whined, panted a moment, then closed her jaws as if in forbearance.

He'd been encouraged by Jess's friendliness in the park. Never mind that she kept calling him Jordie (he hadn't managed to correct her), she'd known right away who he was. She'd been the one, actually, to initiate contact. Well: as far as *Jess* knew, she'd been the one to initiate contact. That was what mattered.

In fact he'd taken Ebie walking in Memorial Park several times over the past ten days, at calculatedly varied times, in hopes of "running into" any of the Ryries. He'd spotted Jess that morning first thing on arrival, and if he'd had any doubts that it was she, Ebie dispelled them by trotting right over, tail awag in recognition. He'd called her sharply away, mortified to think the dog's forwardness might be construed as his own.

And then, although he'd observed from the corner of his eye Jess prop herself on her elbows and study them, Gordie had pretended not to recognize her: he'd given Ebie all his attention, immersed himself in this game of stick throwing with unusual intensity, the result being every aspect of it felt foolish, artificial. *Here I am, athletic and good-natured. Here I am, loving my dog, who loves me. Here I am, lovable.* Despite the knowledge that he was straining, that the whole thing was a bit of a charade, what singing good fortune he'd felt in his heart. To be noticed, to be aware of being watched, was like having a long thirst slaked. And she did watch, he saw. Once, she laughed. He felt elated and ashamed. It was very like another time he'd successfully gained notice through contrivance: last year when he'd tripped over a root in the woods in front of Hugh Chaudhuri.

Hugh Chaudhuri was built like Gordie, short and lean, with dark hair he wore shaggy and glossy dark eyes that had the power to melt anyone, girl or guy. His androgyny was undeniably part of his appeal, even as it added to Gordie's confusion about his own proclivities. There'd been a drinking party in the woods— Gordie's virgin foray into that kind of thing, the unsanctioned gatherings high schoolers held in locations lacking proper addresses ("the rez," "the Hook," "behind the tennis courts"). The invitation had come about by fluke: some people talking about it in the hall before industrial arts, where Gordie, too, had gathered, waiting for the previous class to be let out; Hugh mentioning he had room in his car for one more. He'd looked right at Gordie as he said it, smiled just so with his Junior Mint eyes, and minor explosions detonated throughout Gordie's bloodstream. Was that the signal you wanted to be kissed? Gordie did not know what he wanted, but he had gone along, only to be disappointed later when he found himself consigned to the periphery of the gathering. The group, when they arrived, seemed already enmeshed, as though they shared a kind of fascinating, impenetrable history, forged long before Gordie had entertained even a flicker of desire to join. He'd stood at the edge of the schnapps-passing, lighter-flicking activity, pretending to enjoy the encoded dialogue, taking a long swig each time a bottle was inadvertently passed his way, trying in vain to think of something witty or admirable to say.

When it had been decided (somehow, as if by an unseen signal) that it was time to go, Gordie had almost cried with self-recrimination. He'd blown his chance to charm Hugh, a chance surely implicit in the offer of a ride. It would have been his first attempt trying to charm anyone, male or female, and the mechanics of the attempt had taken no concrete shape in Gordie's mind beyond a vague notion of a look exchanged and then Hugh's mouth closing in on—but never quite making contact with—his own. Did Gordie want to kiss? Or did he *want* to want to kiss?

On the way back to the road, sorting out his genuinely tipsy way between the trees, he'd grown aware of Hugh keeping pace just behind him, and in a last, desperate attempt to provide a romantic opening, Gordie had half willed, half allowed himself to stumble and fall flat on his front. When Hugh said, "Whoa! All right?" and paused above him, Gordie'd felt a rush of guilty triumph. When it turned out he had scraped and bloodied his wrist going down, he'd felt something like relief at acquiring this mark of authenticity, as though it absolved him of falsehood. But Hugh's interest never rose above that moment, that mannerly pause while Gordie got back to his feet—he hadn't even held a hand out to help Gordie up—and although they said hi after that whenever they passed in the halls, it was never more than perfunctory.

Being noticed by Jess, innocent of the fact that his and Ebie's game of fetch was being performed for her benefit, was therefore similarly bittersweet, his sense of victory tainted by self-reproach, the knowledge that he had contrived this opening. Ebie, once she'd caught wind of Jess's approach, had forestalled it with an onslaught of hospitality, bounding across the grass and bringing herself up short just before barreling into the girl, then wagging her hindquarters mightily while conducting, at her opposite end, olfactory operations of an almost surgical delicacy.

"Jess, right?" Gordie, wandering over, feigned uncertainty. "I didn't notice you there."

"You're easy to spot, with your dog." She wore an oversized sweatshirt—the very one, Gordie realized with a flush of embarrassed pleasure, that he'd worn the other day, while his own shirt dried—and a cotton skirt the color of tea.

"Oh. I guess, yeah." He'd ruffled the fur at the back of Ebie's neck. Was the motion ever so slightly different from the way he might normally have done it? Did his voice sound just a little altered, lower, perhaps, more clipped? Or was it only that he was watching himself, listening to himself, differently? "She's easily spotted, anyway." Did it come out resentful? Christ—did he sound jealous of his dog?

The odd thing was that his awkwardness, his hyper-consciousness, instead of tightening its stranglehold—as he was used to it doing whenever it latched on—had ebbed in Jess's prolonged presence. No: the odd thing was that she continued to be present, just as if she were enjoying his company, as if she didn't have anything else she'd rather be doing.

They'd walked downhill, past the fenced playground and the field with its wide gazebo where bands played in the summer-time, down to the water's edge. Jess had her clogs in her hand all this time, right up until they reached the rocky bank, at which point Gordie could no longer restrain himself. "I gotta tell you," he said, "there's broken glass, crack vials, dog crap, goose crap . . . rats, too, actually; you see them sometimes, even in daylight. You have to put on your shoes." He was rather pleased with the way this came off: cool, commanding. The novelty of issuing an im-perative made him feel strangely confident.

"Yes, Grandma." But she did as he said. The first shoe went on all right, while she stood storklike on the other foot, but she went wobbly trying to slide her foot in the second and flailed, teetering, until he gripped her arm and steadied her.

"Thanks," she'd said, once fully shod. "Pregnancy does a number on your sense of balance."

He'd nodded. Then a full beat later: *"Oh."* Embarrassed comprehension washing over him. Was the embarrassment on her behalf or on his own? He felt the same quaking heat in her presence as he had in Hugh's, the same dizzying recognition of possibility. But was it, in both cases, a feeling predicated on the reassuring certainty that nothing would come of it?

"Almost eleven weeks," she added.

Gordie nodded again, as if it were commonplace, as if *most* girls he knew were somewhere in their first trimester.

They'd exchanged quite a lot of vitals then, during that hour hanging out by the river, most of it spent perching side by side on the back of a bench. She was going to be a single mother, she said. As one might announce the intention of becoming a doctor or an artist. Gordie didn't know what to make of it.

"My dad was a single parent."

"Yeah? What happened with your mom?"

"Died. Some kind of infection. When I was a baby."

"Grim," said Jess.

From their bench, as they chatted, they marked the rheumatic progress of a garbage barge as it made its way under the bridge, carrying its load toward Manhattan and the open sea. At last Jess announced, "My butt's sore," and stood up. "You have a car, don't you?"

"A car?" Gordie scrambled after her onto the rocks, where she was picking her way precariously in those clogs. "Yeah."

"We should go somewhere. You want?"

"Sure, maybe. Where?"

"New York."

"The city? What do you want to do there?"

"I don't know. Walk around. Get lost."

She wasn't looking at him but out at the water. A sailboat tacked to and fro. The river was at its widest here, nearly three miles across, and there was something quaint about the opposite shore at that distance; it was like a scale model in a train store, or a landscape in a tintype, glimpsed back at through time.

"What would I do with Ebie?"

They both looked around for the dog. Some twenty yards away, she was rolling around ecstatically at the water's edge. "Ah, shit," said Gordie. He jumped off the rocks and jogged toward her.

It was a dead seagull, its fetid body spread out on a patch of asphalt and weeds. Gordie had to use his sharpest tone to persuade Ebie to abandon her rapture. When at last she did, she bounded around, tongue lolling, as though to say, "Aren't I a pip?" She reeked.

"Stop," Gordie barked at Jess, who was progressing swiftly toward them. "You don't want to get any closer."

He experienced a flicker of satisfaction when she did, immediately, halt. Unaccustomed as he was to wielding authority, he felt he was doing it rather well, casually and in good cause. Evidently, though, he had not stopped her soon enough.

"*Dude.* She smells like a horror show."

Ebie wagged her tail, guilty and low.

Gordie looked at her. "That's right, you dope," he said softly. Then, "So much for going to the city," he called back over his shoulder. "At least, today." He didn't know if he was more disappointed or relieved.

"What will you do now?"

He shrugged. "Bathe her."

Jess walked along with them back up the hill, through the park, toward his dad's car. "Want help?" she asked, once Ebie had climbed in on top of the blanket in the back.

"With what?"

"Giving her a bath."

"Are you serious?"

Jess flipped up her palms, shrugged.

Gordie thought about what it would entail. No one had been over since his dad got sick. Not that Gordie had lived in utter and complete solitude these months. He'd met up with a few of his dad's friends in diners, dropped in at a couple of house parties held by former classmates. People had reached out, a handful of acquaintances left over from senior year: the dregs of the class, like him, people who hadn't gone away to school, hadn't moved on. But he'd had no one over.

He looked at Jess, in John's great droopy sweatshirt and her petal-light skirt, her dark eyes (very like Hugh Chaudhuri's, he noticed) squinting and watering a little in the sharp path of the sun. She had suggested going somewhere with him twice in the space of fifteen minutes. Was it that she wanted to be with him, or was it that she wanted to go?

"You sure?" he asked. "I mean. The car . . . the smell . . ."

But she was game. They drove through town with the windows rolled down and the fan blasting a potpourri of fresh air and stale cigarette odor at their faces. Something new had happened.

At the condo complex Gordie pulled into their numbered parking space. He wondered if Jess was surprised, if she'd been expecting a house, a single-family in town instead of a brick complex by the thruway. Inside, the stairwell was dim; a bulb was out. "Two flights," Gordie said. Beneath poor Ebie's stench Gordie could smell the regular odor of the hallway, not unclean exactly, but heavy and close. His awareness of it was sharpened by Jess's presence. A soap opera was audible behind a neighbor's door. It hit Gordie, as he unlocked the door to their own unit, that the kitchen was full of trash he hadn't taken out, dishes he hadn't washed. He was glad, at least, that the radio he'd left on for so many months, loath to end something his dad had set in motion, was no longer playing: he did not think he would have been able to bear being exposed at that level.

They stepped inside, Ebie pushing past them to inspect her bowl. Never had the condo looked so shabby to Gordie, at once eccentrically cluttered and just plain grungy. The sun was coming in at just the angle to best illuminate the crumbs on the Formica countertops; the vinyl flooring was sticky underfoot. A fly, trapped between two panes of glass, buzzed in the window above the sink. Just as the previous week he'd wondered if John Ryrie's other daughter might be afraid of him, afraid of getting into a car with a strange man, now he wondered if Jess was having misgivings about getting herself into this situation, finding herself here in a seedy-looking apartment with a man she did not after all quite know. A sense of unfairness, bitterness, and defeat clamped down on him, as though she'd already changed her mind.

"I'm going to stick Ebie on the balcony while I fill the bath," he muttered.

"Okay."

He could feel her watching uncomfortably as he wrestled the

foul creature outside and slid shut the heavy door. Ebie looked up at him and wagged slowly, smudging the glass with her nose. Jess said, "Is anything wrong?"

"I'll start the water," he said, going into the bathroom.

He turned on the taps, found the bottle of dog shampoo. He smelled his plaid jacket, shed it. In the mirror he saw a furrow between his eyebrows. He relaxed his muscles; it went away. He splashed water on his face. The little room began to fog. He felt the water in the tub, switched off the taps.

When he came back to the kitchen, it was empty. He glanced out to the balcony; Ebie met his gaze and gave a short whine. "I'll be back," he told her through the glass. He was relieved when he found Jess in the living room, not gone after all, not hitching a ride on Route 59, but standing with her hands clasped behind her, perusing the shelves. His father's dioramas crowded there, long unattended, furnished with dust and the occasional cobweb, in places two deep, in places stacked one upon another.

"You made these?" Jess did not turn.

"No."

He felt her reverence, her absorption, like a rise in barometric pressure. As he watched she stooped, then knelt, in order to peer into the ones on a bottom shelf.

"Is there more light?" It was a request.

He switched it on.

She whispered something he did not catch, did not think he was meant to. She said, "Your father?"

"Yeah. My dad."

Looking at her looking at the boxes, he apprehended something about them. They were the root he'd stumbled on, the root his dad had left purposely sticking up.

"Are they based on stuff?" she asked. "This one looks like, from the *Odyssey*, you know, that island with the pigs. And there was another like Hansel and Gretel, a trail of bread crumbs in the woods?"

"They are from books, some of them, if that's what you mean. A lot he just did from his imagination."

"He was an artist."

"Postal worker."

"Serious?" She turned.

He nodded.

She turned back to the boxes. "Oh. Jordie, how long ago did he die?"

"In January. It's Gordie, actually."

"Oh, God!" She swiveled to him again, covering her mouth. "Sorry!"

"It's all right. He'd been sick awhile."

"No, I mean—yes, I'm sorry about—but I mean, I've been calling you the wrong thing *all this time*?"

"That's okay." He coughed. "I should check the bath."

After Ebie had been bathed and toweled, they went out on the tiny balcony and ate peanut butter crackers and sour pickles, the best Gordie could muster from the derelict cupboards and fridge. "Is this a joke?" Jess asked when he first brought forth the food, and he thought she was riding him about such poor offerings. But she laid a hand on her stomach, on what he now recognized as a meaningful protrusion, and he recalled the cliché:

the pregnant woman's craving for pickles and ice cream, and he wished he'd intended the wit.

Ebie lay at their feet, her drying fur redolent of doggie shampoo and sunshine and also, faintly, something gamier: salty and dark. Jess sat in Will's old chair and used Ebie's hindquarters as a footrest. She ate like a farmhand, ravenously, steadily, one peanut butter cracker after another, and then polished off the pickles, and Gordie began to fear he'd run out of food before she ran out of room. But at last she'd settled back in her chair, hands folded over her small bulge, and tipped her face to the sky.

Gordie took advantage of her eyes being closed to study her. He couldn't decide whether she was pretty or not. He was trying to think what his dad would say if he came home to find Gordie out here with a girl. He'd be glad, relieved of the great worry he'd been too tactful ever to voice. "Well done," he'd say. "Yer a sly one, then, eh?"

"Do I have food on my face?" she said, eyes still closed.

"No."

"Then why are you staring at me?"

He turned away, leaned his arms against the railing and looked out over the other buildings in the complex, the other cars, each parked in its numbered space.

"No, really."

"I don't know," he said. "I just was."

Before he took her home she asked to look at his dad's boxes again. This time he looked, too, rediscovering a few old favorites: Peter Rabbit hiding in Farmer MacGregor's garden; a candy shop whose peppermint sticks were red and white embroidery floss, twisted together and stiffened with glue. A newsstand with stacks of newspapers that had been painstakingly folded from real pieces of newsprint.

"What will you do with them?" asked Jess.

"I don't know. I wasn't thinking that was a question."

"It is," she said. "It is a question. These should be somewhere people can see them."

"Can I ask you something?"

"What?"

He wanted to know why she had come back here, what about him seemed worthy of her interest.

"What?" she asked again.

"Do you really think they're good?"

"I think they're heartbreaking."

She moved to the last shelf on the end. Gordie moved with her. Newer stuff. He looked over her shoulder and saw the last box his dad had ever made, the one begun a year ago, after that final surgery. How faithfully his dad had copied the scene from the photo album: the table all laid out, just as in the picture. Gordie saw his dad's fingers, blocky and hairless (even the coarse hairs on the back of his hands having bowed to chemo), the knuckles densely whorled, the nails thickened and discolored from the drugs, yet clean and trimmed, as ever. He saw his dad's hands working the tip of a pencil over the play dough, molding the icing, raising icing roses as if by sleight of hand along the rim of the tiny cake.

"Can I help?" he'd asked. He'd never helped in the past, never asked to.

And "No," his dad had said. Just like that.

But then had added gruffly, "You can't, because I'm making this one for you." And that had never happened before either.

Gordie'd swallowed hard, and made his escape from the sudden welter of feeling building up in the small room by going off to walk Ebie.

Now, looking together with Jess into the one box that was above all *his,* wondering whether it was worth telling her so, he saw something he'd never spotted before. Something different about the wedding cake, a tiny detail he could swear hadn't been there when his dad finished the box last spring and presented it to him. He must have added this bit later. When, and why? And why silently?

In the center of the balsawood table, atop the antimacassar tablecloth and the silver-dollar platter and the three-tiered wedding cake that rested upon it, two tiny figures stood. Two painstakingly painted grains of rice. A groom and a groom.

4.

John pulled into the driveway at two-thirty, wishing it really were the start of the weekend. It was Friday, yes, but the only reason he was home so early was that he had to be back at work again in a few hours; *For Colored Girls* was opening that night. The set he'd designed was spare: a dozen flats painted to look like graffitied segments of a brick wall. Behind them, a cyclorama, lit with different colored gels over the course of the play, from rosy-yellow to celestial blue. It had come off without a hitch and he was pleased with it. No finishing touches remained to be added, nor did he anticipate any last-minute repairs, but he always made a point of being on hand for opening night.

Usually on opening night he'd stay through curtain, too, out of respect for the actors, but he thought he might duck out earlier this evening. He had a nagging feeling he'd been neglecting something at home. Their lives this past year had not been very happy, but they had been steady, predictably chugging along. Now he had the sense of changes afoot, changes he did not quite grasp or see. He was aware, mostly, of a sharp longing for family, never mind that they'd all had supper together every night since Jess had arrived. Perhaps the feeling had to do with Jess, the way her presence bespoke his failings. Or served to remind him that all children grow up and leave home. Or served to remind him that *not* all children grow up, forcing comparison with the baby they'd lost and his dreadful, thin scrap of life. Or maybe the feeling had nothing whatever to do with Jess; maybe it was all to do with Ricky.

For the arrival of Jess had also, coincidentally or not, heralded the renewal after long absence of what John thought of wryly as "marital relations." Why wryly? Why wasn't he simply glad? He sat there in the driveway, in the truck, motor off, keys in hand, mulling over these past nights.

It had begun after their talk with Jess, that Friday night— or really, it had been the small hours of Saturday by the time Ricky's fingers slipped through the unstitched slit of his boxers. In the milkiness of the streetlamp she made patterns on his skin, drew lace on him with her nails, unhurried, agonizingly light, until he could not *not* say through his teeth, "Harder," and then she tugged his boxers down. Lowered her face to the damp curling hair between his legs and rubbed her cheek and jaw bones hard against him like a cat. Later, she rose to straddle him, her face luminous and distant as an antique silver-print. She did not smile, not even with her eyes.

Each night since had seen a repetition. A new iteration. Theme and variation. It was not so much a renewal of their marital relations as a reinvention of them. He should have been ecstatic, should have been delirious. Well, he was. Was anyway swept away, overcome by the tidal force of the thing—even now, in the truck, he'd grown aroused inside his jeans. The ferocity of their sex had no history he could think of; the source of its ruthlessness he did not understand. This lovemaking felt punishing, retributive.

Yesterday morning, going to the bathroom, John had discovered a bite-shaped bruise at the top of his thigh. Its provenance took a second to dawn on him, and when it did he became light-headed. He felt awed by the maroon ellipse on his skin, awash in unfamiliar tenderness. Unfamiliar because it was directed toward himself, a feeling for his own vulnerability. It occurred to him, in a bizarre rush of association, that if Ricky were in some fatal accident, injured beyond recognition, the mark on his thigh could be used to identify her, a kind of dental record. That night he showed her what she'd done. He turned on the bedside light, knelt over her, one knee on either side of her waist, and, grasping the back of her head, steered her face to the spot. She made no expression of remorse. She touched the bruise with her thumb. Grazed it with her lips, salved it with her tongue. But within moments she'd abandoned this posture, her fingers digging into him from behind, her teeth pressed to his front. He winced, and, with a speed that surprised him, pressed her back against the pillow, kneed her legs apart.

John did not know what to make of any of it. He was fascinated and repulsed by what had been brought forth in him. For so long Ricky had related to him as obtuse, wanting, incapable of not letting her down. Now suddenly she needed him, demanded him—but that was not the whole of it: it was this specific version of him she demanded. Inarticulate, brutish.

John got out of the car. The day was mild for mid-April—hard to believe that only two weeks ago bits of snow still lingered. Going up the steps to the porch, he bent to retrieve a mug, presumably left by Jess. Hours ago, from the look of it: an inch of cold coffee sloshed in the bottom, and its walls were coated with milk scum. It was the alphabet mug Paul had made in second grade. John dumped the liquid over the railing and held the empty mug by its lopsided handle—he could picture seven-year-old Paul sculpting it with slack-jawed concentration, the gumdrop-tip of his tongue protruding—as he pushed through the door.

"Hello!" he called. "Hello?"

Paul was due home from school in a matter of minutes; Biscuit not for a half-hour. It was Jess's response he listened for. The afternoon sun slanted through the diamond-shaped window on the second-floor landing, draping a column of light across the stairs: dust motes and hush. She was out, then. When she got home he'd speak to her. She simply could not stay vaguely on this way, all open-ended, hapless fate, all whichever-way-the-wind-blows and time-will-tell. Last night at supper Ricky had come down on Paul for asking Jess point-blank when she was leaving, but John had thought the question legitimate, if not, perhaps, felicitously phrased. If her parents really had kicked her out, he supposed they would have to make a place for her here, as Ricky kept insisting. One way or the other, he wanted it said, acknowledged.

And why *did* Ricky keep insisting? He couldn't work it out. But then, it had been a long time since he'd felt he understood what Ricky desired. Nearly a year had passed since the revelation of her second infidelity, but his memory of that night remained sharp: the way he'd lurched home late, after having slept off most but not all of the tequila on the love seat in his office, and pressed her to divulge the secret she'd been keeping, the secret whose content he had not come close to guessing, but of whose existence he had finally become convinced—or at any rate had become freed, perhaps by drunkenness, to posit. The way she'd proven him right and shocked him at the same time. Really shocked him, with a truth he'd never have imagined. The way he'd finished out that night on the den couch, not sleeping at all but staring into the dark, which had a textured, binding quality, like a cheesecloth in which were caught many wild thoughts like so much flotsam and jetsam: thoughts of her workplace affair before they married, thoughts of her holding on to their short-lived baby in the big pink hospital chair. Thoughts of the crib he'd put together, alone, on a Sunday afternoon, whistling, Allen wrench in hand, screws strewn across the floor.

He no longer remembered how many nights he'd spent on the couch last spring—four? five? a dozen?—or what exactly had precipitated his return to their bed, only that it had been nothing transformative, no sweet, relief-filled instance of reconciliation. A certain atmosphere of normalcy was hard to avoid, frankly, in a family where the kids needed their reading logs signed, the laundry needed folding, the fridge restocking, the plants watering. Daily business, if not a balm, was at least a broth in which they'd been swept up and eddied along. His hurt and anger had gotten pulled into the current, as had Ricky's, apparently: had become just a regular part of the larger brew.

It was tempting to trust her again. He wanted to give himself over to her reanimation these past few weeks, her general move toward good cheer, her excitement over Jess's baby, her unexpected fervor in bed. But John could not, quite. Why? He put a hand on the newel post, touched the alphabet mug to his forehead. He thought of the night of the baby's conception, a night all too easy to pinpoint in the sea of touchless nights stretching in either direction from it. That night, he recalled, had held the brief whiff of renewal. Their hands, their bodies, knew painfully well what to do, as if to mock the small coolness that had come to mark their waking hours. Their hands, their bodies, seemed to belie their daylight moods and gestures, to flout what they'd become, to insist, *Here is the root of your marriage, undiminished, unchanged.* He had been roused that night by her touch, had woken aflame to his own erection in her hand, and had turned to her, already responsive, before he'd had sufficient time to register surprise. The baby had been conceived in the slippery sweat of nostalgia, and the truth was that John had spent the next several months wishing its existence away. Perhaps it was not Ricky he was now afraid to trust.

He lowered himself heavily onto the stairs. And why had Jess come? Could she be trusted when she said she sought nothing from them? She must want something. Whatever it was, he had little doubt he owed it. He wished she would say what it was, wished he could give it and be done. He pictured her, his eldest child, not well known to him: her eyes, first, behind their glasses: serene, modest, the eyes of a fawn, a novitiate—and then her thickening abdomen. Was she beginning to show? He tried not to notice, tried actively to avoid studying the size and condition of whatever small swell was visible: evidence at once inarguable and unfathomable of a more experienced life.

Another image came to him, one he hadn't thought of in many, many years: day-old Jess. Still in the hospital, swaddled in a receiving blanket, her face a bit compressed still from the trials of birth. Her eyes had looked to him Inuit, dark and almond-shaped; her cheeks had been broad, her chin a little nub, and her hair—he remembered thinking, with a private, triumphant thrill, that she'd got his hair!—had been profuse: black, curly, so silky-fine it looked damp.

A nurse had handed her to him. He had been amazed at how light and yet dense she was, and when, in her sleep, in his arms, she had moved slightly, shifting—with such *authority*—the un-imaginably complex muscular-skeletal system within the tight package of her bindings, he had been overcome by pride and gratitude and fear, because only in that moment did it truly hit him that she was a real person, her own person. He'd been nine-teen, and in awe.

Deena hadn't wanted him to hold the baby at all. Or that is what she'd claimed from where she'd sat propped up in the hos-pital bed, her long wavy hair gathered back in a giant banana clip, her eyes looking oddly naked without their usual black liner, their fringe of mascara. She'd worn a Hofstra sweatshirt over her johnny, and had tiny red dots under both eyes: burst blood vessels from pushing, she'd informed him, piquishly, when he inquired.

"You look like you've been in the ring," he'd said, hoping for a smile.

She'd stared at him, whether annoyed, confused, or simply exhausted he did not know.

"The boxing ring." He mimed a one-two.

They'd started dating in college the previous July. Both their discovery of and interest in each other had been abetted, no doubt, by the scanty summertime population in the dorms. Deena, going into her senior year, had stayed on campus because she was a rampant overachiever who'd enrolled in some kind of academic enrichment program virtually every summer since junior high; John, entering his sophomore year, because he was given free on-campus housing with his job working as an admissions rep.

"I don't think it's a good idea," Deena had said doubtfully when John, hovering near the threshold of her hospital room, asked to hold their daughter. "What do you think, Ma?" She'd turned to Mrs. Levin, sitting in the visitor's chair refolding three infinitesimal outfits she'd just held up to show Deena. On the floor beside her sat an enormous Saks Fifth Avenue shopping bag; there was a sight gag, John thought, in the relative proportions: the reverse of the clown car at the circus.

"Of course he should hold his baby," Mrs. Levin said, shrugging her heavy shoulders and pursing her lips, although not looking at either of them, but only at the impossibly small, pink-and-white terry-cloth sleep suit she dangled by the shoulders. "Why shouldn't a father hold his own baby?"

And John had felt a shot of hope, not because she'd come to his defense (he felt fairly certain her verdict was unrelated to any warm feelings toward him) but because Mrs. Levin was so

palpably annoyed with them both, he felt it might serve as a reminder to Deena that she and he were really allies, at least in
this sense. They were not getting married, as the Levins wished
them to do (never mind that John wasn't Jewish, never mind,
the Levins said, that they were both still in college, both still
kids, both, for that matter, idiots: a baby needed a mother *and* a
father).

The thing is, John would have stepped up. Or caved in. Either
way: he would have wed. It was Deena who'd held firm in saying no. Deena, two years older than John, had managed to attend
her commencement less than a month earlier, huge under her
black gown, squinting migraine-ishly against the slamming metallic sunshine, shifting her weight from foot to foot long after
the end of "Pomp and Circumstance," all through the part of the
ceremony when the graduates stood waiting to receive their di-
plomas, supporting the weight of her bulge with fingers laced
tightly together beneath it. It was she who'd put the kibosh on
their getting married. She who'd said categorically it would be a
mistake. A disaster. The worst thing they could do. So that even
as John had felt relieved—even, to be fair, as he'd privately acknowledged she was right—he'd felt snubbed. Diminished.

Deena had been adamant not only about marriage; she'd
made it clear he was to have no role whatsoever in the baby's
life. "I'm going to be a single mother," she'd informed him back
in the fall. "You won't be part of us. I'm going to raise her on
my own."

When he'd protested (though again, he wasn't sure he quite
meant to protest; he hadn't figured out whether her decision
constituted more of a deprivation or a reprieve for him), she'd

pointed out, not unkindly, "I could have not even told you I was pregnant. I could have told you it was someone else's."

She was pre-law, Deena. Years later, after getting her J.D. and passing the boards and marrying Bernard Safransky, whom she met at Cardozo and who specialized in intellectual property law and who made shitloads of money, it seemed, from the get-go, she would chuck it all for throwing pots. But back then, whether he was sitting at Sbarro's with her in the student center or standing on the doorsill of her private room at North Shore University Hospital six months later, clutching a bouquet of pink carnations rather too hard, John couldn't help deferring to the future attorney in her, the litigator against whom it was useless to fight—and it was her, not Mrs. Levin, to whom he appealed for permission to hold the baby, this once.

"Well . . . okay," Deena said with an eye roll that seemed to imply, devastatingly, that it didn't even really matter, and she'd rung for the nurse to bring the baby, who was staying in the nursery between feedings so that the new mother could get some rest.

Mrs. Levin, whether in protest or out of consideration, had vacated the visitor's chair in pursuit of a cup of decaf, so John had a comfortable base from which to support his infant daughter, whom he held reverently for twenty minutes—or five, or forty; he was out of time, lost in time—until Deena had looked up from the pages of the magazine she was flipping through and said, with unexpected gentleness, "You'd better go now, John."

Obediently he'd risen, then looked around, at a loss for what to do with the baby in his arms. Carry her back to the nursery? Ring for the nurse?

Deena patted the bed. "Bring her here."

He'd passed his daughter, in a kind of slow motion, into Deena's arms. Only once his own arms were absent the specific weight of her body did he have the sickening realization that the baby had slept the entire time. He thought of asking permission to wake her, so he might see her eyes open just once. But Deena had already fitted her, neat as a puzzle piece, in the crook of her arm, the little face tucked in against her mother's breast so that all he could glimpse now was the smoothness of her cheek, the round back of her head.

Then he'd been standing once more on the doorsill, threatening to combust with a grief he hadn't anticipated, barely able to answer when Deena wished him luck.

The rush of years between that moment's pain and this blindsided him. No one, not once in all the intervening time, had ever suggested what he'd done was wrong. But that changed nothing. On the stairs, cradling his son's mug, John bent his head, closed his eyes. The air smelled acrid, as though the memory secreted actual physical properties into the environment.

He wondered if everyone, in the end, found himself in need of redemption.

Jess had not, of course, been his only accidental offspring. The baby they'd lost had been unplanned. He was conceived, plain and simple, out of haste and lassitude—John aware that if he paused to get a condom, Ricky might lose purchase on the moment's rare passion; Ricky, aware that she played bad cop all too often, wanting the relief of playing good cop this once. And although, some weeks later, when their risk had proven consequential, and they had agreed to make room in their family for the manifestation of that consequence, they had not done so enthusiastically. John had been guilty during the first trimester of contemplating (with, yes, something like hope) the increased risk of miscarriage in women over thirty-five. When he, as if in penance for this unvoiced fantasy, offered the idea that Ricky might like to give up her job and stay home with the children, she had not fallen into his arms in gratitude. She had said, "And live on what? What you make?" They had argued then, wantonly, imprudently, about money and responsibility, about who worked harder and who wanted what, bringing up never-before-aired grievances and naming weaknesses that were close to the core of each other's character. And later all of this seemed to have set the stage for the baby's death, as if his swift passing out of their lives came in horrifying deference to their wishes.

If suffering could ever be considered payment for wrongdoing, he did not know. But he knew it had been a mistake not to speak these things earlier, not to insist he and Ricky speak of them together, all their ugly, half-hidden truths. He should have confessed from the start his lack of desire for another baby; his fear that if he told her she would despise him; his fear that she had grown to despise him anyway; his suspicion that her refusal to express anger signified a withdrawal of her love—or worse, cast aspersions on his love, called it into question. And how much did he love her? These days. Did he even know, or was that something else he'd lost sight of, grown insensate to? He remembered then, with a terrible lurch, that he had yet to tell Ricky about Biscuit and the ashes. He felt suddenly afraid, as though through long negligence he'd put his family in a kind of peril.

When the alarm went off, piercing his thoughts, it hit him almost with relief, as though it were something that had been gaining on him for ages, something he'd been staving off but which now at last had arrived. So powerful was this impression that it took him a moment to realize the sound was real, and that what he'd been smelling was smoke.

5.

"Want to go to the Skylark?" Paul was conscious of wheezing a bit. He'd hurried to grab his things from his locker, stuff them in his knapsack, and reach Baptiste at his own locker before he'd gone. He had the feeling of needing urgently to put something right between them, mend a rift, explain himself—even though Baptiste couldn't possibly have known about science class today, the things Prager and Boyd said, the foul coating they'd left.

"Can't." Baptiste, crouching, sorted leisurely through the books on the floor of his locker, all covered in brown paper, all notably unsullied, considering it was three-quarters of the way through the school year. Considering Paul's own textbook covers were worn, ripped, adorned with so many layers of ink and Wite-Out and marker and graphite they stained his palms. Baptiste's books were unblemished, devoid of all marks except the titles, copied out in his distinctive, angular hand. He hefted *The World and Its People,* slipped it into his pack. "My Grann."

Paul clicked his tongue. "Yo, she doesn't even get home till later."

Baptiste shook his head. "I can't, man."

"I got money."

"It's not the money."

It was the same frenzied hallway it always was after the bell, the same bodies jostling, same lockers slamming, same conversations and instrument cases and body odor and lunch tickets, but Paul felt it all fundamentally shift. As though transposed into another language. His baseless fears were not then baseless after all.

"Why?"

Baptiste stood. He closed his locker. Some girl nearby shrieked, shrill as tacks on glass.

"Dude. *Why?*" Yes, his voice did crack as he said this; yes, it did switch registers, making him sound every bit as desperate, as panicked, as he felt.

Baptiste turned and looked at him, close mouthed. So he had heard. Ryrie's a homo. Ryrie's sister's a retard and his parents are freaks. What else? They had a freak baby and it died and now the whole family's wack. What else? Did you see Ryrie checking out Boyd's shorts? Did you see Ryrie checking out Boyd's ass? Did you see him drawing knives and shit in his notebook? Did you see that look he gave you? Did you see the way he looks?

"Yo, if you don't want to go, just say it," Paul said. "Don't say you 'can't.'"

Baptiste sighed. "It's truth, yo."

"All right, then, how come?" Maybe Baptiste hadn't heard. Or maybe he'd heard and didn't care. It hardly mattered, since Paul could not keep from pushing, needing. One day he would tick Baptiste off and then he'd have zero friends. No time like the present. "You can't say why? 'Cause you're lying, that's why."

Baptiste shook his head slowly. He let out a silent laugh. Then he was walking down the hall, but with his pace inviting Paul to fall in beside him. At least that was one way to read it. Together they threaded among the dramas that did not involve them and yet did, that were part of their world: girls whispering, shrieking, whipping their long hair this way and that; boys leaning over them and smirking, then lurching back and throwing things, Yo, catch! playing keep-away with whatever: a juice box, a love note, a cell phone, an Ugg.

Outside, away from the building, Baptiste stopped and turned to Paul. He said, in the manner of someone divulging a great and volatile secret, "My mom's coming. My mom and my little sister. From Haiti." He pronounced it *"Ayiti."*

"Whoa. What, you mean like, today?"

Baptiste nodded.

"I thought you said she died."

"Dude. My other sister."

"I didn't even know you had another sister."

"Tifi. The little one."

"How old?"

"Eight."

They resumed walking and when they came to the spot, veered off the road the buses used and took the shortcut down the grassy hill. The apple trees, remnants of an old orchard, were frilly in bloom. Paul's feet slapped the earth. His Doc Martens, his fat black shoes. *Flam, flam, flam.* Clown feet. Beside him Baptiste walked like a cat.

"They're coming to live? For good?"

Baptiste nodded.

"That's cool," said Paul, but he was not sure. The relief he felt upon learning that Baptiste had real reason not to go with him to the Skylark today was already being replaced by a different anxiety. He was accustomed to Baptiste having only his Grann, the austerely weary Mrs. Lecompte with her superstitions and certainties, her weirdly staunch fear of intruders with knives. He was accustomed to the idea of the dead father, the dead sister, the mother stripping and making up hotel beds on an island so remote and poor she, too, might as well be no more than a memory. True, Baptiste had voiced hope that his mother one day would come to live with him, but hadn't this been understood to be a wan, even obligatory, dream? Paul was accustomed to Baptiste's faint, sweet air of longing, or (*si Bondye vle*) not longing, but resignation to lack. Above all, he was used to being the anomaly in Baptiste's life, the deviation from the mean. He did not know what use Baptiste, lacking loneliness, would have for him.

They were in the thick of the old orchard now, the trees stooped and hunched like crones all around them, their pale blossoms astir with bees. In the distance, a school bus heaved down the road, carrying its burden home. Seen from afar, school buses were happy things. "When's the last time you saw them?" Paul asked, thinking curiosity might be courteous; being also, in fact, curious.

Before Baptiste could answer a voice assailed them: "Hey, Ry-rie. Heard you like chocolate. That true?"

It came from overhead. They both looked up. It was Prager, that sociopath, crouched in the lower branches of a knobby tree. He looked funny, crouched like that, his feet on one branch, a hand hanging on to a higher one; you could spot the primate in him, you could grasp the verity of evolution, seeing him there.

Paul stood still. He heard Baptiste mutter, "Just ignore him, man," could feel Baptiste willing him to move on.

But Paul, working hard to keep his voice in the lower register, responded. "What did you say?"

"You heard." Prager dropped to the ground. He stood a few inches shorter than them, but it played as no disadvantage. The muscular breadth of his chest and shoulders—Paul could picture him lifting free weights in his basement or garage, rep after rep, pumped—struck him as grotesque, not in themselves, but for the way they made obvious a kind of effort and aspiration. Prager's Adam's apple was a protrusive, hypnotic lump; his voice seemed to emanate directly from it. "I asked if you like eating chocolate bars." His eyes flicking to Baptiste.

"Fuck you," Paul said, but breathily, without conviction. A hoot of laughter came from higher up in the tree, and a Slim Jim wrapper floated down. He looked up, trying to appear bored. It was Kenneth, Kenny Something; Paul didn't really know him. He was an eighth-grader, with coppery hair and a leather wrist-band. Paul had admired his skateboarding skills from afar.

"You'd like that, huh?" sneered this Kenny now, clambering down a ways and dropping beside Prager. He'd dropped from so high that his hands touched the ground when he landed, but when he straightened he was taller than any of them, and didn't bother brushing the dirt off his palms.

Paul had not moved. He saw, from the way Kenny regarded him, that while he had imagined his immobility conveyed strength, this was not necessarily so.

"I told you, man," Baptiste said, louder this time, "just walk away from these assholes." He began to do exactly that, stride on through the orchard, and Paul saw too late that he should have followed this advice in the first place.

Still he remained unmoving, even as he watched Kenny's foot come up, watched it connect with Baptiste's backside, watched Baptiste stumble forward and sprawl flat, his backpack flying off his shoulder and skittering down the slope. He watched Baptiste scramble to his feet and swivel around, looking from Kenny to Prager and back as if trying to figure out which had done it. He had grass stains on his shirt, dirt on his face, blood on his teeth. He spat. Kenny and Prager were laughing. Baptiste said something in his language. French, Paul used to think it was, but Baptiste said it was Creole. The words came out in a torrent, rapid and full of vitriol.

"What the fuck is that," said Prager, "voodoo?" and he and Kenny laughed harder and more derisively, as if by cursing in his mother tongue Baptiste had contributed to his own humiliation.

The filthiness of their laughter—the *incongruity* of it, amid all the creamy blossoms, all the languid, unbothered bees—seemed to Paul to break with reason. The world about him reeled.

Justice would have been a black panther springing, saliva pouring from its fangs as it lunged; an invisible, pitiless hulk with a knife, ripping his blade jerkily upward through their spinal columns. So quickly he didn't have words for the action, Paul charged them from behind. He punched Prager in the side of the head, hard enough to make him stagger left, hard enough to feel pain in his own knuckles and wrist, reverberating straight up along the nerves of his arm. He pivoted, his hunger whetted, wakened, lusting now for a second taste of this, but Kenny was fast. Kenny looked older than fourteen, come to think of it, looked like he might have been left back a grade or two. That was Paul's oddly detached thought as Kenny's foot rammed his gut. He heard a dismaying sound come from his throat as he went down: a moist, involuntary expulsion.

He landed on his rump, which did not hurt, clutching his middle, which did, unable to retch for want of wind. The tears in his eyes infuriated him; they were a result of physics, mechanics—not emotion. Or if emotion, then only the cold burn of frustration, of having been robbed; he ached to feel his fist impact Kenny's face. Yet somehow he was down here, an ungainly clod on his ass, the wind knocked out of him, ineffectual once again, while Kenny was up there, sneering. And ugly— so ugly!—all things ugly gathered and amplified in the squint of his eyes, the curl of his soft, freckled lip.

For just a moment then things turned brilliant, became the living realization of Paul's comic book fantasies, as, from nowhere, flashed Baptiste, lissome and gleaming. He seemed actually to enter the frame horizontally, as in a kung fu movie. He grabbed a fistful of shirt and jabbed, and his fist landed with an audible crunch—surely it had made a crunching sound, or maybe that was only the sound of twigs underfoot, or the sensation of Paul's own ribs expanding as air at last rushed to fill the vacuum of his lungs, a sensation at once reassuring and searingly painful. But this much was true: Baptiste's fist came away bloody. This, too, Paul saw as though on screen, the cinematic surprise of crimson glistening on Baptiste's brown knuckles, and the whites of his eyes very bright as he regarded, amazed, what he had done. Kenny, whose face Paul could not see, drew his arm back in what seemed almost leisurely fashion—as if the whole thing were a play-fight, boys acting out their fantasies in slow motion—then brought the point of his elbow smashing against Baptiste's chest. Baptiste staggered several steps back, doubling at the waist. Kenny finished with a kick in the balls and Baptiste dropped to the ground.

Through this Paul was aware, dimly, of other kids not far from them, classmates cutting in twos and threes through the orchard. If any noticed a fight going on (and how could they not?), they gave it wide berth. They were like figures belonging to another world, and they passed as no more than slivers of clothing and fragments of speech through the flower-studded branches. It lent the whole scene an inconsequential, almost serene, air, as if it were no more than a skit or a dream.

In the next instant, though, any illusion of serenity dissolved. Prager, having recovered (sort of: he was openly crying) from the blow to the side of his head, appeared above Paul, raging with a shrillness that bordered on hysteria: "You fucker, you mother-fucking dirty fucking gay retard cocksucking shit . . ."

"Hit him." Kenny's face, too, appeared above him now. Blood ran thickly from his nose. He kept wiping it with his arm. There was something horribly workaday in his tone as he coached Prager: "Get him back."

But Prager, whose fists were clenched at his sides, only continued to choke out filth through a welter of tears.

So Kenny pushed him aside and straddled Paul himself. As he knelt, his knees pinned Paul's arms to the ground. He did it automatically, as though this were how it was done. The weight of Kenny's body, coupled with Paul's grasp of his own helplessness, revolted him. He lay there. During the beating, his attention sought out small things. Parts. He was conscious of minding the sun in his eyes, of feeling inconvenienced by the stone or root that was digging into his shoulder blade. Also of Kenny's breath, which made a sharp hiss each time he landed a punch: it was a piston sound, as regular and impersonal as a machine.

When he was done, Kenny got off and muttered, "C'mon," and he and Prager left. A bird was chirping. It was a chickadee, one his grandma had pointed out a hundred times. According to her, it was saying, *See-me. See-me.* There were warm places and cool places on Paul's face. That was interesting. He adjusted his body so that the stone or root no longer pressed so painfully against his scapula. He closed his eyes against the sun. That was better. Something smelled sweet. Apple blossoms? Or just spring. It was nicer with his eyes closed and the thing not digging into his bone. *See-me. See-me.* He didn't always like his grandma, but the thought of her seeing him as he lay like this on the ground, the thought of her outrage and shock and concern filled him with sudden tenderness for her, even pity.

A shadow crossed his face. He opened his eyes. Baptiste was squatting beside him.

"Yo, man. You okay?"

Paul sat up. He did not cry. He used the front of his shirt to wipe his nose, which felt wet. The shirt came away bloody and he began to touch his face gingerly, visiting each quadrant in exploratory fashion.

"It's not your blood," Baptiste told him. He added, unable to keep a trace of pride from his voice, "I think I broke his nose."

Paul considered his shirt again in light of this revelation, and then his fingertips, which had picked up and smeared speckles of blood as he'd touched his own face. *"Gross."* He touched the area around his left eye, his fingertips gloriously cool on the skin. "I look bad?" His lip felt hot and puffy; he touched there, too.

Baptiste considered him with some thoroughness. "No. But hold still." He reached toward Paul's hair. When he took his hand away, he held an inchworm on his fingernail, tiny, and bright, bright green. He transferred it to the ground where it reared up its front end, probed the air unhurriedly, then latched onto a blade of grass, sliding its back end along. A wind stirred through the grizzled trees above them. The blossoms shook on their branches like mute bells.

"I'm sorry," said Paul. He looked at the inchworm, not Baptiste.

"What are you talking about?"

"What they said," he near-whispered.

Baptiste sucked his teeth. "Don't be a fool, yo."

But no. Everything was different. A vast chill came over Paul. It was like entering a cavern: a dank, essential coldness pervaded him. He was as somber, perhaps as sad, as he had ever been. The boys stood and retrieved their backpacks, along with the cell phones and loose change and lunch tickets that had fallen from their pockets, and continued down the hill.

He was like Biscuit now, Paul thought. Beyond pretense. For the past year and a half, he'd spent so much energy sustaining the frail hope of being popular again, of being liked. Of not being disliked. Every insult he'd pretended not to hear, every snub he'd pretended not to mind, every missing invitation he'd pretended not to have wanted—all of these had drained him, but none so much as the act of dissembling to himself. Prager and Kenny, Boyd and his cronies at the pizza shop, even Fiona Conley— who, in sticking up for him had been the most hurtful of them all, as singularly devastating as only a nice girl could be—Paul had them to thank, in a way. It was done.

They walked a long way in silence, Paul and Baptiste. They crossed 9W, went over the overpass, turned down Depew. It was not bad walking like this: the wind cool on his swollen eye and lip, his somberness upon him, him free and unaccountable for it. Halfway home it came to Paul there was something lush about giving up hope, something peaceful, even powerful, in it.

"You sure you okay?" asked Baptiste as they turned onto Elysian Avenue. His house stood at the end of the block.

"Yeah."

"You got him good in the head, man." He stopped walking and turned to Paul. "Yo, man, he *cried* in front of you. Don't worry about the other guy. He's like twice our age. A'ight? Prager knows he can't give you shit anymore."

Paul almost managed a smile.

"Look, you want to come in, get some ice?"

"So I do look bad."

"Not that much."

Paul hesitated. He cupped a hand around his left eye. In the time it had taken to walk here, it had swollen up so much he could barely see out of it.

"My Grann wouldn't mind."

At that, Paul did smile. And, perceiving the lie, declined.

6.

Further offerings are dedicated to the soul.
Its last earthly ties are severed by
the symbolism of burning a string
and breaking an egg.

Nearly two weeks ago she'd broken the egg, cracked it right into the Hudson. But the string—Biscuit had burned it many times over in her mind, but not yet in real life. Until last night, she hadn't known what string to burn. She'd been rehearsing mentally on different strings. Lying in bed at night she'd ignite the cord on her window blind, see it burning straight up like a fuse. In the car on the way to school she'd set fire to her shoelace, or to the loose thread dangling from the cuff of her sleeve. In the bathroom, getting ready for bed, she'd incinerate a curl of dental floss someone had discarded in the waste-basket. And yesterday, sitting at her desk, Biscuit had missed the whole of that day's lesson on the Sugar and Stamp Acts of 1764 and 1765, so caught up had she been in the fantasy of burning each strand of fringe, one by one, on her teacher's scarf.

Her brother's birthday had passed and the anniversary of his death had come and gone and no one but Biscuit seemed to care or even realize. She was positive of the dates because she had written them down in her denim-covered diary that had its own tiny lock and key. It was last year's diary, but she'd taken good care not to lose the key. She always put it back, together with the diary, in one of her mother's old figure skates, the pair of which Biscuit kept under her bed while she waited to grow into them.

On his birthday she'd wondered if there was going to be a cake. She knew it was probably a silly idea—the sort that, if she gave it voice, would make Paul laugh at her, not nicely—but she couldn't help imagining the scene in different ways, each admittedly more overwrought than the next: her parents baking a small round angel cake and writing *Simon* on it in yellow cursive, both of them holding the tube of icing together, her father's right hand over her mother's left. She saw them finishing the *n* and saying, "He really would've liked that," and each of them wiping a tear. In other versions, her mother alone wiped the tear, her father then putting his arm around her. In still others she saw them casting their eyes heavenward, but this really was silly, as no one in her family believed in such things.

When Simon's birthday passed unremarked, Biscuit had gotten down on her stomach and ventured in halfway under her bed, shoving aside Clue Jr. and electronic Battleship, a deflated inflatable easy chair, her mother's old figure skates, several markers without their caps, and the dust-furred plaid skirt she'd pretended to have lost so she wouldn't have to wear it to her fifth-grade chorus concert, and located the book of funeral customs. She'd stolen it from the library when Mrs. Mukhopadhyay didn't come back to work after having her baby.

She had told Biscuit she would come back. She'd go on maternity leave in June, then to Bangladesh in the autumn to visit relatives, then come back to work early in the new year. Biscuit knew when the baby was born. One day after school let out for the summer she'd been at the library and saw a birth announcement on the circulation desk in the children's room. It was a whole display, pasted on green construction paper, with a photograph of a big-headed baby with lots of dark hair, and a card announcing the arrival of Arun Jason Mukhopadhyay, 7 pounds, 11 ounces, 21 inches. Ounces and inches, like the results of a science experiment.

In January she'd begun keeping an eye out for Mrs. Mukhopadhyay, but each time she went, Biscuit saw only the same old assistant librarian who'd been filling in since summer. Then in February another woman appeared behind the circulation desk of the children's room, a white woman with white hair cut in a heavy bob that hung and swung about her face; it looked as though she were wearing a wig too far forward on her head. The same woman kept being there each time Biscuit went in. Finally in March Biscuit had asked this person if she knew when Mrs. Mukhopadhyay was coming back.

"Who?" the woman said.

"The librarian."

"I'm the librarian. Can I help you find something?"

"That's okay," Biscuit mumbled.

"I'm sorry?"

"No, thank you," Biscuit said, a little louder, moving away from the desk.

She didn't even know where Mrs. Mukhopadhyay lived, Nyack or one of the other towns, or indeed if she had ever returned from Bangladesh. Biscuit missed the sound of the librarian's silver bracelets, missed twirling herself in the librarian's plush swivel chair, watching her stir the fruit up from the bottom of her boysenberry yogurt. Standing before her bedroom mirror, she tried speaking to herself in Mrs. Mukhopadhyay's Bengali accent, but had lost the way the rhythms went, lost the lilts up and down the scale.

So she stole the book. She returned to that part of the stacks where she remembered finding it a year earlier. She didn't remember the title or author or call number, and it took her some time to locate, but locate it she did, and zipped it inside her parka. She walked past the circulation desk the way her father had coached her to walk through the hospital corridors a year earlier: like she owned the place, and she timed her walk through the electronic sensors to coincide with a man who was checking out a sizable armload. When the alarm went off, the man returned to the circulation desk with a beleaguered sigh, and Biscuit continued outside.

That had been a couple of weeks ago. Now she sat on the edge of the bathtub with the book open on her lap. Having located at last, after much paging, the passage that had provoked Mrs. Mukhopadhyay to comment, "That has a beautiful sound to it," Biscuit read it aloud to herself now:

At sunset the embers are quenched, and any charred
bones and fragments are mounded, covered with palm-
leaves, and placed in an urn fashioned from a coconut
shell and covered with a white cloth, for carrying to
the sea. When the procession reaches the shore, the
priest enters the water, and after having begged it to
bear the ashes safely away, scatters them on the waves.

Further offerings are dedicated to the soul. Its last
earthly ties are severed by the symbolism of burning a
string and breaking an egg.

The acoustics in the bathroom were very good. Biscuit was
confident Mrs. Mukhopadhyay would have been equally pleased
with her reading today. She had done the first bit of the ritual—
minus the coconut shell of course, and using proxy ashes (she
had no knowledge of what had been done with her brother's
body after he died, nor was it anything she dared to ask)—and
the last bit, with the egg. All that was left was burning the string.

Biscuit was shy of fire. She'd lit a match only twice in her life,
both times holding the stick so timidly, and conducting it along
the strip so lightly, that she'd had to strike it several times before
producing even a spark, and all the while cringing so exaggerat-
edly Paul had made fun of her, scrunching up his own face like
a drawstring bag. Paul was the opposite. He was, as he liked to
say, a real pyro. Whenever their mother set the table with candles,
he'd ask to light them. Same with jack-o'-lanterns, same with
birthday cakes. He'd let the match burn down so far that Biscuit,
watching, would feel dizzy. The front part of the stick would

blacken and crumple while the living flame stole closer to his fingers, spreading just before it a line that gleamed like moisture, as if the wood had begun to sweat. Once he'd gotten them lit, Paul couldn't keep his hands off the candles. He'd stick his fingertips in their pools of wax and let the wax cool into hard little caps, with which he'd tap out muted rhythms on the table. Biscuit would look on jealously, wanting but afraid to stick her own fingers in the liquid wax. Sometimes Paul let her have the little caps when he was done; she saved them in a special box she kept in one of her mother's figure skates.

Only if their parents were not looking, Paul would pass his finger back and forth through the flame, quickly at first, then slower, slower, at last so slowly he'd stop a moment and hold it still in the flame. Then he'd hold up his finger and show Biscuit the black mark that did not seem like it could be anything other than what he told her, grinning, it was: his own singed epidermis.

"Paul!" she'd cry, as much in reverence as reproach.

"What? It doesn't hurt." And he'd lick his finger and wipe the blackness on his pants.

He was swagger and she was swoon. She understood that the role she played in it was key, and also that it was part sham.

Still, at least some of Biscuit's fear of fire was real, as was all her lack of experience. She set the book on the floor next to the box of matches. The house was still. She could feel its stillness through and through, feel it right inside her bones. If she were the gray lady, she'd be able to sense even more things. The emptiness of all houses. The contents of people's dreams. The causes of their sadness, as revealed by the shapes left behind in their sheets.

Outside the bathroom window light played through the shadows of branches. Scraps of Hudson glinted blue. It was a little past two. She had not skipped the whole day; she'd gone dutifully to school that morning, arrived on time, handed in her homework, done her math worksheets and her language arts exam and gym, then slipped quietly away after recess.

A great mistake people made about Biscuit was to assume her unpragmatic. She was not. She was capable even of being strategic. She had, for instance, carefully timed the event of the burning of the string. She knew perfectly well, sitting on the edge of the bathtub, gathering up the box of matches now with shaking hands, that her father was due home from work at any minute.

Yet there was whimsy about her, and caprice; people were right in this. She had not known, for example, that she would do this part of the ritual until just last night, when Jess brought home a cake from the bakery. Jess kept bringing things into the house, little gifts: candy necklaces, pints of ice cream, colored soaps in the shape of flowers, a pink Depression glass vase from one of the antique shops in town. "It's fun giving things," she'd say with a shrug when they thanked her. She'd act like it was nothing. Biscuit's mother had made quite a fuss over the little vase, which found a home on the windowsill above the kitchen sink. She'd made more of a fuss over the little vase than she had over the mandolin Biscuit's father had given her a week earlier. And they'd all made a fuss over the bakery cake (which had been, in point of fact, exceptional: chocolaty and dense and decorated all around the rim with orange buttercream roses)—but it was the sort of fuss you made with guests, Biscuit noticed. It didn't matter that they really liked the cake; their exclamations had a ring of artifice, of striving, a note of form's sake. Just as Jess's shrugging off the importance of things—the cake, the vase, the soap—was not real.

At any rate, there had been no birthday cake for Simon, but then soon after Jess had brought home this cake, and it was in a bakery box tied with bakery string, which she snipped off right at the table, and Biscuit had thought, *Aha*. She pocketed it, only at that moment hatching her plan. She smoothed the string across her lap now. It was thin and festive-looking, candy-striped. She climbed onto the rim of the bathtub and looped the string around the shower rod. She thought she'd been admirably responsible in choosing for her site the most fireproof room in the house.

Climbing down, Biscuit retrieved the box of matches from the floor. She took one out, being careful to shut the box again. She slid the match along the phosphorous strip. Not even a spark. She tried again, willing herself to press harder, strike faster, and then again and once more: nothing. She wiped her hand on her jeans, tried again. The match broke. She bit her lip. "There, there," she said. She fished out a new match, struck it. It flared with a sharp hiss. Biscuit felt heat seize her finger like teeth. She dropped the match with a cry.

Because she had not remembered to slide the box shut after extracting the second match, it sat in her hand with its inner compartment jutting far out, like the lower jaw of a hungry dragon, and this dragon, right before Biscuit's eyes, snapped up the falling match quite neatly, even greedily, upon which all its rows of skinny teeth burst into flame.

With a scream she flung the box away. It landed on the doorsill, burning brightly. Her palm was hot and she pressed it to her chest, inside of which her heart pounded. But as she stood there, recovering from the shock and fright, watching the flames and seeming still to feel the heat, the way it had come alive so suddenly bright and hissing in the palm of her hand, a peculiar thrill came over her, a scandalous, scoundrel excitement: this was more than she had hoped for.

Black smoke, flecked with ruby sparks, writhed upward. The wooden doorsill, painted white, had begun visibly to scorch in the area around the blazing box. Even if she were to douse the fire immediately a mark would be left. She stood where she was. Something like a laugh trembled in her throat. It was all wrong, both what she'd done and this urge to grin, to laugh, but the plainer the problem grew, the lighter she felt. It was beyond her. Beautifully, blissfully beyond her. Someone else would have to fix it.

Not until the smoke alarm went off did Biscuit come out of her state of exhilarated paralysis. Coughing, aware of a rawness in the back of her throat, she went to the sink. Her eyes stung. She turned on the tap, dumped all the toothbrushes out of the toothbrush cup—in her agitation scattering them all across the floor—and held the cup under the faucet.

The sudden presence of her father—although expected, although precisely planned for—was like something out of a dream: there he loomed in the mirror over the sink, where a moment earlier there had been no one. He looked large and angry. Biscuit loved him for it. His lips were set tight in his beard.

He snatched the cup from her hand, pushed her aside with forgivable roughness, crossed the bathroom in two large steps, trodding on toothbrushes as he did, and poured water over the fire, creating an instant cloud of steam and smoke, within which orange tongues still flickered. Paul should have been here, thought Biscuit. He would have been in heaven. The alarm keened and keened. Her father tossed the cup in the sink, threw a towel in the tub, ran the water, got it soaked, and laid it out over the whole blackened, still smoldering doorsill. Then he crossed the hall, disappeared for a moment into Paul's room, and came out carrying Paul's desk chair, onto which he climbed in order to reach the smoke detector, which he ripped from its mount with such force the plastic cracked. A piece fell to the floor and the house fell quiet. Her father stood there a moment, holding the smoke detector in one hand, inspecting the other, on whose index finger Biscuit saw a small gash.

She stepped over the doorsill and came tentatively to him.

He climbed down, breathing heavily.

In the meekest of voices: "Is your finger okay?"

"*This* is not okay! This is not *okay*!"

She stared. He'd yelled. His eyes were wide, his nostrils bull-like, flaring, and nothing about him was not furious. She didn't know the last time her father had been angry at her like this. Never.

"What are you even doing *home*? *Again*. During *school*."

She looked at the floor. Her heart was a mouse curled in a ball. Yet even now, the truth was she was not sorry; or she was, a little—sorry about his finger, anyway, and sorry to have him angry with her. But not that she'd caused a fire, not that she'd caused notice.

"You cut school again."

She didn't answer.

"What are Mom and I supposed to do?" The hallway stank of doused flame, wet charred wood. "Can you tell me?" Loud, loud was his voice. Clanging. "HELLO?"

She was studying the wooden floorboards, the grain, the way it made patterns and the way those patterns got interrupted, and also repeated. She was making herself as tiny as the grain, intricately traveling along its traverses and swirls.

He threw the broken smoke detector across the hall. The sudden motion made her startle. It smashed apart. The battery skidded across the floor and into Paul's room. She looked at him, indignant, awed. "You skip *school,* you put yourself in *danger,* I don't know what you were trying to do at the Hook the other day but you could have *drowned,* now you're setting *fires*—what? Is this"—he broke off, and a terrible kind of laugh escaped him—"is this a cry for help?" Sarcasm edged his voice. "Do we not give you enough *attention*? Do we not give you enough *love*?"

Biscuit, quiet Biscuit, quiet, noticing Biscuit who did not yell, who never talked back, opened her mouth as though some hidden catch had been released. "You don't! You don't! You don't! You don't! You don't! You don't! You don't! You don't! You don't! You don't! You don't! You don't! You don't!"

The words like claws sprung from her throat. The tendons in her neck were copper wire. She could not stop repeating it, over and over, and each time she did the truth of the words shone plainer and plainer.

"And I didn't fall in!" she screamed, finding a break in the rhythm at last. Her voice pitched high and metallic, offensive to her own ears. "I did it on purpose! I wanted to go in the river!"

The confession erupted with the ferocity of an accusation. Which it was.

She was aware of the surprise on her father's face, a look of stunned concern that seemed to siphon off his anger, leaving him as if physically depleted, smaller in his skin.

Biscuit turned and tore down the stairs, smacking the treads with violent, headlong force. As she neared the bottom the front door swung open, and what she saw there stopped her.

"Dad!" she called. *"Dad!"* and the quality of her voice was altogether different.

Paul entered slowly, his T-shirt torn at the neck. One of his eyes was swollen shut and his lip was split, crusted with blood.

Biscuit hadn't known her father was capable of such speed; almost before she said Dad a second time, he'd passed her on the stairs and landed in the hall.

Paul raised a hand, deflecting him. "I'm all right," he said, the words stiff: his fat lip. He let his backpack drop to the floor, then screwed up his good eye and cocked his head. "Do I smell smoke, or are you just happy to see me?"

7.

As soon as she got in the car, Ricky slipped off her shoes and tucked them beside the glossy black shopping bag perched so improbably on her briefcase. She hadn't driven in stocking feet in years, and the feel of the ridged pedals against her soles plunged her back into her twenties. Her first car: a white Fiero with no air conditioner. How tangled her hair would get in the wind. She'd put the volume up, slide her sunglasses on, guide the stick silkily through its positions. At red lights, reapplying lipstick in the rearview mirror, noticing who among the other idling drivers was noticing her. The game of switching lanes, the game of downshifting, upshifting, her foot so smooth on the clutch even she could barely feel the moment the gears engaged. Working the shift, the feel of its slick round knob, hard and tight in the hollow of her palm.

John had not owned a car when she first met him. He'd lived in Hell's Kitchen, near the theater district, and been an avid subway man. On summer weekends they'd take her Fiero out to Jones Beach, or to the Hamptons if someone had invited them; in autumn they'd tool up to Westchester to pick apples or to picnic at Storm King. Once, in late September, she'd driven him all the way up to Split Rock Hole, an old haunt she knew from her SUNY New Paltz days. "Where are you taking me?" he asked, as she led him through the woods. "You'll see," was all she would say until they reached the swimming hole. They'd gone in, cold as it was, with nothing on. They'd fucked in the water, a feat, a coup, for the water had been shockingly cold—so cold, John gauged, pinking up a little through his beard, he didn't think it would work. But Ricky had told him yes it would, and she had proven right.

Wherever they had gone in those days, Ricky would always drive. They both liked what it did to them: the effect of her in control (at twenty-three she looked seventeen, her body that small and sleek, her hair hanging midway down her back) and him passive (at twenty-eight he could have passed for late thirties, already burly and bearded, with eye crinkles she liked to trace with her fingernail), a reversal they played with, pushed to exciting limits.

Now driving was a drudge, something she'd grown to detest. The wasted hours, the isolation, the unvarying commute back and forth across the river—it had become the opposite of motion, had become the very emblem of her stasis.

The traffic leading up to the tolls was stop and go, as always on Fridays. Ricky put on the radio, tried a few stations, shut it off. She checked her cell phone, checked her fingernails, checked the gas gauge, turned the radio back on. The fact of impatience was not unusual but the degree of it was; she had decided to make a formal proposal to Jess that she move in, that she live with the Ryries not only throughout her pregnancy but beyond. She'd mentioned the idea to John that first night Jess had arrived, and had floated it in a nebulous, noncommittal way with Jess herself on various occasions, but today she would issue the invitation outright, in practical, unmistakable terms. All week she'd been giving the issue of space serious thought and had determined they could convert the little den downstairs into a bedroom. It would mean having the TV in the living room, something she'd sworn would never happen, but none of the rest of the family would mind, and she could tolerate it. Jess could sleep on the couch at first, and slowly they'd refurnish the room—how perfect that this was the beginning of yard sale season. It wouldn't need much, just a proper bed, a dresser, some curtains for the French doors (visions of Ricky and Jess going together to the fabric store, never mind that neither of them could sew). Eventually, of course, a crib. Ricky saw it over against the far wall, underneath the windows. Pine, maybe, and unpainted, finished with only a light stain.

The walnut sleigh crib John had found for a hundred bucks on Craigslist last year, driving across the county by himself one Saturday to pick it up from someone's house over her protestations that they didn't need a crib right away, that the baby could sleep in a dresser drawer its first several weeks; the crib he'd nevertheless insisted on assembling in a corner of their bedroom, and furnishing with a new mattress and flannel sheets, and in which he'd stacked a few bags of disposable newborn diapers and a box of wipes, along with the assortment of little outfits, onesies and booties and ladybug hats that had been gifts from coworkers and friends and which were still wrapped in their tissue paper and boxes; the crib upon whose side rail he mounted the mobile he'd impetuously gone out and bought, a plastic mobile with plump blue-and-yellow felt moons and stars that perambulated slowly to the tune of "Twinkle, Twinkle, Little Star"—that crib they'd sold for forty-five dollars after the baby died.

But Ricky would not think of that crib, whose incriminating hulk she'd worked hard to ignore during the last days of her pregnancy. She would not have to think of that crib because there was a new crib to think about, a clean new crib with simple straight lines and the palest of stains. It would sit beneath the den window. The great thing (without even meaning to, she was rehearsing her pitch) was the light; the den got the prettiest morning light, and a view of the river, as well, at least when the trees were bare—as they were in November, when the baby was due. A rocking chair, they'd want, too. Ricky could picture sitting in it, looking out the windows, a few leaves the color of pumpkin still clinging to the trees; the river already looking wintry, opaque; the new baby, that most tender of weights, tucked deep inside its own slumbers.

Ricky was not stupid. She was not deluded. She did not think that if Jess said yes, her baby would somehow become or replace the missing Ryrie baby. Nor did she suppose that by nurturing John's daughter and grandchild she would redeem herself in her husband's or anyone's eyes for all that she'd done or failed to do during this past year. If anyone were to suggest these motives,

Ricky would have balked. But fantasies are by their natures reductive. And the wonder of it was that these past few days, her indulgence in the fantasy had caused a shift inside her, had brought a real sense of movement. It wasn't that she put faith in the fantasy. It was that she put faith in the shift.

Would John?

That was the question, and the real cause, she realized, of her keyed-up impatience on this particular drive home. He had not been alive to her (nor she to him), had not taken unchecked pleasure in her (nor she in him), for a very long time. It was not a matter of simply a year. This reached back well before the baby's death. She tried to remember the last time it had been all good between them, free of fear and recrimination, free of anger and artifice. What came to mind were nights at Cabruda Lake when the children were fast asleep in the cabin, and she and John would lie on the floating dock, a loon's laugh rippling the air, a hundred fish stirring the black depths beneath them. They'd watch the bats flit overhead, mark the occasional lonely airplane coursing between them and the stars. What came to mind were nights in empty theaters when he'd let her hold the pounce bag and work the nail gun, and amid the smells of sawdust and talc, and the sound of The Doors, he'd spread a blanket on the dirty stage floor and lower her down under the work lights' glare. They'd discover things to do with each other among the half-built sets, something new, it seemed, every time. Even then, had it been "all good"? Ricky wanted badly to think it.

She glanced over at the diminutive black shopping bag atop her briefcase. The bag's very smallness thrilled her. She pictured how she would dazzle John with its contents—dazzle him, perhaps, in spite of himself. The proposal she was planning to make Jess was also meant, more important, to proposition her husband. Look, John, she would really be saying, even as she mouthed the invitation to his firstborn: I can open my heart. Look, John, you have not led a blameless life. I have made mistakes, but so have you. You have made mistakes, and your mistakes have led to other mistakes and look, John: see how I open my heart to them, see how I admit them into my home, the fruit of your mistakes. If I were truly unworthy, if I were beyond reach of your love, could I do such a thing?

Still stuck at the tolls, Ricky leaned over and parted the cream-colored tissue that crested the bag. Inside, cocooned with inordinate care, in more layers of tissue, were a chemise of black silk trimmed in velvet, and, encased separately (as if they were not scraps of lingerie but pieces of china or crystal, or Fabergé eggs) matching panties. Ricky had never ventured inside this boutique before, although she'd noticed it often, always cordoning it off in her mind as an establishment she had no cause to frequent. And then yesterday, passing it on the way back to her office with her tuna hero and Fresca from the deli on the corner, her gaze had flitted over the window display as it had a hundred times, only this time, instead of continuing apace, she'd stopped and allowed herself to drink it in. A reclining mannequin wore a navy tulle bodystocking; another, on tiptoe, wore a dove-gray balconette bra and matching culotte, both of which were trimmed with intricate pleats and ruches; a third stood angled coquettishly away in order to show that its black bustier laced up the back with trailing pink ribbon.

Silly things: but no. Cheap: but in fact terribly expensive. The midday light had cast a glare on the plate glass, so that Ricky's reflection appeared alongside the mannequins, and again instead of glancing away she let herself look. Her swimmer's body was still lithe; her hair, in the sun, showed its maple-syrup tones. Her eyes looked tired, shadowed and even sunken, but that might have been due to the partial quality of the reflection. She'd had no time left on her break, but resolved then to go inside the shop the following afternoon. And she had; today she'd spent her entire lunch break fingering the delicate garments, gently parting the hangers on their racks, selecting an armful to try.

"Shall I put those in a room for you?" the girl had asked, and Ricky thanked her with the casual ease of one who shops regularly for high-end lingerie. Only in the privacy of the fitting room, which was (the affectation, the whimsy made Ricky laugh aloud when she saw it) round and appointed like the inside of a genie's bottle—a love seat mounded with apple green cushions, swaths of pink-gold fabric draped from the ceiling—only as she stood naked before the trio of angled mirrors had Ricky blushed, not from embarrassment but from pleasure.

This past week had been a revelation. A return to touch. She'd known a resumption of sex was inevitable—that or the dissolution of her marriage. And she'd known it would have to happen soon: a year's abstinence was no small thing. What surprised Ricky was her own appetite, not simply its strength but its very existence. She'd thought it lost, gone forever with the baby. Gone with what she'd done, the choice she'd made. She'd assumed that whenever she initiated touch (that the responsibility for doing so fell to her seemed obvious), she would do it uncomplainingly, proficiently, and absent any desire. Her lack of desire might even help their marriage: a penance for a wrong. This is what she told herself, gearing up for the act. And then Jess had appeared, her presence a reminder of her entitlement, and if that was the spur, if Ricky's final motivation came down to territory, came down to staking claim, so be it.

The revelation was that after the bowls of ice cream, after the news that Jess was with child, after Ricky and John had shut the door to their own bedroom and lay whispering past midnight in the light of the streetlamp, when Ricky cupped her husband's head and guided it to her breast; when she let him lie there, rising and falling with her breath, her fingers moving through the curls at the back of his neck with a gentle, proprietary pressure, as if to assure them both that he belonged there—she was stirred as she had not expected to be, repositioned. Her own movement toward him had opened her.

She blushed to think of it: the moment she'd guided him back into her after more than a year. Through the tolls at last, she glided over the bridge, the girders splitting the late light, piecing and repiecing the smoky-looking sky. So vivid was the memory, she felt John as if he were there with her, there in her, and was still blushing as she exited the thruway and looped around the ramp. At the traffic light she looked at herself in the rearview mirror. Her eyes were bright, her cheeks darkly pink. She remembered something she'd once heard about blushing.

Three times, after the baby's death, she'd gone to see a psychiatrist. The referral had been among the discharge papers she'd received at the hospital; the obstetrician had urged her to go, and she had, rather sullenly and dutifully, made the first appointment. The psychiatrist's office was in the hospital; perhaps she'd gone in hopes of running into Dr. Abdulaziz. In any case, she was put off by the psychiatrist, who was not the gentle elderly person she'd expected but a younger man, hardly older than herself, with, she thought, a critical and even combative manner. He didn't ask her about the baby. Ricky supposed he was waiting for her to bring it up. It was like a game, like fencing or chess. It made her want to win, which she decided she would do by revealing nothing, and so they passed many long minutes in dead silence, punctuated by fragments of random conversation, like inept guests at a cocktail party. Midway through the third appointment he'd asked, apropos of nothing as far as she could tell, "Do you carry a lot of shame?"

"What? Why?"

"You blush a lot."

"I do?" She cupped her face. "No, I don't." What had they just been talking about? It escaped her. "I don't think I do. Anyway, shy people blush. I mean—what, blushing means you're ashamed?"

The psychiatrist had shrugged, as if it were nothing to him. "That's how we generally read it."

She'd been incensed. Who was he to bring up shame, when she had gone to him in grief? At the end of the fifty minutes, he asked whether she'd like to set up another appointment.

"I don't think so," she said, as if it were nothing to her.

Only after he did not try to convince her otherwise did she realize she'd been relying upon him to do so. In the car afterward she'd sobbed. Though she had not even liked him, she felt bereft.

Now at the light, which had turned green, as she sat remembering that day from last spring, Ricky filled with a cold, wringing anguish. Its source was a terrible realization and it seemed to saturate her, slowly, as though she were sinking in it, drowning. She had been banking on Jess as a kind of second chance, an opportunity to remind John of her own goodness. But she had been banking, too, on Jess's being an artifact, a living reminder of how things had been, of who John had once been, the old self he still carried folded within, as we all must eternally carry our previous iterations: not blameless, not good only.

But what Ricky now saw, as if it squatted leering at her through the windshield, was the fault in her own arithmetic. The idea that Jess somehow balanced the equation, that John's being responsible for her paternity equaled or canceled out Ricky's infidelity, was false. They were not the same at all. She'd been trying so desperately to convince him of it, willing him to sign on, to adhere to this logic. Wasn't that the very thought she'd been attempting to press into him the other night when she bit him, branding the flesh of his thigh: that we are all helpless before our bodies? And the next night, when he showed her what she'd done—lifted her head to see the mark, stark against the white skin, patterned there with sparse black curls: the purple stain of her bite—wasn't it clear, when she bit him there again, that it was only a kind of surrender, an admission of her own baseness; a return, blameless and profound, to what he'd first loved about her, a boring back into pure element? And in spurring him to be rough in turn, eliciting from him a like carnality, she'd meant only to win her case. To win him.

The car behind her honked and Ricky drove on. Not until she'd pulled into their driveway did she realize what she'd done: for the first time in a year, crossed the Tappan Zee without rehearsing the nearness of the guardrail, the number of degrees she'd have to turn the steering wheel, the force with which she'd have to accelerate in order to drive off the bridge.

INSIDE THE HOUSE she heard the television going, quick bursts of sitcom laughter. Looking through the living room, through the French doors that led into the den, she saw the silhouetted backs of Biscuit's and Paul's heads; they were snuggled close together, sitting as they had often done when they were small, on the listing old couch, watching TV. She felt a flash of remorse; they had no idea the den was about to become Jess's room. It was the same difficult remorse she'd felt ten years ago, on the eve of Biscuit's birth, knowing Paul was about to be robbed of something: his place in the sun, his unchallenged primacy. She remembered his innocence of the fact, how his three-year-old's inability to comprehend what was about to happen and what it would mean to him had made him more tender to her, more terribly lovable.

They looked just so to her now: soft, ingenuous, mesmerized by the flickering light of the screen, lost to themselves and to the world. Paul was wearing his ridiculous hat, the filthy one he'd bought himself at the street fair last fall. Biscuit—when had Biscuit gotten so tall?—had her head inclined slightly toward her brother, as though she might in a moment rest it against his shoulder, a thing Ricky could not imagine her doing, nor Paul tolerating. Yet their postures, their proximity, made them look like close siblings. Were they? Ricky was not used to thinking of them as close. She was struck by an impulse to touch them, to see their faces before she went to find John, before she went to find Jess and ask her to stay. She would just say hello to her children first.

The sound of John's voice stopped her.

"That's crazy," he said, from the kitchen. He was not quite yelling.

Ricky tensed. He must be arguing with Jess. There was a silence.

When he spoke again, his anger—a thing he rarely displayed—was more distinct. "Well, then, the policy's nonsense."

She glanced toward the den again; the television volume was high and the children seemed oblivious. She strained to hear whatever Jess was saying in reply, but could not make out even the murmur of her voice. Ricky realized she was standing with her shoes still in her hand, like a guilty person, a spy. She set them down, along with her briefcase and the glossy black bag, and walked into the kitchen.

Jess sat at the round table beside two large shoe boxes—boot boxes, more like—both of them made over into little scenes. For a moment, Ricky mistook them for her husband's work. John had made dozens of set models over the years, many of which resided at the college, but some of which had found a permanent home languishing in their dampish basement, on the shelves next to the washing machine. On second thought, she realized they were nothing like John's work. These were more like a child's school project. There was something at once rough and precious about them: the scale was off, and the workmanship imperfect, yet the overall result signaled a degree of investment, of care, that was beguiling, and which placed them, on third thought, in a whole other realm: these could hardly be the work of a child. Even at a fleeting glance, Ricky realized these were not models for something else but creations in their own right.

Jess turned as Ricky came in and gave her a rather wan smile, wan and something else—sympathetic? condoling?—before facing around again toward John, who stood with his back to them both, the cord of the wall phone snaking out from under one arm, so that Ricky realized it was not Jess who had raised his ire but the unknown conversant on the other end of the line. For that she was relieved. Ricky found herself placing a hand on Jess's back. She brimmed with the urge to tell her about the plan, the proposal: how they would remake the den, visit yard sales, procure rocking chair and cradle, about all the care Jess would receive if she stayed. It was more important than ever that she say it in front of John; he had to hear her make the offer. She pursed her lips, willed him to finish his call, whatever it was.

After a long silence he spoke again. "Well, then I'd like to talk with the superin— . . . I said if he's not available, then I'd like to talk with the superintendent. . . . No, before Monday."

A pause. Ricky tried to work out what was going on. The superintendent. It must be Biscuit, the truancy thing. Had she been skipping again?

"Then give him *my* home number and ask him to call me." John's voice was frighteningly deliberate, the words paced with unnatural evenness. "That's correct."

This silence lasted longer. John, though he must have heard her come in, still did not turn around, and Ricky, despite her impatience, found herself drawn to him for this very reason, his single-minded dedication to the matter at hand. Steadfast, she thought, taking in his broad shoulders and large dark head with something like pride. John was steadfast. She had always felt (and wasn't it odd?) both attracted to and rebuked by this quality in him. Perhaps—very likely—it was the chief reason she'd married him. It could not be—she would not believe it—too late for them. She prepared to take him in her arms once he was off the phone, to hear the story of his frustrating dealings with school officials, to soothe and admire him, show she was grateful—and then to invite his daughter to stay, and receive his appreciation, his gratitude, for that.

"No," John said now, and his voice nearly shook with the effort to contain his emotion, "what I *said* was, if you'd seen his face, you'd realize that can't be the whole story."

Silence again, and something swift and burning clouded Ricky's mind like smoke in a bowl.

"Yes," said John. "Yes . . . I'd appreciate that. Thank you." He hung up.

When he turned and met her eyes, his own were cold. He filled her in with a tone of indifference that made her head pound. That had been the school principal on the phone. Not Upper Nyack, no; this was not about Biscuit. Although she had cut school that afternoon and set a fire in the upstairs bathroom. This was about Paul. He'd been in a fight on school grounds, which meant a mandatory three-day suspension. The other parent was insisting Paul had thrown the first blow, and although Paul would not say why he'd hit the other boy, he had not disputed the parent's claim—although from the look of him, he'd received the worse beating. John had considered bringing him to the emergency room.

"When did this happen?" Ricky's breath came shallow and short. "What did you mean about setting a fire? Is Paul all right?"

It happened right after school. Paul seemed all right; he was icing his eye. No, he wouldn't say anything about the cause of the fight. Fuck if he knew about the fire, Biscuit wouldn't talk, either. And now—John checked his watch—he had to go.

"Go?"

"The theater. I have an opening." His words were clipped, as if it disgusted him to grant her even the length of his vowels. "Bye, Jess," he said, differently. "Thanks for all your help this aft."

Jess reached up a hand and he squeezed it, and the ease of the gesture wrenched.

Ricky followed John into the front hall, almost tripping to reach him before he left. The fear sprung from deep in her gut. She felt she might vomit. "Why didn't you tell me this was going on? Why didn't you call me at work?" An image came to her mind of where she'd been earlier, not at her desk but in the lingerie shop for an extended lunch break, turning this way and that before the three-way mirror. "Why didn't you call my cell?"

John grabbed his jacket from the coatrack and put his hand on the doorknob. His face looked gray and shuttered, but when he spoke his voice came out without bile and was the more devastating for it. "What difference would that have made?"

"I could have come home, John."

He regarded her.

"I would have come home early. What?"

"You haven't been home in a year." He said it very quietly. The door closed behind him.

"Oh, God," whispered Ricky in the empty space. Her heart hammering violently, she leaned her forehead against the door. "Thank you for noticing that."

PART FOUR

Eight Years Ago

Paul begins the game out of boredom, out of the blue, forty miles outside of Albany. "Apples or applesauce?"

His mother, seated directly in front of him, draws a long breath, as if it's a tricky decision. "Apples." Within seconds she volleys back: "Raincoat or flip-flops?" She is the one who taught him this game.

Paul looks out his window. He is five, buckled into his booster seat. The sun on the stretch of blasted rock at the side of the road is so bright it makes his eyes ache. The sky is blue like the public pool. Black puddles glimmer on the highway ahead. Every single one of them vanishes just before they reach it.

"Raincoat," he says. And then, "Kangaroo or roach?"

"Kangaroo. Balloons or pizza?"

"Balloons."

"Why?" asks his father, who is driving.

"There's no why in the Or Game, John." His mother turns around and rolls her eyes at Paul, and then she turns and makes a silly face at his father, too, so he will know she is only teasing.

His father glances at his mother and frowns.

It's the end of August and they are going camping, as they always do, for two weeks. Not real camping in a tent, although Paul has wished for a tent ever since he got to go inside one in his friend Alexi's backyard. Alexi's tent was tan and inside it smelled like an old glove, and the sun lit up the cloth walls like the insides of a peach or, he imagined, like the insides of his own cheeks, and there were many zippers and you had to take your shoes off before you could go in.

At Cabruda Lake they camp in the cabin his mother's grandparents built. The walls still have bark on them. It has no bathroom, only a privy down a path, full of moths and daddy longlegs. Baths and toothbrushing you do in the lake. The lights are not like at home; his parents turn them on with matches and they make a soft pop and then a hissing noise, and you make them brighter or dimmer with a metal key. Mornings are cold even in summer, and the cabin has a woodstove for heat. Every morning Paul sits by it and drinks his milk while looking into the miniature orange city that burns beneath the logs. His milk comes from the short fridge, which runs on the gas they have to bring with them in a red tank. Water comes from the spigot attached to a tree out front. The spigot's metal handle is rusty and Paul can't turn it by himself. The cabin is one big room and two little curtained-off nooks for sleeping, one for him and Biscuit, one for his parents.

This year is different because he has a new sister who is coming with them. He has never met her. She is fifteen. He told Alexi this and Alexi didn't believe him. They are picking her up not at her home, which would take them too far out of the way, but in a city near her home, called Albany, which is a fine name, smooth and pale; he imagines tall towers, white as soap, rising steeply from a hillside. The sister's name is Jessica and she will sleep (he has asked) in her sleeping bag on the couch in the cabin's main room.

"What time is it?" asks Paul.

"Ten twenty-eight," says his mother.

"What time did we leave?"

"Around nine."

He figures it out, drawing an invisible clock on the window. "So we'll be there in thirty-two minutes?" He'd been told the ride from their house to the Albany train station was two hours. Then another three to Cabruda Lake.

"I don't know. Something like that, if we don't hit traffic. I don't know if we left exactly at nine."

"Is Biscuit still sleeping?" asks his father.

His mother looks over her shoulder. "Biscuit is."

Biscuit is fat. She is strapped into her car seat, which is stained with cranberry juice and gritty with graham cracker crumbs. Her face is pink and her wispy hair is curling and damp at the temples, even though she is wearing nothing but a T-shirt and a diaper. Thin red crescents made by her pacifier mark her cheeks, but when his mother tries to slip the pacifier out, Biscuit, without waking, begins sucking on it hard. "Paul, honey, are you hot back there?"

Paul shakes his head, forgetting she cannot see him.

"Paul?"

"I said no."

"You didn't say anything," says his father, rubbing his fingers down the side of his beard as Paul has seen him do hundreds of times. "You have to answer when someone talks to you."

"I did," says Paul, but in a voice too low for anyone to hear.

Biscuit has stopped sucking again, her mouth gone slack. They drive another mile. Paul pinches the ring on the pacifier. He holds perfectly still while the trees rush by the window; then, quick as lightning, he plucks it out. At first Biscuit does nothing. Then she smacks her lips. She makes a sound like a creaky gate and scrunches up her face. Here it comes. He can feel the pressure mounting like excitement in his own chest. She kicks out with both legs and, even before she has completely awoken, begins to cry.

"What's the matter, little one?" says their mother, her voice all of a sudden musical, pastel, all pinks and blues, a voice she uses often for Biscuit, never for Paul or for his father. Paul studies the back of his father's head, the slice of profile he can see from where he sits. He is frowning, concentrating, both hands on the wheel.

"Were you sleeping?"

"Pie-oo." Biscuit can talk all right, but when she first wakes up she refuses to.

"We're still in the car, sweetheart. Did you have a nice nap?"

Biscuit grunts.

"In a little while we'll stop, and you can get out of your car seat."

"*Pie*-oo."

"Oh, her pacifier. Paul, did it fall down under her? Would you please feel around for it?"

Paul turns toward his sister and grins. One of his bottom teeth is missing. The other one is loose. He wiggles it at her with his tongue. She scowls. He brings out his hand from behind his back. The pacifier dangles from his fingers.

Biscuit's eyes widen. "Mm!" she says, one fat heel thrusting forward.

He is grinning so broadly his cheeks hurt.

"Did you find it, Paul?"

He doesn't answer. Biscuit is making short, furious shrieks, like dog yaps.

"Give it to her."

He circles it slowly in the air, closer and closer, before popping it in her mouth. Instantly she resumes sucking and it is quiet except for the rhythmic, rubbery squeak. "You're not my only sister," he whispers. She blinks at him slowly, like a bored queen. Already her lids are growing heavy again, her eyes glazed. "I'm your only brother. I have two sisters. You only have one." She lets her head rest back against the wing of her car seat. Paul watches without blinking. They are having a staring contest, which he officially declares in his head, starting: *now*. He is confident; he is the master of staring, and he stares and stares. Sure enough: her eyes fall shut.

IN THE MIDDLE of their first night at the lake John gets sick, throwing up on the flat stone just outside the cabin door, which is as far as he gets before being overcome. Paul and Biscuit do not wake. Jess does and calls softly from her sleeping bag, spread out on the couch, "What's the matter? Should I do something?" but Ricky, having followed him out, replies in a low voice through the screen door, "No, it's all right—go back to sleep."

Ricky has never known John to vomit, not in all the years they have been together. She would like to stand behind him and hold his forehead, as she would if he were one of the children, as he has done for her on many occasions during her pregnancies, but he is too tall, even crouched over; she cannot both stand clear of the vomit and reach his brow.

"Poor John," she murmurs instead, between her husband's heaves. She'd been angry with him when they'd gone to bed, and cannot help feeling a little glad that he has gotten sick, not because she is still angry but because it makes him helpless, makes him *hers,* and draws forth her desire to forgive him.

She'd been angry because of the way he treated her all day: meanly, or at any rate, grouchily. At first, as they drove toward the Albany train station, where they'd arranged to pick up Jess, Ricky had chalked up his mood to anxiety over successfully completing the handoff. Once they arrived at the station (on time, without getting lost), she thought he'd relax, but as she began to unbuckle Biscuit, expecting they'd all go in and meet Jess together, John had said, *No, wait here,* and strode off quickly, stranding her in the hot car with the kids. He'd been grouchy in the little diner outside Lake George where they'd had lunch, grouchy again when she asked him to pull off the road so she could change Biscuit's diaper, and of all things he'd snapped at *her* when *he* missed the turnoff for the cabin.

He did begin to lighten up after they'd finally arrived, but by then Ricky was too hurt to forgive him easily. They'd made supper and washed the dishes and taken the kids down to the dock to brush their teeth and all of that they'd done side by side, but later when he climbed into the double sleeping bag beside her, she'd turned away from him. Ricky knows it is a kind of fear that caused his foul temper today. She believes this fear is also what has made him throw up. She believes, too, that it is Jess who has brought out the fear—not through her actions but through her existence. But the fear predates Jess. Ricky does not know how she knows this. She has not seen John like this before. But she recognizes what she sees: John is afraid of being revealed in a poor light, afraid of being found unworthy, small. Who in his past has made him feel this way? Ricky does not know.

She rests one hand on the small of his back and looks up at the tall night sky. It is starless, black, and rimmed by the silhouettes of treetops that are blacker still. The silhouettes of trees are like shapes cut out of folded paper. They remind her of a stage set, not the kind John builds but the one that was part of a toy theater she had as a child. It folded out of an album like a pop-up book, and came with its own paper actors and props. Her mother would help her put on little plays at the kitchen table. Sometimes they'd set up a row of tea lights at the foot of the cardboard stage.

Her father never took part in the plays, except as an audience member, but he loved to tell stories, mostly the same handful of stories over and over again, sometimes from books and sometimes from memory, and as he told them she saw the action unfold in her mind as if in a play. It was here at Cabruda Lake, some twenty years earlier, that he first told Ricky the story about the rabbi of Nemirov. She'd been lying on the dock well after dark, her head on her mother's lap, her father's corduroy shirt spread across her legs like a blanket, her father sitting beside them. They'd come to watch the Perseids, but there was cloud cover. To entertain her while they waited and hoped, her father retold the I. L. Peretz story "If Not Higher." It was one of his favorites, and she heard him tell it many times throughout her childhood, but it remains always fastened for her to this place, to the night sky and the tall trees here at Cabruda Lake, where she first heard it.

Ricky thinks she would like to tell John the story. She tries to recollect the way her father told it:

The rabbi of Nemirov always disappears one day a year, always during the High Holidays. On this day he cannot be found—not at home, not at the synagogue, not at shul. The villagers would always explain this absence by saying the rabbi, on this day, must ascend to heaven, to plead with God on their behalf. But one day a Litvak comes to the village, and he scoffs at this explanation.

("What's a Litvak?" young Ricky had interrupted.

"A scoffer," her father replied. "May I please continue?")

On the eve of the High Holidays, just before the Day of Atonement, the Litvak nervously hides under the rabbi's bed. He's determined to discover wherever it is the rabbi goes. The next morning the rabbi rises, dresses in rough clothing, and grabs an ax and a thick rope. The Litvak, with fear in his heart, follows the rabbi into the woods. As he watches, the rabbi chops up a tree and ties the wood into a bundle with the rope. He carries the bundle to the shack of a sick old woman and knocks on the door, pretending to be a peasant selling firewood. When the woman protests she hasn't any money, the rabbi says he'll lend it to her. When she says she may never be able to pay him back, he scolds her for having so little faith in God. When she asks who will make the fire for her—she's too sick to get up—he does it himself, reciting, as he does, the penitential prayers.

From this day forth, the Litvak becomes a disciple of the rabbi. From this day forth, whenever he hears someone repeat the rumor that during the High Holidays the rabbi of Nemirov ascends to heaven, the Litvak does not scoff. He only adds quietly, "If not higher."

Ricky hears these last words as if her father is speaking them now, and recalls how his voice had seemed to hang above them for a moment, like the wire of black smoke after you blow out a candle.

("Why," young Ricky had asked, "didn't he just give her the wood?"

"He did," said her father.

"But he makes it sound like she has to pay him back."

"Because he knows she won't accept charity."

"Why did he have to dress like a peasant? Why didn't he just let her know he was the rabbi?"

Her father turned to her mother. "What am I not saying in English?")

And this is the problem with the story, as well as the real reason she has thought of it now. Ricky cannot recall the story of the rabbi without reinvoking the memory of disappointing her father. This is how it always went with them: he forever offering her something he clearly regarded as a precious gem; she forever failing to grasp the crucial thing about it, always apprehending, instead, its poorest facet. She knows a thing or two about being seen as small, as wanting.

John retches again.

"Sweetpea," whispers Ricky.

His vomit steams on the cold ground.

Above them, above the steely black of the pines, the sky's black is soft as a plum. Ricky listens to the tuneless chorale of the insects and the faint clues—twigs snapping, leaves rustling— that weightier creatures are awake in the forest. Her breath comes out as feathery fog, silver in the air before it disappears. Between the trees, Cabruda Lake shows yet another sort of black: slick as obsidian glass. Tomorrow they will take the canoe from the shed.

The need comes over her to make a vow. Standing with her husband, her palm on his waist while he is sick at their feet, she pledges silently to be the one who will always see in him the large. No matter what, she will be that one. The private nature of her vow, the fact that he is unaware of this new promise, her new obligation, fills her with a kind of solemn awe.

When he is finished, Ricky ushers him carefully over the prickling pine needles and hard roots to the little washstand set up between the privy and the cabin. Here is a jug of water, a chipped enamel basin, a hand towel. She helps him wash his face, rinse his mouth. When he is done she flings the wash water across the path, into the pines. Then she walks him inside, guides him over to the bed, covers him. She feels his forehead; it is not hot.

"You're nice," whispers John, in fetal curl, within the flannel-lined sleeping bag.

She whispers *"ssh"* into his beard.

There is a metal pail, which they use to heat dishwater; she takes this from atop the woodstove and places it on the floor by

John's head, just in case. Then she pulls on one of his wool sweaters, slides into her flip-flops, and goes back outside. They keep an identical pail by the big stone fireplace built into the clearing in front of the cabin. Ricky carries this down the path to the lake, walking across the strip of sand and right out to the edge of the floating dock, which sways beneath her as she kneels. She dips the pail, and the black water that swirls into it is warmer than the air.

Lugging it back to the cabin, she feels her shoulder being pulled earthward, has a graphic sense of the muscle within the casing of skin, the ligaments and bone. Her burden relieves her; she is as light—as happy—as she's been all day. She pours the lake water back and forth over the door stone, washing it clean.

PAUL BRINGS HIS bucket up from the shallows and dumps the treasure, along with a fair amount of water and sand, unceremoniously onto Jess's towel.

"Dude," she says, scrambling to sit up, and—"Peh!"—spitting sand from her mouth. She has been lying with her head on her rolled-up sweatshirt, reading one of the library books she brought from home.

With a small, sticky hand, Paul helps brush the sand from her face. He's thorough about it and surprisingly gentle. She closes her eyes and holds still. When he finishes, she opens her eyes to find him looking back at her. He is both slender and sturdy, like a young barnyard animal, a calf or colt. He's wearing red swim trunks and, in his hair, the wreath of white clover she wove that morning. Jess is in her bathing suit, too, a modest black one-piece. Over this she wears a large blue oxford she will not take off, not

even to go in the water; earlier she went wading in it, and yesterday, when it was warmer, she jumped off the dock with it on.

"So what's this stuff ya dumpin' on my head?"

"I didn't dump it on your head," he corrects reasonably, and,
kneeling, sorts through the jumble. "Shell, shell, plastic thing,
shell, pink grass, rock with a line in it, bottle cap, more shells . . .
here." He holds up the glinting item, the prize he has apparently
come in order to show. She takes it from him with respect.

"That was down by the water? That's dangerous." She points
out the tiny barbs that make the fish hook so dangerous, and
shows him, using a fat blade of beach grass, how once the hook
pierces something it cannot be pulled out again without causing
greater damage. "Good thing you found it."

He puffs out his chest. His skin is tawny from a summer's
worth of sun, his hair streaked white and yellow as the bicolor
corn Ricky and John cooked last night. Jess and Paul had
shucked it themselves, sitting on the big log outside the cabin,
with "help" from Biscuit, who had mostly waved around her ear
of corn like a maraca, pulling off a husk or two and biting into it
raw before flinging it into the cold gray ash of the fireplace. Paul
had scolded her perhaps too severely for this—"No, no! *Never*
throw anything in the fire!"—which had so offended her that
Biscuit had been compelled to respond with an immediate re-
bellion, throwing in after the corn the handiest thing available:
her pacifier, as it turned out, direct from her mouth.

It had been, objectively speaking, high comedy, watching the
consequences of her action dawn on her. At first, she'd looked
slyly pleased with her insurgence. Then came the double take,
and after a shocked delay, the tears. Jess, biting the insides of her

cheeks in order not to smile, had fished "pie-oo" out of the ashes and gone to rinse it under the spigot. By then Biscuit had begun to wail so hysterically that John came dashing from the cabin, where he'd been making chili, wooden spoon still in hand, and Ricky, emerging from the woods with an armload of kindling, had dropped the sticks by the fireplace, scooped up the squalling girl, and taken her into the hammock for comforting.

Jess, having delivered the clean pacifier and come back to sit by the bag of corn, caught Paul's eye in such a way that the two of them had burst into laughter, which they tried unsuccessfully to squelch and which earned them Biscuit's disdainful refusal to acknowledge their subsequent apologies. The quality of laughter was novel to Jess, not because she'd never experienced it before but because she'd experienced it only in cahoots with a girl-friend, someone her own age, not with a little kid, a mere five-year-old. She looks at Paul now, sitting across from her on the towel, grains of dry sand dusting his shoulders like sugar. She wonders if the quick closeness between them could be a result of their shared blood.

The others are in the cabin now, Biscuit having her nap, John and Ricky washing the dishes. It's become a routine, Jess bring-ing Paul to the beach after lunch, just the two of them until mid-afternoon, when the others wander down. Jess wonders if Ricky and John use the time to make love. She is embarrassed to be capable of such a thought, but she can't help it. Lying at night on the couch in the cabin's main room, she has heard them whisper and shift within their sleeping bag, and to her mortifica-tion she has strained to pick out the sounds she imagines might be associated with sex. She has not been able to, and wonders if they are abstaining because of her, and if so will they abstain the whole two weeks, and if so, how difficult is it? She has heard it can be painful, especially for a man.

As a couple, John and Ricky are enormously interesting to her, which is repulsive because this means she is having inappropriate thoughts about her father, even though he isn't her *father* father. She's shaken enough by her own inability to stop thinking about such things that she has been avoiding John. She thinks he is feeling bad about this, hurt, but what else can she do? They are so different from her own parents, who, though peaceably wedded, seem not particularly interested in each other. Or interested: yes; but intrigued, entranced: no. John and Ricky have the crackling charge of film stars. They speak in funny little half-sentences, call each other Baby and Sweet Pea, and carry on their own secret dialogue of glance and touch, right in front of Jess and the kids. There is a palpable complexity, as though the air between them has been folded into many layers, within which lie all the artifacts of their history together. Jess tries to monitor her gaze so as not to look at them too long at any one time.

Not, evidently, a concern for Paul, who has been regarding her unblinking these past several moments.

"What are you looking at?"

He shrugs.

She mimics the gesture, but he continues to stare. "Here. Look at that." She holds the fish hook out on the flat of her palm so that Paul can better see its tiny, wicked barbs. He brings his face in close. She can feel the breath from his nostrils flowing against her skin in two distinct streams. He remains in this position, surely too close to the hook to be able to focus on it—in fact, she notes, he seems to have half shut his eyes—inhaling deeply. "What are you doing? It's not *food*."

"You smell like eggs."

"Great."

"Easter eggs," he says appreciatively.

Jess runs her tongue over her braces. "I'd like to take you home and show you to my mother."

A skeptical crease appears between his eyebrows. "Why?"

"'Cause you're a kick."

What she'd really like is to show her mother herself: her, here, with the Ryries. She is something new here, something shiny, different, at the lake with this family. She feels older somehow and also excitingly young, aware of the possibilities of her youth, the great array of things she might eventually be and do. The only thing missing from the experience is a witness, someone who knows her in real life and could perform the task of saying: yes. This is all true. This could all be true.

"So," says Jess, holding up the hook. "What are we going to do with this sucker?"

"Throw it away?"

"When we go back, but for now, I mean."

"Put it someplace safe?"

"Here." She picks up her library book, a romance novel, one of seven she has brought. She consumes one every two days. They are, she knows, essentially all the same, and not what she would de- scribe as good, but that's beside the point; they seem to be a kind of requirement for her these days, as basic as bread. This book's protective film, she sees, has somehow been infiltrated by sand, sharp grains of it denting the plastic from the inside, a fact that should make her feel guilty but gives her perverse satisfaction: she has marked it, this piece of public property, with a bit of herself. The sand physical evidence of the book's journey from Elsmere Public Library to Cabruda Lake. Jess opens the back cover and slips the fish hook into the empty card pocket. "Good?"

Paul nods. The clover wreath on his head slips over one ear and she settles it back on his crown. She can feel his infatuation extending toward her in waves as distinct, as palpable, as earlier she'd felt the twin streams of his breath on her palm. Her feeling of love for this little boy is like a new frequency she's discovering, a new channel within her. She is awash in it, shining and addled. He's cross-legged on her towel and as golden, as bitable, as a toasted marshmallow. It's yesterday again and they are dissolved in laughter in front of the cold outdoor fireplace, strands of corn silk strewn all around, edges of the sky seeming to tilt and spin them together. It's tomorrow and she'll wake to him sitting on her legs, on her sleeping bag, drinking his milk in front of the woodstove. She is fifteen and experiencing for the first time what she thinks of as grown-up love. It turns out not to be the thing described in her romance novels. Nor is it the thing John and Ricky have, although what they have continues to fascinate her, to make her both wistful and uncomfortable. But what she has discovered is another variety altogether, almost another species. This love, she thinks, is selfless, beyond self, mature.

"WHAT ELSE?" John is taking down the shopping list that Ricky dictates. So far he's written milk, tomatoes, hot dogs and garlic, butter and chocolate bars and toilet paper.

"And more of that corn," says Ricky. "The corn was good."

The time is flying. Already they are more than halfway through the vacation. Although she wasn't expecting it (not this summer, not with John's daughter on the scene), Ricky realizes there have been a few stellar days, or parts of days: moments that seemed instantly to become emblazoned in her mind as postcards she will look back on. Scavenging for late-season blueberries, and Biscuit turning out to be the best seeker of them all. Playing cards all day, the day it rained without stopping, and eating popcorn straight from the metal pot. Hiking on the blazed trails and logging roads that suddenly opened up and as suddenly stopped, like ghost boulevards in the old forest; the sun filtering down as if in slow motion through the crown cover, the light somehow altered, distilled, as though it had been sent from a long time ago. The evening paddle with John in the bow, Ricky in the stern, Jess and the children sitting on boat cushions in the bottom of the canoe. They'd seen a whole family of deer drinking from the lake, and also, on a branch that stretched out into the water, a prehistoric-looking creature that Ricky said was a turkey vulture. Paul, wondrous and a little frightened, had shrunk against Jess, but Biscuit had been entranced and was barely restrained from climbing out of the canoe; she kept calling lustily, "Bird! Bird, come!"

How strange to discover the pleasure of being five. Five of them instead of four. Fitting together as though *this*, after all, was the natural number for their family. The only thing Ricky wishes for is sex; after ten days she is minding the physical deprivations that are the result of their lack of privacy.

The cabin at this hour is cool and dim. Jess is at the beach with both kids; Biscuit having been delivered there after her nap.

Ricky has come back to the cabin to change into her suit and figure out with John what they need from town. As she finishes dictating the shopping list, she begins to strip. She throws her jeans on the bed and reaches for her suit, which is hanging over the alcove curtain, still damp from her early-morning swim. She likes going alone, partly for the solitude but also for the peculiar beauty that seems uniquely enabled by the solitude: the needle sharpness of the light, the champagne chill of the air, the hushed skin of the lake.

This morning Jess asked Ricky if she could come. They'd left John with the children and gone down the path as silently as though it were a library corridor. They deposited their towels on the sand and went to the end of the dock, Jess still wearing a man's button-down shirt over her suit. "You don't want to wear that to swim in," Ricky said. She understood the girl was modest, and said it in a careless voice, squinting out across the lake.

Jess turned away to undo her buttons, and then, tossing the shirt quickly behind her, plunged in ahead of Ricky, who jumped back, startled by the cold spray of the splash. Now in the cabin Ricky pulls off her sweater and, in her bra and damp bathing suit bottom, says, "Why don't you pick up a bottle of wine, too?"

John adds wine to the list.

Ricky covers his fly with her hand. They stand like that. The warmth between her palm and the denim grows.

"You can't just do that," says John, shifting his hips. After a moment, he whispers, "You're so bad."

He says the same thing whenever she arouses him. *You're so bad.* He says it always the same way, back in his throat, and every time the words unsettle her. In what sense does he mean it? It seems to her the words are at once approving and indicting. They draw her to him, lay claim. They mark some private knowledge between them that is neither entirely pleasing nor entirely unprecious. Sometimes she thinks what holds them together is just this: his minor distrust, the permanent crack in his faith.

She unhooks her bra, lets it fall. John looks at her a long moment in something like pained reverence, then shakes his head.

"Just quickly," she says.

"You told Jess you'd be right down."

She turns back to the alcove, finishes putting on her suit.

"Ricky."

"What?"

"Don't be mad."

"I'm not mad."

"It's not that I don't want to."

"Okay."

"Ricky."

"It's fine." She moves briskly through the cabin, gathering the crossword, her sunglasses, a couple of juice boxes. She can feel him tracking her, trying to figure out what he should say. She says, "You have the list?"

"What? Yeah." He looks at the paper in his hand, puts it in his pocket. "I may get a haircut, too." He always does, during their annual two weeks in the Adirondacks; there's an old-style barbershop he likes. "Bye, baby." The screen door smacks behind him. Minutes later the engine starts.

When Ricky gets to the lake she sees it is bustling with

activity, both in the water and along the shore, which is sprinkled with other cabins, some of them evident only in the mornings and evenings, when columns of smoke rise from their chimneys. There are clusters of dots on the various small beaches, and many small craft skimming about: Sunfish and rowboats, catamarans and JetSkis. The party boat is out, too: a flat-bottomed boat people rent by the day, recognizable at a distance by its blue-and-white-striped awning.

Ricky stands at the place where the path meets the beach, as yet unnoticed by her children and Jess, savoring the luxury of giving her attention without its being demanded. Jess and Paul crouch in the shallows, remarking on the school of minnows weaving among their ankles. Biscuit, wearing only a diaper, is eating sand, licking it from her palm the way another child might lick batter from a beater. Paul, holding the hems of his red trunks, dainty as a Victorian girl holding the edge of her bathing costume, peers past his knees into the water. A laugh bubbles from his throat—"One *tickled* me!"—and Jess smiles at him in such a way as to raise in Ricky's chest something swift, like a sob. It is the realization that of all the innumerable sweetnesses the world will offer her children, the vast majority will go unwitnessed by her.

"Hey! Mommy!" Paul, noticing her, jumps and scatters the fishes.

Biscuit gives a sandy grin over her shoulder and pops her pacifier back in her mouth.

They all sit together awhile, digging and mounding sand with an assortment of plastic bowls, scoops, and sieves, until Ricky says she feels like going for a swim, and asks Jess if she minds being alone with the kids again. Jess does not, and Ricky wades in up to her waist and then dives.

WHILE JESS AND her brother build up the walls of their castle, Biscuit works on her own project. She has discovered that it is fun to peel at the sticky tape at her hips. She peels one, then the other. When both little flaps of tape are sticking out, like open doors, she stands up. Her diaper does not come with her. "Hey." She speaks around her pacifier. "'ook." This is a good trick. No one reacts. She looks up. Her mother has disappeared into the lake, her father has disappeared into the world, and the other two have disappeared into their castle. She sees them, but they don't see her. Maybe it is she who's disappeared. She looks back down. No, there is her round tummy, there is the dimple of her crotch, there are her feet with their little piggies sticking up pink through the sand. Everyone is missing the diaper trick. "'ook," she says again. "'ook!" And they do. Paul's eyes widen and already she can see him preparing his mouth to speak, to scold. Jess laughs. And here goes Biscuit shrieking with delight, tearing across the sand as they come chasing her. She is tackled and they all tumble down and sand gets everywhere; everyone is laughing now, even Paul. When they get up Biscuit remains where she is: upside down, the crown of her head pressing into the sand so that the sky has become the floor, the lake the ceiling. This is the other world she goes to sometimes. But where are the others? Not in it. They have moved away, outside the frame of what she can see. Now there is another shriek, not Biscuit's, not anyone's, but the ongoing shriek of a siren, the siren that echoes every day across the lake when they are eating lunch, but it's the wrong time, she knows that because she's already woken from her nap, and Paul and Jess have moved away toward the edge of the lake, leaving Biscuit on her own in the upside-down world.

"WE THOUGHT IT was you," Jess says later that evening, when the whole family is gathered around the outdoor fireplace. Ricky and Paul are in the hammock; John and Jess sit on the folding chairs in front of the fire, feeding it handfuls of peanut shells every few minutes. Biscuit is walking in circles around the woodpile with *Scuffy the Tugboat,* which she "reads" out loud to an invisible, rapt audience. Besides the colander full of peanuts they keep passing around, there are plastic cups of wine for John and Ricky, and of cranberry juice for Paul and Biscuit and Jess. A plate of raw chicken parts, slathered in homemade lemon-mustard sauce, sits on a flat rock beside the fire.

"We really thought it was you," repeats Jess, and she has said this already, earlier in the afternoon. They have all been telling and retelling the story, so that by now even John, who was in town getting groceries, feels as intimately acquainted with the way it unfolded as if he'd been present.

First there'd been the siren sound of the noon whistle, echoing oddly in mid-afternoon, and sounding over and over instead of one long blast. Then Jess and Paul had made out small figures clustering at the edge of the public marina partway around the lake; there had been something about the way they clustered that differentiated them from people gathering for sport or play.

And then several of the small craft scattered about the lake were switching course, homing in together on one spot, not terribly far from the Ryries' beach, a hundred yards, maybe two. It was the party boat, with its jolly striped awning, that arrived first at the place where all the other boats were converging, so that it initially looked as though everyone were gathering for some kind of prearranged mid-lake merrymaking. But Jess did not think that was it.

For a while she had been unable to make out much. "What's happening?" Paul asked at intervals, until she picked him up. "I can't tell," she said. "Maybe nothing." But they watched as though neither of them believed it.

After a time, the siren stopped. They saw figures in dark clothes, uniforms, arrive at the public marina and move rapidly into a motorboat. It was difficult to see, with the sun spangling the water, but Jess thought she saw someone dive from the side of the party boat. Occasionally they could hear voices but no words. Then Jess saw another figure jump in, from the catamaran, and she knew they were diving for something.

"What are they looking for?" asked Paul, and she said nothing, and he didn't ask again, and she marked this, and also the fact that neither child had asked for Ricky or wondered aloud how long she'd been swimming.

Jess wishes she hadn't seen them hoisting the body from the water. Though she had never seen a dead body, it was obvious what it was, the sodden weight of it terrible and limp, like seaweed. She saw them lay the body on the party boat, whose flat base, almost level with the water, made it the best-suited for such a purpose. After this she sensed a deflation of energies, nothing like relief, but a kind of uncoiling, as one by one the boats dispersed from their knot, most of them following, at what seemed an unnaturally slow pace, the party boat as it headed for the public marina. She realized she had to set Paul down.

"What was it?" he asked, when he was standing.

"I don't know," she said, and realized he thought whatever it was had passed. Jess was thinking about how long it would take the police to identify the body, and then how long it would take them to make their way out to the cabin, and she hoped John would be home by then. Somehow, both grateful for and a little disturbed by her own ability to act normal, she started playing tic-tac-toe with Paul by drawing the lines in the wet sand. Biscuit came over and chanted, "Ta-ta-toe," and tried to get in the game, mostly messing it up so that they could hardly tell which were the X's and which the O's.

Some ten minutes later Ricky emerged from the water, radiant and exhausted. Jess broke down at the sight of her. Ricky, bewildered, looked first to see that Biscuit and Paul were unharmed, then took Jess in her arms. "What is it?" she panted. "Did something happen?"

Jess sobbed into her neck. The front of her oxford turned dark blue. Drips from Ricky's body ran down her own legs. She felt how strong were Ricky's muscles, inhaled the lake smell that clung to her: silt and algae and deep, mineral coolness. The children's hands were on her, little sandy butterflies lighting upon her calves and thighs, offering oblivious, heartfelt consolation.

It wasn't until John came back from town with the groceries and a too-short haircut that they learned what had happened. A volunteer fireman had come into the barbershop while John was in the chair. In the manner of the local men, who habituated the barbershop more often to chew the fat than groom themselves, he'd related the facts succinctly: single mother, thirty-five, vacationing down from Elmira. Two kids. Here with the sister's family, the grandparents, too, all of them staying in a rental cabin. No history of heart trouble, no history of substance abuse, according to the family. Autopsy would tell. Kids nine and eleven. Girls, both.

Now, sitting by the outdoor fire as daylight drains from the air, waiting for the coals to die down to the point where John can lay the grill over them and cook the chicken, Jess goes over it again in her head: the siren, the convergence of boats, the divers, the seaweedlike mass of the drowned body, the blue-and-white-striped awning that shaded it as it was brought to shore. She thinks of the way Ricky held her and of the way she held Ricky; of the dead mother and the dead mother's children; of her parents back in Elsmere and of the word "orphan." She thinks of little sandy hands patting the backs of her legs, of the chicken and corn John bought and is now cooking, of the solace of food and wood smoke and twilight. Of affection secured.

The shapes of bats flit above, black against violet sky.

JOHN IS BARRED from the cabin. It is switching over from afternoon to evening on their last day at Cabruda Lake. Within the hour they will all sit down to his birthday supper, but for now he is forbidden entry. Something about a surprise, says Paul, standing in the doorway with his arms spread. "You have to stay out, Daddy. You can't see it yet."

Ricky, Biscuit in her arms, appears behind him. She lays a hand on Paul's head, but looks at John as she says, "Nice work, sentry."

"He wanted to get in."

"I see. I'll take over from here."

Paul disappears into the interior, which is smelling like cake.

"We're not quite ready," says Ricky, leaning against the door frame in a leisurely manner.

"You look nice," says John. He is standing on the door stone, flirting with his wife. "You're a fine-looking woman."

Ricky smiles, her mouth closed as if she is holding something wonderful, honey or pearls, on her tongue.

"You're a country wife."

She laughs.

"I don't even know what that means," he confesses.

"Here." Ricky transfers their plump girl from her hip into John's arms. "Why don't you and Biscuit go look for a bear? Come back in twenty."

The cabin door closes. John looks at Biscuit. "Want to walk?"

"Ride."

He hoists her onto his shoulders. They stroll down the path, out toward the dirt road. The early evening is shot through with pale yellow, but this drains away as they walk, leaving the air a granular blue. John whistles. He forgets how good a whistler he is, and how nice a thing it is to do.

Biscuit winds his curls around her fingers. "Gentle," he reminds her after a bit, and reaches up to pry her hand loose. She has tensed; one of her feet kicks out. "See! See!" she commands. A chipmunk, eating something. It sits silkily hunched and bright-eyed, darting glances at them as it chews. His daughter has grown very still on his shoulders, but John feels her avidness, her concentration. She is breathing through her mouth. He is holding her ankles and there is sparkling power in them. He imagines if he let go she would pitch herself forward and rush toward the nibbling, gold-backed creature. There will come a day when what John knows about Biscuit will amount to less than what he does not know about her. That stands to reason. But now a thought startles him: what if that day has already come?

Later, the ban lifted, Paul gives his father a tour of the decorations he has made. "All by my bigself," as he says. They include a circle of pinkish pebbles arranged on the doorstep, a cupful of wildflowers and grass in the center of the table, and at each place setting, one baby pine cone nestled in the bowl of the spoon. They eat hamburgers and salad, and then cake, which Jess presents, carrying it, lit, with some pride to the table, and setting it carefully before him. It turns out she has made it. John is moved, hearing this. This whole time, the whole vacation, she has seemed to want little to do with him. John would be the first to say she owes him nothing, yet he's been hurt by her apparent disregard, jealous of the affection she's so freely showered on the others—even as he's rejoiced in it, been thankful to see her take so warmly to Ricky and Paul and Biscuit, and they to her.

The cake is . . . interesting, as dense and rich as any John's ever tasted, almost alarmingly so. With the first bite he has the sensation of juice running down his throat. "Wow," he says, nodding, reaching for his napkin, aware she is watching him. "That's some cake."

Jess is pleased, when asked, to be able to rattle off the ingredients: flour, sugar, a can of 7Up, a pound of butter, five eggs.

"Really?" John says very politely. "A pound of butter?"

"Four sticks." She turns to Ricky for confirmation. "Right?"

"Ah," he says, with no particular emphasis, and catches Ricky's eye. She keeps her smile expertly contained. Her earrings, little glass teardrops, dangle like beads of sap just below each lobe. John would like to bite them lightly.

Jess has noticed nothing of their silent, amused exchange; she is safe in her ignorance and pleased with her cookery, as innocent, as protected as Biscuit and Paul, both of whom are deeply, utterly invested in their rectangles of cake. It's an art form, thinks John, sui generis: the act of youths eating cake. He feels himself and Ricky gazing together at all three children, all happy at this moment: the happiness of absolute intention.

Biscuit finishes first and asks Jess for seconds; Jess appeals to Ricky for permission. John perceives the shift in allegiance, or in intimacy. Now it is Jess and Ricky who share the knowing smile, who parse each other's tiniest movements of eyebrow and shoulder. John reads in this the history of their afternoon together: their trip to town, their labors side by side in the cabin's tiny kitchen. But it isn't only this afternoon; he sees how in two weeks' time they have made something of their own, Jess and Ricky, something that does not include him and is not about him. It has sprung from and resides in innumerable small intimacies: their playing the Or Game while they do dishes; Ricky teaching Jess how to light the gas lamps, Jess teaching Ricky how to play Liverpool.

After supper, once the dishwater has heated up on the stove,

Jess takes the flashlight and leads Paul and Biscuit, already in pajamas, down to the dock to brush their teeth in the lake for the last time this summer. John presses the length of his body against the back of Ricky's, so that she's pushed up against the enamel rim of the sink, where she stands doing dishes. He moves his lips along the back of her neck, touches his tongue to the glass bead of one earring, holds it between his teeth a moment, as he had wanted to do. He runs his hands along the front of her, murmurs, "After the kids are in bed you and I are going down to the dock."

"We can't," she says, even as she braces her soapy hands against the sink to press herself against him. "I promised Jess. Earlier. I'm taking her skinny-dipping. She's never been."

"But I love you." His lips graze the curve of her ear.

She goes on tiptoe and turns sideways, rubs her face back and forth to nuzzle his beard. "Tomorrow," she promises. "In our own bed."

Later, his oldest child and his wife get ready to go down the path to the dock. John has the Week in Review spread open on his lap, but he's not reading; he's looking at the embers dying in the woodstove and listening to them as they disrobe behind the curtain of the alcove where he and Ricky sleep. They are whispering so as not to wake Biscuit and Paul. Their clothes make small noises, the sound of zippers, of fabric brushing over skin.

When they emerge sheathed in towels, both of them clutching their pajamas in small bundles against their chests, John catches only the ice cream gleam of their bare shoulders before fastening his eyes hard on the newspaper in his lap. The atmosphere of shy adventure emanates strongly, seductively, from them. So unsure of his position is he that when they whisper,

"Bye," he pretends not to hear, and glances only obliquely when Ricky adds, in a hoarser whisper, "We're off." He waves, nods, and turns the page as the screen door closes behind them.

But before the slapping of their flip-flops fades, John casts aside the paper and hurries to the doorway. He catches the last of them as they disappear down the path, the moon lighting their way. His wife in the lead. His daughter, whose braid makes a single dark stripe down her back, following. He pictures, involuntarily, Ricky's body under the towel. He knows it so well: the three little moles below her left breast, the way the right hip is slightly higher. John is riddled with longing and gratitude. The fullness with which Ricky has embraced Jess reveals a quality he would not have guessed of her. It's shameful but true: he thought her smaller than this. He will never confess his crime; it isn't something for which he can openly apologize. But he feels duly chastened. Every day henceforth he will atone silently, actively, he decides, for having underestimated his wife.

Minutes after they have disappeared from view he continues to stand at the door, straining to hear the dock creak under their feet. Nothing. He thinks of the woman who drowned two days earlier—the very words seem improbable, strung together in error—but they are as correct as the woman's death is real, and he thinks of this correctness, this realness, as something tangible, a liquid substance secreted into the lake in which she drowned and now spread evenly throughout it. How many others, he wonders, standing in this lonely way by the screen door, have died in the lake over the years, the millennia? How many have died on the land, in these woods, on the very spot where he stands? Also this: How many are dying right now, at this moment, the whole world over? For just a moment his mind is able to grasp it, the existence of a vast, invisible, yet utterly real community of the dying, and then, it follows, another composed of the suffering, and one of the ecstatic and one of the healing, and one of those in despair and one of those in wonder. Somewhere on this earth, too, there are others like him, others paused at this very moment in contemplation by an open doorway. For just a moment he is able to grasp the perfect truth, of this. Then it is gone.

And he perceives that it will always be this complicated, that life will always contain such quicksilver changes, that it is *composed* of quicksilver changes, those mercurial shifts between understanding and loss of understanding, longing and gratitude, imprecation and blessing. He stands close to the night, listening for a splash, and thinks he has never felt so unafflicted in all his life, so wholly unmarked by fear.

PART FIVE

This Year

1.

Adult lap swim ended at 9:45, or Ricky would've gone on
indefinitely spanning the same twenty yards back and
forth: freestyle, flip turn, breathe in, breathe out. Her swimming
body was a kind of machine, uncomplicated by a multitude of
human attributes. In the pool she was pared down to her unim-
peachable essence, all muscle and method, and everything else
was muffled: thought, sound, even vision, thanks to the chlorine
blur. Swimming caps were required. Hers was white, and
when she caught her reflection, smile-less, dripping, in the
locker room mirror, she was reminded of her mother, and
thought: *so soon*.

She'd come in an effort to exhaust herself—she hadn't been
sleeping—but when she left the Y, going down the steps and
turning onto Remsen Street with her swim bag over one shoulder, she felt damnably awake. The night air seized her head, her

hair wet from the shower and combed flat to her scalp; the cold seemed to latch on, a thin hand steering her forcefully the two blocks home. She wondered whether she and John would have another session tonight, another tunneling nightmare discussion in which she attempted to talk their marriage into resuscitation, into wholeness. Their marriage was a broken body laid out on the bed between them, and she a fraud in a nurse's uniform, trying to make the bones knit through any means she could think of: incantations; sugar pills; sheer, useless will.

It had been this way for two weeks now, ever since Biscuit's fire and Paul's fistfight and suspension.

John didn't want her touching him. Each time she tried, he'd remove her hand, immediately but neutrally, without anger or force, as if his response were less emotional than neurological.

"I can't," he'd say. Factually. He'd said it again last night, when, all out of words, at a loss for any other kind of persuasion, she'd tried once more, in spite of herself, placing a hand oh so carefully—on his knee, his *knee*.

He'd lifted it off.

"You won't forgive me?" she'd croaked. But how many tears had she spilled these past weeks already? Too many for these to gain notice, let alone to move him. "Ever?"

"I don't know. How can I—? It's not something I can know. I'm not *trying* to not forgive you. Tell me how."

These moments were cruelest, when he appeared to be offering her a chance, except she'd tried every answer she could think of and none of them was right. Last night she hadn't been able to come up with anything new, and had only gaped back: dumb, beseeching. The tears had trembled but remained in her eyes as if they, too, were tired of the endless repetition.

The problem was her crime was old. She'd admitted to it a year ago. She'd confessed, apologized, and they'd gone on—only now it turned out he'd never forgiven her, the whole thing had merely lain dormant. She'd tried to claim— No. She *had* claimed, for once, full responsibility for what she'd done, for how her lie had hurt them, harmed them, no excuses tendered.

"But you're wrong about my not having been home in a year, John. You're wrong about that." This had been earlier that same evening, arguing in the kitchen as they'd done dishes, because that was the nature of it now; it had overflowed the bedroom, overflowed any semblance of privacy. Even as domesticity carried them along in its current, the fight had come into the open. Another strange relief.

"It hasn't been only a year," she'd gone on. "Or only two, or only three. And it hasn't been only me. We haven't been home to each other in . . . I don't even know how long. I always think of that summer we went away with Jess, when she came with us, you know, as this golden time? But it wasn't, even then. I don't remember a time when we were living with you not as the for-giver and me the forgiven."

The kids—all three of them, Jess included—had been in the den, watching TV, as they'd been doing far too much of lately, but it wasn't to be helped; Ricky and John kept needing to have these talks. There was no arranging for them, no making a date to converse in private or finding a time when it would be con-venient; the need for talk kept seeming to arrive, like weather:

urgent and unassailable. They tried keeping their voices down, but this, too, was little to be controlled.

"I know what you're thinking," Ricky had gone on. "I know what you're going to say now: that I fucked it up even before we married, with that *thing*, that stupid affair. And fine. Okay. I did fuck up, John. But if you were never going to get past it, you should never have married me. How dare you—oh God, John—how dare you marry me and not trust me? Where"—she'd drawn a rasping breath—"where did that ever leave us?"

He'd dried his hands on the dish towel and turned to face her. "But, Ricky," he'd said, and his voice was not so nice, "I was right not to trust you."

"But don't you think you're a little bit responsible? When you treat me as untrustworthy, when you see me as untrustworthy, what can you expect? It's like, like, a self-fulfilling prophecy."

He'd let out a short disgusted laugh. "That's good. That's convenient. You fuck some other guy, and then you blame me for not trusting you. And, oh yeah, the fact that I don't trust you is what makes you go on being dishonest."

"No, John, no. This is part of your meanness. You always have the upper hand, don't you? You *thrive* on being morally superior to me." How was it that it felt like hell to say and hear these things, and yet was at the same time such an enormous relief? "Fine, then. Let's turn that logic on you. I don't tell you about the baby because I don't trust you, because I don't trust that you'll let my decision be. And then what happens? I do tell you, and it turns out I was right not to trust *you*."

He'd stared at her, blinking. The kitchen light seemed to pulse above them. Or was it the refrigerator, pulsing in her ears? "What are you talking about?"

"You said—God, I'll remember this till I die—'How compromised would it be?' Remember, John? I was comforting you, you had your head on my stomach, and you looked up and you were thinking of the baby being disabled, if it lived, and you said, 'How compromised would it be?' You were horrified. You didn't want it. It was so clear. You would have wanted me to have an abortion if I'd told you earlier. I was right not to trust you."

"No." He'd shaken his head. His face, his beard, his eyes, his voice, all were very dark. The shadow of his bulk seemed to grow darker and the rest of the kitchen to fade almost to white. Ricky'd braced herself against the back of a chair.

"No," he'd said again. "It's not the same. You don't know what I would have said if you'd told me when you first found out. *I* don't know what I would have said. That's the—" He'd broken off, expelled a breath, grabbed her wrist, let it go. "That's the point, Ricky. *We* don't know. You didn't give us a chance to find out. No, not *me*. Not: you didn't give *me* a chance. You didn't give *us* that chance."

The overhead light brightened and dimmed, brightened and dimmed. Her head felt queerly light. "Oh," she'd said, her voice so dry it crept like crumbs. "I wasn't thinking of it like that."

He'd nodded. She wished he would grab her wrist again now, but he didn't. "That's the problem." He looked her in the eye after he said it.

"John?" It had come to her suddenly, with a quick, flashbulb sort of pop. "This is better. Isn't it? What we're doing now?"

But he'd only regarded her steadily. After a moment, said, "I don't know."

THE Y WAS JUST two blocks from home. Ricky turned onto their street now and approached their house, then stopped several yards away. There were a few lights on downstairs, a few upstairs as well. Through the window at the far end of the porch, the bluish shifting light of the television in the den. She backed away, like a painter trying to get a clearer, more comprehensive view; she backed farther and farther until she was standing on the far side of Depew. And was surprised to find herself there. She did not have a particular idea about what she was doing. She had never come home before only to back off like this, and was conscious of feeling scarily free, unscripted. She was, she realized, seeing the house from the angle she'd first laid eyes on it, stepping out of the realtor's car on that sweltering day eleven years earlier. The coup it had been, to obtain this house! The giddy, slightly illicit triumph of it—she remembered it feeling like that, as though they were getting something they did not entirely merit: scraping together the money for the down payment, accepting help from both John's mother and her own parents, declaring their incomes, baring their credit histories, paying for the title search, signing the mortgage papers—all of it seeming to require more daring, more cheek, even, than had the act of getting married.

Ricky retreated farther, walking into the very middle of the park, from which spot she again turned and regarded the house, her home, softly lit, sweetly inhabited, oblivious to her presence. From here it was not hard to imagine her exile, her rightful turning out, which would be a kind of death. And so she imagined dying, and felt again that shot of alarming liberation, and imagined in death keeping watch over the house, and in this state she was all benign, incapable of hurting or lying or failing anyone. She imagined being a soul only, a transparent birdlike thing, living in one of the trees in the park, watching the children, and John, as they came and went. Watching over them. Incapable of speech, touch, anything but bearing witness.

Desolation swept through her, so real she nearly cried out.

Down the hill she heard the sounds of young men playing basketball. Saw by the stone steps the red tips of cigarettes. Conversation lapped around the edges of the park, even this late on a cold spring night. Young people without jobs, old people without jobs, people wanting drugs, people selling drugs, people who were always leaving their used condoms and empty nip bottles in the bushes. Sometimes she felt annoyance toward such strangers, and sometimes she felt them as a threat, but not tonight. She imagined herself as a soul again, a kind of vague guardian figure, flickering and gray, bearing a great tray of cocoa, picking her way through the wet grass, picking her way among the wounded—for wasn't the park full of the wounded, even the joyful ones, even those having a good time tonight—dispensing angelically the steaming cups.

The sky was starless, moonless. Her eyes still stung from chlorine. She remembered a night long ago when she'd lain on the dock at Cabruda Lake, not with John but much longer ago, with her parents, her head in her mother's lap, her father's corduroy shirt spread over her legs. She remembered the Perseid shower, their patience, the meteors that never came. Or did come, sight unseen.

Her father's story about the Litvak, the rabbi with the ax and the rope. Her mother's near-silent laugh. The water lap-lapping.

"Hey, Ma, what up?" A hooded figure brushed by her, turning as he passed to check her out. It struck her as comical, being mistaken for a sexual entity when here she was imagining herself a transparent bird-thing, no body, all spirit. She took no offense but it was her cue to walk again, to move toward her house, from which she had not, after all, been expelled.

JOHN MET HER in the front hall. He was putting on his jacket.

"I'm going out," he said. "If that's all right."

"Of course." She set down her swim bag. "Did something happen?"

"What do you mean?"

"Just that . . . it's late for you to be going out."

"I'm meeting a colleague for a beer. I was waiting for you to get home."

"Sorry."

"Biscuit and Jess are both in bed. Paul's watching TV."

"Okay. Did you give him a time he has to go up?"

"No."

He opened the door to leave.

"John."

He stopped.

"About what I said earlier. We need to decide."

He turned and looked at her. His eyes were cold, but perhaps not as cold as they had been of late. Perhaps they were mostly dim with exhaustion.

"Do you know what I mean?" she said. "About what we're going to do. We need to decide."

He looked at her the same way so long she supposed he wasn't going to respond, but then he gave a nod. And was gone. Alone in the hallway, she worked her fingers through her damp hair, then let herself cradle her face.

From the den came the sound of a muted explosion. Ricky wandered in. Paul, watching *MythBusters,* barely looked up. She stood by the couch, the saggy old thing that was, in some alternative version of events, to have been replaced by now with a bed for Jess. Instead, these past two weeks John had been creeping down to sleep on it each night and as stealthily evacuating it early each morning. The formal proposal Ricky had rehearsed was never delivered, just as the scraps of fancy lingerie were never unwrapped from their tissue paper parcels. The thought of both made her feel worn, now, and ill. She combed her fingers slowly through the tangles at Paul's nape. Ever so slightly, he moved his head away, as she'd known he would; the shake-off had been part of his repertoire for at least a year now.

"It's really cool," Paul said, in a dazed, preoccupied way. Biscuit did this, too, spoke in the same vacuous cadence whenever watching TV. "They're using a whole bunch of roach foggers in this abandoned building to see if it'll explode. If it works it'll be the biggest explosion they've ever had on *MythBusters.*"

Ricky came around and sat beside him. Once, he'd wanted to tell her everything. How he'd gotten a triple in kickball; how polar bears steered with their back legs; how his friend Alexi had a wart on his pinkie but it went away; how he'd dreamed he was a red Lamborghini. He used to relate news from and about his life in so much detail that she had regularly tuned him out while he followed her around the house, chattering on. There had been a time when she'd felt worn out by his relentless attentions. She remembered all those nights—not even two years had elapsed since the last occurrence—when he'd appear in the doorway of her and John's bedroom, the way he'd stand there, shoulders tensed, face red with the effort not to cry, telling them he couldn't sleep, that something "didn't feel right." How weary she'd grown of this routine. She cringed to remember how she lost the ability to escort him back to bed without letting her annoyance show. How she'd made him feel guilty for troubling them, for failing to manage his worries, for being in some fundamental way deficient. Were these his memories, too?

Once, he had not been able to get enough of her. She'd been his favorite audience, requisite witness to all he did and thought. Now, she was honored if he so much as volunteered a synopsis of a TV show.

Ricky stole a sideways glance at his eye. If you didn't know about the shiner, you wouldn't notice anything, but she believed she could see the last cabbage-y green remnant littering the skin under his eye. She had to restrain herself from touching a finger to the spot, from touching her lips to it. She took stock of how his eyebrows had thickened, his nose and jaw become more prominent. His emergent wisps of mustache glowed clearly in the television's unforgiving light. The Braille of his pimples was similarly, heartbreakingly pronounced. How little effort it took to picture him at nine, at four, at one: like a dandelion clock, slender and bright. Little towheaded Paul. Who was now neither little nor towheaded and did not want her touch. Who would not now come to her with his problems under any circumstances.

John, after his initial enraged phone call with the principal, and then a second, more mollifying and illuminating conversation in the principal's office on Monday, had taken Paul aside and spoken with him at length, obtaining confirmation of what the principal's interviews with teachers had suggested: that their son had been the target of increasing verbal bullying for months. The incident in the apple orchard was apparently not an isolated event, but the culmination of escalating provocation. Although it did appear Paul had thrown the first punch, and the mandatory three-day suspension for fighting on school grounds still stood (the principal had said apologetically), the other boys were regarded as the main aggressors; in addition to suspension, they would have to do community service and attend a weekly lunchtime anti-bullying affinity group in the guidance office. "It's great they give the bullies all that extra attention," Ricky had said. "What about Paul?"

"I don't know," John had replied. "Maybe you should have been the one to meet with the principal."

"You're right. I'm sorry."

"I don't want to hear I'm right. I don't want to hear you're sorry."

That was what it kept coming down to these days. A measure of civility; a measure of practical communication around the household and the children. But the least trespass into the realm of their relationship and anger flared, or else he shut her down. She was not allowed to apologize anymore; he was tired of those words' progression from her mouth. For weeks she'd thought in

304 • LEAH HAGER COHEN

the most desperate terms of penance, wishing for a sequence of words she might recite, a splintered board on which to kneel, a hair shirt, good works. Alternatively, she'd rehash the proofs that John was not blameless: he had a daughter he barely knew; he exploited Ricky's income so that he could work at a job he liked; he hadn't wanted a third child in the first place; he wouldn't have understood, had never understood. A wildly assembled list of his wrongs to balance her own.

But life was not a balance sheet. Poor little quant. She'd known better, of course. Against her hopes, all along she'd known. It wasn't a matter of tweaking the numbers to make the equation come out. It was not hers to control. Nor was it his to control. That was what John had kept trying to tell her. *I'm not trying to not forgive you.* That was the hopeless part.

And yet this truth—that neither one of them could script what would happen—was also where hope resided. She'd realized it in the kitchen earlier that evening, and realized it again while standing in the park after her swim, looking at their little house aglow on the dark street. It was what she meant when she'd told John, just before he left, *We have to decide.* A fearsome prospect but a necessary one, and the only one that offered any possibility of sanity or happiness.

"Here it comes," said Paul. "Watch." Ricky turned to the screen in time to see the explosion. A sliding door blew off the building. Flames roiled out. "Yes! Did you *see* that? Wait, they'll show it again."

At the end of the segment she sent him to bed. He went compliantly, yawning, not without letting her put her arms around him first. The difference in their height had become negligible. Within the year, she realized, watching him trudge up the stairs, he would overtake her.

She went to the kitchen, to the pantry, took down the old bottle of vodka, a holiday gift from someone in John's department, and poured quite a lot of it into a jelly glass. Who was it, she wondered, John was seeing tonight? And why had he said "colleague" rather than the person's name? She sat at the kitchen table and listened to the hum: the fluorescent light over the sink, or the fridge, or perhaps the very wires stretched arterially throughout the house behind the plaster. She laced her fingers around the jelly glass and drank it all in several gulps.

The stove clock read 11:47 when she picked up the phone and dialed his cell. It rang a long time and went to voice mail. She broke the connection and hit redial. Same thing. She broke the connection again, dialed a different number. Again it rang several times.

"Hello?"

"Hi, Dad. It's Ricky. Sorry to wake you."

"What's wrong?"

"Nothing. We're all okay. I just . . . I'm sorry, it's really late. I shouldn't have called."

"That's all right. What is it?" His voice, gruff with sleep and the effort to speak quietly, conjured the image of her mother asleep beside him. Simply that—the thought of her mother there beside her father, her parents lying together as they had these past forty years, nested in their own warmth within the worn linens, on their old platform bed, neither fine nor shabby but exquisite in its familiarity, the very bed she'd stood beside as a child when she needed them in the night, the bed in which she'd lain between them when she had measles, when she had mumps, when her ear ached or fever raged or nightmares frightened her awake—the thought of them in this bed now flooded her with longing. She ran her thumbnail around the threaded rim of the jelly glass.

"Well. I was just thinking about that story you used to tell? About the rabbi of—not Chelm. Something? The one with the ax . . ." She trailed off, catching her reflection in the top part of the Dutch door. It looked ghoulish, her eyes no more than hollow pits in a pale oval. She knew her father had wanted, had meant her to be like the rabbi in that story: selfless, ascendant, warming the houses of the sick, bringing cocoa to the wounded, all of it. "The thing is, I guess the thing I was wondering, Dad, is"—her voice was a beggar, scraping and tripping—"do you think I'm good? I mean, am I good?"

"What's that?" He was still working to cast off the wool of sleep. "You're talking about a story? You sure you're all right?"

"Yes. Sorry. Never mind—it's okay."

"What is it, Erica?"

"Nothing. I'm sorry. Go back to sleep."

"You sure?"

"Yes."

"Are you okay?"

"Yes."

"We'll talk in the morning."

"Okay."

She pressed OFF and set down the phone, raised her eyes to her doppelgänger in the window. She gave a start: it had doubled. It hadn't doubled; it was Biscuit, standing behind her in the kitchen doorway, her pale, troubled face an echo of Ricky's own. Ricky swiveled around, conscious of the vodka bottle, ashamed of the jelly glass, her own breath. How long had Biscuit been standing there? Had she heard any of the conversation?

Her daughter stumbled toward her, hair mussed, pajamas rumpled. "*I* think you're good," she said. "You are good."

"Biscuit, Biscuit. Why are you up?" Ricky drew her daughter onto her lap, rested her chin on Biscuit's head and breathed: shampoo, girl sweat, sleep. The ticking clock. The darkness outside. "You should be in bed."

"You're *very* good," Biscuit insisted. A validation. An exhortation.

"Shh, shhh." Ricky almost brutally aware of her daughter's weight, so dear upon her body.

2.

A s I say, they're not my field, but I showed them to Piers and he agrees they're undeniably compelling." Madeleine Berkowitz used her hand to transfer her heavy sorrel mane from the right shoulder to the left, with a commensurate adjustment to the tilt of her head. "I mean they're naive, more folk art than anything. And yet." She took a sip of her drink, a single-malt scotch and water on the rocks.

John, without shifting his gaze from her face, drank from his, the same minus the water. He'd been surprised when she offered scotch, then less surprised when he saw that the bottle was un-opened. It was both flattering and unsettling, the notion she might have purchased it in anticipation of his visit.

They were at Madeleine's place, a small bungalow in Grand-view. He'd never been there before, and it was far more appeal-ing than he'd imagined: unassuming, aged, listing. The downstairs comprised two crooked rooms of exposed brick and bulging plaster. Windows full of wavy glass panes that made the lights across the river wink on and off like stars. A cat, of course (he'd guessed as much), a gray Siamese with Popsicle-blue eyes that lifted its tail at him when he'd first arrived and then condescended to brush, disdainfully, against his ankles. ("He likes you," Madeleine had pronounced.) The place was surprisingly—agreeably, to John's taste—underfurnished. An enormous bunch of bare willow branches, stuck into a metal jug on the floor, reached up and across one wall of the tiny living room. Another wall was books and music; another, windows; the last cut diagonally by the staircase leading upstairs.

Madeleine set her glass on the old steamer trunk that served as coffee table, and with one finger described a circle around the rim. "Piers thinks they have a kind of power, a sincerity." Under the stained glass floor lamp, both the burnished leather of the trunk and the burning amber of the scotch were not unlike the color of her hair.

"Is that right?" John was not proud to discover a twinge of jealousy: who was this Piers?

Madeleine nodded. As if she knew what he was feeling, she added, "I think so, too."

She was speaking of Will Joiner's box constructions. John had given them to her for her appraisal, or at any rate, given her the two Jess had brought back from Gordie's a few weeks earlier, seeking John's professional opinion.

At first he'd demurred. "The world of fine arts, and what I do," he'd told Jess, "are pretty much apples and oranges."

"But these are like sets, aren't they?" she'd pressed, gesturing toward the boxes on the kitchen table. "I mean, what about all your models on the shelves by the washing machine?"

John's old set models, dating back to his repertory and off-Broadway years, had long resided unceremoniously in the cellar, collecting beards of dust and freckles of mildew. He had not thought of them in a long time and was gratified to hear her mention them, to know they had won her notice. But it made him uncomfortable, too, Jess referring so casually to these most obscure objects, located in the nether regions of their house.

She'd been with the Ryries a mere fortnight at that point, and the effortlessness with which she fit in seemed to refute the prediction John had made last year, when Ricky was pregnant, that a fifth family member would strain their household. Jess had just . . . slipped in. Somehow, their small kitchen table accommodated her without feeling unpleasantly cramped. The extra demands on the upstairs bathroom occurred mostly when the rest of the family was at school or at work. Biscuit seemed unbothered by having to step over the air mattress every time she wanted access to her own bed, and although Paul had made an initial show of wariness, even he had settled into apparent comfort with having Jess around. She was . . . *ingrained* was the word that came to mind. She helped with dishes, folded wash, played Mancala with Biscuit out on the front porch, brought home treats from the bakery, watched *Iron Chef* with Paul in the den, and had long chats with Ricky at the kitchen table—mostly about pregnancy, it seemed to John, and impending motherhood; he could not imagine what this must be like for Ricky, a kind of torture, he would have thought, but he did not see how he could shield her from it when Ricky herself invited, even initiated, these talks.

John alone was less than sanguine about all the apparent harmony. He could not escape the feeling that it was a subtle indictment. Anyone who fit in so naturally, so easily, must inherently belong; it seemed proof of her birthright, her due, of which she'd been robbed. He could not look at her without thinking of all the missing years. Not that she ever mentioned or even alluded to this. This made it almost worse: the fact that she hadn't come to lay blame at his feet heightened his sense that he deserved it.

So when she'd brought home Gordie's father's boxes and a request for help, it had come as something of a relief, and John found himself eager to be of service. Still, he told her regretfully, he wasn't qualified to assess them. But there was someone in his department who'd once co-curated a costume exhibit at the Museum of Arts and Design (a bit of trivia he found himself remembering even as he stood before Jess's upturned, hopeful face). Madeleine knew people in the art world, he told Jess, hoping it was true—gallery owners, critics, that kind of thing. "I could ask her to take a look at them," he offered. "If you think that'd be okay with Gordie."

Madeleine had, of course, been *only too happy to assist in any way, John, any way at all*. He'd brought them to work a few days later, delivered the boxes to her office and then braced himself for a ponderous, highly wrought, yet likely knowledgeable verdict. Madeleine had strolled around to the front of her desk and turned the boxes to face out so that she and John could study them together, side by side. Silent, frowning, alternately donning her Adrienne Vittadini eyeglasses and sliding them off and biting thoughtfully on an earpiece, she had considered each, at length, in turn.

The larger of the two, a wooden milk crate that had been painted white inside and out, housed a polar world in which snow was represented by cotton and soap flake and sequin, and at whose center arose an ice castle made of shards of glass, its turrets frosted with what looked to be sugar or salt. A tiny red and gold oriflamme flew from the uppermost spire. Close inspection showed it to have been made out of a postage stamp. Fixed to the back wall of the crate was a gold metal sun. Closer inspection showed it to be a whistle, fitted into a slat in such a way that the mouthpiece was accessible from the other side. If you blew it, it gave the low warble of a mourning dove.

The smaller, a cardboard shoe box whose exterior read "Smartfit Rugged Oxford 8.5," was to John's eye the more compelling. It held a stage (floorboards made of tongue depressors stained walnut brown, red velvet curtains, klieg lights made of film canisters painted silver) upon which a magician sawed a lady in two. It was at once crude and ingenious. Both the magician and the lady were sculpted of wire, stark yet lyrical. Lyrical, John considered, *in* their starkness. A small music box had been duct-taped to the outside of the shoe box, and a length of fishing line had been rigged so that when the music box's handle was cranked, the magician really "sawed" back and forth, while the steel comb struck the pins on the revolving cylinder to plink out a thin melody he could not place, something vaguely operatic.

"They do have a certain power," she'd said. "An integrity. Less Cornell, I'd say, than Finster-esque. Shades of Calder. Obviously, they're highly representational." The glasses went on and off again. "There *is* something . . ." She sipped in a breath and held it, tilting her head this way and that for many seconds before expelling it again. "Well, they're mournful."

This had been so far from anything he might have expected her to say that John had looked at her in some surprise, without the faintly sardonic smile he usually reserved for interactions with Madeleine. She seemed not to notice but stood looking at the magician's box, a whiff of theatrics in her posture, yes, but under this genuine feeling; he believed he could see it in the heaviness of her mouth, the slope of her shoulders. He'd never before sought her opinion, let alone her favor, and felt sharply uncomfortable now, in light of her ingenuous willingness to grant it, about the way he and Lance had always treated her as fair game, the butt of so many unarticulated jokes.

Part of the implicit rationale for mocking Madeleine had always been her aggressively sexualized persona, the way she tried too hard, and the conclusion that she was therefore phony. Yet standing so close to her at that moment, seeing not just the bottle-red hair and the tight cashmere sweater but also the perimenopausal down on her cheek, the fine lines around her lips and eyes, the stray fleck of mascara on her lid, John realized he'd been wrong to construe phoniness. What was trying too hard but evidence of innocence, naïveté? He had been, in spite of himself, moved.

When she'd asked whether she might borrow them, take them into the city to show a friend, he'd agreed. That had been over a week ago. This morning she told him she'd had a chance to get her friend's opinion, and—well, it was *très intéressant*; the friend was eager to see more; Madeleine wanted to pass on his comments in more detail; when would John be free? They compared calendars; no luck. How about sometime after work, then? Why not—tonight? Her place? It made sense; that way he could retrieve the boxes. She jotted down her address; he said he'd call to let her know when he was on his way. It was all so quick and easy, accomplished as though it were nothing, or rather, were something they'd done a hundred times, like agreeing to a date for the next faculty meeting. He knew from the very casualness with which they'd set up the plan that it was not nothing.

A dozen times that afternoon he'd thought about canceling. When Ricky got home from work wearing that brave, effortful smile she wore nearly all the time now and went on tiptoe to rub her nose against his beard. Again when Paul, without being asked, helped him wheel the garbage out to the curb. Again when Jess and Biscuit, standing in front of the living room sofa, folded the laundry together, singing, "There's a Hole in the Bucket," over and over and with great feeling, Jess taking the part of Henry and Biscuit the part of Liza. But then he and Ricky had fought while doing the dishes after supper, and she'd accused him—this was new—of not wanting the baby. She claimed she'd been right not to trust him, right to have withheld news of the diagnosis, and while he knew her logic was wrong— had tried explaining to her why it was wrong, why her presumption constituted the very core of their problem, that by not trusting him to respond as she might have wished, she'd robbed them of the chance to find out, together, how he would, in fact, *have* responded—still, her accusation stung more than she possibly could have known.

And now he sat on Madeleine's gray velvet couch, in her unexpectedly appealing, unexpectedly self-possessed, uncloying little house, and she was leaning forward and asking him something as if for the second time. ". . . if he spoke Italian?" she said. "Your Mr. Joiner?"

"Pardon?"

"Do you know whether he spoke Italian?"

"Oh—no. Not my Mr. Joiner, anyway. Never met him. How come?"

"Because of the way he spelled the name of the song. Did you happen to notice?"

He had no idea what she meant.

"I'll show you," said Madeleine, rising. "They're right up here." She picked up her drink. He took his and followed her to the tiny hall.

How absurd, he was thinking. *Come up and see my etchings.* Was this really how it happened, how people had affairs; was it really so clichéd? In disappointment and excitement he swallowed the rest of his drink as they mounted the stairs. These were narrow and creaky and slanted drastically to the left. They led directly into a room with low sloping ceilings; only in the very middle could he stand up straight. A skylight showed milky clouds in a purple sky, its pane rattling slightly with a draft. Madeleine switched on the light. It was her studio, he saw, a candy-shop mess of fabric and ribbon, artificial flowers and pots of beads, jars of buttons, silks dyed vibrant hues. In one corner a dress model. In another, an ironing board and two sewing machines, one modern, one antique. The walls were papered with costume sketches, some of them watercolored, and pictures torn from magazines or books. John was aware of an urge to lap up these details thirstily, even lasciviously; aware, too, that the urge stemmed as much from his lust for art as for eros. He could see through a dark doorway what must be the bedroom, but knew the room where he already stood was her most intimate space.

On a high drafting table under the skylight sat Will Joiner's boxes. Madeleine switched on a gooseneck lamp and angled it toward the smaller, magician's box. She pointed an eggplant-colored fingernail to where a slim wooden plaque, fixed with tiny gold screws to the front of the stage, bore the words O SOLO MIO. "See that?"

"Yeah. I hadn't before."

"It's the song, you know, that plays on the little music box." She sang a line, badly, then gave an embarrassed smile. "Well, you know. Only it's supposed to be 'O Sole Mio,' S-O-L-*E*, the sun. The way he's got it—I confess I wouldn't have caught it; Piers is the one who pointed it out—it's something like 'My Loneliness,' or 'O Lonely Me.' You have to wonder," she said, turning to look at him, "if it was intentional. Or just a misspelling, a coincidence." Her gaze flitted to and fro between his eyes in the unnerving, too-searching manner of a soap star. "What do you think?" She reached behind the box and turned the tiny handle, as languorously as earlier she'd traced the rim of her glass. The song ticked forth like seconds on a clock, one plucked metal note after another. Onstage the magician, in all his faceless wire melancholy, sawed. The lady lay rigid beneath the movement, a hollow, horizontal twining of unprotesting silver.

John watched, mesmerized, trying to work it out—not just the answer to the question, which seemed bigger, somehow, than Madeleine realized, as if her words were code for things beyond this room (they reminded him of something, what?); but trying to puzzle out, too, what the question itself revealed, not simply about Gordie's dad, but about him and Madeleine and this rickety charmer of a house with the wintry-eyed cat downstairs; about Biscuit's fire and Paul's black eye; about Jess's baby and Jess as a baby. Madeleine turned and turned the tiny handle. The song continued to come and it came to him then, what the words reminded him of. Intention or mistake. It was Ricky's Or Game. Funny that Ricky, the quant, would play such a game, a game that demanded all things be stripped of quantifiable worth, a game in which all answers were permitted and no reasons begged or offered. *Sun or lonely?* he could hear her asking, just as clearly as if she'd said it aloud. And then: *We have to decide,* her voice in his mind as distinct as if she'd somehow come into the room, crept up these crooked stairs behind him and spoken, quietly but with great force of truth, her face lovely and worried and tilted toward his, awaiting his reply.

3.

Since Baptiste's mother and sister had come to Nyack, the ban on his going home straight after school had been lifted.

"Yo, what was that anyway?" Paul finally asked. "The knife thing?"

"It happened to my Grann," Baptiste explained.

"Someone broke in with a knife?"

"A machete. They killed her son."

"Your father?"

"My uncle. A long time ago, man. Before she moved to this country. Gimme one, okay?"

Paul shook a Swedish Fish into Baptiste's upturned palm. They were walking home through the apple orchard, backpacks slogging heavily against their shoulders, the fallen petals of apple blossoms littering the ground like snow. Nothing had turned out like Paul would've thought. He'd figured when he went back to school after his suspension, things would be worse than ever, kids ignoring him, pretending not to notice, then whispering behind his back about the state of his face and how it had gotten that way. The story would be circulated, embellished, cemented; the bruises would act as visual confirmation of a status he'd so far been only provisionally assigned. For five days at home—the weekend plus the three days of his suspension—he had writhed in a kind of private agony, all contained in his gut. He'd had no appetite, hardly been able to eat anything, and shat when he did, all water and nerves.

Most of that Monday and Tuesday he'd done nothing but lie on his bed, drawing with Winsor & Newton Black Indian ink, which got all over his fingers and sheets, or just contemplating cracks in the ceiling, devising ways he wouldn't have to go back. Homeschooling, but both his parents worked. Private school, but the money, plus wouldn't those kids be even worse than public? Play hooky for the rest of the year and hope his parents just confused him with Biscuit. Ha ha. Come down with an illness, something serious, childhood cancer. The Ronald McDonald House. Make a Wish. Simpler yet, die. And he spent long minutes tenderly, solemnly spinning out the idea of his nonexistence, imagining it so deeply that he brought himself to tears, finally, with the thought of his mother's agony. The after-effects of indulging in such a fantasy included shame as well as refreshment, and when he rose from his bed he felt fragile, as though his limbs were spun glass—although maybe that was just because he hadn't been eating.

Baptiste had been suspended, too, but it was not so bad for him, thought Paul, because of his mother and sister having newly arrived. In a way, for Baptiste, it was perfect. Paul pictured the reunion: all smiles, hugs, and tears. Staying up late, everyone speaking hungrily, listening hungrily, every exchange in rapid-fire Creole, the fact of its taking place in another language automatically imbuing the reunion with the quality of being beyond Paul's reach, even beyond the reach of what he could imagine. After three days of tormenting himself with the certainty that Baptiste would drop him, *had* dropped him, on Tuesday Paul steeled himself to make the call: he tried the Lecomptes' house once, two times, three, five, ten: no answer. He tried all day and into the night. Nothing. Obviously Baptiste was screening. Paul wrote a text, last resort—I JUST WANTED TO SAY THANKS FOR FIGHTING KENNY THAT WAS COOL. IF YOU DONT WANT TO HANG OUT I GET THAT BUT DONT THINK WHAT THEY SAID IS TRUE. ITS A LIE EXCEPT IF THEY SAY IT ABOUT THEMSELVES RIGHT? HA HA—and in self-loathing, deleted it without sending.

The next day he'd tried phoning again. This time Baptiste picked right up.

"Man, how you doing?" As if nothing was wrong.

"A'ight. How 'bout you?"

"A'ight. Chillin'."

"So how's your mom, your sister, everything?"

"Good. Crazy. Every Haitian person in like, New York, has been over to pay respects. Yesterday we had to go to Brooklyn to see like thirty of my aunts. I ate so much *food.*"

"So what are you doing today? You want to like, hang?"

"Can't. I got to show my mom and sister stuff, you know."

"Okay, well . . ."

"Yo, how's your *face*?"

"Oh, it's okay. Whatever. So I'll see you in school, I guess."

In fact, the bruising on Paul's face was approaching its dramatic peak. The killer thing about the length of the suspension was that although the swelling had gone down, just in time for his return to school the subdural blood that had pooled under his eye achieved its richest shade of burgundy, flecked with darker spots, like dregs. It was as if the principal had timed it for maximum humiliation. Paul's parents offered to let him stay home a few more days, and Jess offered to apply some concealer, but in the end Paul decided just to deal. The waiting, he figured, the lying there studying the cracks on his ceiling, fantasizing about the horrible things people would say and listening to his intestines lament, all of this had to be worse than finding out for real how it was going to be.

And it had turned out to be so much better than he'd thought. He wasn't exactly greeted like a hero or anything, but whatever story had gone around school in his absence had worked somehow in his favor. Guys who'd all but stopped acknowledging him in the sixth grade nodded at him in the hall and passed him the ball in gym. Girls who'd never acknowledged him at all asked to borrow lunch tickets and see the drawings in his notebook. It was plain strange. Paul didn't dislike the change, but his classmates' inconstancy made him wonder whether he'd overvalued their esteem in the first place, and he was that much more appreciative of Baptiste's friendship. More, he felt less tentative about it, or felt it to be less tenuous than he'd thought. In any case, where once he wouldn't have dared ask about the knife and his Grann, or anything much about life in Haiti and what Baptiste remembered of it, now he did and Baptiste did not seem to mind.

"So, what happened, exactly?" Paul asked, as they crossed the overpass into town. "It was like a robbery gone bad?" He realized not only how long he'd been working to make himself small, but how this had imposed limits on what he knew of his friend. Now he shook a few more Swedish Fish from the package into each of their palms and listened to Baptiste explain about the Tonton Macoutes.

HE THOUGHT AT first the house was empty, but then he heard sounds, strumming, coming from upstairs. He let his backpack slide heavily from his arms and then went up to see, following the sounds to the open doorway of his parents' room. Jess sat cross-legged on the oval rag rug, leaning against the foot of the bed and plucking away at his mother's mandolin. She looked up as he filled the doorway and smiled at him without breaking her song.

"Who said you could use that?"

"Hello to you, too."

He came in and sat on the rug opposite her, crossing his legs like hers, only this had become, in the past year or so, difficult for him to do; he had to use his hands. Her fingers sprang over the frets and darted among the strings with easy authority. Who knew? The music was dancerly and American. It made him think of overalls and chickens. When she came to the end of the song she looked up and made a little *ta-da* gesture with one hand.

Paul put his hands together twice, soundlessly: an ironic gesture of clapping.

"Is she giving that to you?" he asked, having suddenly realized, without knowing how, that this was the case.

Jess looked down and plucked at a few notes. "Yeah."

"Cool." He did not think it was cool. His father had given it to his mother for her birthday. "Can I see it?" He held out his hand.

"You see with your eyes," she said, but self-mockingly, and passed it to him by the neck.

Paul plucked the open strings, fingered the mother-of-pearl inlays, turned it over and ran a hand along the bowl-shaped back. The thing was shaped like a giant fig. It was kind of grand, and also kind of ridiculous in its grandeur, like a man in a silk cravat. He tried in vain to imagine his mother playing it, and felt suddenly embarrassed for his father. He handed it back. "Is it hard to learn?"

Jess considered. "Like anything else."

"How many instruments can you play?"

"Just guitar, really, and then I can kind of pick up other string instruments and scratch something out. Banjo, ukelele. Mandolin. Not well, though."

It sounded good enough. "Play something else."

She did. This tune was more courtly and slow; it made him think of *Masterpiece Theatre*. The bedroom was very dim; it had an eastern exposure and got no direct light in the afternoon. You could see out the window how the sun was shining brightly on the bridge, and this made the shadowy blue of the bedroom seem all the more out of place, or them out of place in it, like they were here at the wrong time. The bed was, as usual, neatly made. The small wicker wastebasket next to his mother's dresser was overflowing with crumpled tissues, a few of which lay scattered on the floor. A few more adorned her bedside table like fat white flowers.

His father had not slept here in two weeks. Paul, with his insomnia, had heard him going down the stairs well past midnight every night. Although he stayed up listening, some nights until three or four, he never heard him come back up again. There was more: he'd heard arguing in his parents' room, the hissing sounds of whispered acrimony. He'd heard the door of the linen closet, which was right outside his bedroom, opening and shutting softly each night; heard the sound of cloth sliding on cloth, and the muted click of the old-fashioned latch, just before his father's footsteps descended the stairs. Every morning when he woke, the house looked undisturbed, his parents' bed already made, nothing out of place downstairs, all the couch cushions arranged as usual. But last night, while watching TV, he'd noticed something between the cushions. And even though he'd already known, it had still been a blow, pulling out his father's actual sock.

"Are you moving in with us?" asked Paul. He'd picked up on stirrings and vagaries about this, but both parents had professed to be in the dark when he'd asked them point-blank. He wondered what, if anything, Jess's presence had to do with his parents' discord. He wondered if she knew that his father had been sleeping downstairs, if she, too, like him and like his parents, was simply saying nothing about it. Maybe it wasn't even that unusual. Maybe Jess's own father sometimes slept on the couch. Maybe that went on in lots of families.

"No."

"*Haven't* you kind of, though?"

She laughed. Then she put the mandolin away, packing it gently into its case and fastening the latches. "Don't worry, I'm going."

"When?"

"Are you so dying for me to leave?"

He shrugged.

"No, seriously."

And she was, it seemed, regarding him with great seriousness. It made him feel thrillingly old, adult. He shrugged again: "No."

For close to a minute neither said anything.

Then he said, "Why'd you cut your hair?"

"My hair? Jeez. I don't know. That's what you're thinking about?"

He felt himself redden and looked down, started playing with the frayed ends of his jeans.

Jess sprang up and went toward the hall.

"Where're you going?" He scrambled after.

She darted into his room—there was play in her movement— looked around, grabbed his porkpie hat from the top of his dresser. She put it on. "This better?"

"Gimme." He made a grab but she held fast, squashing it to her own head with both hands.

"My turn!" she insisted, with a mad little stamp. He backed off. And this was interesting: they were both looking at their reflections in the mirror above Paul's dresser. He was the taller, by an inch. They were very changed from the girl and boy they'd been at Cabruda Lake, but here they were, the same two people

326 • LEAH HAGER COHEN

after all, caught now in the same glass. Jess released the brim of the hat slowly, guardedly, her hands hovering in the vicinity in case Paul should try to snatch it. Her mouth was open, in ready position for a laugh, and she kept darting her eyes at him in the mirror. He'd look off in the other direction then and whistle an innocent tune.

"Let's see here . . ." she said, all singsong and goofy. She began perusing his dresser top, picking things up, putting them down. "Comb," she enunciated, holding it up in the mirror and placing it down again carefully, as though an archaeological find. "Wind-up Martian. USB thingy. Deodorant. Acne spot treatment."

This was too much. Paul grabbed her wrist and tried to wrestle it away. She fought him, squealing. They found themselves surprisingly evenly matched. Several items got knocked off the dresser in the ensuing struggle. He proved the stronger, by a hair. They wound up on the bed. He pried the tube of Clearasil from her fingers.

"Ow," said Jess, and rubbed her wrist, which was, in fact, red. "Look what you did." Holding it up accusingly to his face. She was on her back, half under him. Both were panting, both half laughing. But when he leaned in and kissed her mouth (she tasted of Burt's Bees and salt and plain, sweet spit), and she did not push him off right away but let him put his tongue between her lips and slide it along her teeth, no one could have been more aghast than he.

4.

Gordie was out by the dumpsters, trying to get Ebie to relin-
quish something she'd got in her mouth, part of a greasy
paper bag and also, he had a bad feeling, a chicken bone.

"Ebie, *no*."

She gave her tail a measured wave but did not make eye
contact.

"Ebie, *drop it*." He lunged for her collar. She bobbed her head
and deftly sidestepped. With new distance between them, she
began to work her jaws. Gordie heard a splintery crunch. "*No*,
Ebie! *Bad* girl." He sprang at her and gripped her collar with one
hand, gripped her lower jaw, dripping copious saliva, with the
other. She growled, but it was short and soft, as if she felt bad
about it. In any case, Gordie was undeterred. "Ebie, drop it. NO.
You can't have that." He straddled her closely and with two
hands now tried to pry her jaws open. It was a wet and slippery

business. She held on. There was something infinitely patient in her musculature, her stillness, the way she suffered his attempts without either attacking or giving in, that Gordie, even given his exasperation, had to admire. A moment later, perhaps sensing some minute lessening of pressure from his knees, Ebie twisted her head free and loosed herself from between his legs. She bounded away to the other side of the dumpster, and there, with that large object positioned strategically between them, proceeded to enjoy her plunder. Elongating her neck and holding her head up slightly, so as not to let fall bits of food, she crunched, with effort, the discarded chicken: bones, bag and all.

"Great," said Gordie. "That's great. When you choke, don't come running to me."

"Okay, I won't."

He turned. Jess was strolling toward him, hands in her back pockets. He explained about Ebie while they watched her polish off her snack.

"You let her come out here without a leash?"

"I shouldn't. I was just going back and forth with all this garbage, and she was giving me such a hard time I finally let her come." Gordie jogged back to the place in the parking lot where he'd abandoned his latest load: three black heavy-duty bags. He heaved them over the top of the dumpster.

"Why so much garbage?"

"Aah." He prodded a piece of broken glass with the toe of his sneaker. "Cleaning out a bunch of my dad's things." He wouldn't have expected this to upset her, but evidently it did. Her brow furrowed; she took her hands out of her pockets and pressed them together under her chin.

"What things?"

"God—everything."

"Not the dioramas, though?"

"Everything but. Cigarette cartons. Pill bottles. Calendars from like the nineties. Cassettes. Eight-tracks. Broken appliances. One of those bags"—he gestured with a foot toward the dumpster—"was filled entirely with broken clocks."

She put a hand on his arm, just below the sleeve of his T-shirt. He'd worked up a sweat and her hand was cool. "Is it . . . It must be hard for you?"

Gordie shrugged. He'd been all right until she asked. Now his nose prickled; he wiped it vigorously with the back of his hand. "Hey, Ebie," he called, snapping his fingers. The dog looked up, but, rightly ascertaining there was no real point to the summons, went back to licking the spot of concrete where she'd found the improperly disposed chicken. He cleared his throat. "It's long overdue, I suppose."

"Why," Jess began, and then seemed to change her mind about what she was going to say. "Why'd he have so many clocks?"

"He collected 'em. For his projects. He'd take them apart and use the little screws, the cogs, whatever. Hey, what brings you, anyway?" The full strangeness of her just showing up dawned on him. They'd spent a lot of time together these past weeks, but mostly down in the village center, and never without making a plan first. They'd take Ebie for long walks by the river, then wind up at Turiello's for a slice. They'd hang out on the Ryries' porch, where one day Jess persuaded Gordie to let her cut his hair; then they'd watched as the wind came along and blew away the thatches of reddish-brown fluff, which Jess said would end up in a bird's nest. They'd poke around the bookstore, the health food store, the thrift shop, pick out little presents for the Ryries or each other. Jess bought Gordie old salt and pepper shakers shaped like a cat and a dog. Gordie bought Jess a baby spoon, with worn initials engraved in the handle, the bowl of the spoon black with tarnish. They were two young people with nothing to do. They were a fresh-minted orphan and an expectant mother. They'd found in each other a ready companion, unlikely and serendipitous.

"You walked?" Gordie looked over her shoulder, as if for evidence of a previously unnoticed conveyance.

It was a bland afternoon in early May, mild but not fair; there was a kind of dull haze that made the day seem skyless. A couple of kids were riding bikes at the far end of the parking lot, and an old white woman towed a folding cart full of grocery bags toward the entrance of one of the squat buildings. She progressed with such slowness as to strain credulity, as if the whole scene were an illusion, a film being played at the wrong speed. The sound of cars on the thruway behind them was the aural equivalent of the view: unnuanced, unchanging. Gordie felt, as he often did, conscious of the dismal quality of his surroundings.

"News," said Jess, mysteriously. "And yeah, I walked."

"News?" What news merited her walking this far, every bit of it uphill?

"About your dad, actually. About his . . . projects."

"Oh. Really?" Gordie asked her inside. He wanted, he said, to wash the chicken grease and dog saliva off his hands. But he found himself wanting to stave off whatever she had to say. Because he feared dismissal? But she would not have walked all this way to make the announcement, certainly not with that expression on her face, if the news was dismissive of his dad's work. Well, then, did he fear approbation? That seemed, as his dad might have commented, daft. He snapped his fingers for Ebie, and this time she charged after them willingly, pushed ahead and bounded up the stairs with a kind of fleet cheer, as if to curry favor after her recent transgression.

Climbing the stairs rather more slowly behind the dog, and pausing on each landing in order to turn and gesticulate, and catch her breath in the process, Jess filled Gordie in on the details. John's colleague's friend—or friend's colleague, something like that—knew someone who worked at a gallery, or curated exhibits—Gordie couldn't make out whether this was two different people or one who did both—who had looked at the two and asked to see more. Jess seemed to put a lot of stock in that phrase, "asked to see more," although to Gordie it sounded vague as could be. It might, he thought, signify anything from interest in acquiring them to polite brush-off. "John said if you want to go ahead with it, choose ten or fifteen and he'd get them to the guy, and I thought maybe I could help you de—"

She stopped talking the moment he opened the door to the condo. It was very different from the first time she'd seen it. The surface of the kitchen table was bare and had been sponged clean. The sink was empty, the drying rack full. The window over the sink gleamed. A single yellow dish towel, folded in thirds, hung over the handle of the oven door. On the floor beside the door, more plastic garbage bags were lined up. The boots, shoes, gloves, umbrellas, shopping bags, and the big glass carboy that had previously sat by Ebie's water dish, weighted with coins, were nowhere to be seen.

"Holy shit, Batman," Jess said softly. "Did you do all this today?"

"Today and yesterday, mostly." Gordie washed his hands and filled two glasses with water, which they carried into the living room. Here, too, he'd done a lot of work. Gone was the clutter, the newspapers and books and boxes and extension cords and dirty plates and empty chip bags. The couch was free of all objects except two throw pillows. The carpet, which had previously been a sea of socks, pizza cartons, dead batteries, circulars, loose bills, take-out menus, ballpoint pens, junk mail, clothes hangers, and shot glasses, was not only debris-free but vacuumed. In one corner stood a pile of boxes labeled "GOODWILL." The only thing apparently untouched was Will Joiner's art, row upon row of the dioramas crammed cheek by jowl onto the standard-and-bracket bookshelves that lined two walls of the room.

"Gordie—are you moving?"

He sat heavily on the couch, or as heavily as his light frame would allow. His muscles ached. Sweat stained the armpits of his gray T-shirt. He drained his entire glass of water. "That's the thing," he said then. "I have to."

"Oh, Gordie. The money?" Jess sat beside him, facing him, crossing her legs, nesting her glass of water in two hands.

He shrugged elaborately and made a face intended to convey a sort of Zen urbanity: it's all trivial in the long run—though he had an uncomfortable feeling he might have missed his mark, conveying something more along the lines of inanity. "It's not so bad," he said. "There's money for a while, and Fordham's offering me practically a free ride for next year, based on my 'extraordinary circumstances'—that's what financial aid calls it. Isn't that weird? 'Extraordinary circumstances,' like people don't die every day of the week. And there's my uncle in Canada, who's actually great, he's offered like a hundred times to help out. The main thing is, *I* can't stay. I mean I don't want to."

Ebie ambled into the room, accompanied by the leisurely clink of her tags. She came around the couch and inserted herself between the coffee table and Gordie's legs, laying her chin on his knee. Bits of kibble and beads of water now clung to her greased muzzle. Gordie overlooked this and stroked her wonderful broad crown—incredible what the roundness of Ebie's skull against the hollow of his palm did for his spirits—and she rolled her liquid black eyes up to meet his: an inherently, almost quintessentially empathetic expression, the Newf rendition of the proverbial sad clown.

Jess said nothing, and into this gap, Gordie wandered on. "It's not that the memories are too painful." He made his voice slightly ridiculous for the last four words. "It's not— I *like* having the memories. I like that I think of him when I'm standing at the sink, making coffee, whatever. I *like* sitting in his chair out on the balcony, thinking of how he'd always be sitting out there, smoking his stupid cigarettes. Acting like he was looking out at the friggin', I don't know, French Riviera." Gordie gave the littlest laugh, not at all bitter. He looked up and around the room, seeing and not seeing the many dozens of boxes lining the shelves, seeing and not seeing the many dozens of tiny worlds, the complete and elusive installations his father had left behind. "But it's like, I'm nine*teen*. I can't— I shouldn't be here. You know? Living behind the"—he gestured a little wildly toward the kitchen—"*thru*way entrance, surrounded by all these young families and old people and stuff. It would be like . . . I mean, you know those stories where people go and fling themselves on top of the grave of the person who's died and they never get up? They just lie in one spot and, I don't know, freeze to death?"

Jess shook her head apologetically.

"Whatever. That kind of thing?"

"Like . . . people who don't get on with their lives?"

"Aaghh. That sounds lame. Forget it. I just know I can't stay here." He set his empty glass on the coffee table. He felt her looking at him. He felt her still looking at him. "What?" He glanced sideways.

She was smiling mysteriously, abstractedly, seeming to study at the same time his face and her own private thoughts. Her eyes, he was reminded—remembered thinking—were like Junior Mints. Like Hugh's. Darkly soft. Did she know it? Did she actively *train* that limpid gaze on him, make it all melting on purpose? His own witlessness in the face of such a gaze maddened him. Was he meant to respond in some way? To counter, to match her, to up the ante, what? *"What,"* he demanded.

"No, I was just thinking—"

"That I sound completely lame."

"That you sound completely old. I mean . . . you make *me* feel lame."

The confession sounded honest, shyly so, yet the likelihood that he could cause her to feel lame seemed so farfetched he could not help eyeing her with suspicion. He liked her. It was true. True, too, that she reminded him of Hugh, and he had really liked Hugh, *like*-liked him. Hadn't he? Why didn't he know for certain? He'd pictured kissing Hugh. He was picturing it again right now; how could he help it? Did that mean he wanted to? Was imagining the same as desiring? His dad—for fuck's sake—had made that wedding cake, the two grains of rice on top both men. What had that been, that crazy little message from beyond the grave? A blessing? A knowing wink? It was crap. What had his dad known, or guessed, about him, and why in hell hadn't he ever talked about it with Gordie while he'd been still around? Gordie felt his palms grow slick with sweat.

"That's what I was thinking," she maintained. "And. That."

". . . yes?"

"You're fantastic."

"Oh, please." He snorted. Ebie quirked up her ears.

"No, I—"

"Are you ever just genuine?" He was a little startled by his words; also, by the force with which he spoke them.

"What?"

"Right, though?" Gordie continued as though he had just made a point, which it seemed to him, inside his head, he had. "It's like you're always . . . *flirting* with me, in this half-assed, borderline way that doesn't really mean anything. I mean I know that. It's pointless. Obviously."

His antagonism sprung from a source of which he had no prior knowledge. Without his intending or even anticipating it, the conversation had changed course, become different from any exchange they'd had in the preceding weeks. But it was true, he thought: she was always touching him, small, sororal gestures—a hand lighting on his back, a shoulder pressing against his—punctuated by more devilish, intimate flashes of contact: a finger-flick on the side of his head; or a push, with both hands, knocking him clear off the sidewalk and into a bush. What was that if not flirtation? And yet, what was flirtation if not ambiguous, as likely to be mocking as sincere?

The indirection was bedeviling. Likewise the threat of hope. And how could he fault her for her ambiguity when he himself was so torpidly ambivalent? Could he be attracted to Hugh and Jess both? Or was what he felt something less explicit than attraction, a merely reflexive response to the magnetism of another's coquetry? How on earth did people recognize their own desires? What was wrong with him that he alone seemed incapable of doing so?

"Obviously," he repeated, as though this word somehow contained the crux of his complaint, encapsulated his most concentrated grievance against her.

Jess uncrossed her legs and sat up straight, but although she opened her mouth, words apparently failed her. She gaped a little, fishlike. And even so was not unlovely: her pursed lips opening and closing; her eyes showing rims of white around the pupils; her cheeks dark with rising blood.

"I don't need . . . false flattery, or flirtation." Gordie spat out the fricatives, his own vehemence continuing to surprise him. "I don't need anything false from you."

Jess rose so violently water spilled from her glass. "Fine. Only I'm not false. I'm very sorry you think so. Fuck you," she added, all in the same low, evenly spaced voice.

Gordie stood, too, mirroring her belligerent stance more out of a knee-jerk sense of etiquette than out of any instinct for preservation or to do battle. They stood face-to-face, both of them fairly radiant with anger. Ebie looked from one to the other, wagging her tail, ready to play. Gordie felt unable to recall exactly how they'd come to this point.

"What?" he said.

"What do you *mean*, 'what'?" Her eyes widened as though she were not only incensed but incredulous.

Would she dash in his face the water that remained in her glass? Would she slap him? He had the strong impression that she was, in fact, about to kiss him. So compelling was his conviction that his mind seemed to wander forward a few moments in time and supply the projected sensations: her knuckles hard against his chest as she grabbed a fistful of his shirt, her lips pressed hotly to his, his own mashed up tight against his locked, recalcitrant teeth. His spine, his arms, his legs, all gone rigid, tightened against the implication—but here his mind complicated matters by conjuring an additional tightening in his groin.

Blushing, he stammered, "Wh-what are we fighting about?"

"You just called me a liar."

"I didn't."

"A fake."

"Well," he said. He thought a moment. "Yeah."

She reacted to this admission not by striking or kissing him, but rather appeared to shed, in an instant, all anger, all indignation. It was as though he'd pressed a secret button, so quickly did the change come over her. She set down her glass, seized one of his hands, and began to plead, almost, it seemed, to bargain.

"But I'm not fake, Gordie, really I'm not," she was saying. "That's how they make me feel, but it's not my fault he's my

338 LEAH HAGER COHEN

father. I try, I try, to be nice, and good, and, and, and *liked,* and I know they do like me, but—they don't. Or they don't really let me . . . trust me . . . They don't *talk* about things. Did you know they had a baby die? Last year. And they don't even mention it, never even told me. I mean, Biscuit, she told me, tells me some stuff. But you'd think! And Ricky and I have had all these talks about pregnancy and babies and everything, and then I go and find out she never even mentions this important thing to me, and they're always whispering together, Ricky and John, and they go silent and all stony-faced when I come in the room. And I . . . my God, I mean I *buy* things, you know, and wash the dishes, that kind of thing, try to help, be *helpful,* like with the boxes, I'm trying to help, help *you.* And it's the least he can do, after all these— Isn't it? Don't you think?—really, to help with this one thing I ever asked, not even for me but for someone else, a friend, and after all it's his line of work, I mean he *knows* people. . . ."

She kept talking, or babbling, and he listened, following some of it but not all, noticing in any case less her words than her tone of distress, and also the distressed way she was kneading his hand, pinching up—as if absentmindedly—the loose skin around his knuckles, then smoothing out his joints, tracing the lines on his palm, separating his fingers, sliding her own between them, imploring him. She seemed, for the first time since he'd met her, much younger, rather than older, than her twenty-three years. She seemed about fifteen. Even her voice sounded younger: tentative and high. She was not crying but was in a state that seemed to him like crying, her words, her unstructured, nonsensical speech continuing steadily in the manner of tears.

He'd struck a chord he'd had no intention of striking. She was a stranger—she'd never legitimately progressed beyond that point, no matter how much he might have liked pretending so over the past several weeks—a stranger who seemed at this moment both more and less authentic than ever. But when he folded his arms around her he felt not at all stiff, and barely strange. He was like Ebie coming out onto the balcony and resting her head on his thigh: a body that knew exactly what to do—not forever, not in all situations, but in this moment, for this time. He held Jess and took note of his ease, which was at once novel and native. How amazing. "Shh," he said. "Shh."

5.

As she explained to Ricky, Jess wasn't worried. In fact she felt a little silly mentioning it. In fact she had *not* mentioned it at first, not for several hours after going to the bathroom at Gordie's house and wiping and seeing the blood on the toilet paper. One reason she wasn't worried, as she explained to Ricky two or three times (it seemed worthy of repetition; an important, determining fact), was that the blood wasn't bright red. It was only a pale brown stain, like what you see (she said) when you're about to get your period but it hasn't really started yet. Another (this had seemed even more decisive a fact) was that each time she'd gone back to the bathroom since, there'd been no sign of blood, neither on her underwear nor on the toilet paper. Also, she'd read somewhere, hadn't she (in one of the books on Ricky's shelves most likely, one of the pregnancy books to which Ricky had specifically and generously drawn her attention), that a little harmless spotting in early pregnancy was common, or at least not unheard of.

All of this Jess told Ricky in an embarrassed and strangely excited rush, in the upstairs hall that night, not long after Gordie had given her a lift home. To Gordie she'd said nothing. She'd taken stock in his little bathroom with its pill-pink fixtures and fluorescent lighting, staring at the piece of toilet paper with a kind of detachment that was at odds with her racing heart—first seeing: a mechanical, strictly synaptical act; then absorbing: the process of sight becoming reality; then evaluating: trying to assess the image's possible import—in steps as distinct and methodical as that—the information contained in the definite but faint smear of blood, as innocuous in color as a residue of coffee around the rim of a mug. She had, after several moments, risen and flushed the toilet and washed her hands and washed her face and examined in the medicine-cabinet mirror her own face, which appeared the same as it always had, and as she always envisioned herself: practical, plain, steady of gaze. Then she'd walked back into the living room, where Gordie was kneeling before a low shelf of his dad's boxes, and, kneeling beside him, did not mention the blood but resumed the conversation they'd been having about dollhouses and letter carriers, babies and art.

It had seemed important to go on responding, if obliquely, to his charge of falsity, and several times during their conversation she edged close to telling him about her mother and father, how they hadn't really kicked her out; how they wanted her home again; and how she missed them, and wasn't sure herself why she was sticking around the Ryries, what it was she was waiting for, hoping for. She came close to telling him, too, how Paul had kissed her earlier that afternoon—wasn't it terrible?—and how she was ashamed for him, and also sorry for him. But that wasn't quite right. The truth (though she did not come close to telling Gordie this) was that she was ashamed of herself for letting it unfold as it had: the progression from mandolin to hat to wrestling match to bed. Panting and laughing, laughing and panting, pink and breathless and the bedsprings squeaking—as though she had been curious about her own power, had wanted to see if she could bring him to that point.

Nor did she tell Gordie how she lay every night on the air mattress beside Biscuit's bed making up stories, fashioning lies. A white vinyl purse, a sequined insect. Canadian coins. Mints. A chipmunk tame enough to eat from their hands. How effortlessly she'd gotten Biscuit to collude in those lies, to enjoy them, initiate them; how they invented together, night after night, weaving, in the glow of the night-light, a fake history: half sister and half sister both hungry for threads.

Nor did she tell him how splendidly, wickedly easy it had been to gain Ricky's affection; that simply by showing up pregnant she had gained a foothold on this most daunting task. More than a foothold—she'd reaped bequests. A turquoise bottle of prenatal vitamins; a mobile that played "Twinkle, Twinkle, Little Star" while cloth moons and stars perambulated; a half-shelf of books advising what kind of fish not to ingest, what kind of oil to massage into stretch marks, what to name one's baby. All of these offered with an almost eager flourish, as though Ricky had been expecting her, or at any rate aching for someone to whom she might pass these things along.

Even had she wanted to, she would not have had the means

to tell how John, for all that he was unfailingly courteous, seemed in subtle fashion to disparage her, or despair of her. Or maybe what she sensed was simple distrust. She sensed it not in spite of his courtesy but as a result of it, the quality of his courtesy toward her being so careful, so considered. A few times she'd caught him looking at her with nothing in his expression—not admiration, or regret, or wonder, or even *interest,* really—but a kind of wary bemusement. Jess did not have words to describe this, not even to herself, nor to describe the pain it caused, a pain made sharper by this dearth of language.

Instead of telling him any of these things, Jess had found herself talking about the baby, that invisible, impractical, incontestably real presence within her, as if it were the best, the ideal, response to Gordie's accusation of phoniness. "In another month, about, I'll be able to feel it move," she mentioned, and, "The button on my jeans is definitely getting hard to fasten." She noticed how rapidly each mention of the subject induced in Gordie an air of deference, a kind of carte blanche respect verging on awe and which seemed to assume her own superior fortitude, her sparkling, staggering grit. And she saw how it would be this way, how having a baby young and solo would assign her, in the minds of observers, certain qualities—or not simply qualities, but a certain command. She felt rich with it, fat and pleased with the creamy, private thought. She imagined herself with the baby—visible at last!—itself fat and creamy in her arms as she went about her business, walked down the street, mailed a letter, stood in line to buy, what?—milk, crackers, bananas—and no one able to accuse her of being fake.

Reminding Gordie she was with child suited her purpose in

another way, too, since pregnancy seemed (antithetically, when you thought about it) to exempt a woman from her sexual status, and therefore from behaving in any way that could be construed as flirtatious. With their tiff in this way safely put to rest, Jess had stuck around to help Gordie bring out the rest of the trash bags, after which they wound up ordering pizza (she was, she thought, just as glad not to sit opposite Paul at supper tonight), and then they had worked to identify the dozen boxes they imagined John's colleague's friend's etc. would find most interesting, or relevant, or meritorious from an artistic point of view or whatever. After some congenial debate, they packed their selections into the back of Gordie's dad's station wagon and delivered them to the Ryries'.

It was by then a little past nine. John had helped carry the boxes in. Biscuit, pajamaed, had clunked to her knees and flung her arms around Ebie, submitting to copious, adoring slobber. Ricky had put the kettle on, and they'd all wound up in the kitchen except Paul, who chose to remain in the den, his pork-pied head a stolid silhouette against the aquatic glimmer of the TV screen.

It wasn't until Jess was getting ready for bed that it happened a second time—she wiped and there was blood on the toilet paper, again not red and again not much, though more this time than last.

For several seconds she just stood in the darkness outside John and Ricky's room, underneath the closed door of which a bar of light shone, and argued sternly with her thudding heart against leaping to conclusions. Then she knocked.

"Yeah?" It was John.

"Um . . . Ricky?" Jess asked softly.

A pause. The sound of pants. A man's pants. Funny that such a thing had its own inimitable sound. The cuffs mutedly smacking the floor, the heaviness of the fabric being drawn up, the jostle of coins in the pocket. Involuntarily, wistfully, Jess pictured her own father, his distracted look as he dressed for work, his thoughts forever remote from things like pants.

"What's up?" John's face appeared in the door. He wore jeans. His broad chest was covered in tufts of curly black, streaked heavily with gray, much more so than the hair on his head.

"I'm sorry." She was whispering. "Could I just talk to Ricky a sec?"

He raised his eyebrows, stroked the wiry beard on one side of his face, then turned, opening the door wider as he did. Ricky was not in bed, as Jess had imagined, but sitting on the window seat, her knees pulled broodily to her chest. When she saw Jess she sprung up at once and pulled a robe over what she'd been wearing: not much, Jess glimpsed. Ricky came to the door, exchanging first glances, then places, with John.

"Do you mind if . . . well, in private?" begged Jess.

Ricky closed the door behind her and they moved toward the linen closet, away from all the bedrooms. There was one window at this end of the hall, set high in the wall, and through it a mingle of streetlight and moon washed her features as she listened to Jess whisper her news. Her robe, white terry, looked like snow in the light. She offered no reassurance but laid a hand very kindly on Jess's cheek, and that is what started Jess shaking.

....

THE QUESTIONS—"How many weeks do you think you are?"
"What was the date of your last period?" "Have you had your
pregnancy confirmed by a doctor?" "When was your last prenatal visit?" "Did you hear a heartbeat at any earlier exam?"—
for all that they were put neutrally by the succession of healthcare
professionals, those at Ricky's own ob-gyn office and then by
the nurses and technicians and doctors at the hospital, seemed
to carry the air of the courtroom, of the cross-examination. Jess
found herself responding as though she were covering for a lie,
could feel herself reddening in a lady-doth-protest-too-much
way, and on several instances she turned to Ricky, who sat un-
waveringly beside her in each of the waiting and examination
rooms (who had taken the day off work in order to ferry her to
these appointments), and repeated the answer she'd just given,
adding desperately, as if seeking to persuade, "My mother was
with me! The doctor said it."

Although Jess was now thirteen weeks along, no heartbeat
could be heard on the doppler, not even with the intravaginal
transducer. She was sent for ultrasound, which confirmed the
lack of heartbeat and put the gestational age of the fetus at seven
weeks. "Seven?" Jess repeated hoarsely, and felt the world swing
away from her. That meant it had been dead before she ever
showed up in Nyack. Perhaps before the Greyhound left San
Francisco. "Could be seven and a half," the short man in the
short white lab coat, whoever he was—she never saw his name
tag—allowed, but he said it with such terrible, futile compassion
that Jess understood it to be a kindness only.

When they left her alone in the room—"You can dress"—
she stood wiping off the gel in slow motion, staring at the now-
black monitor. Gone was the initial, unpardonable giddiness
she'd felt when she first saw the blood. (What had that been
about? Adrenaline? Gladness for any event linked to her pregnancy, any kind of outward manifestation of what until then had
been a silent, unembodied, phantom fact? Or was it gladness for
any event that called attention to her, period, anything that war-
ranted her asking for help, for attention, from Ricky, from John?)
Gone, too, was any sense of perpetrating a sham. Now that the
authorities had detected proof of her failed pregnancy, she no
longer found herself in the position of having to insist she really
was pregnant. There was something, she recognized mechani-
cally, funny in that. But she seemed to have lost, along with the
giddiness and the queer sense of shame, something like proximity to her own emotions. In their stead was a well-water stillness,
a thing deep and hard, with an aftertaste of sulfur.

No, she replied blandly, obediently, to their questions, she had
not "passed" any more "fluid," "colored discharge," "tissue," or
"clots." She had not experienced any "pain or cramping" in her
"abdomen or lower back." She had no fever, no chills. Her options, she was informed, were "expectant management" (go
"home" and wait for her body to "expel the fetal tissue" by itself;
this could take "a few days" or "weeks") or a "dilation and aspiration," which, contrary to its hopeful-sounding name, referred
to a "procedure" that used a "suction curette" to "empty the
uterus." Did she have a "preference"?

"Jess?" Ricky prompted.

She said, "I have a dead baby in me." It was not properly

either a question or a statement, but the dumb parroting of a sentence that had formed, seemingly all by itself, inside her head, and now required expulsion. "Take it out."

THEY WERE ABLE to schedule her for the following day, a piece of information delivered not quite grudgingly but with the clear implication that she was lucky in this regard. This still left nineteen hours from the time she and Ricky got home from the hospital to the time she was scheduled to arrive at the day surgery. Nineteen hours, stretched before her like a bridge, a grim, girdered span extending into heavy fog, appearing to lead nowhere. Yet crossing it turned out not to be hard, only joyless, only dull. She sat with the family at supper, ate a little chicken. Biscuit cleared her plate for her, and gave her a pat as she passed behind her chair again on her way to the den. After dinner Jess retired to the living room couch with her father's paperback Whitman, which she thumbed but did not read. Paul, having apparently decided to play off their brief, mortifying entanglement as if it had never happened, stopped before her and said in a voice that might have been pitched for sincerity but came out sounding drily comic, "Uh, sorry about"—tongue click—"you know." He had his hands clasped behind his back in what looked like mock-formality. "The pregnancy thing." Perhaps it was simply a teenage boy's valiant, dissonant effort to introduce levity into all situations, the sadder the situation, the more pressing the urge. She turned up the corners of her mouth dully. John had cleared off the mantel in the living room and lined up Will Joiner's boxes in a row. He had not, he said, made the call yet to the art world friend, but he would, he promised, soon. Now, this evening, he stood before the boxes, examining them at length, making frequent appreciative comments, and Jess felt it was for her benefit and was not ungrateful.

Ricky came to her later, knelt by the couch. "You must want to call your mother."

Jess shrugged.

When Ricky continued to look at her searchingly, her brows tilted up in encouraging inquiry—as if what she sought was not simply an affirmative response but the whole story behind the purported estrangement, the mystery revealed, the offenses confessed—Jess proffered a tiny, empty smile, shook her head and turned her face into the couch. The truth was she wanted nothing more than her mother now, but how to make that happen when it would mean everyone finding out she'd been telling tales? That was the real unnavigable bridge, the span leading into blind mist.

SHE WOKE FROM the anesthesia in tears and shivering. Her teeth chattering. "Do you kn-kn-know . . . ?" she tried, but it was difficult because of the crying, which seemed different from her own crying. It was like a foreign species of crying, something she hadn't remembered encountering but must have acquired while traveling far from home. "C-c-c-could you t-t-tell . . . ?"

"All right, Jessica," someone soothed, a woman, who adjusted something at the side of the shiny hard bed, and looked at something, a monitor, mounted high over her head.

"C-c-could you t-tell if it was a b-b-b-boy or a g-girl?"

There was the doctor on her other side now, she recognized him: Asian, elderly, with a wonderful mane of white hair and a peaceful, wrinkled countenance. "No," he said quietly. He seemed to be taking her pulse, or maybe just trying to steady her.

"I kn-kn-know . . ." Jess meant to say she'd known the answer, she didn't want him to think she was ridiculous; she'd known the fetus got suctioned into a tube, came out unrecognizable as anything human; it had just not been possible not to ask. But these tears, this sobbing: it was hard to get any words by this kind of crying, so virulent, so *thorough* was it. A warmed blanket was placed over her shivering legs, and both the heat and the weight reminded her of being buried in sand at the beach.

"Okay, Jessica?" said the woman again, or a different woman, but with the same professional brightness; there seemed to be various bodies, busy, unconcerned, moving efficiently about the bed. "We just want you to rest now," said the woman, moving in and picking up a tube, something to do with the IV. "Okay? Just relax."

THE NEXT TIME she woke they brought her apple juice, and after she drank it they brought her Ricky.

"How you doing?" said Ricky from the foot of the bed, and Jess started to cry, but this time it was regular, her own normal crying, close to soundless.

Ricky, haggard-looking, smiled sadly at her. Jess wondered how long she'd been in the waiting room. This whole time?

How much time had passed since she'd come out of the anesthesia and then gone back to sleep again?

"Sweetheart, I spoke with your mother," said Ricky. "I thought—we both thought—we owed your parents a call. Both of us talked with your mom, and John also talked with your father. You know, Jess, they're not mad at you."

The intensity of her crying, though not the volume, increased. "I know," Jess got out, though whether intelligibly or not she wasn't sure.

"They never kicked you out." It was a statement, but one seeking confirmation.

Jess managed a nod, pushing away the tears as they fell. "I'm sorry."

Ricky sighed.

Jess cried and cried.

"Poor Jess." Ricky looked at her, touched her ankle through the blanket. "You're young," she said eventually. "You have so much time. And you know it's common, don't you? It doesn't mean you won't be able to have children."

All of this only made her cry harder. She managed to choke out, "It isn't that."

Ricky came around closer. She perched on the wheelie stool beside the bed and brought her face near Jess's. She took over the clearing of tears, stroking them away with her thumbs. Very gently, she asked, "What, then?"

Jess's whole face crumpled. She held her hands over her mouth.

"It's hard to let go of *this* baby, even if there'll be others," guessed Ricky.

Jess shook her head more vigorously: no, not that.

"What, then, sweet girl?"

It was too much. Jess looked up, horrified. "I'm *not* sweet! I'm *relieved*." It was as though a scream were being forced through a whisper-sized tube: an ugly, scraping sound from her throat. "I didn't want it. I didn't *want* it." This was a truth she had not previously allowed herself to know, and now it had come out she felt fear creep into its place. The fear was not vague. It took the form of a certainty: from now on anything might happen to her and no matter how terrible it was, the worst part would be knowing she deserved it.

Some time passed before the sobbing abated. Ricky did not touch her or speak, and Jess took this as a sign of disgust. But when she finally lifted her face from her slippery fingers, gulped a long shuddering breath and used the edge of the hospital sheet as a handkerchief, she saw that Ricky had not wheeled the little stool any distance from the bed but sat as close as before, gazing at her with sorrow and without judgment. And now Ricky plucked thoughtfully at her own lip, and drew a breath and gazed hard at the blanket, seeming to lose herself in contemplation of some deep and powerful interest, as though whatever she was working out was not for Jess's sake only. When she looked up she said: "That might be harder."

Jess did not follow.

Ricky spoke slowly, deliberately, as though the words would require time and great focus to comprehend. "Losing a baby you don't want might be harder than losing one you did."

All around them were clean things: sterile, aseptic, hygienic. White and black and red and blue, metal and plastic, wired and motored, nesting and depending. Expensive things, each with its own highly specialized purpose, each invented, manufactured, purchased, and employed in the service of preservation of life. Tubing, buttons, calibrated dials, casings and liners, speakers and lights. *They* were the living things in this room, or not room but cubicle, this makeshift capsule enclosed by curtains on metal tracks. They, Ricky and Jess, possessed—*were*—the life that was the object, the sole point, of all these pieces of equipment, none of which could know or grasp or approach how muddy, how complicated and ignoble such lives might be.

Jess let her head rest back against the pillow and closed her eyes, and the hot tears flowed again, bathing her already salty cheeks. "I don't have the right," she whispered.

"What?"

"I don't have the right to cry." She spoke in a low, rusty voice, as if she were loath for anyone else to hear, to learn what they were, both of them, guilty of. Yet the thought that she was not alone, that Ricky must be speaking from her own experience, was also a relief. Crying blindly now, she reached for Ricky's hand. Ricky held on, tightening her grip as Jess tightened hers.

After a while Ricky spoke. "Listen to me."

She waited until Jess opened her eyes.

"Are you listening?" Ricky's eyes were dry. "It doesn't have anything to do with right."

6.

When she woke there was the sun already high in the sky, dappling the slim spriggy branches outside her window. The leaves still had that dainty, new-green look, the tree equivalent of baby teeth. Biscuit lay there, yawning, and saw there was a rolling wind that lifted the branches high and set them down at close intervals. There was something else, too, though she could not at first remember what.

The space beside her bed was bare: no raft of an air mattress beached broadly upon the floor. The duffel bag that had lolled like a giant sausage in one corner of her room, and which had, week by week, gradually disgorged its guts as piles of clean and dirty clothing scattered and bunched and stacked in the area around it, was also gone. As was, she knew, though its absence could not be marked in her room, her mother's mandolin, bestowed hastily in the moments just before Jess's departure and last seen being handed into the back of her father's pickup.

It had been a loosely, laggardly frenetic departure, with no one directing it and none of them seeming sure how it was to be handled. There had been Jess, her hair still wet from the shower, a small cloth bag slung over one shoulder, sunglasses perched on top of her head, Congers Community College travel mug in hand, first standing by the open door on the passenger side, then going back in the house to the bathroom, then wandering out again and turning a small circle on the front walk, as if to take everything in one last time. There had been Gordie, insisting on carrying Jess's duffel down from the porch, then struggling with it across the little lawn before handing it to Biscuit's father, who would be driving Jess to LaGuardia, and who relieved Gordie of the bag and lofted it easily into the truck. There had been Ebie, trotting down to sniff at the bushes by the sidewalk, then doubling back in an ear-inverting bound to see where Gordie was headed with that bag, then putting both paws up on the tailgate as if debating leaping onto the truck bed, then bumping instead over to Biscuit for a stroke of reassurance before mounting the porch stairs to investigate the sound of someone else coming out. There had been Biscuit's mother, who'd been outside earlier but disappeared mysteriously back into the house without explanation, reemerging now with the mandolin in its figgy case, and a flush traveled up her neck as she bent at the waist and spoke inaudibly to Jess, sitting on the bottom step, and then transferred the instrument onto her lap. There had been Paul, hanging back in the shade of the porch; he showed signs of having woken up only recently, but managed to deploy this sleepiness in the service of cool, with his bare feet, his ragged jeans, his undershirt and porkpie hat, which he'd slapped rakishly over his pillow-mussed hair. There had been Biscuit's father, securing the tailgate, checking his watch, scowling across the patch of grass (that scowl a stranger might have chalked up to the sun's brightness, but which everyone in the family understood to be a sign neither of anger nor of glare, but of knowing a particular emotional response was expected, and not knowing how to deliver it), looking caught off guard when her mother approached and, on tiptoe, slid her arms around his neck and pressed the side of her face against his chest, right below the throat. Seconds had passed; then he'd gone ahead and slid an arm around her waist. More seconds, and then he'd slid the other. Then he put his face down and rubbed his forehead, just lightly, back and forth, across the top of her mother's hair. They'd stood like that for what seemed a peculiar length of time; so peculiar Biscuit felt she was expanding, as though helium were being poured into her body, filling it so completely that her toes might lift up off the porch and she might go floating out over the little lawn.

It had been Paul, sitting on the porch railing, his big white feet half obscured by twining wisteria, surveying them all from above, who'd finally intoned, his groggy voice even lower than it had become naturally over this past year, so that it sounded like a radio announcer's, gravelly and imposing, "Uh, not to break anything up, but does anyone here have a plane to catch?" Then Biscuit's parents had dissolved their embrace, but slowly, her father turning back toward the truck, pulling a tissue from his pocket and blowing his nose, and her mother blinking and wiping her eyes with an embarrassed laugh and a comment about how bright the sun; and Jess rose from the porch steps, and Gordie held his arms apart as though someone had asked him roughly how big a Chihuahua was, a gesture Jess somehow understood was meant to initiate a hug. She disregarded the intended size of the embrace, though, instead flinging her arms around him with such abandon that she managed to whack him with both her shoulder bag and travel mug in the process. Then she'd turned toward the porch, shading her eyes. "Where are you guys?" Paul had shuffled down the steps onto the grass and removed from his pocket his right hand, which he extended in a gesture at once awkward and debonair. Jess stared a moment before taking it; while it was still in her grasp, she leaned in rather quickly and kissed him on the cheek. Then, "Biscuit?" she called. So Biscuit emerged, too, slowly, from behind the wisteria, which had in the past days begun unfurling its pale shag of purple clusters. Why now did she feel shy? She came down the steps into the sunlight and Jess kissed her cheek, leaving behind a tiny damp spot and the scent of coffee and of coconut shampoo.

Biscuit's mother was last to say good-bye, the one Jess saved for last. It had seemed to Biscuit, watching Jess go and present herself to Ricky, and on some level watching the rest of them watching—Paul, Gordie, her father, even Ebie—that this final interaction was like a little show, like a scene played out for them, the audience, if only because they *were* all watching. In any case it played out differently from the rest. Instead of throwing her arms around Biscuit's mother, Jess clasped herself around the middle. She was smiling, but seeming to bite the inside of her lip at the same time, and her shoulders were hunched forward, her knees a bit bent and her nostrils flared. Biscuit watched as her mother put her hands on Jess's elbows and brought her own forehead close, closer, until it touched Jess's. They stood this way. Biscuit couldn't hear what words, if any, her mother spoke, nor could she be sure Jess was crying. She did know that this good-bye, for all that it didn't include a full embrace, was in some essential way more intimate—more adult, she supposed—than the others had been, and she had a peculiar reaction to this, a mixture of jealousy and relief, that in turn made *her* feel more adult.

That had been a week ago. Now it was Saturday again; again not an ordinary Saturday, large and comfortably shapeless (in Biscuit's mind "Saturday" evoked the color, texture, and amiable homeliness of a brown paper grocery bag), but one charged with purpose, with plan. She knew this much, lying supine, stretching her limbs luxuriantly, absorbing the fact of the trees tossing their newly frilly branches against the window; she knew it on the level of bones and tissue, of rapidly dissipating dreams, before she remembered in practical terms what that purpose was. Slowly it dawned, or rather solidified, the particulate energy that had been tingling, shimmering at the edges of her awareness gathering and assuming form: today was the funeral. She got out of bed. She pulled on her pilly robe.

Downstairs she found her father sifting flour over the green mixing bowl. He wore not his ubiquitous costume of jeans or painty overalls but a pair of charcoal trousers, creased sharply down the middles, and a shirt with collar and buttons. And a necktie. Biscuit was pleased to see the tea towel slung over his left shoulder; it comfortably undermined the formality of the look.

"Where's Mom?" she asked. And without waiting for an answer: "Are we still doing it?"

"Good morning." Her father turned and smiled.

"Good morning," she complied. "Are we? Still doing it today?"

His smile had a deliberate quality, its production seeming not so much forced as conscious, willed. Flour dusted his beard like fake snow in a school play. Gesturing behind him, he announced with delicate grandeur, "Pancakes."

"What's wrong? Are we not doing it?"

"Nothing's wrong. Mom and Paul just went to the store. They should be back any minute. Come crack an egg."

The eggs were already on the counter, ensconced in their clear plastic bubbles: two rows of pale dun. Some were freckled and some clear, some scabrous and some smooth. *A suitable specimen*, approved the white-coated scientist as Biscuit selected one with a smattering of little bumps. She broke it against the side of the bowl and pried the halves apart. The yolk dropped cleanly out. The whites drooped after. She saw the egg she'd cracked into the Hudson that rainy day over a month ago. *Its last earthly ties*, intoned the scientist, *are severed by breaking an egg.* She saw the twin jagged cups of shell floating on dark, pointy waves. Strange to think of what had happened since that day, the day Gordie came, and Ebie, and Jess with her baby inside her, hidden and already dead. Suppose her poor ritual, so full of substitutions and never properly completed, had actually set something in motion?

"Beautiful," said her father. "Do another."

Biscuit cracked the second egg into the bowl, then went and perched up on the radiator, its cold metal pleats pressing against her thighs, and watched her father mix the batter with a long wooden spoon.

The egg in the Hudson was no longer a secret, nor were the fireplace ashes and chicken bones, the stolen library book, or her reason for setting fire to the upstairs bathroom. Revealing all had been something of a relief, but not nearly so great as the relief of having been, at last, *made* to tell. This had happened a week ago, just after her father came back from taking Jess to the airport. "Come on," he'd said, "take a walk with me," and she'd followed him down the street to the river, where they sat on a bench looking out at ruined pilings and the distant shore. It had been late afternoon by then and the water was sapphire, cold-looking on a cold spring day. Brave, early sailboats, just a smattering, tacked this way and that. They could hear, sporadically, the shudder and snap of the sails on the ones nearest them.

They hadn't said anything for a while. Some Canada geese had been strutting in their proud, ungainly way along the water's edge. Biscuit admired their handsome black heads and white chin straps, but they seemed ill-tempered, almost devoutly humorless, and when they drew near she slid over on the bench a little closer to her father. At last he spoke.

"The thing is, you can't skip any more school," he said. "It was wrong of me to let you get away with doing it so much."

"It's not your fault."

"Right. The skipping's not. But not doing more to end it is. You can't do it anymore, Bis. It stops. That's one thing."

She sat curled tightly beside him, her sneakers up on the bench, tucked against her bottom, her arms locked around her shins. Her parents couldn't stop her. That was a lonely, terrible truth, one which she'd discovered this year and which made her hate them a little. But he had gotten her attention. She was interested in the way he said it, the way he spoke as if he *could* stop her, as if his forbidding her were enough. They might pretend together. Though if she did stop cutting class, it wouldn't be pretense, would it?

"The other thing," he went on, "is I need you to tell me what you've been doing when you skip school. I don't just mean 'I was at the Hook,' or 'I was home.' I mean: doing what?"

Across the river a train was gliding along the water's edge. There were people in it, going north. She could not see them, but she saw their train and she held the idea of them in her mind. They could not see her, a speck on the bench on the opposite shore, but she was here, nevertheless; and she, too, was traveling, in slower fashion, following a kind of coastline, too, as faithfully and inexorably as they. It would lead somewhere else. Someday she would be someone else. A grown-up lady. As distant to her present self as were the strangers on that train. That truth, too, was lonely and terrible. She thought of the gray lady: sad and just and mute. Who marked her now and marked her then, who was acquainted with everyone she knew, including her future self. Perhaps—the idea caused in her a startling gladness—the gray lady was a piece of her future self.

"It's not a choice, Bis. I need you to explain."

He'd looked at her, stern and unwavering. She'd waited for this for so long. Biscuit looked away from him, watched the train recede from view. It faded into the landscape's curves, its metal glint melding into the shimmering, scalloped distant shore. *Good-bye, my darling,* she bid it as the train disappeared, and whether she thought these words to the gray lady or as the gray lady she was not sure, but there were long pearl-buttoned gloves in the voice, and a hat with a veil, and expectance. And acceptance. *Fare thee well. Until we meet.*

Biscuit unfolded her legs and stood.

Her father touched her arm. "Biscuit." He looked angry but sounded weary. "Tell me."

"I am. You have to come," she'd said, and led him back up the hill to their house, and to her room, where she had gotten down on stomach and elbows and disinterred from the assorted heaps under her bed the pilfered library book. She'd shown him the page with the bones and the ashes, the white cloth, the egg and the burnt string. He'd sat holding the book on his lap at the foot of her bed, while she'd huddled at the head with a stuffed animal clutched to her chin (a powder blue rabbit; she'd never been sentimental about any one stuffed animal, but retained a sizable menagerie to which she felt attached as a group), and watched him read, her view increasingly obscured by blue fur as she shrank lower onto her pillow. She saw the light dawn, saw him connect her antics, each successive transgression, with one of the funeral customs detailed in the book.

"Oh," he'd said at last. "This has all been about"—after a small hesitation he pronounced the name nobody ever said—"Simon." A long, cleansing sigh. "I didn't know you thought about him." He'd leaned back against the wall, squishing a bear, a cat, and a large velour grasshopper in the process, and pulled his fingers mullingly down the side of his beard. "I think about him, too. We didn't— Biscuit, why are you hiding behind that rabbit?"

She'd shrugged, unable for the moment to speak. She was in some peculiar fashion overcome—with an urge to laugh, it seemed, although that did not begin to cover it. So much was happening. All her imaginary scripts coming to life.

"We never did have a funeral," her father continued slowly, nodding as though agreeing with something Biscuit had just pointed out. After a minute he'd picked up the book again and began paging through it. "Listen to this," he said, and read aloud a description of a Ukrainian practice. Then a silence, interrupted by a new find: "This one's interesting." From Senegal. More minutes, more page turning, then something from Bali. He read aloud to her the varied customs of grief, from this country and that, from one people and another. Biscuit, listening initially from behind her rabbit-screen, but eventually surrendering this and moving in close to lean an elbow on her father's knee, let him curve an arm behind her back and snuggled close against him, in the way she used to when she was small and he'd read to her of Scuffy and Maisie and Pooh.

The steps by which last Saturday's unplanned private encounter had led to this Saturday's planned family event remained unknown to Biscuit, part of the whole impenetrable world of adult communications and machinations, a world she was, on the whole, perfectly content not to comprehend.

Simply, on Wednesday night at supper her parents had asked what she and Paul would think about their having a small family funeral for the baby. Okay, the kids had responded, both immediately shy. Whether Paul knew the question had been prompted by Biscuit she did not know and was in no rush to say. But he refrained, amazingly, from cracking any jokes, and her parents were full of solemnity, and for a dismal moment Biscuit had thought the whole thing was to indulge her: a sham funeral complete with sham mourning, like what they'd done for her years ago—because she could see now that it had been an indulgence, kindly meant but still essentially fraudulent—when they'd all gathered in their best clothes and helped her lay the fallen bird to rest in its poor, shabby grass-lined shoe box beneath the bridal wreath bush.

But then she'd seen the fork trembling in her mother's hand, and her mother had dropped the fork with a clatter and put both hands quickly in her lap, where she seemed to be pressing them together. "I'm sorry we didn't do this before," her mother said, her gaze flicking swiftly to Biscuit's father, then back to Paul and Biscuit, each in turn, before ending up vaguely in the area of the butter dish.

"That's okay," Paul had been quick to assure her, and Biscuit had chimed in, "Yeah, that's okay."

"This'll be our time," her mother had added, very softly, but with a kind of resolution, "to say good-bye as a family."

The words had seemed to travel out and hang above the table, ominous, peculiar, with a singing sharpness. *Good-bye as a family.* Biscuit turned the words around in her head like marbles in her mouth, helplessly, over and over, until they grew as smooth and lost the distinction of meaning, were reduced to raw sound.

She resurrected them now, sitting on top of the cold radiator and watching her father cover the bowl of pancake batter with plastic wrap. *Good-bye as a family.* Was this morning's ceremony about more than laying Simon, the idea of Simon, to rest? Simon. Simon Isaac. She had seen him once. In the hospital. The day she'd learned to walk like she owned the place. Her father had taken her and Paul to visit their mother; that's what he had said—not "Mom and the baby," just "Mom"—and Biscuit had been anxious about seeing her in a hospital bed; but when they arrived in the room her mother had been sitting in a chair by the window, and she had not been alone, as Biscuit imagined, but held the baby—Biscuit's brother—in her arms, wrapped all in white wrappings like a mummy, sort of, a tiny mummy with just a bit of exposed face, teacup-fine and still: porcelain eyes shut and porcelain lips shut and minutely curved nose, with its nostrils, so black and elegant, small as peppercorns.

Was there, Biscuit wondered, turning a freshly apprehensive eye on her father's creased trousers and necktie, on the somber solicitousness with which he was now setting the table, handling the juice glasses and the plates with suspect care and caution, moving as though to avoid incident, accident, unnecessary harm—was there another purpose to the family's gathering today?

People thought she was little but she was not so little. People thought she was always lost in her fancies, her private conversations, the things she made up to believe in her head. But she saw. She heard. She'd known something was wrong—more wrong, extra wrong—between her parents these past few weeks. Hardspat whispers behind their bedroom door. Mistimed hugs, incompletely reciprocated. Stealthy footsteps on the stairs: too late at night, too early in the morning, always traveling in the wrong directions. The mandolin handed off in front of them all. The clear, heavy, rectangular bottle on the table that night when Biscuit had woken from her sweaty dream and crept downstairs, reaching the threshold to the kitchen in time to hear her mother's terrible question, the words that had cracked from her throat and spilled backward like salt into the holes of the phone: *Am I good?*

7.

What more is there to tell? What else ought to be, must be, said? If it were to end here, would anything of importance remain in doubt?

Would it, for example, make any difference to know that Ricky and Paul came home just then, he with his index finger hooked through a gallon of orange juice; she with an armload of blooms: five sunflowers, one for each Ryrie, as long as her arm, their heads, bright, fiery as hammered brass, poking out of a paper cone? That Ricky and Paul were each, like John, dressed in formal best, and that Paul had washed and combed his hair (and forsaken his hat) so that the high white dome of his forehead showed clear for the first time in months? That a tripping, trilling laugh nearly erupted from Biscuit to see him this way, in such a state of spit and polish, and that this laugh trembled and faded from her throat, supplanted by a stronger feeling, a staggering lunge of gratitude, of pure, unstrained affection—or no, name it: love?

That when her mother said, "Still in pj's?" and Biscuit hopped off the radiator and ran, her lavender robe flapping, upstairs where she wriggled into her sole skirt, her sole blouse (fetched from the general pile of debris beneath her bed), she was overcome by such a tidal wave of feeling, a mix of dread and perverse gaiety all at once, she had to steady herself with a hand on the banister as she went back downstairs, admonish herself to don a solemnity suitable to the occasion?

That when Biscuit reached the front hall and found her family waiting there, her mother holding a small, corrugated cardboard box, smaller, even, than the bird's coffin—a box whose existence had not been known to her but whose provenance and purpose she instantly apprehended—she did not have to work to don that solemnity, because it fell heavily, decisively upon her?

Or—leap forward—would it make a difference to know that at the edge of the river, where the family processed with its small, difficult burden, it was John who extracted the inner sack from the box in Ricky's hands, who undid the twist tie and stretched open the clear plastic mouth, and that he offered it first to Biscuit? That her insides became jelly at the sight of the contents, their mottled grayness and their paucity; that she croaked, "With my hand?" and Ricky said, "Oh, John . . ." but then Biscuit did it, thrust her bare hand in and gathered a handful of milled ash and bone? That Paul went next, then Ricky and finally John, who finished by tipping up the bag and shaking the last of its contents into the river, and that they all bent then at the rocky shoreline and washed their hands in the water, rinsed the cremated body of their brother, their son, all together, each at his or her separate, identical task, the way they'd used to wash up at Cabruda Lake, brushing their teeth and soaping their hands and faces at the end of the dock?

What else could need telling? That they met Gordie and Ebie as they walked back up the hill, that Gordie acted embarrassed about catching them in their relative finery, but that his real embarrassment was over being caught himself: patrolling yet again outside their house, where he continued to feel drawn even with Jess gone? That they invited him in for pancakes; that Paul, for once, was affable toward him, struck up a conversation, asked him questions about his dad's boxes, which were still lined up thickly along the Ryries' living room mantel as though they'd put down runner roots and were proliferating there, this cache of alternative worlds; that Ricky and John said little and ate less, but found one another's hands beneath the table and that this unpublic intertwining of their fingers was the most intimacy they'd shared in more than a year; that Biscuit, noticing the former but not the latter, and fancying she felt her brother's ashes on her tongue, and the gray lady's gaze upon them all, found herself also less than hungry; that Ebie sat throughout the meal resting her muzzle on Biscuit's knee, and that she alone ate well?

And what of the boxes? Would it alter the course of understanding in any meaningful way to know whether Madeleine's Piers was able to get the Joiner Boxes a show, either in a museum or a gallery, or to persuade the friend's colleague (or colleague's friend) to buy one, or two, or the entire lot? What, for that matter, of Madeleine? Is it necessary to know whether she and John kissed that night, whether they took off all their clothes up under the skylight in her crooked little bungalow, or whether John found himself so moved, so shaken—by the wire magician; or by the dead man whose hands had wrought it, whose loneliness had conceived it; or by Madeleine Berkowitz herself and the realization, the revelation of how small he had been and how shamed he was to have ridiculed her all these years; or by the thought of his wife, his troublesome, troubling wife, at that moment still wet-haired from her swim at the Y and waiting for him, with her mix of ingenuity and ingenuousness, her unpardonable absence and her irremediable presence, her lies and fears and honest, enduring appetite for him—that he excused himself in a jumble of apologies and went home chaste?

Could it be that attempting to answer any of these questions might amount to arrogance, to a kind of conceit verging on blasphemy? Could there be a point beyond which it would be hubris to proceed?

We know more than we pretend to know. More than we presume we know. Even so, what we know would fill a teaspoon.

Here, perhaps, is all that's left to say:

Elsewhere in Memorial Park, as the four Ryries kneel by the river, rinsing from their hands the ashes of the fifth, a teenage girl in an army jacket is writing curse words on her wrist with a ballpoint pen. Six boys in muscle shirts cut a diagonal across the grass, making noises in imitation of drunkenness. A girl who lost a tooth last night executes her first cartwheel. A man who lost his virginity last night tries to assemble a kite. A young woman with a cane bends to drink from the fountain. A little boy, poking in the dirt, finds what he is sure is a diamond.

An old man, scrunching his sandwich wrapper, throws it toward the trash, missing by a foot.

And now as the Ryries start the climb with their hollow box, heading for home where the pancake batter stands mixed and ready to pour, a red-haired man comes down the hill. He holds the leash of a large black dog, and as they draw even with the middle house on the block, they slow, both of them, man and dog, almost involuntarily, almost without noticing, and turn their heads in concert—a movement inadvertently beautiful, also comic—to look openly, hopefully, toward the door.

ACKNOWLEDGMENTS

To Sue and Oscar, for everything;

to Dr. Richard Barakat and Dr. Carol Aghajanian, for time;

to Betty Brock, for being a paragon of children's room librarians and for being ours;

to Stuart Pizer, for his step-grandfather;

to Caroline Heller, Lynn Focht, and Martha Nichols for their most felicitous balance of kindness and intelligence;

to Mary Page, for being an exquisite reader and a teacher to the bone;

to Gillian Richards and Florence Marc-Charles, for help with Baptiste and his Grann;

to Ted Simpson, for help with stagecraft;

to Cathy Jaque, Matt Spindler, Erin Edmison and especially Inge De Taeye, for their icebergian talents and labors, of which I know I glimpsed no more than the proverbial tip;

to Sarah McGrath, Geoff Kloske, Sarah Stein, and everyone at Riverhead, for their thoughtful and rare care in making this into a book;

to Barney Karpfinger, for helping me come to understand not only the work but also myself better, and for his increasingly vital friendship these past twenty years;

to Joan and Arnie and Tam, for coming into the picture;

and to George, Rosy, Joe, Barley and Mike, for everything else:

thank you.